Also by A.J. MacKenzie

The War of 1812 Epics

The Ballad of John MacLea
The Hunt for the North Star
Invasion

The Hundred Years' War

A Flight of Arrows
A Clash of Lions
The Fallen Sword

A Clash of Lions

A.J. Mackenzie is the pseudonym of Marilyn Livingstone and Morgen Witzel, an Anglo-Canadian husband-and-wife team of writers and historians. They write non-fiction history and management books under their own names, but 'become' A.J. MacKenzie when writing fiction. Morgen has an MA in renaissance diplomacy from the University of Victoria, but since the late 1990s has concentrated on writing books on leadership and management. Several of his books have been international bestsellers. Marilyn has a PhD in medieval economic history from the Queen's University, Belfast. She is a musician who writes music and also plays in a silver band and sings in an a capella trio. They have written two books of medieval history together, and also several novels, including the Hardcastle & Chaytor mysteries set on Romney Marsh during the French Revolution.

A.J. MACKENZIE

A Clash of Lions

CANELO

First published in the United Kingdom in 2021 by

Canelo
Unit 9, 5th Floor
Cargo Works, 1-2 Hatfields
London, SE1 9PG
United Kingdom

Print ISBN 978 1 80032 484 8
Ebook ISBN 978 1 80032 284 4

Look for more great books at www.canelo.co

Printed and bound in Great Britain by Clays Ltd, Elcograf S.p.A.

1

To the Bonner family, with whom we almost had a tour of the battlefield at Neville's Cross before lunch and a bottle of red wine intervened. It was warm spring afternoon just after lockdown ended, and spending time with friends seemed more important than historical research. We'll get there one day!

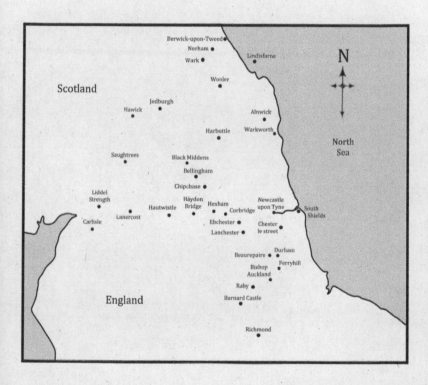

Anglo-Scottish Borders, 1346

Dramatis personae

Accompanying Merrivale

Simon Merrivale, herald to the Prince of Wales and queen's envoy to the north

Mauro, his servant

Warin, his groom

Diccon, his groom

Tiphaine de Tesson, Norman noblewoman and daughter of an executed rebel

Peter de Lisle of Chipchase, the herald's apprentice

In Kent and London

Reginald, Lord Grey of Hargate

Lady Grey, his wife

Lady Mary Grey, his daughter and wife of Sir Richard Percy

Philippa of Hainault, Queen of England

John Stratford, Archbishop of Canterbury and president of the council

William de la Pole, banker and merchant

John Pulteney, banker and merchant

The Percy family and relations

Henry Percy, Baron Percy of Alnwick

Lady Idonia, his wife

Harry Percy, their eldest son and heir

Richard Percy, their younger son, currently fighting in France

John Grey, her brother, currently fighting in France

The Disinherited

Edward Balliol, claimant to the throne of Scotland, now defeated and in exile

Gilbert d'Umfraville of Harbottle, Lord of Redesdale and claimant to the Earldom of Angus in Scotland

Lady Joan, his wife

Jamie Hall, hobelar from Redesdale, in Umfraville's service

Thomas Clennell of Hesleyside, claimant to the Lordship of Selkirk in Scotland

Thomas Wake, Baron Wake of Liddell

Walter Selby of Biddlestone, captain of Liddel Strength

William Selby, his son

Robert de Lisle of Chipchase, father of Peter de Lisle

David Harkness of Blackfell

Northern lords and their followers

Ralph Neville, Baron Neville of Raby

Thomas Rokeby, High Sheriff of Yorkshire and royal commander in Berwick

Tom Rokeby (Young Tom), his nephew

John Coupland, border landowner

John Stryvelyn, keeper of the castle at Berwick

Roger Heron, Stryvelyn's deputy

John Croser (Kalewater Jack), hobelar in Heron's retinue

Eckies Nickson, hobelar in Heron's retinue

Eustace de Manenghem, Lord Rowton

Ecclesiastical figures

William de la Zouche, Archbishop of York and Warden of the Marches

Thomas Hatfield, Bishop of Durham, currently with the army in France

Hugh de Tracey, treasurer of Durham Priory

John of Bridekirk, prior of Hexham

Gilbert de Tracey, formerly the king's banker, now a canon at Hexham Priory

Oswald of Halton, Dominican friar

John of Bothcastle, prior of Lanercost

John of Eskdale, abbot of Jedburgh

Alexander Seton, preceptor of the Order of Saint John in Scotland

Merchants and traders

William Blyth, merchant of Newcastle-upon-Tyne

Oliver Woodburn, man-at-arms in Blyth's service

Adam Murton, alderman of Newcastle-upon-Tyne

Egidia Murton, his wife

Kristoffer Tielt, Flemish merchant resident in Newcastle-upon-Tyne

John Brotherton, merchant of Berwick-upon-Tweed

Henry Cheswick, merchant of Berwick-upon-Tweed

Oppicius Adornes, banker in Bruges

Scots

David II Bruce, King of Scotland

Niall Bruce of Carrick, his half-brother, illegitimate son of Robert the Bruce

Patrick Dunbar, Earl of Dunbar and March

Agnes Randolph, his wife, Countess of Dunbar and March and Lady of Mann and Annandale

Lady Mora of Islay, shieldmaiden in the service of the Countess of Dunbar

Somairle of Mann, man-at-arms in the service of the Countess of Dunbar

John Randolph, Earl of Moray, brother of the Countess of Dunbar

Sir William Douglas of Liddesdale

James Craig, Master of Kinross

Archibald Graham, Lyon Herald

John Graham, Earl of Menteith

William Murray, Earl of Sutherland

Robert Keith, Marischal of Scotland

Rollond de Brus, Norman nobleman and cousin of the Scottish Bruces

Guy Dampierre, Count of Béthune and Lord of Hamilton in Scotland

Yolande of Bohemia, Countess of Béthune, his wife

I

The Narrow Sea, 3ʳᵈ of September, 1346
Midday

The wind picked up halfway across the short crossing from France to the Kent coast, and the horizon of grey-white cliffs and cloud-speckled blue sky rose and fell at speed. Simon Merrivale stood firmly on the deck of the roundship *Grace-Dieu*, braced against the buffeting of the lively waves. The warm rays of a late summer sun shone on the little flotilla of ships ferrying a number of Englishmen, and at least one Frenchwoman, along with their horses and baggage back to England.

The travellers were a somewhat mixed group. Some had been sent by King Edward III to take home the news of the great victory at the battle of Crécy a week earlier; others had sought permission from their king to return and look after urgent personal or estate business. Merrivale, perhaps uniquely, had been sent on a secret and sensitive mission for the king. He was not, at least in name, one of the king's own servants; his official master was Edward, Prince of Wales. But, as Merrivale had observed several times in the past few months, when a king called, a prince's servants still jumped to serve.

If he was honest, Merrivale thought, it suited him very well to be away from the prince's entourage for a while. The prince and his friends were very full of the spirit of victory. A young man who had begun the summer uncertain and awkward with the reins of power had been transformed into a battle-hardened commander, who felt invincible and was flexing his muscles.

As the prince's herald, Merrivale was one member of the household who found this tedious. The regular drinking and gaming that accompanied most evenings had little appeal for a man half a generation older than most of the prince's court. So when King Edward requested his presence, Merrivale had greeted the invitation with some enthusiasm, albeit tempered by the knowledge that the king usually had more than one scheme in mind at any one time.

–

'Come in, Merrivale,' the king had said. They were in the royal pavilion in the middle of the camp on high ground overlooking the town of Wissant, which the army had reached earlier in the day while making its leisurely way north from Crécy.

The king gestured towards a bench. Normally one stood in the royal presence. *Mmm*, thought Merrivale, *if he wants me sitting down, I really do need to watch out.*

Edward III was, like his son, still flush from his recent victory. His short coat speckled with fleurs-de-lys sparkled in the sunlight coming through the walls of the tent, and his manner was even more confident than usual.

'So, Merrivale. Do we think Edward de Tracey's death means an end to the plotting against us?'

Merrivale had given this question a great deal of thought in the days following the battle. 'Honestly, sire, I do not. Even though many of those on the French side perished, I cannot feel comfortable that all the tendrils of this plot are cut off. It had supporters in several parts of Europe, and some of the plotters will be keen to continue. They have a plan that they hope will bring them power and riches. Despite what happened at Crécy, they are unlikely to forego it.'

'I agree,' said the king. 'Therefore, I am sending you back to England to track down any more of these tendrils, as you call them.'

'What about my duties with the prince, sire? Is he aware that you require my services?'

'Yes, yes, of course. My son can do without his herald for the moment, and I have need of your knowledge and skills. It is highly likely that Tracey had co-conspirators at home, working against us. We need to hunt them down and we need to do it promptly, before the attacks from the north begin.'

'Attacks?' Merrivale asked.

'The Scots will launch against us soon, we can be certain of that. It is part of their pact with the Valois adversary, to raid from the north while most of our men are in France. I need you to go to London and meet with the queen and council, describe the plot as you have uncovered it and work with them to rid England of this cancer. We have enough enemies outside the country, we don't need them inside as well.' The king took a sip of wine from a cup standing at his elbow. 'Where do you intend to start once you land in England?'

Nothing like making up plans on the spur of the moment, Merrivale thought. 'I would start with de Tracey's family, sire, especially with his brother Sir Gilbert, the banker. His position would provide ample opportunity for fomenting plots and he has the funds to support them. Of course, he might be completely innocent, but even so he may know something that will be useful.'

The king nodded. He knew Gilbert de Tracey well; the banker was one of the most prominent men of commerce in London, a merchant of the Staple and a force to be reckoned with. The king himself had borrowed money from Tracey on a number of occasions. 'Agreed, that is a good beginning,' he said. 'My formal messengers to London are preparing to leave, but I would like you also to carry some special letters to the queen on this affair. As you well know, you may depend on her wise counsel in all matters. She has already seen your reports on the summer's events. You shall have special passes as usual to speed your journey, and the *Grace-Dieu* is in port at Wissant, ready to take you across to England.'

'Yes, sire. There is one small matter, however. If I am to return to England I am reluctant to leave the Demoiselle de Tesson here without my protection. She has been under my care since Carentan, and has no family here to support her. I want to take her with me to England for her own safety.'

'Under your care?' The king looked amused. 'Well, if the lady is agreeable, by all means take her with you. Although from what I hear of the lady, it is likely to be her decision and not yours.'

'Indeed, sire,' Merrivale said patiently. 'I think she will be willing to leave with me. One of the conspirators, the Seigneur de Brus, appears to have survived the battle. Brus hates her and has threatened her life on several occasions. I don't think much persuasion will be needed.'

The king waved a hand. 'Then tell the *demoiselle* to go with you. An army is no place for women.'

Ah, thought Merrivale, thinking of the two young archers who had been his guards during the summer, *if only you knew how many women your army is harbouring...* The king stood up, signifying the meeting was over. 'Concentrate on ferreting out the remaining plotters,' he said. 'The queen and council will provide you with whatever information they have. Report to them regularly, as you did to me. That's all.'

–

The cliffs of the English coast were drawing closer now. Merrivale shook himself from his reverie and went back to the stern of the ship to find Tiphaine. He had been right; she had not needed much persuading to come with him. The knowledge that Brus was still alive provided a strong compulsion to put the width of the Channel between herself and the vengeful Norman baron.

He found her leaning on the rail, gazing at the thin line of coast to the south where the cliffs fell away. 'Have you been out of France before?' he asked gently.

'No. I was sent to the nuns while very young, and lived with them for most of the time until my capture and imprisonment.

This is also my first time on a boat.' She smiled a little. 'It is a day of many firsts. When shall we reach Hargate?'

'Lord Grey's castle is only a short ride from Dover, five or six miles.'

She smiled wryly. 'Ah, then I have not long until I meet my fate.'

Ever since he had first found Tiphaine on the streets of burning Carentan, filthy from her long imprisonment and in imminent danger of being raped by English soldiers, Merrivale had been obsessed with finding her a place of safety. It was Sir John Grey, one of the talented young captains in the English army, who had suggested she go to Hargate, his family home. His sister, Lady Mary, was married to his fellow captain Sir Richard Percy, son of the powerful Northumberland baron Lord Percy, and was about the same age as Tiphaine; she would, Grey said, make a suitable companion.

'I trust that Lady Mary will not fall into the category of "your fate",' Merrivale said. 'According to her brother, she is a very intelligent and friendly young woman.'

'I am certain she is. But how will she like having an unknown Norman woman thrust upon her? And what will the rest of her family think?'

Merrivale smiled. 'If Lady Mary is anything like her brother John, she will begin by submitting you to a rigorous examination of your reading habits with a view to gauging the gaps in your knowledge. Being convent educated, I am sure you will pass with honours.'

She looked at him. 'I am certain she will also be kind and welcoming,' Merrivale said.

'Mmm,' said Tiphaine. 'Well, time will tell.'

Hargate, 3rd of September, 1346
Late afternoon

Time, in this case, was about three hours. Letters from Sir John Grey ensured that Merrivale, Tiphaine and their three servants were made welcome. Lord Grey, an amiable, square-built man of about fifty, and his gentle, sweet-natured wife enveloped the travellers with kindness. The daughter of the house, Lady Mary Percy, was small, humorous and sharp-witted. She eyed Tiphaine's red hair, hanging rough-cut to the shoulders of the ragged boy's tunic she had worn for most of the last six weeks. 'Is that the newest fashion in Normandy?'

'I had to cut my hair off when I came out of prison,' Tiphaine said. 'Things had begun to build nests in it.'

'Prison? What did you do? Wear red shoes to church? Teach a pig to become a lawyer?'

A small spark began to glow in Tiphaine's eyes. 'Something like that,' she said.

'Come and tell me all about it. And for heaven's sake let's find you some decent clothes. Did you see my husband before you left France? Was he well?'

She bustled Tiphaine away. Another servant took Merrivale to his lodgings, a small room above the hall, and he sat down on the edge of the bed for a moment, feeling weary. Unlike the rest of the army, he had not celebrated much in the aftermath of Crécy. Too many things were still worrying him, too many cares resting on his shoulders.

Crécy had opened poorly healed wounds. Old adversaries, men he had not met or even thought of in years, had reappeared. Some were dead now; King Jean of Bohemia, who had once ardently desired Merrivale's own death, had fallen on the battle-field. But many others had escaped, and now they were gathering in the shadows once more. He could feel their presence, invisible, ominous.

Yolande would be in mourning now, he thought. She had always looked well in white...

A servant interrupted his reverie, calling him for supper. Rising, he went out and found Tiphaine on the stairs. He blinked; he was unused to seeing her in skirts. He held out his arm as they reached the hall and said, 'Come, my lady, supper awaits us.' She performed an ironic curtsey and swept with him into the hall where a table was set for dining.

As well as the family, Lord and Lady Grey and Lady Mary, there were two other diners, a grave man in a grey Franciscan habit and another in a coat of expensive Cambrai cloth lined with silk and trimmed with vair, with several rings on his fingers. Merrivale thought he looked familiar. 'Here are our guests just arrived from France,' Lord Grey said cheerfully, introducing Merrivale and Tiphaine. 'They bring good news, which you will be delighted to hear. Sir Herald, *demoiselle*, may I present our chaplain, Brother Reynard? And this is Sir Gilbert de Tracey from London.'

Merrivale stopped abruptly. 'Sir Gilbert de Tracey, the banker?'

'The very same,' said the other man, smiling. 'The Grey family and the Percys are among my clients. I have called to transact some business with Lord Grey and also Lady Mary on behalf of her husband. I am glad to meet you, Sir Herald.'

Merrivale bowed. *How glad will Tracey be*, he thought, *to hear that the last I saw of his brother, he was stretched dead across the back of a horse with an arrow sticking out of his back?*

2

Crayford, 5ᵗʰ of September, 1346
Afternoon

The cavalcade of a dozen riders had passed Rochester and Dart-
ford and was now, after nearly two days of travel, approaching
London. The party was rather larger than originally planned. It
had been intended that Merrivale and Lord Grey should go, the
former to report to the queen and council, the latter to attend
the opening of parliament scheduled for later in the month. Then
Lady Mary had decided that she and Tiphaine would join them,
and once she had decided, that was that; Lady Mary might be
small and young, but she was every bit as formidable as her much
larger soldier husband, and she would not be moved from her
purpose once she had formed it.

Gilbert de Tracey was travelling with them too. Now that he
had finished his business in Kent he was anxious to get back
to London, he said, to look after his brother's finances in the
wake of the terrible news of his death. Merrivale was hard put
to decide whether the banker was more shocked by the death
of his brother, or by the news that he had joined the Knights of
Saint John shortly before his death and attempted to put all his
worldly goods into the military order's hands. As a banker, the
herald thought cynically, gazing at Tracey's back, he would likely
be more concerned about the latter. Whatever the reason, like
Merrivale, Tracey wanted to get to London as soon as possible.

Lady Mary's motives were harder for the herald to discern.
Certainly there was no reason for her not to join her father,

but judging by her mother's surprise at Lady Mary's intentions, this was not a normal occurrence. Perhaps she was simply, as she claimed, keen to visit the city for pleasure and help Tiphaine get some new clothes. Whatever her reasons, she had thrown herself into the visit, sorting out baggage and arranging for the passage of larger items by water up to London. Her skills were impressive; Merrivale thought she behaved like a confident matron, not a bride of less than a year.

Any suggestion that the ladies go by cart was firmly rejected. 'We shall ride,' declared Lady Mary. 'A cart will take weeks to get there. The *demoiselle* and I are used to riding.'

That was true; Tiphaine, certainly, had spent many hours on horseback crossing Normandy and northern France last summer. So here they were, Merrivale with his three servants, Baron Grey and his escort, Tracey and two more servants, and Lady Mary and Tiphaine with a groom and a maidservant. Two of Merrivale's servants had been with him for years; Mauro, his Spanish valet, was clever and capable and Warin the senior groom was a solid, reliable man who, like Merrivale himself, hailed from Dartmoor in Devon. After Tiphaine joined them there were more horses to care for and Merrivale had engaged a second groom, another Devonian named Diccon Luxton, from Lydford.

The low hills and marshes stretched around them. Ahead was a final river to cross, the Cray, with the village of Crayford huddled around a ford in the river. It was late summer and the river was low, the water barely a trickle over its stony bed.

As the group prepared to cross the ford, a rumbling noise behind them drew their attention. Tracey and Merrivale, riding at the rear, turned to see a horseless farm wagon careering down the hill towards them, gathering speed. 'Get off the road!' Tracey shouted at the others, but there were houses and shops lining the road; there was nowhere for them to go.

Merrivale and Luxton the groom leaped down from their mounts and ran towards the oncoming cart, looking frantically for anything that might stop or at least slow down its progress towards the vulnerable mounted party trapped on the road ahead. Baron

Grey and his men grabbed the bridles of the women's horses and sped them down the slope to the river where they could spread out and let the wagon pass through; Mauro, Warin and Tracey rode behind them, shielding them with their bodies and those of their horses. One of Tracey's men had dismounted too, and he grabbed a wooden stool sitting outside a shop and threw it in front of the wheel of the wagon. The stool splintered but the wagon slowed slightly, buying the party in front a little more time. Merrivale's horse, panicked by the oncoming vehicle, added to the confusion by racing neighing through the party, jostling other horses out of the way as it escaped towards the river.

Luxton seized a broom leaning against a fence and thrust it between the front wheel and body of the wagon. It turned sharply, crushing him between the wheel and the fence, knocking part of the fence down. The groom screamed, adding to the noise and confusion, but the wagon came to a halt, its iron-rimmed wheel resting on the groom's legs. Merrivale and Tracey's man scrambled to move the cart off the howling man while at the same time preventing it from rolling down the hill again. Mauro came running with several saddlebags in his hands and shoved them under the wheels, while a shopkeeper ran out with a bench and jammed it under one wheel too. Further disaster had been prevented.

With the wagon secured, Merrivale knelt beside his moaning groom. The young man was slumped against the broken fence, his breathing ragged. His legs were bloodied and broken. As Merrivale reached him, a woman appeared from a nearby cottage with cloths and a jug of water. Between them, the herald and the woman tried to move Luxton into a position that would not add to his pains.

'Here you go, lad, have a sip of this,' said the woman. She held the jug to the lips of the injured man, but he struggled to drink. She turned her attention to the damaged legs and started tearing up cloths for bandages to staunch the blood. Merrivale ran his hands gently over Luxton's torso, but a scream of pain stopped him.

'I can't feel my legs,' the groom moaned. He coughed, and blood ran down from the corner of his mouth. Merrivale and the woman exchanged looks and she laid down the bandages, knowing there would be no need for them.

Warin arrived. 'Is everyone else safe?' the herald asked.

'No one else was hurt apart from a few chickens who were behind the fence when it collapsed,' said Warin. He gazed in horror at Luxton, whose breathing grew more shallow with each passing moment. The woman knelt beside the young man, holding his hand and murmuring soft words of comfort as his breathing slowed and gradually ceased. She remained kneeling in prayer as Merrivale bent down, crossing Luxton's arms across his chest and gently closing his eyes.

After some moments the herald stirred. 'Is there a priest here, who could give my man a decent burial? He has no family in this part of the country, and burial here would be gentler and kinder than taking him to London with us.'

The woman nodded. 'I'll send my lad to fetch Father John. He might be on the way already, if he's heard the noise.'

A black-robed figure came hurrying up from the river, threading his way through the mounted party and local onlookers who had gathered to look at the scene of disaster. He saw Merrivale's tabard bearing the royal livery, three red leopards on a field of yellow, and bowed, then knelt beside Luxton and began to pray for the dead man's soul. After several minutes he rose again.

'Will you bury him?' Merrivale asked. 'I will defray all costs, of course.'

The priest bowed again. 'He will be safe in our hands. The coroner will want to make a report about what happened here today.'

'Our party are due in London as soon as possible. I am instructed to meet the queen and the royal council and Baron Grey has been called to parliament.'

'I understand, Sir Herald. If you are able to write a report, I will see it safely delivered to the coroner. He will of course be able to ask local witnesses for their testimony.'

Merrivale nodded. He looked again at Luxton. Too young, he thought; too young to die in such a way, thanks to someone else's stupidity. This was a wasteful and avoidable death.

–

Anxious to reach London as soon as possible, Tracey and his servants rode on. Merrivale spoke to the banker before he departed, and while Luxton's body was being prepared for burial, he spoke also to the woman and the shopkeeper and as many locals as he could about what they had seen and where the wagon had come from.

After the funeral service the party reassembled and rode on, but instead of continuing on to London they made a stop at Bexley where there was a decent, if rather small inn that could house them for the night. The last stage of the journey tomorrow would be a short one. As they sat at the table for their evening meal there was only one topic of rather subdued conversation.

'So *nobody* knew how that wagon had broken free?' asked Tiphaine.

'No one would own up to it, at any rate,' said Baron Grey. 'The wagon's owner was half a mile away in a field, overseeing the cutting of the last of his rye crop. The oxen had been left to graze on the stubble and the wagon was waiting unattended to take away yesterday's harvest.'

'But someone must have set it on its way,' Tiphaine persisted. 'Wagons do not move on their own.'

'True,' said Lord Grey, 'but whoever set it moving wasn't seen, either by the farm workers or by us.'

Tiphaine snorted. 'Well it was certainly not a farm worker I saw lurking beside the road when we rode back to find you. Or do your farm workers wear heraldic devices here in England?'

Merrivale looked up from his plate. '*Demoiselle*, what do you mean by heraldic devices? What did you see?'

'Ah,' she said, 'our herald's attention is caught by the thought of heraldry. I did not see the device clearly, but there was some

14

part of a coat of arms of red and possibly yellow. It was worn by a horseman, just at the top of the hill. He was there, half hidden by a tree, for about ten minutes. When the poor boy's body was taken away, he rode away to the east and disappeared.'

'A device,' Lord Grey said thoughtfully. 'I assure you, *demoiselle*, it is not common for farm workers to wear such things on their clothes. Curious, very curious indeed.'

There was a short silence. 'So,' said Lady Mary, 'do we believe this was not an accident? It was a deliberate attack?'

'That is quite possible,' said the herald.

She looked completely unfazed by this. 'Any thoughts about which of us was the target?'

After most of the party had gone to bed, Merrivale found a quiet corner. Mauro brought his writing box and he settled himself to make sense of the day's events and write a report for the coroner.

> *Notes on the event at Crayford, co. Kent on the Vth day of September, in the twentieth year of the reign of King Edward III*
>
> *Item, at Crayford in the county of Kent, a runaway wagon was apparently aimed at the party consisting of myself, Simon Merrivale, herald to Prince Edward and special envoy of his Grace Edward III of England and France; the Demoiselle Tiphaine de Tesson; Lord Grey of Hargate; his daughter Lady Mary Percy (wife of Sir Richard Percy of Maldon); Sir Gilbert de Tracey, banker and merchant of London; and our servants. One of my men, Diccon Luxton of Lydford, was killed when the wagon crushed him against a fence on the road to the river crossing at Crayford.*
>
> *Item, the wagon belonged to a local freeman, but the wagon was not attended by him or his servants. The free-man, Walter Coster, and his men were working in the field*

some distance from the wagon and none saw it move or saw anyone near it.

Item, the Demoiselle Tiphaine de Tesson has deposed that she glimpsed someone with a heraldic device on his coat but could not identify the device as it was only partially seen. No other person saw anyone near the wagon at the time of the incident.

Item, myself and my servants and Sir Gilbert de Tracey were riding at the rear of the party. However, there is at present no evidence to suggest which member or members of the party were the target of this attack, if attack it was.

Simon Merrivale, heraldus

When the ink was dry he rolled the parchment and sealed it with a blob of wax. The final clause of the report opened the possibility that this had been nothing more than a tragic accident, but he did not believe it, and he knew Tiphaine did not believe it either. This was something more.

'And so, it begins,' he said aloud.

3

On reaching London the party split. Merrivale and his two remaining servants took a boat upriver to Westminster, where they would remain while the herald had his consultations with the queen and her council. Baron Grey, Lady Mary and Tiphaine were bound for the Temple quarter, and headed across the crowded bridge and into the city of London. Lady Mary had made it clear before leaving Hargate that she intended to stay at the Percys' rented London house. Her mother had been horrified. 'You cannot just show up on their doorstep with a party and stay for an indefinite time.'

'But mother, Richard's sisters are in London. They say they are happy to have me stay.'

'You, yes, but you have not told them you are bringing the *demoiselle.*'

'Tiphaine can share a chamber with me. I am sure they will be thrilled to meet someone who spent the summer with the army. I know I was.'

So Lady Mary got her way, as usual, and Lord Grey escorted her and Tiphaine to the Percy house just outside the city's western walls. Her sisters-in-law were indeed delighted to welcome her; they were even more excited to meet the exotic *demoiselle*, and pressed her for news. Tiphaine was economical with the details of her own exploits during the summer campaign, but was happy to tell the Percy women about what she had seen of their brothers,

Sir Richard and Sir Harry. That, it transpired, was what they were mostly interested in.

Tiphaine found it strange to be part of a family household. The lives of Lady Mary and the Percy sisters were far removed from her own girlhood convent life, then two years in prison. She felt like she was a different species. Mary was concerned for her husband and did not know when (or if) she would see him again, but she had the support of family and friends. The two young Percy women lived much of their lives on the northern frontier of the country, but again had the cushion of family and money to fall back on and the prospect of marriage and children to come. Tiphaine was not envious, but did wonder what it must be like to have such comforts to depend on. Reluctantly, she had accepted some money from Merrivale, realising that she could not live on air and at the very least would need clothes. Her hosts greeted this news with delight and promised to help her replenish her wardrobe over the next few days. They kept their promise with enthusiasm.

The house was full of comforts and her new friends were full of kindness. But for Tiphaine something was missing. She wondered what the herald was doing, and realised she was irritated that she did not know.

London, 7th of September, 1346
Morning

The queen had yet to arrive from Windsor. Parliament was due to begin its sitting in four days' time and the barons, prelates and knights of the shires were arriving steadily in London. Merrivale used the time to gather information, in particular listening carefully for any whispers about the 'man from the north' who had defied identification during the Crécy campaign. His efforts were hampered by the absence, with leave, of many of the northern barons and prelates; even the Archbishop of York, recently appointed Warden of the Marches, was absent. The threat

18

of renewed war with Scotland was talked of everywhere. Rumour was rife, but actual information was scarce.

In search of better intelligence, Merrivale went into the city. Merchants like Sir John Pulteney and William de la Pole had interests across the whole country and de la Pole, whose origins were in Yorkshire, was a sure source of up-to-date knowledge about the northern part of the kingdom and its troublesome neighbour. These men also knew all about the finances of their fellow merchant and rival Gilbert de Tracey; and, surprisingly, his brother.

'Both the Tracey brothers have had complicated finances for many years now,' commented John Pulteney, who was himself no stranger to complex financial dealings. 'Latterly Edward was doing many deals in the Low Countries and France, which was risky given the political situation. He must have been making a good rate of return in order to compensate for the risks and transaction costs of doing such business. But his position as one of the king's favourites may have shielded him from accusations of removing sterling from England.'

This was news to Merrivale; the late Edward de Tracey had claimed that his income came from land, not trade. 'Exporting currency is illegal, of course,' de la Pole said.

'It is,' said Pulteney, 'although everyone does it. The coming parliament is going to discuss the subject, or so we are informed.'

Merrivale nodded. 'The king has been very concerned about this, particularly when there seems also to be so much false money about. Counterfeit money just adds to the expense of wars. But the two of you would know all too well about the high cost of war-making.'

Pulteney and de la Pole gave wry smiles. As pragmatic men and important lenders to Edward III for many years, they were well used to the vicissitudes of war finance and the dangers associated with getting on the wrong side of the king in matters of money. 'Do you know whether Gilbert de Tracey was involved in his brother's activities? Did he follow Edward overseas?'

'Not so far as I am aware, no,' replied de la Pole. 'He has concentrated on providing banking services to many of our barons and earls. The Percys are one of his clients, so he is well versed in the ups and downs of business on our northern border. I believe he has made somewhat of a speciality of working with the Disinherited lords. He apparently likes to live dangerously. Though there are rumours that he may be changing his mind.'

'Oh?' said Merrivale. 'In what way?'

De la Pole and Pulteney exchanged glances. 'It is only a rumour,' the latter replied, 'but it is said he intends to retire from the world, turning all his goods over to one of the holy orders. Seems that sort of thing runs in the family.'

'Which order?' Merrivale's voice was sharp.

'I did not hear. Perhaps the Knights of Saint John like his brother? But I don't know for certain.'

'If you hear anything further, I would be very glad to hear of it,' said Merrivale.

'We shall pass on any news if we hear it,' said Pulteney. 'You are staying at the palace?'

He was indeed, staying in the old palace near the queen's apartments in a small suite of chambers kept for the use of the Prince of Wales. During the prince's absence, Merrivale noted, his sisters had begun to encroach on their brother's space. The prince would want to have words with them when he returned, the herald thought. A London palace was being prepared for the young prince, but it would be some time before it was ready.

Lambeth Palace, 8ᵗʰ of September, 1346
Morning

Lambeth Palace was just across the river from Westminster, and as instructed by the king, Merrivale went to consult John Stratford, Archbishop of Canterbury and president of the royal council; the council's titular head was the king's second son Prince Lionel of Antwerp, but he was only eight years old. The archbishop welcomed him; they had known each other since Merrivale first began in royal service. Like de la Pole and Pulteney, Stratford's relations with the king had not always been smooth. As with most churchmen his role as archbishop was as much political as spiritual, and while he had not suffered the fate of his famed predecessor Thomas Becket, he had incurred the king's anger more than once. His appointment as president of the regency council had been a surprise to many.

Baron Grey was with the archbishop. 'His Grace and I are old friends and campaigners in parliament,' Grey said. 'He was kind enough to offer me a comfortable place to stay whilst we wait for parliament to assemble.'

Stratford smiled. 'Lord Grey prefers the air on this side of the river to the heady atmosphere of Westminster. I hope your time in London has been profitable, Merrivale? I must say you arrived rather quickly. The official party from the army in France is not expected for a few more days.'

'His Grace has given me some particular tasks to undertake and a small party travels swiftly,' Merrivale said. 'I understand the queen is due shortly?'

'Her Grace will arrive from Windsor tomorrow and stay at Westminster for a few days before journeying on to join the king in France. She is taking her eldest daughter with her.'

An army is no place for women, Merrivale remembered the king saying at their last meeting. Unless, that is, you are Edward III, in which case the rules don't apply. 'Your Grace, I wish to speak to you about a rather delicate matter.'

'Oh, yes?' Stratford glanced at Baron Grey. Merrivale shook his head.

'Lord Grey knows much of the story already. It concerns Sir Edward de Tracey, who was killed the day after the battle at Crécy-en-Ponthieu. Tracey had left the army unexpectedly before the battle. After his departure, it became clear that Tracey had joined the Knights of Saint John. Equally, it became plain that he had been plotting against the king in concert with Jean de

Nanteuil, the French prior, and others including John of Hainault, the king of Bohemia and the lords of Genoa and Monaco.'

Stratford said nothing. Merrivale wondered how much he already knew. 'Unsurprisingly, the king is concerned to know whether the Knights had any role in this treason. In your opinion, do we need be concerned about the loyalty of the English Knights of Saint John?'

'Tracey never struck me as one suited to the religious life, not even in a military order,' said Stratford, and Grey stifled a snort at the thought. 'Far too keen on the pleasures of the flesh he is, or I should say, was. He was equally keen on wielding influence and power at court. That might have been tricky to accomplish in an Order already full of powerful, influential men. Hmm. Curious.'

Merrivale waited while the older man considered the news and watched as the archbishop turned over options in his mind. 'Is Philip de Thame in London?' Grey asked.

Thame was the grand prior of the Knights in England. 'He is at the priory at Clerkenwell,' Stratford said. 'I shall arrange to see Thame and see if he has anything of interest to say.'

'Indeed,' said Merrivale. 'Thank you, your Grace. I am most grateful for your help.'

Westminster, 9th of September, 1346
Morning

There was, as always in Edward III's palaces, the sound of children in the background. Nearly twenty years of marriage to Philippa of Hainault had brought forth ten children, of whom an astonishing eight had survived infancy. It may have been the newest and youngest princess, Margaret, born only a few weeks ago, whose lungs were being exercised so lustily nearby.

The queen sat straight on a simple throne, surveying Merrivale as he approached with intelligent, somewhat cautious dark eyes. As always, she was beautifully dressed in fine embroidered pale fabrics that contrasted with the warmth of her skin. She had a broad, unremarkable face with a short, slightly snubbed nose. She was, by some distance, the most formidable woman in the kingdom.

Merrivale bowed low. 'I hope my reports were informative, your Grace.'

'As always,' she said. 'You are a diligent servant, Merrivale. My husband tells me you believe this conspiracy is still active.'

'That is correct, your Grace. John of Hainault survived the battle, as did a number of the others, including Rollond de Brus, a cousin of David Bruce of Scotland. Most importantly, the Englishman we know only as the man from the north has not been identified. I am convinced he is the leader of the conspirators.'

The queen's eyebrows raised. 'The man from the north?'

'He speaks with a northern accent, according to one who has heard his voice. That is all we know of him.'

'Not much to go on,' she commented.

'No, but his hand has been apparent in many of the problems that beset our army this past summer. It is important to identify and neutralise him.'

'Indeed. I trust that this shall be one of your key tasks in the coming weeks. What then is this connection with the Knights of Saint John?'

'That is not yet clear, your Grace. It is possible that the plot was confined to the French priory, and the involvement of the Knights ended with the death of Jean de Nanteuil, the prior. I have asked Archbishop Stratford to examine whether the prior of England might also have been involved.'

'A wise precaution.' She was still watching him, studying him.

'The other loose end concerns the banker Gilbert de Tracey, the traitor's brother. I don't know whether he had any involvement in the plot, but I hear rumours that he is planning to liquidate his business and withdraw from the world.'

'The rumours are accurate,' said the queen. 'I was informed only this morning that he intends to take holy orders at the priory of Hexham in Northumberland. He has made arrangements to give his entire fortune, some thirty thousand marks, to charity.'

Merrivale looked puzzled. 'I would have thought Sir Gilbert was worth more than thirty thousand marks.'

'I don't just think it, Sir Herald, I know it. Tracey has, or had, one of the largest fortunes in the country. I have already asked the Chancery clerks to look into his affairs, and parliament will take this up as well when it meets. If Sir Gilbert is giving money away in secret that is his affair. But if he is hiding it to avoid taxes, or smuggling it out of the country, that is rather different.'

Merrivale nodded. 'Is it known why he chose Hexham? It is rather remote.'

'Perhaps that is what appealed to him. But I agree, it is a strange choice. There is a truce with Scotland, but it expires at Michaelmas. In three weeks' time we will be at war again, and Hexham is almost on the border. Our spies have heard rumours of forces mustering at Perth, but we do not yet know how many men the Scots will raise. We expect a season of heavy raiding along the borders, to say the least.'

'Hopefully the northern barons, the Percys and Nevilles and their allies, can hold them back.'

'Yes,' said the queen. 'Hopefully.'

There was a long pause. 'What is it that your Grace is not telling me?' Merrivale asked.

Her lips twitched a little. 'You always were impertinent, even when you were a messenger. Very well. There are other rumours too. They suggest there is disaffection among the northern lords, particularly the Disinherited.'

'That is not surprising,' Merrivale said. The Disinherited were a faction of northern barons and knights whose families had served under the king's grandfather during the English occupation of Scotland, and been given lands there. After the collapse of English rule those lands had been confiscated by the victorious Scots, but fourteen years ago a party led by Edward Balliol, the English-backed claimant to the throne of Scotland, had invaded the country again. After a second brief occupation they had been thrown out, but they still claimed their lost lands.

'If I may speak plainly, the Disinherited feel abandoned,' Merrivale said. 'The war with France has taken English attention away from Scotland. They feel that their claims are no longer supported by the government in London, and they have been cast aside. Lord Wake, Sir Gilbert d'Umfraville, Sir Robert de Lisle and the other leaders are angry. If I were in their shoes, I might feel the same.'

'Fortunately, you are not,' the queen said coolly. 'I have a commission for you, Merrivale. Unless the king has commanded your return to France?'

'Not immediately, your Grace. My instruction is to identify the remaining conspirators.'

'Then you can kill two birds with one stone. Our officials will look into Gilbert de Tracey's financial affairs. You will go north and continue your investigation. You will also observe the Disinherited and the other northern barons, and uncover any evidence of disloyalty among them. If there is treason in the north we need to know about it.' The intelligent dark eyes watched him. 'Do you think the conspirators might try to stir up trouble in the north?'

Merrivale nodded. 'The Disinherited would be an easy mark,' he said. 'And time is pressing. With your leave, your Grace, I shall depart as soon as possible.'

'I will send warrants so you may use the messenger service. Call on Archbishop de la Zouche on your way. And there is a banker in Newcastle whose services I use, and whom I trust. His name is William Blyth, and I have asked him to give you any assistance you desire. Godspeed you, herald.'

On his way back to his own chamber Merrivale was surprised to encounter Tiphaine, Lady Mary and the Percy sisters. Tiphaine wore a gown with an embroidered girdle that reminded him of a Giotto fresco, and though she was unmarried, a scarf over her chopped-off hair. She looked uncomfortable, he thought.

'What brings you here?' he asked.

'We have come to call on Princess Isabella,' said Lady Mary. 'She and her mother are going to join the king at Calais shortly, and she is not happy about it. She demanded to see her friends one last time before she goes into exile. Her words, not mine. I brought Tiphaine because she knows France, and might be able to tell her Highness what to expect.'

'I suspect the princess will find plenty to amuse her,' Merrivale said. 'Are you going with them?'

'No.' Mary frowned. 'I have other things to occupy me,' she said. 'I have just seen my brother-in-law, Harry. Did you know he had returned from Calais?'

Sir Harry Percy was the elder son and heir of Lord Percy, the most powerful of the northern barons. 'No, I didn't,' said Merrivale. 'How is he?'

Tiphaine plucked at the sleeve of her gown. 'He was enigmatic,' she said.

'He was shifty,' said Lady Mary. 'He said he was going north, where he had some business to do with Scotland. Then he closed his mouth and wouldn't say anything more. The Percys don't do business with Scotland. They hammer Scots into the ground and use them for tent pegs.'

'That has always been my experience,' the herald agreed. 'As expected, I am going north myself for a while, and must bid you farewell. I may not return for a few weeks. *Demoiselle*, I am certain that you shall enjoy your time with Lady Mary.'

Tiphaine pulled a face at him.

'If you see my brother-in-law, keep an eye on him,' said Lady Mary. 'He's just stupid enough to get into trouble, and not quite smart enough to get out of it.'

II

4

Cawood, 19th of September, 1346
Evening

High clouds cast a veil over the sun. Summer's heat was gone now, and the north wind hissing across the fens was full of autumn chill. Merrivale and his servants pulled their weary horses to a halt in the courtyard of the Archbishop of York's palace, and grooms came running to take their bridles as they dismounted. A steward appeared, his tunic bearing the arms of the archbishop, white crossed keys on a field of red. 'I seek an audience with his Grace,' the herald said. 'My name is Simon Merrivale.'

'Yes, sir. You are expected.'

Servants conducted him to a guest chamber, handsomely painted with a fire already lit on the brick hearth to keep out the damp. A narrow arched window looked out across the River Ouse and its marshes. A ship, a big North Sea cog, was moored next to a pier in the river and he could see men hard at work around the ship, loading it with a cargo of cut stone brought down from quarries further inland. Why the archbishop chose to reside in this bleak damp place rather than in the comforts of York a few miles north was a mystery.

He stood and watched the work for a while, feeling weariness etch its way into his bones. It had been a hard ride from London, changing horses every few hours, wanting to stop and rest but knowing he was desperately short of time. His week in London had hardly provided much rest after the intense physical and mental strain of the six-week campaign in France. *I thought a herald's post would be a sinecure after ten years as a King's Messenger,* he thought with mild humour. *It would seem I was wrong.*

Old memories stirred, fatigue releasing them from their bonds. He thought of other journeys in Savoy and Brittany, Spain and Florence, and of the good friends and comrades who had ridden with him. Very few were still alive now. He was not entirely certain how he himself had survived.

He thought of Yolande, the woman who had once been his whole world. He wondered, as he did every day, where she was now and whether he would see her again. For both their sakes, he hoped not. But her loss was a pain that would not fade, a blood-red rose that bloomed and never died.

—

A servant brought him hot water and a towel, and he washed the dust of travel from his face and hands. Opening a bag he took out his glittering tabard, smoothing out the wrinkles and pulling it over his head. The steward knocked at the door. 'His Grace will see you now, sir.'

Crossing the courtyard, he followed the steward into the great hall where servants were clearing away the remains of dinner, and upstairs to a solar. Tapestries depicting hunting scenes lined the walls, and a coal fire burned in another grate. A reliquary cross on a polished oak side table was the only sign of religious devotion in the room.

William de la Zouche was a tall man in his late forties, flecks of grey in his tonsured hair and a stubborn cast to his mouth and jaw. He and Merrivale knew each other slightly; their paths had crossed in London years ago, when Zouche was Lord Treasurer and Merrivale a King's Messenger.

'Let's get to the point,' he said bluntly as Merrivale bowed. 'You are Queen Philippa's watchdog.'

'Her Grace has entrusted me with several commissions,' Merrivale said. 'Inquiring into the loyalty of the northern lords is one of them.'

'Does the queen have reason to doubt their loyalty?'

'Yes,' said Merrivale. 'Else I would not be here.'

Zouche stared at him. 'Am I one of the men she doubts?'

Merrivale considered this for a moment. 'Your Grace has been appointed Warden of the Marches, guardian of the frontier with Scotland. Does that not suggest that you are in high favour?'

The archbishop snorted. 'Hardly. The warden's post is a poisoned chalice. I don't have enough men or money to keep out the Scots, and when they come over the border and to burn and pillage again, it is me that will get the blame. Meanwhile, Percy and Neville are boiling over with resentment because they were wardens for years until the king snatched the post away from them. They're just waiting for me to make a mistake so they can take it back again. I'm damned, whatever I do.'

'And you will have to do something,' Merrivale pointed out. 'The truce expires in ten days' time. The queen's spies tell her the Scottish army is mustering at Perth. Do you know how many men?'

'At least fourteen thousand. Possibly more.'

Merrivale stared at him. '*Fourteen thousand?* Are you certain?'

'The latest report came through from Rokeby yesterday. All of the mormaers and earls and barons have been called up. The fact that Moray, Menteith, Dunbar, Strathearn and the Lord of the Isles have all mustered tells you how large their army is. Moray is their war leader, a man whom the entire army respects. Sir William Douglas and the border reavers are also gathering at Jedburgh. The French have sent help too.'

'Do you know how many men have come from France?'

'Not many, but they have sent weapons and we hear of large sums of money. Their leader is David Bruce's French cousin, Rollond de Brus. They mean business this time.'

At the mention of Brus's name, a cold finger ran down Merrivale's spine. 'This is not just a raiding campaign,' he said. 'This is an invasion.'

'Yes,' said Zouche. 'That is Sir Thomas Rokeby's conclusion as well.'

They faced each other for a moment in the lamplight. *He looks exhausted*, Merrivale thought, with bags under his eyes, and deep-etched lines in his forehead. His career had taken him straight from Oxford into the royal household, where he had served as Keeper of the Wardrobe, Lord Privy Seal, Lord Treasurer, Dean of York and now archbishop; it had not prepared him for this moment. He had absolutely no experience of military command.

'Do we know what their objective is?'

'Not yet. Rokeby's spies are trying to find out. It's likely to be either Carlisle or Berwick. Carlisle is the easier target; Douglas burned it just last year. But Berwick is the key to the border.'

'What steps have you taken so far?'

'I have called on all the northern barons to muster their men at Richmond.'

Too far south, Merrivale thought. 'How many men can they raise?'

'I don't know,' Zouche said. 'Quite frankly, Merrivale, your guess is as good as mine. Whatever it is, it's probably not enough. The queen's suspicions are correct. I don't know which of the barons I can trust. If any.'

The fire flickered. Tension crackled in the air. 'Tell me,' said the herald.

'Percy and Neville are jealous of me, but there is more to it than that. Someone is working on them. I don't know what they are being promised, but there is a strong rumour that when the Scots come over the border, Percy and Neville will stay on their own lands. And if they do, many other barons will follow their lead.'

'They will protect their own,' Merrivale said. 'Especially if they don't believe there is a chance of defeating the Scottish army in the field. What about the Disinherited?'

'They are receiving special attention. David Bruce is trying to woo them over to the Scottish side. The word is that Umfraville has been promised restoration of all his Scottish lands, and the earldom of Angus. Lands and titles have been promised to the others as well.'

'What about the ecclesiastical lords, and the towns?'

Zouche shook his head. 'I'm raising troops from my own estates, of course. But the priory of Durham has refused to help, and the towns are nearly as unreliable as the barons. The Scots are also working on some of the merchants of Berwick and Newcastle, trying to persuade them to turn traitor. All of this is familiar, of course. We nearly lost Berwick last year when the Scots bribed some of the townsmen to open the gates. But this time the plot is more widespread, and more serious.'

'Do we know who these merchants are?'

'Not yet. Rokeby is investigating in Berwick, and I have asked William Blyth to do the same in Newcastle.' The archbishop paused for a moment. 'At least we have some reliable men. Just not enough of them.'

'And Durham? Have the Scots managed to influence the prior and his monks also?'

'Possibly. I don't know.' The archbishop paused for a moment. 'Something is strange, Merrivale. Very strange.'

'What do you mean, your Grace?'

'David Bruce is young and lacks experience. His nobles are hot-brained and ambitious, and apart from Patrick of Dunbar, none is particularly competent. Of late they have done little more than raid across the border and burn a few towns. But now Rokeby says they have a unity of purpose he has not seen before, not since old Robert Bruce died. Someone has pulled them together and stiffened their backs. Rokeby says it isn't Dunbar. So who is it? Do *you* know?'

'No,' said Merrivale. 'But I have heard the same thing from other sources. We need to find out who is behind this, and eliminate them.'

'We don't have a prayer,' the archbishop said abruptly. 'Unless our nobles stand together, the border is wide open and the Scots can walk in any time they wish. And there is not a damned thing we can do about it.'

'I do have one possible line of inquiry,' the herald said. 'Are you aware that Sir Gilbert de Tracey has taken holy orders and entered the priory at Hexham?'

'Yes. I saw him on his way north.'

'He called here? May I ask why?'

Zouche shook his head. 'He lodged here for one night on his journey. We knew each other quite well once, when he first came to London and started lending to the king. I negotiated several loans with him.' The archbishop paused. 'Do you believe Gilbert was mixed up in his brother's treason?' The archbishop, of course, had his own sources of information at court.

'I don't know, yet. That is what I need to find out. What do you make of him? As a man?'

Zouche considered. 'He is likeable, if somewhat distant. His father was a wicked and cruel man, and his brother... Well, we know how he turned out. But Gilbert seemed an honest man. For a banker, that is.'

'Do you know why he chose Hexham? He's a Devon man, or at least he was. Northumberland is a foreign country to him.'

'He told me he didn't want to return to the scene of his father's crimes. He wanted a place of peace, where no one knew him or his family, so he could dedicate his life to God's service.'

Merrivale raised his eyebrows. 'Peace? Hexham is only a few miles from the frontier. A strange place to look for tranquillity.'

'Perhaps God called him there,' said the archbishop. 'It does happen, you know. But there may also have been a family connection.'

Merrivale raised his eyebrows.

'Hugh de Tracey,' Zouche said. 'Gilbert's uncle. He is an obedientiary at Durham Priory. Did you not know?'

Although an ordained priest, Hugh de Tracey had worked hand-in-glove with his brother, Sir John de Tracey of Dunkeswell, during the anarchic final years of the old king's reign. Proscribed along with his brother and nephews, like them he had been pardoned in 1332 when the young Edward III decided to wipe clean the slate of the past. 'I knew he had taken monastic vows,' Merrivale said, thinking hard. 'I did not know where.'

'Then your lot should have kept better track of him. He is treasurer of the priory now, and likely to be the next prior. With his fingers on the purse strings he controls the priory. And the priory controls the cathedral, and the cathedral controls the County Palatine of Durham. Brother Hugh and the priory have a great deal of power, and they recognise no master.'

Merrivale stood silent for a moment, feeling the tension increase. Hugh de Tracey controlled Durham. His nephew Gilbert was a short distance away in Hexham. *What if they too were following the orders of the man from the north?*

'What about the bishop?' he asked. 'Surely it is his cathedral.'

Zouche snorted again. 'The bishops of Durham are ciphers, little more. The last one, de Bury, spent more time with his books than he did on diocesan business. The present fellow, Hatfield, is interested only in his career at court.'

'Why should there be any connection between Hugh de Tracey and his nephew? The monks at Durham are Benedictines, and the canons at Hexham are Augustinians. The two orders don't have much to do with each other.'

'Up here they do,' Zouche said, a little grimly. 'The religious orders are the largest landowners in the north of England. Even the estates of the biggest magnates like the Percys and Nevilles are tiny by comparison. And the orders ensure their domination by sticking to each other like glue. It's not just land, either. Salt, coal, iron and lead, they have it all sewn up between them.'

'So Hugh de Tracey may have procured a place for his nephew at Hexham. But why not Durham? A place could have been found in the priory there, surely.'

'I don't know,' said the archbishop. 'And on reflection I don't really care. I have more important things to worry about. So, I suspect, do you.'

Outside the sun was setting, a red ball over the marshes of the Ouse. Tendrils of mist were rising from the river. 'Your Grace may well be right,' Merrivale said. 'I will take up no more of your time. With your leave, my servants and I will depart in the morning.'

'You're too late for dinner, of course. I'll have food sent over to your lodging. Merrivale?'

'Yes, your Grace?'

'I'm glad the queen sent you,' Zouche said abruptly. 'I would rather she had sent a thousand men-at-arms, or a dozen companies of archers. But if she only sent one man, I'm glad it was you.'

5

Durham, 21ˢᵗ of September, 1346
Afternoon

The road north from York had been busy, clogged with wagons loaded with corn and pig iron, bordered by fields of stubble where wheat and flax had just been harvested. At Darlington the air smelled of linseed, and sheets of linen hanging in the air flapped in the wind like sails on a ship. It was after nones on the second day out of Cawood when they reached Neville's Cross, the waymarker for pilgrims heading for Saint Cuthbert's shrine at the cathedral rising above the River Wear. Turning their horses, they rode down to the river and across Framwellgate Bridge into the town. As they reached the busy marketplace, Merrivale turned to his servants.

'Given all that has happened, I am unlikely to be made welcome at the priory. See that inn? Take rooms for us there and wait for me.'

'You are going alone, *señor*?' Mauro asked. 'Is that wise?'

'I am a herald,' Merrivale said. 'No one will dare to harm me.'

'He always says that,' Mauro muttered as they watched their master ride up Fleshergate towards the cathedral.

'So far, he has been mostly right,' said Warin.

'*Sí.* But one day, I think he will go too far.'

Above the gatehouse the banner of the Bishopric of Durham, four silver lions on a crossed field of blue, rippled and snapped in the cold north wind. Merrivale looked up at the colossal bulk of the cathedral, its towers reaching towards the dark, wind-driven clouds. Compared to it, the bishop's castle on the far side of Palace Green looked small and rather dowdy. That was almost certainly no accident, Merrivale thought.

The porter, a black-robed monk standing outside the gatehouse, held a long wooden staff in a manner that suggested he knew how to use it. Another, a boy novitiate, stood hesitantly just inside the gate. 'Who are you?' the monk asked, looking at the herald's tabard. 'What is your business here?'

He must have recognised the royal coat of arms, the yellow embroidered leopards on a field of red blazing even in the dim light, but the challenge was also a statement: *you have no authority here.* By a quirk of history, the bishops of Durham held their lands not as tenants of the crown but as a palatine, independent of royal control. With the passage of time, their own authority had been eroded and the priory had seized power instead. As Zouche had said, the priors of Durham recognised no master.

'I am Simon Merrivale, herald to the Prince of Wales and personal envoy of her Grace the queen. My business is with Brother Hugh at the priory.'

'Brother Hugh sees no one without an appointment.'

'He will see me,' Merrivale said. 'I wish to speak to him about his nephew, Edward de Tracey.'

The porter hesitated for a moment, then turned to the boy novitiate. 'Run to Brother Hugh, and tell him he has a visitor. Quick now!' he shouted, shaking his staff. The boy hitched up the skirts of his cassock and raced away towards the cathedral. The monk turned back to Merrivale. 'Leave your horse here.'

The vast interior space of the cathedral was flooded with light from the high windows and hundreds of lamps and candles reflecting off the painted walls and carved columns. The air was full of competing smells: incense, tallow, unwashed bodies. From a chantry chapel came the sound of voices reciting the mass. Pilgrims arrived in a quiet steady stream, uncovering their heads as they entered the church. Some were barefoot penitents with their hands clasped in prayer, others hobbled on crutches.

Curious, Merrivale followed them towards the east end of the church.

Behind the high altar lay the shrine of Saint Cuthbert, an immense gold reliquary lit by banks of flickering candles. Gemstones glowed with coloured flame, blood-red rubies and garnets, the eye-aching blue of lapis lazuli, emeralds green as spring grass and the purple fire of amethysts. At the centre of the shrine was an image of Cuthbert himself, black-robed, bearded and tonsured, holding a Bible and cross; above him was another, much larger image, Christ enthroned in majesty with blue robe and golden halo, and neat red stigmata on his feet and hands.

The hum of soft prayers filled the air. Some prayed for the souls of the loved ones they had lost, or the restoration of health or sight; others for absolution for sins they had committed, or would commit... Prayers complete, they rose and found the sacristan and his assistants ready to guide them to the stall where they could buy little red splay-armed crosses, badges to remind them that they had made the holy and noble pilgrimage to Cuthbert's shrine. The badges cost sixpence each. *Nothing is free in this life*, the herald thought, *not even forgiveness. Especially not forgiveness.*

'Have you said your prayers, herald?' a voice said quietly beside him.

Merrivale turned. The man who had spoken was in his fifties, with keen dark eyes and a long thin nose. He wore a black habit with the hood thrown back, girdled with a leather belt, and a gold ring on his finger set with a cabochon ruby. His grey hair was tonsured, but unusually for the fashion of the time he wore a carefully trimmed beard. In another convent that might have been considered a luxury, but as the archbishop had said, Durham made its own rules.

There was enough family resemblance to recognise him. 'Brother Hugh de Tracey,' the herald said. 'Thank you for agreeing to see me.'

'In the eyes of the Lord, Brother Hugh is sufficient. Come with me.'

Taking a candle from a nearby stand, Brother Hugh led the way back through the cathedral and out into the cloister. Opening a heavy iron-bound oak door, he ushered Merrivale into the library. More odours floated in the air, leather and parchment and the bitter gall of ink. Parchment rolls and bound books with heavy cover boards rested in wooden racks around the room. A Bible stood open on a lectern, the margins of its pages decorated with bright painted scrollwork.

Brother Hugh lit more candles. 'I presume you have come to tell me about Edward. Save your breath. I have already heard what happened.'

Merrivale nodded. 'Then please accept my condolences for the death of your nephew.'

'Why? He was a traitor. No one should mourn him.'

'Not even his wife and children? Surely they should be pitied.'

'God will provide for them,' said Brother Hugh.

The ruby ring on his finger would have fed Tracey's widow and her daughters for more than a year. 'Let us hope so,' the herald said. 'As for the rest of his family, his brother has resigned his business and taken holy orders. And what about you yourself, brother? I am told you have ambitions to be the next prior of Durham. Considering the disgrace that Sir Edward has brought upon your family, do you think this is now likely?'

The prior's bearded face was full of hostility. 'I am the instrument of God's will, and I go where He calls me. Edward's crimes have naught to do with me.'

'Well said. But I wonder if the king will believe it.'

'What the king believes is of no consequence. I answer only to the prior, and the prior answers only to God.'

The herald nodded. 'Having such close connections with the Almighty must be useful,' he commented. 'Did you by any chance use your influence on behalf of Sir Gilbert, to find him a place at Hexham Priory? That too must be convenient, having your only surviving nephew just a day's ride from here.'

'When I entered this convent fourteen years ago, I renounced my family utterly, herald. This convent, this cathedral, they are my life now. The brothers here are my family. The outside world is of no consequence to me.'

And yet he has not actually denied helping Gilbert, the herald thought, *any more than he denied having ambitions to become prior, another degree closer to God.* 'Did Sir Gilbert call on you when he came north?'

He was surprised by the answer. 'Yes,' Brother Hugh said reluctantly. 'I didn't particularly wish to see him, but courtesy demanded it. We met briefly at the gates, and I congratulated him on his new vocation and wished him well. That was all.'

'I see.' The herald paused for a moment. 'He didn't happen to mention what he had done with his money?'

Brother Hugh stared at him. 'What are you talking about?'

'When he liquidated his bank, Sir Gilbert stated that he had donated his entire estate to various religious houses and hospitals, Hexham Priory included. We know the value of these donations, and it is nothing like the full amount of Sir Gilbert's wealth. Tens of thousands of pounds are missing.'

'So? What is this to do with me?'

'Do you know of any other donations he made? To Durham Priory, perhaps?'

'No. If he had, I would know of it.'

'Of course, you are the priory's treasurer. And Durham is already rich enough, isn't it? You have vast investments in land and coal and iron, as well as the pilgrim trade. From what I have seen this evening, I imagine Saint Cuthbert's shrine has a very steady yield. You do not need Sir Gilbert's money.'

The monk said nothing. 'Another thing puzzles me,' Merrivale said. 'When the Scottish army comes over the border, as it will do very soon now, Hexham will be in danger. Why did Sir Gilbert choose the priory as his place of retreat?'

'I don't know,' said Brother Hugh. 'Why don't you go to Hexham and ask him yourself?'

That was exactly what Merrivale intended to do. 'One last question, brother. Archbishop de la Zouche is raising troops to fight the Scots, and he needs money and men. Why has the priory refused to help him?'

'Because it is not our place to do so,' Brother Hugh said. 'Nor is it Zouche's place. He is a man of God. He should never have become involved in secular affairs, and we will not follow his example. We do God's work here, not the work of man.'

'I see.' Merrivale's voice hardened. 'And were you doing God's work twenty years ago, when you rode out with your brother to terrorise the people of Devon and Dorset? The piracy you engaged in, the ships you plundered, the murders you committed, the men and women you robbed; was that the work of the Lord?'

He had lost his temper, and that was a mistake. Brother Hugh gazed at him for a long time. 'This interview is finished,' he said calmly. 'I regret I cannot offer you accommodation. As you have seen, we have many pilgrims to house.'

'Doing God's work, I know. But when the Scots come, brother – not if, but when – the lords of the north must pull together, all of them, secular and spiritual. If they do not, then Durham will burn, and Hexham, and Newcastle, and the Scots will spread fire and the sword all across the north of England. Will you do nothing to protect your own people?'

'When the time comes, we will follow the will of God.' Ironically, one hand sketched a cross in the air. 'Go in peace, my son.'

–

After Merrivale departed, another man stepped out of the shadows at the far end of the library. Unlike Brother Hugh, he wore the long white tunic and black cape of the Dominican order of friars.

'Did you hear all that?' Hugh asked.

'Every word. Is he dangerous?'

'Very. I've had a full report on him.'

The friar crossed his arms over his chest. He was a portly man, his belly straining at the fabric of his cassock. 'What do we do about him?'

'Watch him. Report his every move to me.'

The friar nodded. 'The usual fee?'

'Of course.'

The door closed behind the Dominican. Brother Hugh walked over to the lectern and stood for a moment, looking down at the Second Book of Samuel. *Thus shalt thou say unto Joab: Let not this thing displease thee, for the sword devoureth in one manner or another; make thy battle more strong against the city, and overthrow it; and encourage thou him.*

Crossing himself, Brother Hugh raised his eyes towards heaven. 'Thy will be done,' he said aloud.

Chester Moor, 22nd of September, 1346
Morning

The wind had veered east, bringing with it the cold chill of the sea. A buzzard circled overhead, riding the wind. Merrivale could see occasional glimpses of the Wear off to the right, water glinting pale in the light. There were coal workings on the far side of the river, black scars across the fields. In the distance lay the houses and church tower of Chester-le-Street; from there it was only a few more miles to Newcastle, their destination.

They passed two groves of trees that had been felled completely; piles of woodchips and a few pale, axe-bitten stumps were all that remained. Up ahead, woodcutters were working on another grove, logs piled up by the side of the road, and he heard the dull thud of axes and the rasp of a saw. He watched the cutters, puzzled at what the men were doing. Ordinarily, timber men only took the best trees and left the rest standing. These men were cutting down everything in sight.

Merrivale's interviews with the archbishop and Brother Hugh had each been unsettling in their different way. It had been nearly twenty years since the Scots had last mounted a full-scale invasion of England, and London had foolishly assumed that it would not happen again. The queen had been more concerned about plots among her restless nobles than any real threat from the north. But if Zouche was right, the kingdom faced two threats at once. The crisis was deeper and more dire than even the queen had imagined.

It had been particularly disconcerting to find Hugh de Tracey in a position of power and influence. Not for the first time, the herald wondered how he had managed to slip into the priory and rise to prominence in such secrecy. Of course, this was the County Palatine of Durham. No one was accountable here; no one had to make reports or render accounts to the crown. He was quite certain that Hugh had lied to him about almost everything.

Near the end of a long journey, when travellers are tired and let their guard down as they think of the comforts that await them, is the moment of greatest danger. One moment the road was empty; the next, men were swarming out of the trees. Merrivale turned his horse, but too late; hard hands dragged him out of the saddle, hurling him to the ground and knocking the wind out of him. He heard Mauro and Warin struggling nearby and looked up to see a man standing over him. The sword in the other man's hand was a silhouette, a dark cross against the background of trees and sky.

He sucked in air and managed to speak. 'Your business is with me,' he said. 'Let my servants go. They have done you no harm.'

The man said nothing. He raised the sword above his head, preparing for a killing stroke.

Someone whistled sharply. The swordsman hesitated, turning his head. The whistle was repeated, and suddenly Merrivale could feel the drumbeat of approaching hooves reverberating in the ground beneath him. The man stepped back, slamming his sword into the scabbard. '*Sauve qui peut!*' he called, and the attackers turned and ran. As quickly as they had arrived, they were gone.

Still winded, Merrivale struggled to his feet. The woodcutters were watching open-mouthed. A party of horsemen came sweeping through the trees, gentlemen in bright coats and hose with feathers in their hats, accompanied by an escort of mounted archers. Some of these had arrows at the nock, and were surveying the woods for targets. The leader of the party rode up to the herald and stopped. 'Are you hurt?' he demanded.

Merrivale looked at Mauro and Warin, who were dusting themselves down. 'Thanks to you, sir, we are unharmed. But we are deeply in your debt.'

'Think nothing of it. Lucky for you we happened to be hunting nearby.'

Merrivale looked at his coat, white with three black lions rampant. 'Sir Thomas Clennell of Hesleyside. You are hunting a long way from home, sir.'

The other man laughed. 'Trust a herald to know everything. I'm the guest of an old friend who lives nearby. I'll send someone to round up your horses, they won't have gone far. The rest of us will see if we can track these brigands down.' He smiled again. 'One kind of hunting is as good as another, hey?'

'Once again, you have my thanks,' Merrivale said. 'We owe you our lives.'

Clennell raised a hand in salute. 'Think nothing of it. I will detain you no longer, Sir Herald. Journey safely.'

He wheeled his horse and rode away, followed by his men. One had an unusual coat of arms, two gold chevrons on blue with a red crescent on the lower chevron. An archer arrived a few minutes later, leading their horses, and they mounted and rode on. Mauro waited until they were out of earshot of the woodcutters. 'Those were not robbers, *señor*,' he said. 'Those were assassins.'

'Yes,' said Merrivale. 'Possibly. Or possibly not.'

'What do you mean, sir?' asked Warin.

'Sir Thomas and his friends arrived at exactly the right time, did they not? And Sir Thomas, of all people. What exactly *is* he doing here?'

'Do you know him, sir?'

'I know who he is. Sir Thomas Clennell of Hesleyside, three black lions on white, claimant to the lordship of Selkirk and one of the leaders of the Disinherited. His English lands are in Tynedale and Coquetdale, up in Northumberland. But today of all days he just happens to be hunting down here in Durham.'

'He said he was the guest of a friend,' said Warin.

'Perhaps he was. And perhaps what we just saw was a mummery staged for our benefit. It stinks like week-old fish. Mauro, Warin, when we reach Newcastle, find out who this friend of Sir Thomas's might be. And learn anything you can about who might have hired a gang of cut-throats to attack a party of travellers on the Great North Road today.'

6

Newcastle was booming. Ships crowded the wharfs along the banks of the Tyne, loading cargos of coal and iron and lead, leather and timber and corn, and offloading bales of Flemish cloth and chests of pepper and ginger. The east wind brought the acrid tang of the salt pans at South Shields a few miles away. Were the merchants of Newcastle oblivious to the sword hanging over their heads? Merrivale wondered. Or were they just determined to make as much money as they could before the storm broke?

They crossed the long stone bridge over the Tyne and came to the gatehouse. Here there were clear signs of preparation for war. The gatehouse was stuffed with armed men, and the wooden arms of stone-throwing engines protruded above the battlements. The captain of the guard gave them directions, and they rode up the slope past the castle to Westgate and the fine house of William Blyth, the queen's favourite merchant.

Courteous and quietly efficient, servants took their horses and guided them inside. The steward met Merrivale in the painted great hall, bowing. They were expected; their accommodation awaited them. The master was abroad in the town on business, but would return soon. Mauro and Warin were taken away to the kitchen and Merrivale was shown to a room in one of the corner towers, finely furnished with painted walls, its own fireplace and a feather bed. Lancet windows looked out over town walls and cropped fields towards a distant line of hills to the west.

Hot water was brought for washing; the towels that came with it had been warmed over a fire. The steward knocked at the door. Dinner would be served as soon as the master returned, but meanwhile might Sir Herald care to take refreshment in the solar? The other guests were already waiting.

'Guests?' said Merrivale.

'Indeed, sir. The lady Mary, wife of Sir Richard Percy of Maldon, and her companion the Demoiselle Tiphaine de Tesson.'

'Good God,' said Merrivale. There did not seem much else to say.

The steward conducted Merrivale up a polished wooden stairway into an octagonal room with white painted walls. The wealth on display made Merrivale blink. Carpets from Badakhshan and Artsakh hung on the walls, colours glowing bright as the jewels on Saint Cuthbert's shrine. Lustrous maiolica pots gleamed in the light of candles burning in gilded torchères. Delicately painted Greek ikons in gold frames jostled for position with Venetian mirrors in filigree glass frames. The floor tiles looked like they had been lifted from a Moorish palace, and probably had been. A pair of linnets perched on a rail above the arched windows, twittering brightly.

The other guests rose from their seats as he entered. Lady Mary was dressed in a vivid green gown with her hair tucked up under a wimple; Tiphaine wore a simple blue kirtle with a pair of brown kid turnshoes with pointed toes, her red hair loose but tidily trimmed and brushing her shoulders. 'Surprise,' said Lady Mary brightly.

'Yes,' Merrivale said. 'It is. How did you get here?'

'You mean, how did we get here ahead of you? We came by sea.'

His eyebrows raised. 'Was that not dangerous? The seas are full of pirates at the moment.'

'I know. We sailed with one, an old ruffian called John Crabbe who changes allegiances more often than his linen. But he is also a great friend of my brother, so we were perfectly safe.'

A servant brought him a glass of wine, and added water from a silver jug. 'And now, you are in danger again,' he said. 'A Scottish army is mustering on the far side of the border, and in a week's time we shall be at war. Was coming here wise?'

'Someone has to pull my idiot brother-in-law's fat out of the fire,' she said crossly. 'After you departed, another report reached London claiming that Sir Harry Percy is in correspondence with the Earl of Dunbar. The queen wanted to have Harry arrested and flung into the Tower. I persuaded her to let me speak to him first. So, I came north.'

'And I came with her,' Tiphaine said.

'I seem to recall something about you going to a place of safety? Never mind. Lady Mary, have you managed to clear your brother-in-law's name?'

'No,' she said, sounding more cross than ever. 'It turns out the rumours are true. The fathead really has been writing to Dunbar. Crabbe, my brother's pirate friend, knew all about it. The whole thing is my brother's fault, as you might imagine.'

'Oh? How is Sir John Grey involved?'

'Because everywhere he goes, he sticks his nose into things. He is practically a legend in these parts, you know. Ask anyone north of the Tyne and they'll tell you all about the Battle of Windy Knowe, or the Hot Trod in Teviotdale, or any number of other tediously heroic narratives. At some point he captured the Earl of Dunbar and negotiated his ransom with his wife.'

'Agnes of Dunbar?'

'The very same. She took a fancy to him, and although he has never admitted it, I'm quite certain they played the beast with two backs. The point is that she and Dunbar were already thinking about how to arrange permanent peace between Scotland and England, and she recruited John as an ally and go-between. After John left the borders, Harry decided to step in and maintain the contact. Being Harry, he didn't bother to get leave to do this, he just went ahead and did it.'

Merrivale thought for a moment. 'Where is Harry now?'

'Here in Newcastle. He was about to go north to the family seat at Warkworth, but I insisted he wait and see you.'

'If there really is a peace party in Scotland and Harry is in touch with them, this could be helpful.'

She made an impatient gesture. 'My brother, for all his faults, is a subtle and clever man. Harry has trouble fastening his own garters. Agnes will cut him into collops and serve him on toast.'

Merrivale nodded. 'Can you arrange for me to meet Harry? If so, I would be grateful.'

'He is lodging at the castle. I will send my maid with a message.'

'There is no need,' said a pleasant voice from the door. 'My servants will be happy to oblige.'

The newcomer was a man of medium height, with an unremarkable face save for a pair of intelligent brown eyes, clean-shaven with carefully trimmed hair. His silk coat was a rich and expensive blue trimmed with sable. 'Sir Herald,' he said, bowing. 'My apologies for not being here to welcome your arrival. My house is yours.'

'Master Blyth,' Merrivale said. 'I am grateful for your hospitality.'

'Her Grace has informed me of your mission,' said Blyth, 'and Lady Mary has given further details. I am entirely at your service. If there is anything I can do to assist, you have only to ask.'

'Thank you. What is the latest news?'

Blyth walked forward, taking a sip from the cup of wine a servant offered. He took something from the pocket of his coat, and Merrivale saw it was a small handful of birdseed. He whistled softly, holding out his hand, and the linnets fluttered down to perch lightly on his outstretched fingers and peck the seed from his palm.

'The Scottish army has completed its muster at Perth,' he said. 'They have not broken the truce, not yet, though we expect that any day. The first blow is likely to fall in the east, probably on Berwick. Then it will be our turn.'

'Are you prepared?'

Blyth smiled. 'You mean the bustle you saw on the river? Everyone is scrambling to ship their last cargos before the Scots come. Do not fear; when they do arrive, they will find us ready. The walls are strong and well-defended, and we also have plenty of money.' He smiled again. 'If we cannot resist the enemy, we will buy them off. And I have already sent my most precious valuables, my wife and children, away to safety in York.'

He shook his hand gently and the linnets flew away to light on the rail again. 'Ah, here is my steward coming to announce dinner. Shall we go down?'

—

They ate in the great hall, its walls painted with rural and hunting scenes under dark wooden rafters. A coal fire glowed in the huge fireplace. Servants brought them salmon pie with figs and damsons, chicken in almond sauce, meatballs glazed with saffron, a sweet cake flavoured with rosewater and elder-flower, a dish of rice with raisins and cinnamon that Merrivale had not tasted outside of Italy, and bowls of fruit and candied nuts and sweetmeats, all beautifully presented. A dog wandered in partway through the meal, glanced once at the guests, and stretched out on the mat before the fire and went to sleep.

Blyth talked of Newcastle and its trade, telling them about his fellow merchants and the cargos they shipped across the North Sea and into Scandinavian waters. 'Wool is important and always will be. But the new industries we are developing up here, coal, iron and steel, salt, lead; that is where the new wealth is coming from. Given time, we will rival Bruges and Hamburg for prosperity.'

'What about Durham?' Lady Mary asked. 'I understand the priory is rich, and becoming richer every day.'

'Yes, the monks of Durham are formidable rivals. But they will overreach themselves, I think. Their pursuit of wealth is reckless, and they are squandering resources. Farming land is being turned over to mining, but many of their seams are in boggy ground and cannot be mined deeply. And because they can sell coal at a good profit, they are turning to charcoal for their smelting operations. They have already felled most of the woodlands in Weardale, and are rapidly depleting the rest. Some of the other religious houses are following the cathedral's lead.'

Merrivale thought about the woodcutters. 'What will they do when they run out of woodlands?'

'It is an excellent question. The peasants had rights to use those forests for wood-gathering and pannage for their pigs, but now those rights are gone. It will cause unrest, I am certain of it.'

At the end of the meal they sat drinking glasses of spiced hippocras. The glow of the fire reflected orange light off Tiphaine's gown. 'Tell me how I may help you,' Blyth said.

'The truth is, I barely know where to begin.' And that really *was* the truth, Merrivale thought. 'My commission is to investigate the reliability of the northern lords, and remind any waverers where their duty lies. But I am also informed that there are doubts about the loyalty of some of the townsmen. I understand his Grace the archbishop has asked you to investigate.'

Blyth seemed reluctant to answer. 'His Grace has honoured me with his trust,' he said finally. 'I fear I have done little to earn it.'

Merrivale waited. 'There are two separate questions,' Blyth said. 'If their interests were threatened, would our merchants negotiate with the Scots? Would they pay blackmail, or even offer their allegiance to the enemy, in order to protect their businesses and their lives? The answer is yes, many of them would. I will be quite candid with you, my friends. In the right circumstances, rather than let everything I have worked for over the past twenty years go to waste, I might do so myself.'

'So might any of us,' Merrivale said quietly.

Blyth was startled. 'Even you?'

Merrivale could feel Tiphaine watching him. 'The instinct for preservation is a strong one,' he said. 'There are times when it overrides everything else. What is the second question?'

'Whether any of the merchants of Newcastle are deliberately plotting with the Scots. If they are, I don't know about it. I know all of my fellow members of the Guild Merchant personally. I know their wives, their families, their business interests, who they trade with and in what ports. Not one of them has had any trade or correspondence with Scotland since hostilities began two years ago. And yet, the rumours of Scottish influence persist.'

'That influence may not be coming directly from Scotland,' Merrivale said. 'There may be intermediaries involved. In Durham, for example, or in Hexham.'

'Hexham?' Blyth looked startled for a moment, but then comprehension came. He nodded. 'You mean Gilbert de Tracey. Do you think he is a traitor like his brother?'

'That is one of the things I am endeavouring to find out,' said Merrivale. 'Do you know him?'

'I have done business with him in the past. I made some investments in the Staple through him, and I also helped him invest in a shipping venture to transport sea coal to London. But I cannot say I know him well.'

No one did, Merrivale thought. He asked the same question he had asked the archbishop. 'What did you make of him?'

'He was always very correct and fair in his business dealings. As a man, which I think is the question you are asking, I did not find him particularly likeable. But he was an excellent business partner.'

'Have you heard if Tracey made any large investments or transferred any large sums of money? Especially during this past summer?'

Blyth shook his head. 'The London merchants would know more, of course, but doubtless you have already asked them. So far as I know, his business, like that of most moneylenders, went quiet over the summer when the king and most of his court were away in France. My London office made a few small loans to the queen, and I believe Tracey did the same, but there was little else. Then word came of the victory at Crécy and the death of his brother. He announced he was taking orders and began liquidating his business. I understand he gave everything to charity.'

Merrivale shook his head. Mary and Tiphaine watched him. 'The Chancery investigated his gifts to charity. Between the first and tenth of September, Gilbert de Tracey gifted twelve thousand marks of silver to Saint Paul's Cathedral, a further three thousand to his own London parish church, and five thousand to Hexham Priory.'

Blyth raised his eyebrows. 'That will keep the canons in cakes and ale for a good few years.'

'His landholdings were transferred directly to Saint Bartholomew's Hospital,' Merrivale continued. 'Along with other smaller donations to shrines and religious houses, the total comes to about thirty thousand marks, or twenty thousand pounds. That is less than one-fifth of his estimated total fortune.'

Blyth looked incredulous. 'He was certainly worth more than twenty thousand, but a hundred thousand?'

'At least. As you suggested, the London merchants helped to build up a fairly complete picture of his investments and holdings. And that is on top of any portable wealth such as coin, ingots and jewellery. All of that has vanished as well. The question is, where is it all? What did Tracey do with it?'

'Have you asked him?'

'I intend to. But if you have heard anything useful, I would be grateful.'

'If you were going to hide a large amount of money, where would you hide it?' Lady Mary asked.

'Overseas,' Blyth said. 'I know it is illegal, but there are ways of doing so. Have you checked with the foreign merchants, the Italian banks and the Hanse merchants at the Steelyard?'

'The Chancery is looking into it,' Merrivale said. 'They had found no evidence before I came north.'

Blyth was silent for a moment. 'There is another possibility,' he said. 'If Gilbert de Tracey was in league with his brother, it is possible that he was also financing whatever scheme Edward was involved in. In which case, the money may have already been spent. What Gilbert liquidated and gave away was all that remained.'

'Edward was also raising money,' Merrivale said. 'He was buying up plunder from the common soldiers at a high discount and reselling at a profit.'

Blyth nodded. 'It's a common practice. But Edward de Tracey would have needed more money than that.'

'Yes,' the herald said, ignoring the look on Tiphaine's face. 'I suspect he would. What you are suggesting is certainly one possibility. But I need to be certain.'

'I can make inquiries,' Blyth said. 'I have my own connections with the foreign merchants. Licit or illicit, the transport of large quantities of coin and bullion always attracts attention. Someone, somewhere, will know something.'

He drained his cup and rose to his feet. 'And now, ladies, Sir Herald, if you will forgive me, I have a large number of letters on my desk requiring attention. Shall we gather after vespers for supper and a glass of wine? I have engaged a lutenist to play for us, a Flemish player whom I first heard in London. He is excellent.'

'Your hospitality does you great credit, sir,' said Lady Mary sweetly. They waited in silence until the door had closed behind their host, and Lady Mary rolled her eyes.

'Honestly!' she said. 'He feeds birds out of his hand! Exquisite taste, beautiful house, fine clothes, food that could have come from the king's table; oh, and he can call up stray Flemish lutenists at a moment's notice. Really?'

'I wonder what his wife looks like,' said Tiphaine, starting to giggle.

'Oh, I can guess what she looks like,' said Lady Mary. 'Tall, *very* blonde with blue eyes and skin like new milk, and one of those prim little mouths like you see on badly painted madonnas. He probably feeds her out of his hand, too.'

She looked around the brilliant painted hall. 'I don't like this place. I prefer my husband's household, with people brawling and shouting at each other and throwing bones at the dogs. And speaking of the Percys, where *is* Harry?'

Harry Percy arrived ten minutes later, brushing dust off his coat as he entered the hall. He was a big, square-jawed man in his mid-twenties with a shock of untidy fair hair. 'Sorry, sister,' he said, kissing Lady Mary's hand. 'Only just got your message. Came as soon as I could get away.'

'Where have you been?' she demanded.

'Corbridge,' said Percy. 'The captain received a report of a Scottish raiding party coming over the border. Someone thought they had seen them around the old Roman wall. He asked me to ride out and take a look.'

'Did you find them?' Merrivale asked.

'Not a sign. Just a rumour, this time,' Percy said soberly. 'Give it a few days and the rumours will be real enough.' He looked at Lady Mary. 'Why did you want to see me?'

As usual, she came straight to the point. 'What's all this about you being in correspondence with the Earl of Dunbar and his wife? Don't try to deny it. John Crabbe told me all about it.'

Harry Percy's face fell. 'I'm a bit thirsty after all that riding,' he said. 'I don't suppose there's a glass of wine handy, is there?'

Lady Mary picked up a handbell from a side table and rang it. A servant arrived with wine, and Harry drank half his glass at a gulp. 'It's like this,' he said. 'My brother told me John Grey had been in contact with the Countess of Dunbar, about possibly opening peace negotiations. After John and Richard went south, the whole venture seemed to lapse. I thought I'd try to revive it.'

'Why?' Merrivale asked bluntly.

Percy was silent for a moment. 'I looked at my father,' he said finally. 'He is a violent, bitter old man who hates the Scots and will fight them until the day he dies. So do most of his friends, and so do many on the Scots side. And that's the problem, you see. They're just fighting and fighting, and they have no idea why any more. John Grey talked with Countess Agnes, and they decided it had to stop. I didn't understand at first, but I have done a lot of thinking since, and I agree with them.'

Merrivale studied him for a moment. Clearly, Harry Percy was nowhere near as unintelligent as his sister-in-law made him out to be. 'What contact have you had with the Countess of Dunbar?'

'Not much, so far. I wrote to her last winter and suggested a meeting, and she replied that she was considering the matter. Then I went off to France with the army over the summer, but I wrote again when I returned home. This time she offered to meet me.'

'This could be a trap,' Lady Mary said immediately.

'It could,' said the herald. 'When and where is the meeting?'

'Tomorrow afternoon, at a bastle house called Black Middens. It's in Tarsetdale, north-west of Bellingham. I am to go alone.' He looked at Lady Mary. 'Of course I know it could be a trap. I'm not stupid, you know.'

Tellingly, Lady Mary said nothing. It could indeed be a trap, Merrivale thought, part of a plot to discredit the Percys; or Sir Harry might genuinely be in league with the Scots. The third and least likely alternative was that all of this was true, and Agnes of Dunbar really was holding out an olive branch to her enemies.

There was only one way to find out. 'I will go to Black Middens in your place,' he said. He raised a finger to forestall Percy's protest. 'No, Sir Harry. I hold the queen's writ in this matter. You will abide by my decision.'

'And what am I meant to do?' the other man demanded.

'You will go to Warkworth, where you will help your father raise as many men-at-arms and archers as possible and bring them to join the archbishop's army. That is the queen's command.'

'Don't be an ass, Harry,' said Lady Mary. 'You are neither a spy nor a diplomat. This is Master Merrivale's profession.'

Sir Harry looked unhappy, but he recognised *force majeure*. He swallowed the rest of his wine and set the cup down. 'I shall take my leave, then,' he said. 'Er... Sir Herald. Will there be any trouble about this? My writing to Lady Dunbar, I mean. There is a truce, after all. I really was trying to do the right thing.'

'I understand,' said Merrivale. 'Good evening, Sir Harry.'

The lutenist was every bit as good as promised. Afterwards they made polite small talk for a while, and then Blyth departed to feed his birds. Lady Mary and Tiphaine retired too. Merrivale sat for a while and stared at the glowing fire, piecing together everything he had learned today and on the ride north.

He had seven days before the truce expired. Seven days to find out whatever the Countess of Dunbar was plotting with Harry Percy, unravel the mystery of Gilbert de Tracey's money, and persuade the northern barons and the Disinherited to stand firm in their loyalty. The first should probably be easy enough, assuming the meeting at Black Middens was not an ambush. The second two were beginning to feel like the labours of Hercules.

He rose and went up to his chamber. Tiphaine was standing in the middle of the room, still in her blue gown, hands at her sides. They looked at each other. 'Your hair has grown,' he said after a while.

'Perhaps the sea air was good for it,' she suggested. 'Are you any closer to knowing who he is? The man from the north?'

'I suspect he is not Harry Percy. Apart from that, no. And time is running out.'

'How do you think Master Blyth knew that Edward de Tracey needed more money? He knows more about Tracey's plot than he says, I think.'

'Yes, I noticed that too. He spoke fairly well of Gilbert de Tracey, but he knew the latter had secrets, and I suspect he knows, or has guessed, at some of them. Men of commerce spend quite a lot of their time spying on one another. What Blyth said today could be a way of letting me know obliquely that Gilbert was involved, without giving up his own sources.'

She walked towards him until she was standing about a foot away, looking up into his face. 'You were very frank with your questions today. About the money, and Sir Gilbert. Everyone knows who you are, and what you are searching for. Is that not dangerous?'

'It is kind of you to worry,' he said gently. 'But the only people who matter already knew who I am, long before I left London. The man from the north certainly knows I am searching for him. There is little point in concealment.'

'You will draw lightning around your head.'

'That is what I am hoping for. In order to attack me, they will have to come out of hiding.'

She took his hands in hers and, in a surprisingly soft gesture, lifted them to her lips and kissed them. 'Be careful,' she said. 'I am not ready for you to die, not yet.' She looked at him, very seriously. 'I know I am not the woman you dream of. The woman you lost.'

His scalp began to tingle. 'I have never asked you to be.'

'Another man might have done so. You have never told me her name.'

'She was called Yolande,' Merrivale said after a moment.

'A beautiful name. But then, I imagine she was a beautiful woman.'

Her fingers began undoing the laces at the neck of her gown. The tingling increased. 'I cannot promise much,' he said. 'There has been a lot of hard riding in the past few days.'

A smile lit up her face. 'What a pity,' she said. 'For tonight, all I have to offer is more of the same.'

Merrivale laughed. Reaching out, he caressed her face with gentle fingers. 'What do you see in me?' he asked.

'Hope,' she said, and she reached up and kissed him, with feathery softness, on the lips.

7

Newcastle-upon-Tyne, 23rd of September, 1346
Morning

Six days until Michaelmas; six days until the truce expired, and the sword fell on the outstretched neck of northern England. In Newcastle the merchants and traders counted their takings, and despite the high walls and stone-throwing machines that defended them, thought about places to bury their money when the invaders came. From the defenceless villages around the city came a slow trickle of people carrying their moveable goods on their shoulders, looking for places of safety before it was too late. The air was heavy with premonition.

Restless and on edge, Tiphaine put on a pair of pattens and a dark cloak with a hood to cover her hair and went out into the town. The wind was still fresh from the east but it had blown the clouds away; the sun shone brightly in a burnished blue sky. The streets were full of traffic, wagons and porters shouldering heavy loads, and from nearby she heard the clang of hammers and smelled the hot tang of charcoal. She walked past the hospital towards the church of Saint Nicholas, brooding.

She was worried about Simon. He had departed at dawn, without taking Mauro or Warin; he had been bidden to come alone, he said, and alone he would go. He had said nothing about the attack on the road near Chester-le-Street, but Mauro had told her and she had been furious. 'Why did you not tell me yourself?' she demanded as he mounted his horse in the courtyard. 'Do I mean so little to you?'

'On the contrary,' he said, looking down from the saddle. 'I am trying to protect you.'

'I have told you, many times. I do not wish to be protected.'

'I know,' he said gently. 'But you must forgive me if I wish to extend my protection all the same. Call it a selfish desire on my part.'

There was no answer to that. He had ridden away towards this horrible sounding place, Black Middens – she had been in the north country long enough to know that a midden was a dungheap – leaving her to fret resentfully about the injustice of a situation where he was allowed to take risks and she was not. She tried to tell herself she regretted going to his room last night, but she knew that was a lie.

Up ahead was the great market, packed with people selling eggs, salmon, cheeses, baskets of apples, late season vegetables. Trade was brisk, but the voices around her were anxious and faces often turned towards the north. Although she had learned a fair amount of English during the summer campaign, the burred, clipped local dialect often defeated her, but she did not need words to tell her what was in the air. She could smell the fear around her.

She spotted a man walking ahead of her, wrapped in a dark cloak like her own with the hood pulled forward. He walked stiffly with one arm pressed close to his side as if in pain, and it was this that first caught her eye. But there was something about him that seemed familiar too, and then she stopped suddenly, breath hissing with shock. No, she thought, it *can't* be! But then the man reached up and pulled his hood back a little, and she saw a gleam of golden hair. Shock hit her again, so hard she felt briefly nauseous.

Rollond de Brus was not with the Scottish army mustering at Perth. He was here, walking through the streets of Newcastle.

Shivering, she forced herself to be calm. She looked around for the town watch, but there was no one in sight; of course, she thought, constables are never there when you need them... On the other hand, if Brus was arrested now, they would never know why he was here. Sinking her teeth into her lower lip, planting her feet carefully in the wooden pattens and putting as many people as possible between him and herself, she followed Brus out of the market past another big church and then up a long street lined with inns and stables towards the north gate of the town. People surged around her; she used the crowd as cover, following the distant figure of Brus. Her heart was beating very hard.

Opposite the Franciscan friary was another inn, a big two-storey building of stone with timber jetties. Rollond opened the front door and went inside. Tiphaine watched for a few minutes, but he did not come out again. She turned and hurried away.

Back at Blyth's house she ran up to her chamber. In amongst the clothes she had bought in London was the outfit she had worn through the summer campaign in France, a man's shapeless coat and shirt several sizes too large for her, both faded and a little ragged, hose patched at the knees, badly scuffed leather boots, a plain girdle, a long knife in a wooden sheath and a leather cap. Changing quickly, she checked to see if the stair was clear. It was; the household were all hard at work elsewhere. She ran down-stairs and out into the street, walking back towards the market. Anonymous in her baggy coat, no one paid her any attention.

Back on Pilgrim Street she took up position where she could watch both the door and the gate into the inn's courtyard. Pilgrims walked past, wearing dark cloaks and broad-rimmed hats decorated with badges from the shrines they had visited. A man driving a cart loaded with firewood swore at her and told her to get out of the way, but mostly she was ignored; just another lad idling in the street. She watched the inn, waiting.

An hour passed, and she began to think he must have left the inn while she was back at the house. Just as she was preparing to give up and go home, the gate to the courtyard opened and Rollond de Brus came out, leading a saddled bay horse. She watched him mount, grimacing with pain and holding his ribs as he settled into the saddle. So, she thought, not without satisfaction; he may have survived Crécy, but he did not get away scot-free.

Brus rode slowly down the street towards the river. There was a stable next to the friary. Tiphaine ran inside, accosting a startled groom and mustering her English. 'I need to hire a horse. How much?'

The groom looked at her ragged clothes. 'A penny an hour, in advance. And there's a deposit.'

Reaching into her pocket, she pulled out a handful of coins and pressed them into his fist. 'Take all of it. Bring me a horse, now.'

A moment later she was in the saddle, riding down the street and looking around for her quarry. She caught sight of him near the big church, heading down the slope towards the bridge. The guards at the gatehouse paid him no heed, nor did they do more than glance at her; they were interested in people coming into the town, not going out. Once across the bridge Brus spurred his horse to a canter and turned left, passing the coal pits of Gateshead and picking up the road towards the coast. Puzzled, she followed him.

South Shields, 23rd of September, 1346
Midday

South Shields was a huddle of fishermen's cottages along the south bank of the Tyne. Boats were drawn up on the foreshore and nets hung on wooden racks drying in the sun. A single church tower jutted up from the marketplace; on the hilltop behind it, the crumbling ruins of a Roman fort overlooked the village and the sea.

Seeking a vantage point, Tiphaine turned her horse and rode uphill to the fort. The ramparts were like broken teeth protruding from the ground, brought down in some places by weather and in others by scavengers looking for building stone. The interior buildings were mostly just grassy mounds of rubble, but the old double-arched gatehouse still stood, roofless but solid. Dismounting and tethering her horse to a lump of stone covered with weathered inscriptions, she climbed cautiously up onto a section of wall and stood looking around, shading her eyes against the sun.

Below, the village squatted on the banks of the river, its chimneys smoking. She saw a few people, a woman feeding chickens, a man chopping wood, another sitting outside mending a fishing net. There was no sign of Rollond or his horse. Turning, she looked towards the sea. Here was a greater bustle of activity, people and horses and wagons all busy on the golden sands of the beach. Close to hand was a saltern, big rectangular evaporation pools full of seawater separated by narrow stone dykes; next to them were open-sided sheds wreathed in smoke where the thick, treacly salt sludge was scooped out of the pools and boiled down to get rid of the last moisture. Beyond the saltern people were hard at work gleaning the beach for sea coal, some raking the sand and piling up the precious black lumps in little heaps, others plunging into the sea and dragging the bottom. Wagons moved slowly across the strand, collecting the harvested coal.

None of this was new or strange to Tiphaine. She knew all about sea coal, prized for its exceptional heat and the cleanness of its flame, and there were salt works on the west coast of Normandy not far from what had been her family home. She shaded her eyes again, scanning the beach. One of the coal wagons, half loaded, had pulled to halt and the driver had climbed down from the bench and stood holding the horses' heads. Rollond de Brus was standing just beyond the wagon, talking to a big man in the dark cape of a Dominican friar. With his hood back, the Frenchman's fair hair glinted like minted gold in the strong sunlight. Further on she spotted three more men whom she guessed were watchers, placed to ensure that the two could talk in private. Brus's horse was away near the saltern, its reins held by a fourth man.

Tiphaine's stomach fluttered briefly, but then a cold calm descended as she assessed the situation. The watchers were on the seaward side of the wagon, keeping an eye on the coal gatherers to make sure they did not come too close. If she came in from the landward side, using the wagon as cover, she might get close enough to hear what Rollond and the Dominican were saying.

Slipping out of the gatehouse, she scrambled down the grassy bank to the head of the beach. Keeping the saltern to the left, she walked casually towards the wagon, head down as if she was combing the beach. Fortune favoured her; she came across an abandoned wooden rake and began dragging it through the sand. After a moment she found a lump of coal, jet-black, hard and as big as her fist, and dropped it into her coat pocket. Rollond was beyond the wagon, hidden from view, and its team obscured the driver. All three watchmen had their backs to her, still watching the coal gatherers.

At first the voices were an indistinct murmur carried on the wind, but as she drew closer the words began to come more clearly. She squatted down as if examining something she had found in the sand, listening.

'Man, you look in a bad way.' That was the friar speaking, in French with a heavy local accent. 'What have you done to yourself?'

'I broke two ribs when my horse went down at Crécy,' said Brus. 'They haven't fully mended yet.'

'Are you sure you're fit to carry on?'

'Mind your own business. What orders were you given in Durham?'

'To follow the herald and report his movements. That's what I was doing when you summoned me out to this desolate spot.' The Dominican sounded annoyed. 'As a result, I've now lost him. God knows where he is.'

'I know where he is,' Brus said. 'He is on his way to Bellingham. Don't worry about him, he is no longer any concern of yours.'

'Durham might beg to differ. As a matter of interest, was it your lot who tried to kill Merrivale on the Great North Road yesterday morning?'

There was a short pause. 'What in God's name are you talking about?'

'A gang of bandits attacked him. They were about to finish him when a hunting party happened along and saved the day. Clennell and Harkness were both with the hunting party, by the way.'

Brus's voice sounded puzzled. 'Why in hell did they interfere?'

'Maybe they didn't realise it was Merrivale's hide they were saving. So nothing to do with you, then?'

'No. As I said, forget about Merrivale. He no longer exists.'

'What do you mean by that?'

'I mean, he will be dead by sundown.'

Tiphaine's hand closed hard on the handle of the rake. 'They won't like that in Durham,' the friar said sharply. 'A dead herald means trouble, and they don't want trouble, not at this stage.'

'I don't give a damn what Durham wants. I give the orders here.'

'Oh, aye? If you want their cooperation, that's not the way to get it.'

'I don't want their cooperation,' Brus said. 'I want their obedience. Durham will come to heel, or I will burn their cathedral and hang the monks in their own cloister. Do I make myself clear?'

'Very,' said the friar, his voice heavy with sarcasm.

'Good. Now, I need your services, Brother Oswald. I pay better than the priory, remember.'

There was a moment of silence. 'All right. What do you want me to do?'

'I need a messenger to deliver a letter to Lord Percy and his son at Warkworth. Tell them I want a reply, and make sure they give it to you. At the same time, get message to the leaders of the Disinherited. Tell them to meet me in Berwick in three days' time, at the usual place. They are to understand that this is an order, not a request.'

'I'll pass the word.'

'And come to that meeting yourself, too. I will need you again.'

The meeting was coming to an end. Tiphaine knew she had to get away, and she rose and started back towards the fort. One of the horses saw the movement from the corner of its eye and snorted, rearing up in the traces. Cursing, the driver came around to calm the animal, and as he dragged the horse back down he saw Tiphaine.

'You! Boy! Come here, you little bastard!'

Leaving the horses he ran towards her, drawing a knife from his belt. In a flash Tiphaine pulled the lump of coal from her pocket and threw it hard and accurately, hitting the driver on the point of the chin. He stumbled and fell flat on his face on the sand. Even as he went down, Rollond de Brus came around the end of the wagon, sword in hand, his face wild with anger. The Dominican friar followed him, armed with a heavy wooden staff and moving to cut off her escape to the fort. Tiphaine turned and fled.

She could hear Brus's harsh breathing behind her and knew he was very close. Putting her head down, pumping her arms, she ran until her own breath was burning in her lungs, across the beach past the piles of sea coal where men turned and stared at her. She knew the three watchmen were running too, one cutting across to intercept her, two more giving chase and further barring her escape route. Ahead lay the evaporation pools. She realised she could no longer hear Brus, and she slowed her pace a little and turned her head. He was down on one knee a hundred yards behind her, head down and clutching at his side. *Good*, she thought, *I hope his ribs break again and puncture his lung.*

But the first of the watchmen was close upon her. She ran down the narrow stone dykes between the evaporation pools, full of milky sludge glistening in the sun. Fast as she ran, the other man gained on her; now she could hear his breath too, in her imagination almost feel it on the back of her neck. Reaching a crossing between dykes, she turned and slashed at the man with her knife. He dodged the sweeping blade, but his boots slipped on the salt-encrusted stone. Arms flailing, he fell into an evaporation pool with a heavy splash. She saw him struggling to get up, the thick liquid clinging to his clothes and clogging his eyes and nose, and realised she had lost track of the other two, and the friar. She turned and ran towards the boiling sheds, hoping to use them as cover.

The air in the sheds was hot and acrid with smoke and fumes. Salt pans bubbled over low fires. Men moved around them, stirring the contents and feeding the fires with lumps of coal; they glanced at Tiphaine and returned to their work. Breathing hard, she moved from one shed to the next, looking for a way of escape, picking up a wooden spade to use as a weapon as she went.

A bank of smoke wrapped around her, and she coughed. When the smoke cleared the second watchman was standing in front of her, a big man with long red hair and beard and a dagger with no cross guards in one hand. He grinned at her, showing gapped yellow teeth. She smiled back, winsomely, and swung the spade at his head, but he seized it and ripped it out of her hands, then stepped forward, dagger upraised. Grasping her own knife firmly, Tiphaine ducked low and stabbed him in the leg. The big man bellowed with pain and turned, lashing out at her, and in turning he stumbled over the spade. His injured leg gave way, and he lost his balance and fell backwards into one of the boiling salt pans.

By the time the screaming started she was out of the tent and running hard towards the fort. She knew the third man would have circled around to intercept her, and was unsurprised when he stepped out from behind the last hut, barring her way. Choking on smoke and fumes she did the last thing he expected, running straight at him and stabbing him in the belly before he could move. Shouting, he staggered back, clutching at the wound and she raced on up the hill, bloody knife in her hand. She reached the crest, sprinting towards the gatehouse, and then stopped dead. A bulky man in Dominican robes carrying a wooden staff stood in the gatehouse arch. It was Brother Oswald.

'Well, well,' he said, grinning. 'What have we here? Is it a boy, or… can it perchance be a girl? Aye, if they're young and tender enough, what difference does it make?'

He advanced towards her, raising the staff. Tiphaine let the knife fall to the ground, dropping to her knees and clasping her

68

hands in supplication. 'Please,' she cried. 'Don't hurt me, I beg you! I've done nothing wrong.'

'Maybe not yet,' said the friar, grinning. 'But you'll have plenty to confess at your next churching, sweetheart.' Dropping the staff, he hauled his robes up around his waist and reached out to push her onto her back. She seized his hand and bit it hard, teeth crunching through skin and flesh. Oswald yowled with pain, jerking his hand back, and Tiphaine snatched up her knife. She stabbed him in the arm and then raced through the archway. Untethering the horse, she flung herself into the saddle and rode hard for the gate. As Oswald ran towards her cursing and holding his arm, she kicked the horse hard and drove it straight at him. At the last moment the friar jumped aside and Tiphaine galloped away downhill towards the road.

Newcastle-upon-Tyne, 23rd of September, 1346
Afternoon

'They're going to kill Simon,' she said.

Lady Mary was calm. 'Something tells me that gentleman will take quite a lot of killing,' she said.

They were in the solar of Blyth's house, sunlight streaming through the windows and glowing off the carpets and glass. Tiphaine had cleaned the blood from her face and hands and changed her clothes, but she was still shaking with shock. 'We must do something,' she said.

'We'll ask Master Blyth to organise a rescue party,' said Lady Mary. 'That's about all we can do.' With sudden gentleness, she took Tiphaine's hand. 'My dear, he knows the risks. There's nothing you can do to stop a man like that. I should know, I'm married to one.'

'I wish I could be as calm as you,' Tiphaine said.

'Oh, believe me, it's all on the surface. Underneath I am quaking in my boots, just like everyone else. What else did Brus say?'

'Something about Durham, which I did not understand. And he asked the friar to carry letters to the Disinherited, and another to Lord Percy and Sir Harry.'

Lady Mary let go of her hand. 'The Percys? What does the letter say?'

'I do not know. The friar was to wait for a reply.'

'Idiots!' Lady Mary stamped her foot on the rush mats. 'Don't they know that even accepting correspondence from the enemy is treason?'

'You are not at war with Scotland,' said Tiphaine. 'Yet.'

'But we *are* at war with France, and Rollond de Brus is an envoy of the French crown. Damn it! I will not let the Percy family destroy themselves, or this country.'

She looked out the window. 'Make ready to travel, my dear. I am going to see the captain of the garrison. It is too late to depart today, as we should not arrive before dark, but in the morning we are going to Warkworth.'

Tiphaine looked blank. 'We?'

'I promised the herald I would keep you safe. I want you where I can keep an eye on you, and not let you go wandering off again.' Lady Mary bit her lip. 'God's blood. I only hope we are not too late.'

'Yes,' said Tiphaine, thinking of Simon riding alone across the wild hills. 'So do I.'

8

Black Middens, 23rd of September, 1346
Late afternoon

Wind whistled through the grasses on the high slopes of Kielder Moor. Apart from the distant cawing of a crow and the thud of the horse's hooves on turf, all was silent. A line of trees marked the course of the Tarset Burn down to his left; otherwise, the hills were wide open under an enormous blue sky. Merrivale watched the skyline as he rode. He was only a few miles from the border now; one day very soon Scots raiders would come pouring over these hills and down into the settled valleys below.

Perhaps today would be that day. The truce had not yet expired, but Merrivale had little faith in truces. He rode on, the air and land seeming empty around him.

From Hexham, where Gilbert de Tracey waited should he return from this venture, Merrivale had ridden across the Roman wall and up the valley of the North Tyne. South of Bellingham he had met a boy out shooting, who confirmed Harry Percy's directions. Leaning on his bow, the boy gazed in awe at his embroidered tabard. 'Are you a herald?'

'I am.'

'My name is Peter de Lisle. I want to be a herald one day. I am already studying.'

'Very laudable,' said Merrivale, smiling.

'I know the coats of arms of all the northern lords. Ask me, and I can name any of them for you.'

Merrivale glanced up at the sun. 'My young friend, I would love nothing more than to stop and discuss heraldry with you, but I have an errand that cannot wait. I wish you good sport with your bow.'

Passing through the little war-scarred town of Bellingham, he turned north-west towards the moor. Another hour brought him to Black Middens, a square stone bastle house surrounded by a walled enclosure of the kind they called barmekins here in the north. As he drew closer he could see the wall had been breached, and the house no longer had a roof beyond some scorched timbers.

He rode through one of the gaps in the barmekin wall and halted, waiting. His herald's tabard gleamed in the sun, a splash of colour against an otherwise austere landscape. Wind ruffled the tabard, making the red leopards stir a little. The silence lasted a long time, long enough to wonder if he had the right place or the correct day. Then he heard the whicker of a horse, and two men walked around from behind the bastle house. Both wore mail coats and steel caps, and were armed with swords and leaf-bladed spears. Their red surcoats were blazoned with a white *triskeles*, the three armoured legs of the Isle of Mann.

'Who are you?' demanded one of the men.

'I am Simon Merrivale, envoy of her Grace Queen Philippa. I have come in place of Sir Harry Percy to meet the Countess of Dunbar.' He held out his hands. 'As you can see, I have no weapons.'

'Let him enter, Somairle,' said a female voice.

The man who had spoken bowed his head. 'Come with me.'

A little stiffly, Merrivale dismounted and followed the man called Somairle up the stone stair and through an empty doorway into the hall. Charred roof timbers lay strewn across the floor, and the walls were stained with bird droppings. A woman stood in the middle of the chamber, two more armed men in attendance. She wore a long moss-green cloak with a hood framing curly black hair; her face was a warm brown colour with high cheekbones and arching eyebrows over long-lashed black eyes. This was Agnes Randolph, Countess of Dunbar and March, Lady of Mann and Annandale, and the most powerful woman in Scotland.

Merrivale bowed his head. 'Greetings, my lady.'

She surveyed him. 'You are unarmed. Is that wise? The borders are a dangerous place.'

'Heralds are not permitted to carry weapons,' said Merrivale. 'We are ambassadors and messengers, who come in peace.'

Her lips twitched with sudden amusement. 'According to the rules, you are allowed to wear a blunted sword.'

'A blunt sword is a thing a child might play with,' Merrivale said. 'When I became a man, I put away childish things.'

She nodded in acknowledgement. 'Why have you come instead of Sir Harry?'

'Sir Harry has many admirable qualities, but I was a King's Messenger before I became a herald. I understand diplomacy.'

'Do you? Consider this room is now a chessboard. I am black, you are red. You make the first move.'

Merrivale paused for a long time. 'I was going to ask a question,' he said finally. 'But then, I realised I already knew the answer. You opened clandestine negotiations with Sir Harry because you recognised what your king and his councillors have not; that in the long run, even with French support, you have very little chance of winning a war with England. And now, with France crippled after the battle of Crécy, that chance has dwindled to nearly nothing.'

He paused again for a moment. 'Forgive me for saying this. The Scots have courage, that is undeniable. But England has more men and more money. Courage alone will not bring you victory.'

Behind her, one of the men-at-arms stirred. The countess stilled him with a motion of her hand. 'I need no lectures on courage, herald,' she said coolly. 'I held Dunbar for a hundred and eighteen days against Lord Salisbury's army, and in the end Salisbury crept away with his tail between his legs. At the moment, things are running in our favour. I think we have a very good chance.'

'A very good chance,' the herald repeated. 'Yet Sir Harry Percy claims you summoned him here to talk about making peace with England.'

'Yes,' the countess said calmly. 'A permanent peace, once the conflict is over. England and Scotland have been at war for fifty years. Enough blood has been shed, and enough treasure has been expended. It is time to make an end, a permanent end, for the good of both nations.'

'You talk of peace, when your army is poised to invade England,' Merrivale said. 'A curious contradiction, my lady, is it not?'

'I thought you said you understood diplomacy,' she challenged. 'Military victory will give us a stronger hand at the bargaining table. Surely that is not difficult to comprehend.'

The herald nodded. 'Are you putting pressure on Sir Harry and his family to change their allegiance?'

She laughed, which was unexpected. 'The Percys of Northumberland, joining forces with Scotland? The Percy lion will never lie down with the Scottish lion. They would rather fight to death.'

Merrivale shook his head. 'The Percys will look after their own, that is certain. If it suits their ambitions to make common cause with the Scots, they will do so. And at present, someone is pressing them to do exactly that. Is it you?'

'No,' said the countess after a moment. 'But if we are to achieve a lasting peace, we need the support of the barons on both sides of the border, to persuade them to hang up their arms. I offered to meet Sir Harry to find out whether this might be possible.'

'Are there others in Scotland who are also thinking about peace?' Merrivale asked.

'Yes,' she said directly. 'But I will not tell you their names, or how many they are.'

He gazed at her for a moment, thinking. 'But yours is not the party in power in Scotland,' he said. 'Otherwise, you would not have to conduct these negotiations in secret. There is another party, urging war, and I hear that David Bruce is listening to them. I can guess at some of their names: Sir William Douglas of Liddesdale, and your brother, the Earl of Moray. Who are the others?'

The countess said nothing. 'Tell me their names and I might be able to stop them,' the herald said.

She laughed again, genuinely amused this time. 'Why would I want you to stop them? Edward of England has neglected his northern defences for years, and his best fighting men are away in France. Now is our moment. As I said, victory is within our grasp.'

'Yes,' said the herald. 'But you know as well as I do that any victory you win will be pyrrhic. As soon as King Edward takes Calais, his victorious army will return to England and march north, and once more you will be outmatched. Any gains you make this year will be wiped out, and the English will pillage and burn Scotland up to the eyebrows.'

He paused for a moment, letting this sink in. He recognised all too clearly the emotions behind her proud face. 'I believe it is your move,' he said.

'The man who leads the war party, and who planned the current campaign, is the envoy of King Philippe of France,' she said. 'He has only recently arrived, but has been at work at a distance for many months. His name is Rollond, Seigneur de Brus, and he is also King David's cousin. I see you know him.'

'We have met,' said Merrivale. Things were clicking into place, the pieces of the plot coming together in his mind. 'Are there others?'

'The king's half-brother, Niall Bruce of Carrick, is a close ally of Brus. There is another Frenchman too, Guy of Béthune. Those three, along with my brother and Douglas, have the king's full confidence. He listens to them, and them alone.'

Merrivale's hands clenched suddenly. 'Guy of Béthune,' he said. 'What is he doing here?'

'He also holds lands in Scotland, the lordship of Hamilton. His brother, the Count of Flanders, was killed at Crécy. Béthune wants revenge against the English.'

'Of course,' said Merrivale, his voice suddenly weary. 'Everyone wants revenge for something. It is the one thing we all have in common.'

It took him a moment to collect his thoughts once more. He could see the countess watching and appraising him. 'And so, they have agreed a new strategy,' he said. 'Not just the usual border raids to keep England occupied, but an all-out invasion.'

'That is the condition for French support,' said the countess. 'We are to raise every man we have and launch them across the border, to seek out the English army and defeat it in battle.'

'But that makes no sense,' said the herald. 'For most of the past two decades, you have been very successful against us by avoiding large-scale warfare. You have used the razor, not the hammer, slicing away our possessions in Scotland. You have launched lightning raids over the border and retreated before our captains can respond. Why change now? Why are Brus and his allies urging you to risk everything on invasion and pitched battle?'

'Because Brus thinks we have a very good chance of winning,' she said. 'And he has persuaded the king and the others that he is right.'

The herald shook his head. 'There is more to it than that. There must be. Archbishop de la Zouche believes the French are paying you a subsidy to make war on us. Did the Seigneur de Brus bring this money with him?'

She said nothing, her lips compressed. 'My lady, you must tell me,' he said quietly. 'If what I think is true, then Scotland is in even greater danger than you can imagine.'

'Yes,' she said finally. 'How much money, I do not know. But enough to raise an army, and to pay bribes to your nobles and the Disinherited.'

'Where does this money come from?'

'The French treasury, I assume.'

'But that treasury is empty. War has bled it dry. Last summer, Philippe was unable even to pay his foreign mercenaries. So, where has this money come from?'

She stood, silent. There was an obvious answer, he thought, but he was not about to share it with the Countess of Dunbar, not yet. He studied her face intently. 'You are afraid of Brus,' he said.

One of the men-at-arms started forward, but again the countess motioned with her hand. 'You are too bold, herald,' she snapped. 'An unarmed man should choose his words more carefully, I think.'

'On the contrary,' said Merrivale. 'Because I bear no weapons, I am able to speak freely. You are right to be afraid. Rollond de Brus may be your king's cousin, but he is no friend to Scotland.'

'What do you mean?'

'Brus thrives on chaos,' Merrivale said. 'He is acting as Philippe's envoy, but his true loyalty is not to France. He is part of a group of ruthless men, bankers, nobles, cardinals and priests, who seek power only for themselves. Last summer they tried to overthrow the kings of both England and France. I fear that they now mean to bring about the ruin of Scotland.'

'I have never heard of these men. Why should I believe you?'

'Because if I truly wanted to see Scotland brought to ruin, I would have said nothing and let Brus and his friends do their work. I am giving you a warning, countess. It is up to you whether you heed it.'

She was still angry. 'You have said enough. My patience is not limitless. It is time for you to go.'

Merrivale bowed. 'I apologise if I have given offence,' he said. 'I shall say one more thing. I agree with what you said earlier. This war has brought nothing but harm to both of our nations, and it is time to make an end. If you genuinely desire peace, and if you can persuade your king to offer proposals for an end to the conflict, I will be happy to carry them to London. You will always know, I think, where to find me.'

–

The sun was sinking towards the moor when Merrivale walked back into the courtyard. The Manxman holding his horse saluted as he stepped into the saddle. He wondered, briefly, where the man's own loyalties lay; the Isle of Mann was one of the debateable lands, claimed by England as well as Scotland. *We live in fractured, broken times*, he reflected, *when no one's loyalty is certain, and greedy, ambitious men like Rollond de Brus are taking full advantage.*

His intention was to ride to Hexham and take lodging there for the night, and in the morning call at the priory to interview Gilbert de Tracey. Finding the banker's money had taken on a new urgency. Blyth was probably right, and the money had gone overseas; given time, the Chancery's Argus-eyed investigators would probably pick up its trail, but they didn't have time. Michaelmas and the expiry of the truce was just six days away. It seemed very likely now that the missing money was already in the hands of the man from the north; and that some of it, at least, was funding the Scottish invasion.

But what else? What other plans did Brus have? What orders had he received from the man from the north? Everything he had done so far pointed to a carefully planned and prepared invasion; the raising of the army, the careful concealment of its strategic intentions, the wooing of the Disinherited, the bribery and intimidation of local nobles. But there would be more to it than that. Brus and his allies never did anything that would not profit themselves. Scotland, damaged and impoverished by decades of war, was fragile and vulnerable. So why would the conspirators expend so much time and treasure?

Merrivale did not doubt that Brus and the man from the north had some plan to spread chaos in Scotland. The question was, did their plan include England as well?

And finally, what about Agnes of Dunbar? What she had told him was likely to be true, or mostly true, but there were also a great many things she had *not* told him. She was clearly reluctant to speak freely about Brus. Was this because she was afraid of him, as the herald himself had implied? Or was she playing some game of her own?

He forded the River Rede where it came down to join the North Tyne. The sun was low on the horizon now; it would be dark by the time he reached Hexham. He saw a flicker of movement on the track ahead; a single horseman trotting towards him, a typical border hobelar in leather jack and cap, carrying an upright lance. The man wore no device on his jack. Something prickled on the back of Merrivale's neck, and he turned to see two more horsemen coming up behind him.

He looked around. To his right were the rippling waters of the Tyne, full of rocks and boulders; the river was fordable, just, but he would have to pick his way across slowly and if his horse stumbled and fell, the horsemen would spear him in the water. To the left rose a line of bare hills; he might be able to get away over these, but even as he looked three more horsemen topped the skyline and came riding down towards him.

This was growing tiresome, the herald thought. Three attacks in less than a month. Even if one of them was fairly obviously a pretence, it seemed excessive. He dismounted, turning his horse to use it as a shield, and studied the oncoming riders, noting the speed and angle of their approach, working out how he would attempt to deal with each in turn. As they drew closer, he realised this would not be easy. They were keeping pace with one another, timing their rides so that all six would arrive on top of him at once.

Every time we ride out, it could be the last time, his old friend Geoffrey of Maldon had once said. Perhaps this was that time. Unbidden, a woman's face flashed through his mind, and to his mild surprise the face was that of Tiphaine, not Yolande. On the heels of the thought, an arrow came hissing through the air from the direction of the river and buried itself halfway to the fletchings in the chest of one of the riders.

The man fell from the saddle, rolling over once and then lying still while his horse bolted in fright. Another horse went down thrashing and kicking, its rider scrambling to his feet and reaching for his lance. Merrivale turned to see the boy Peter de Lisle running across the fields, bow in hand and nocking another arrow. 'Sir Herald! To me, sir! I will defend you!'

Merrivale ran towards him. The boy halted and shot again; this time the arrow missed. Cursing under his breath, the boy pulled another arrow from his quiver. The ground vibrated to the drumming of hooves; the enemy were almost on top of them, and then out of nowhere four more horsemen piled into the fray, attacking the hobelars with sword and axe. The man on foot tried to run, but one of the newcomers rode after him and chopped him down with a single brutal cut of his sword. The boy raised his bow, but Merrivale saw the white triskeles badge on a red field and put a hand on his arm.

'Hold fast. These are friends.'

The fight was over in less than a minute. The Manxmen circled their horses, lathered from hard riding. A female voice said, 'Is this all of them, Somairle?'

'Yes, my lady.'

'Make certain they are all dead. I want no witnesses.'

The Manxmen dismounted, bending over the bodies. One man struggled up, trying to run; Somairle kicked him to the ground and cut his throat with a single smooth motion. Agnes of Dunbar rode up to Merrivale and the boy, halting her horse and pulling back the cowl of her cloak. The herald bowed.

'Thank you,' he said. 'How did you know they were following me?'

'I had scouts out watching the hills. They reported six men came over the border above Redesdale. I thought at first they were looking for me, but when they bypassed Black Middens, I knew they must be coming for you.'

Her horse stirred at the smell of blood, and she calmed it with a hand on its neck. 'Who wants you dead, herald?'

'There is a list,' said Merrivale. 'These men were Scots?'

'I recognise the one Somairle dispatched just now. He was in the household of Niall Bruce of Carrick. The king's half-brother, and Rollond de Brus's close friend.'

Merrivale nodded. 'I understand why you wanted no witnesses. May I ask why you decided to rescue me?'

'I thought about letting them kill you, but then I realised you might be useful one day. Now I have a question of my own. What is Guy of Béthune to you? I saw your face change when I mentioned his name.'

He had tried to avoid thinking about Guy of Béthune during the ride down from Black Middens. 'An old adversary,' the herald said. 'I thought he was buried in the past. Hearing his name again was... a surprise.'

'Not a pleasant one, I think,' said Agnes of Dunbar. She raised one gloved hand in salute. 'Go carefully, Sir Herald. Night is coming, and there may be others on your list out there waiting.'

She motioned to her men and they turned and rode back up the valley to the north-west. The red surcoats flashed once in the last of the sunlight and then faded from view.

–

Twilight was already hovering over the eastern hills and Hexham was still two hours away. The herald turned to the boy. 'I have not yet thanked you,' he said. 'You risked your life for me. I am deeply in your debt.'

The boy blushed under his sunburn. He was about fifteen, still at the slightly gawky stage; he reminded the herald a little of his own master, the young Prince of Wales. 'It was nothing, sir. But why were those caitiff wretches trying to kill you? And the lady who saved us; was that... was that really...?'

Merrivale raised a finger. 'Not a word to anyone,' he said. 'Take this secret to your grave. But yes; that was Agnes of Dunbar.'

The boy's eyes were round with astonishment. Merrivale could see other questions bubbling up inside him, but the boy remembered his manners and checked himself. 'The lady is right, sir. It is not safe to travel after dark. My father's house at Chipchase is not far from here. Come with me, and we can give you shelter for the night.'

Merrivale looked at him. 'Chipchase? Your father is Sir Robert de Lisle.'

'Yes, sir. Do please say you will come, we receive so few visitors these days. Well, apart from the ones who come to steal our cattle.'

Sir Robert de Lisle was one of the most prominent members of the Disinherited. If the information received in London was correct, he was one of those who had been approached about switching his allegiance to Scotland in exchange for restitution of his lost lands. *By going to Chipchase*, Merrivale thought, *will I be stepping out of the frying pan into the fire?*

Once again, there was only one way to find out. 'I should be delighted,' he said.

9

They reached Chipchase as dusk began to fall in the valley, although the higher hills still shone with light. The house was rather larger than Black Middens, a tower house with battlements on the roof, and the barmekin wall was high and in good repair. Merrivale dismounted in the courtyard and followed Peter through a doorway and up a narrow stair to the hall. A white-haired man seated before the fire and wrapped in a long fur-trimmed robe looked up sharply as they came in. 'Peter! It's about time you were home, lad! And who have you brought with you?'

'It is Master Merrivale, father! Herald to the Prince of Wales!'

'A royal herald?' The old man reached for a stick and struggled to his feet. 'Now what possesses such a man to go riding alone through Tynedale? Never mind, never mind, questions can wait. Run to the kitchen and tell the servants to bring food and wine.' Peter disappeared, and the older man looked at Merrivale.

'Let us introduce ourselves properly. I am Sir Robert de Lisle, and of course you've met Peter, my son. We're proper northern de Lisles, not like those nose-in-the-air bastards down south.'

Merrivale, who had met the de Lisle family of Rougemont in Bedfordshire, smiled. 'My name is Simon Merrivale,' he said.

'Merrivale... From Dartmoor, in Devon? Are you Reginald's boy? Aye, you've his look about you. I knew him quite well, back in the old days. Is he still alive?'

'Yes, though life does him no favours.' Losing his wife and daughters in the Great Famine and his lands a few years later had crushed Reginald Merrivale's spirit; these days he lived in a world of dreams and memories, not knowing what day it was, unable to recognise his only son.

'I'm sorry to hear it. I heard about your mother and sisters too. It was a bloody awful time, the famine, and then the years of chaos around the old king's death. People today complain about hard times. They don't know how lucky they are. Sit down, lad, sit down.'

They sat. A book bound with wooden boards rested on a stand beside the table; Cicero's *The Dream of Scipio*, Merrivale saw. To his relief, de Lisle changed the subject. 'What brings you up here?' he asked. 'I'd have thought you'd be in France with the prince.'

'The queen asked me to come north and look into certain matters,' Merrivale said. 'I ran into trouble on the road today, and your son was kind enough to help out.'

'What kind of trouble? Scots?' Merrivale nodded. 'So they're over the border already,' the old man said. 'It was to be expected, of course. Bloody truces don't mean anything up here, never did.'

Peter returned, followed by a servant bearing a platter of bread, cold beef and chopped herbs, with a flask of wine, a jug of water and a glass. 'Make sure the watch at the gate stays alert,' Sir Robert instructed his son. 'And check that the horses are secure.'

'Aye, father.'

'He's a good lad,' Sir Robert reflected after the boy had gone. 'My only remaining son and heir. My wife died giving birth to him. His brothers are gone too, the eldest killed at Annan, the second died on pilgrimage many years ago. Peter is all I have left.'

'He is brave as a lion,' Merrivale said, cutting a piece of beef.

'He is. Yet strangely, he has no interest in tales of derring-do and courage. The military exploits of our forefathers don't interest him, not at all. He's fascinated by heraldry, that's all. He knows every kind of armorial device there is. Give him a name, and he can not only tell you the man's coat but what its history is and where it comes from.'

Merrivale smiled. 'He has an extraordinary talent. Sir Robert, may I ask you a question? I understand you are one of the leaders of the Disinherited.'

The old man waved a gnarled hand. 'Once upon a time, perhaps, but not anymore. These days I am so crippled with arthritis I hardly leave the house. You're going to ask me if I have received offers from Scotland. This will be the queen's business that brought you north, no doubt.'

Merrivale sipped his wine. 'Your son saved my life, and I am a guest in your house. I will not compel you to tell me anything.'

'Oh, I've nothing to hide. I won't tell you who made the offers, because I believe the man was well-intentioned and I don't want to draw trouble down on his head. I was promised restitution of the Scottish lands I once held in Nithsdale and Dumfries, and a sum of money besides. Quite a large sum.'

'You turned them down,' said the herald.

'I don't want the lands,' the old man said, 'not any more. And I've enough money to see me by. My interest in Scotland ended in 1332, when Edward Balliol fled bare-arsed out of the camp at Annan and left his men to die. My son included.'

Merrivale waited. 'I was part of a great adventure, once,' said de Lisle. 'I was a new-minted knight when I followed Edward Long-shanks to Scotland and we brought her king back a prisoner to the Tower of London. Those Scottish lands were my reward. We thought that was the end, Scotland subdued, peace in our time. But the Scots kept fighting and Edward's son, our present king's late and unlamented father, let them win it all back. Fourteen years ago, we tried again. I followed Balliol to the slaughterhouse at Dupplin Moor, and we established ourselves as masters again, thinking we had turned back time. It lasted four months, before Balliol's stupidity led us into disaster and I lost my lands for the second time; and my son. That was enough. I am done with this venture.'

'Perhaps not,' said Merrivale. 'The boot is on the other foot. When the Scots come, they will remember their enemies as well as their friends.'

De Lisle shook his head. 'That's fortune's wheel for you. If they come, they come, and all I can do is hold them off for as long as I can and make the best end my aching bones will allow.'

'You could make your life easier by accepting their offer.'

'Possibly. Possibly not. I don't really care, to be honest. I just think I've had enough. You see things more clearly when you're near the end of your life. You understand what truly matters in the eyes of God. I want to see my son make his way in the world. Nothing else really matters to me.'

'What about the rest of the Disinherited? Do they feel the same as you?'

The old man shook his head. 'The Disinherited feel ignored and betrayed. When the present king first came to the throne he promised support, and for several years he gave it. Every summer, regular as the turning of an hourglass, English armies came north to fight the Scots, though they never seemed to accomplish much. Then the king decided that the crown of France was the shiny new bauble he was going to pursue, and all the men and money were diverted to the French war. The Disinherited have been cast aside. Edward Balliol is a broken reed, everyone knows that. But Umfraville and Wake and Clennell, in particular, wanted to continue the fight. Now, they are beginning to wonder why they bother.'

'And they may be tempted by the Scottish offer,' said Merrivale. 'I can understand that.' He paused. 'Would you be willing to do a service for the crown? Speak to Umfraville and Wake and the others, and persuade them to follow your example and reject the offer?'

De Lisle paused for a long time before replying. 'No,' he said. 'I won't. There's two reasons. First, I am so damned crippled that I doubt if I could ride as far as Redesdale or Coquetdale to find them. Second, I have made my own decision, but I have no idea if it was the right one. What right have I to expect others to follow my example?'

'You could remind them of their loyalty,' said Merrivale.

'Loyalty isn't something you demand, my boy. It's something you earn. Even kings need to realise that. Who or what you give your loyalty to is a matter for every man's conscience. I will not decide for them.'

From outside came the sound of voices, the guard at the gate challenging, another answering. Booted feet on the stair and Peter de Lisle burst into the room. 'Father! There's a party of men-at-arms at the gate, demanding entrance!'

'Go and find out who they are,' Sir Robert said calmly. 'If they're English, admit them. If they're Scots, we'll give them another kind of welcome.'

The new arrivals were in fact English. Their leader, attired in mail coat, breastplate, vambraces and bascinet with a plain white surcoat, raised a hand in salute as he entered the hall. 'Sir Robert, my apologies for disturbing you at this late hour. Sir Herald, my name is Woodburn and I am in the service of Master Blyth. He sent me and my men to discover whether you were safe, and if so to escort you back to Newcastle.'

'It is good of you to come,' the herald said, 'and good of Master Blyth to send you. Why did he think I might be in danger?'

'The Lady Tiphaine overheard a French spy talking this morning. He appeared to indicate that an ambush had been set for you. She informed Master Blyth, who gave me my orders. We have called at every house since Hexham, looking for you.'

Merrivale considered this for a moment. 'It is too late to start for Newcastle now,' he said. 'Sir Robert, would you be able to accommodate Master Blyth's men overnight?'

'Of course,' the old man said equably. 'Peter, fetch the steward, if you please.'

Woodburn looked disconcerted. 'We're ready to go now if you wish, sir. We can pick up fresh horses in Hexham.'

'Thank you,' said the herald. 'But I have had a long and wearying day, and I will stay here and rest for the night. In the morning I am riding to Hexham, where I have business that will take some time.'

'That's quite all right, sir,' said Woodburn. 'We are at your disposal. Our orders are to bring you back to Newcastle safe and sound. If we don't, we must answer to Master Blyth.'

'And to the Lady Tiphaine?' suggested Merrivale.

'Yes,' said Woodburn with feeling. 'Yes, that too.'

Hexham, 24th of September, 1346
Morning

Five more days until Michaelmas; five more days to war.

At dawn Merrivale departed for Hexham, accompanied by Woodburn and his men-at-arms and by the effervescently eager Peter de Lisle. This last, Merrivale realised, should have been expected.

'I want you to know how much I admire you,' the boy had said as they took bread and weak watered wine in the hall that morning. 'You have travelled so far on your embassies, and seen so much of the world, and you have studied the coats and devices of great nobles from all over Europe. Oh, I would give so much to live a life like yours.'

'I was also once tied in a sack and thrown into a river,' Merrivale pointed out.

Peter looked blank for a moment, and then smiled. 'It is a good joke, sir. I do admire your sense of humour.'

'Don't you want to be a knight like your father?'

'No,' the boy said simply. 'I want to be a herald.'

Later his father had taken Merrivale to one side. 'Could you use an apprentice, perhaps? You don't have to pay the boy, he is well settled. Just teach him what you know, and perhaps one day help him find a post. He'll serve you well and faithfully.'

'If I take him away, who will look after you?'

'I have a steward and plenty of servants.' De Lisle leaned a little closer. 'If the Scots do come,' he said quietly, 'I want the boy out of here. Keep him with you, herald, and keep him safe. He is the last family I have left.'

That settled the matter, and Peter de Lisle packed a saddlebag, fetched his bow and quiver and rode away from his family home without a backwards glance, intent on the sparkling life of adventure that awaited him. Woodburn, informed that there would be an additional member of the party, looked briefly nonplussed before replying that of course the protection offered to Sir Herald extended to his attendants as well. Nevertheless, Merrivale thought he looked put out, and he and his men rode in silence all the way down to Hexham.

Peter on the other hand talked volubly throughout the journey. 'Will we join the army when it musters, Sir Herald?'

'Very likely,' said Merrivale.

'Oh, I do hope so! So many lords and knights and gentlemen will be gathered there, and it will be so exciting to observe their coats and banners. And the Scots too; perhaps we will go on an embassy to Scotland? I should love to see all the Scottish coats and devices. And France; will we go to France when your work is done here?'

Merrivale smiled. 'One thing at a time,' he said.

—

Hexham lay a few miles south of the Roman wall, near the confluence of the northern and southern branches of the Tyne. The town was unfortified; only the priory was walled, and riding through the streets Merrivale saw many of the stone and half-timber houses were tightly shuttered. Their occupants had either fled or had shut themselves up inside. They had reason to be fearful, Merrivale thought; for centuries, Tynedale and neighbouring Redesdale had been the principal high roads used by raiders coming out of Scotland.

They crossed the deserted marketplace and dismounted outside the gates of the priory. Men-at-arms with halberds and axes guarded the door. 'I wish to speak to the prior,' Merrivale said.

The men looked at his tabard. 'You may enter, Sir Herald,' said the leader. 'But your companions must wait outside.'

A postern door opened to admit him. Passing through the courtyard Merrivale saw preparations for defence, baulks of timber bracing the main gate, buckets of water prepared to deal with fire arrows. There were more guards outside the prior's lodging. The prior, a short, black-robed man with a Cumbrian accent, greeted him apologetically. 'Father John of Bridekirk, at your disposal, Sir Herald. I apologise for the warlike preparations. I know they are not seemly in a house of God, but Hexham has been attacked many times before.'

'I think you are wise to take precautions,' Merrivale said. 'Father, I wish to speak to one of your canons, Brother Gilbert.'

The prior looked suddenly wary. It struck Merrivale that he was not entirely happy about the new servant of the Lord that had been foisted upon him, despite the five thousand marks of silver he had deposited in the abbey coffers. 'I will send for him, of course. Has he... Has he done anything wrong?'

'I don't know,' Merrivale said truthfully. 'That is what I am hoping to find out.'

'Of course, of course.' Father John rang a bell. 'Wilfrid,' he said to the servant who appeared, 'fetch Brother Gilbert at once, if you please. You will find him in the scriptorium.' He looked at Merrivale. 'Do you wish me to be present at the interview?'

'If it is all the same to you, Father, I would rather speak to him in private.'

'Of course, of course.' The prior looked relieved. 'I must go and check on the workmen who are repairing the walls. Good men, God's children all, but prone to idleness if not closely supervised.'

He disappeared. Merrivale sat for a moment, looking around the lodgings. The room was pleasant, with white painted walls and a little private altar in a niche and a silver chalice and pyx and a reliquary crucifix with a fragment of the True Cross in a crystal case. One of tens of thousands of such fragments scattered around Europe, Merrivale thought; put them together, and how many actual crosses would they build? Geoffrey of Maldon had once asked that question, he remembered. He thought briefly of Geoffrey, back at his home convent recovering after a spell in a French prison, and wished he was here.

The door opened and Gilbert de Tracey walked into the room and stood, arms folded across his chest. The past few weeks had changed him, Merrivale saw. Gone were the Cambrai cloth and silks and fur; instead he wore the black woollen robe of his order and rough sandals on his feet. He looked older; the cropped and tonsured hair were part of it, but there were lines on his forehead and around his eyes, and his cheeks were hollow. His nose and forehead ridge stood out in sharp, hard angles against the rest of his face.

Merrivale pointed to a stool. 'Please, be seated.'

'Thank you, but I prefer to stand.' The other man's voice was hostile, his eyes sharp and angry.

'Very well. How are you enjoying your new life? Have they given you work to do?'

'I have been set to work in the scriptorium,' Brother Gilbert said after a while. He held out his hands, showing ink-stained fingers. 'I am currently engaged in copying the *In principium Genesis* by Bede the Venerable. I leave it to you to judge whether I am enjoying it. May I suggest you dispense with the small talk and tell me exactly what you want from me?'

'You were among the richest men in England. You were a banker, a merchant, a respected advisor to the king and his council, and yet you turned your back on everything to retire here. I doubt very much that you were motivated by a sudden desire for poverty and simplicity. So what did happen?'

'My brother's death, of course. And the accusation of treason. How long do you think my business would have lasted once Edward's actions become public knowledge? No one would want to do business with the brother of a traitor. The king and court would have turned against me, and the rest would have followed. My choices were to liquidate now, or go bankrupt later.'

'It would have taken you some time to go bankrupt. Before I left London, the Chancery investigated your former business. After your public bequests, they reckon there is still over eighty thousand pounds unaccounted for, not including any moveable wealth. What has happened to it?'

'Why is that any concern of yours, or the Chancery's? Unlike my brother I had committed no crime, and I chose voluntarily to withdraw from the world. My wealth was mine to dispose of.'

'Unless you gave it to the men with whom your brother was plotting treason,' Merrivale said. 'Did you?'

'I have no idea who my brother's confederates were. After I settled in London I rarely saw him. And I am *not* a traitor.'

'That is easy to say,' said Merrivale. 'Can you prove it?'

'Can *you* prove otherwise?' Brother Gilbert challenged.

'Let me put it this way,' said Merrivale. 'You took holy orders, I assume, because you believed they would give you some form of protection. You were wrong. I have only to snap my fingers, and the men-at-arms of my escort will drag you out of this priory and take you to Newcastle, where you will be interrogated with fire, water and the rack. Or you can save us all the trouble and tell me the truth here and now.'

They stared at each other, the canon's fists clenched at his sides. Finally, reluctantly, he spoke. 'The money is safe,' he said. 'I have put it out of reach of the king's agents.'

'Why? If you are innocent of your brother's crimes, then as you said, you can dispose of your wealth as you please and the king will have no claim on it.'

Brother Gilbert sneered at him. 'You think the king and his officers will abide by the rule of law when there is eighty thousand pounds at stake? If you do, you're a bigger fool than you look. Some excuse will be found, some charge will be trumped up against me, and my fortune will be confiscated. That's the way it always is with bankers. Kings love them until they have no more use for them, and then—' Gilbert drew his finger across his throat.

'Very well,' Merrivale said, 'the money is out of reach. Where is it?'

'In Bruges,' said Brother Gilbert. 'Lodged with a banker I know well, and can trust to see my requests carried out.'

'Who is this banker?'

'Oppicius Adornes. You may have heard of him.'

Merrivale nodded. After the collapse of the Italian banks last year, Adornes was one of the most powerful and wealthy bankers in Europe. Not coincidentally, he was also one of the few who refused to lend money to the English crown. 'You do know that exporting currency is illegal.'

'I do. And I know merchants who do it every single day, and the crown looks the other way. So long as we need to import cloth and spices and wine, we will send money out of the country to pay for them. I am prepared to defend my actions.'

'Shipping eighty thousand pounds out of the country is hardly the same thing. You mentioned requests. What are they?'

'Why should I tell you?'

'Brother Gilbert, I am not interested in your currency dealings. I have other, more important things on my mind. Tell me the truth, and I will leave you in peace.'

Gilbert looked disbelieving, but he answered the question. 'When the crown seized my brother's lands, his wife and daughters were left destitute. They are innocent of any crime, and it is wrong that they should suffer. On my instructions, Adornes will pay a pension to his widow, and settle dowries on the daughters when the time comes for them to marry.' Brother Gilbert's mouth twisted a little. 'Adornes is of course charging a sizeable fee for this service.'

It was plausible, Merrivale thought. Indeed, if you did not know the history of the Tracey family – or if you did not know that Edward de Tracey's widow came from the fabulously wealthy Fitzalan family, the Earls of Arundel, who would hardly let one of their own starve on the street – it was almost believable. 'You lent money to the Percys, as we know. How many other northern families did you do business with?'

'Most of them. The Nevilles, and Selbys; quite a few others. Not regularly, but from time to time.'

'You mentioned the Selbys. What about the rest of the Disinherited?'

'All of their leaders, yes.'

So Gilbert de Tracey had financial connections with all the nobles and knights the Scots were attempting to bribe. His close knowledge of their financial affairs and their worth meant he could have calculated fairly exactly the amount it would take to bribe them. 'What about Durham cathedral priory?'

Brother Gilbert shook his head. 'I have never dealt with them. Their banking arrangements are unknown to me.'

'Uncle Hugh never sought to put a little business his nephew's way?'

'No.' Gilbert's voice was dry. 'You will have gathered, herald, that we are not a close family.'

Merrivale's eyebrows rose. 'And yet you were happy to take your father's inheritance and use it to start your bank, the foundation of your own fortune. That inheritance came from the proceeds of piracy, murder and worse. Did you know your father acted as a broker for the Norman raiders who sacked Southampton in 1338? He helped them sell girls and boys captured in the raid as slaves. That's your inheritance, brother.'

Gilbert was impatient. 'Men commit sins, money does not. Money is fungible, it has exactly the same value no matter how it is earned or acquired. My money does not mean I am tarred with the same brush as my father, or my brother.'

He looked at the herald, his eyes still angry. 'I know you don't believe me. I know you think I was mixed up in the same treason as my brother. Do you know what, herald? I don't care. Arrest me, drag me away, torture me; I don't give a damn. Whatever Edward did, whatever my father did, is in the past. I have made a new life for myself here. I would hope that a decent man would respect that, and leave me in peace. If you don't,' and Gilbert spread his ink-stained hands again, 'then there is nothing I can do about it.'

The herald watched him for a moment. 'I asked you this question at Hargate,' he said. 'I will ask it again now. Did Edward ever talk to you about the scheme he was involved in, or mention the names of his associates?'

Brother Gilbert folded his arms again. 'If I give you a name, will you leave me alone?'

'It depends on the name.'

The other man let out his breath. 'He was in contact with a Norman nobleman named Rollond de Brus. Some sort of cousin to David of Scotland, apparently. Edward made several payments to Brus last winter, about four hundred marks in all. I queried him about the legitimacy of the payments, but he assured me it was all above board. Brus was one of the Normans in rebellion against France and the king had approved the payments.'

For a banker, Merrivale thought, he lies surprisingly badly. The intriguing question was, why of all the names he could have dropped, why Rollond de Brus? *Because Brus is in Scotland and we cannot touch him?*

The thought came suddenly. *Or because he is not? Is there a chance that we could find Brus and arrest him? Is he trying to betray Brus?*

'You don't belong here,' he said aloud.

For the first time, the other man looked startled. 'What do you mean?'

'Why retreat from the world? Why take the vows of poverty, chastity and obedience? None of the three suits you. You don't belong here, and you know it.'

'What choice did I have? My business was ruined. No one would deal with the brother of a traitor. I had to liquidate and get out, before the whole thing collapsed around me.'

'But in time,' the herald said, 'other, greater scandals will erupt and the name of Edward de Tracey will be forgotten. When that time comes, you will leave your monastic cell and return to the secular world. Oppicius Adornes will have kept your fortune safe for you, and you will resume your old life. Your withdrawal is a tactical retreat, while you wait for fortune's wheel to turn once more.'

'You know nothing of me,' said Brother Gilbert. 'Absolutely nothing.'

'I know this much. If Rollond de Brus is using your money to bribe the Percy family and the Disinherited, they will put your head on a spike on the Micklegate Bar and feed the rest of you to the dogs.' The canon said nothing. 'As for your friends, I don't advise you to rely on their goodwill either, or the protection this priory can offer. From the moment your brother's involvement in the conspiracy became known, he was expendable. They sacrificed him without a second thought. They will do the same to you.'

Still Gilbert stood silent, his eyes burning. 'An archer from your brother's own retinue killed him,' Merrivale said. 'His orders came from the leader of the conspiracy. I don't yet know the name of that leader, only that he comes from somewhere in the north of England. But he will be found. I will find him, and pull this entire conspiracy down. Think about that, Brother Gilbert, and consider where your own self-interest lies.'

–

Outside he found Father John directing a party of workmen building a stone buttress to reinforce the barmekin wall. 'I must ask you a favour,' he said quietly. 'If Brother Gilbert receives visitors, or letters, please inform me at once. You may send word to me through Master Blyth of Newcastle.'

'I shall do so, of course,' said Father John. 'Is this man a danger to our priory?'

'I don't know,' Merrivale said. 'It could be that he is also a danger to himself. Keep him close, father, and keep an eye on him.'

10

Warkworth, 24ᵗʰ of September, 1346
Afternoon

The sun shone once more as Lady Mary and Tiphaine rode up the Great North Road, accompanied by a small escort of men-at-arms procured from the castle. Blyth had offered the services of his men, but Lady Mary had refused. 'I intend to make an entrance when we reach Warkworth,' she said once they were on the road. 'I want a proper troop of horse with me, not some shop-bought mercenaries. They need to know I am a force to be reckoned with.'

'I don't think there will be any doubt about that,' said Tiphaine. She was glad she was here in Lady Mary's company. Simon had not returned, nor had the men Blyth had sent to find him, and her nerves were twanging like harp strings. 'What will you do at Warkworth?'

'Tell them some plain truths,' said Lady Mary. 'And hope to God they listen. I had word from the castle before we departed, by the way. The man who fell in the salt pan is dead; nicely salt-baked by the sound of it. He carried nothing to identify him. The rest have vanished without trace, including Brus.'

'Give the devil his due,' said Tiphaine, 'he is clever.' She shuddered. 'How could I have ever fallen for a man like that?'

'We all make mistakes, my dear. What about you and Simon? Have you reached an understanding yet?'

Tiphaine looked uncomfortable. 'We have not spoken about it.'

'Why not? There is no time like the present.'

'Because I know his heart and soul are tied to his past,' said Tiphaine. 'And he is not yet free of it. I don't know if he ever will be.'

Lady Mary looked down her nose. 'And how long will you allow him to live in that past? You're probably the only person who can help him escape it.'

'Mary, I do not know my own mind, let alone his. You are talking about things like love, but what do I know about love? I thought I was in love once, but that man betrayed me and tried to kill me.'

'That was Brus.'

'Yes. Sometimes, I feel like I have lived forever, Mary, and yet for no time at all. I went from a convent school to a dungeon. I spent two years in a prison cell with no one but rats for company. I don't really understand anything about life. As for Simon… his past enfolds him like a tapestry, scene after scene re-enacting itself, over and over again. He cannot escape it.'

'But you are not part of his past,' said Lady Mary. 'Perhaps that is a good thing.'

'Good for whom? For him, for me? How can I tell? I am not as wise as you, Mary.'

The other woman smiled. 'How my family would laugh to hear you call me wise. But I don't want to see you miss an opportunity for happiness.'

Shortly after midday the towers of Warkworth came into sight, and Lady Mary turned again to her companion. 'I hope this won't be too dreary for you. I'm afraid there are going to be a lot of discussions about treachery and family politics.'

'I am from Normandy,' Tiphaine said. 'I am used to both.'

'Yes, but in a much more subtle and gentlemanly fashion, I suspect. The Percys are about as subtle as the Nibelungs.'

In fact their welcome could not have been more pleasant. Warkworth Castle, surrounded on three sides by the river, looked austere from the outside but the great hall, set against the curtain wall in the bailey and overlooked by a circular keep, was warm and comfortable. The furniture was rather battered, as one would expect in a household full of boisterous young people and dogs – as Tiphaine was ushered to a bench seat, she looked down to see a puppy sprawled on its back, chewing on the table leg – but the wall hangings were rich and bright with colour and the wine cups were made of silver. The wine was good, too. The household was overseen by Lady Idonia, Lord Percy's wife, who managed servants, guests and husband with well-oiled ease. *In the unlikely event that I ever become a chatelaine*, Tiphaine thought, *I shall apply to her for lessons.*

Lord Percy was a gruff man of about fifty with a face carved out of the stone of his own castle, but he treated Lady Mary with respect and was surprisingly tender towards herself; it turned out that Sir Harry had told him something of her history. Sir Harry was there too, along with various other members of the household whose names Tiphaine heard and promptly forgot.

They talked border politics in English, belatedly switching to French when they realised she was struggling. She gathered that the Scottish army had completed its muster at Perth and was now moving down to Edinburgh; it was expected on the borders within a few days. Opinion was divided on which way it would come next. The Scots might strike in the east, attacking heavily defended Berwick, or they might move to the less well-protected west; only a castle called Liddel Strength could be expected to put up much resistance. The border clans were already moving, Harry said, and Douglas of Liddesdale was mustering his followers at his castle, the Hermitage. Niall Bruce of Carrick was with him.

Although everyone talked calmly, there was an undercurrent of unease around the table. It was not hard to guess why. At one point Lord Percy and his son broke off into a side conversation of their own, speaking so quietly Tiphaine could not hear, but they watched Lady Mary as they spoke.

Dinner ended and the board was cleared. Lady Mary looked at her father-in-law. 'My lord,' she said, 'may I have a word with you? And Sir Harry also?'

Recognising her cue, Lady Idonia rose. 'I have some sewing to attend to,' she said. 'You are welcome to join me, *demoiselle*, or there is a garden below the keep where you may take some air. The pinks are quite heavenly at the moment. And help yourself to damsons, we have far more than we can eat.'

'Thank you,' Tiphaine said. 'I think I will take a little air.'

The rest of the household rose and went out. Lady Mary waited until the door had closed behind them, and then rose to her feet and stood looking down at her husband's father and brother.

'The first rule of treachery is this,' she said. 'If you are going to betray your country, do it properly. Plan carefully, make thorough preparations, and above all keep it *secret*. Don't wander around like headless geese drawing attention to yourselves, like you are doing now.'

Sunlight shone through the high windows, painting stripes across the table and the rush mats. The men looked at her in shock. 'Treachery is a harsh word,' Harry Percy said sharply.

'Yes,' said Lady Mary. 'Isn't it? And yet, it is exactly the word they are using in London. I heard it myself from the queen's lips, when discussing whether the northern barons would remain loyal to the crown. She *knows* the Scots are in correspondence with the Nevilles and the Percys. She *knows* they are attempting to seduce you from your loyalty. And what is more, she knows you are considering their offer.'

'How does she know?' asked Lord Percy.

'Because she is a highly astute woman who keeps her ear to the ground,' Lady Mary said. 'Look, both of you. If you want to drag yourselves down to ruin, that is your affair. But if the Percy family turns traitor you will drag my husband down too, and very possibly me and my own family with you. And there, I draw the line.'

'Harry is right. You need to temper your language, my lady,' said Lord Percy. 'No treason has been committed. But we have to be realistic.'

Lady Mary's fine eyes opened wide. 'Realistic? Is that what we are being? Very well, then. Show me some realism.'

'The facts are plain. The Scots have mustered fourteen thousand men at Perth. At the utmost, after reinforcing the garrisons of our own towns and castles, we can put half that many into the field. On top of which, the king has seen fit to appoint the Archbishop of York as Warden of the Marches. A quill sharpener, a clerk who has never commanded men in the field, to go up against battle-hardened captains like Moray and Douglas. He doesn't stand a chance.'

'He might,' said Lady Mary, 'if he had you and Lord Neville alongside him. If your men are there to stiffen the archbishop's army, then there is a chance of victory.'

'We have to be realistic,' Lord Percy repeated. 'This is the largest army the Scots have put in the field for a generation. Northumberland and Cumberland are wide open to invasion. We must protect our own lands, our own tenants. We have a duty to them.'

'A duty,' Lady Mary said, as if she were having trouble believing her ears. 'Your duty to your queen, I suppose, is a matter of only passing relevance. Very well. May I see the letter? The one delivered by the friar?'

Harry Percy looked apprehensive. 'How do you know about that?' Lord Percy asked after a moment.

'Never mind.' She held out her hand. 'Show it to me, please.'

Lord Percy took a small parchment roll from his purse and handed it to her. She read the script, and a shiver ran down her spine.

> To the esteemed and noble Henry, Baron Percy, and to his son Henry Percy, miles, greeting. On Michaelmas day, the truce between England and Scotland will expire, and war harsh and cruel will once again engulf your land. The armies of Scotland will lay your estates waste, and spread fire and sword from the Tweed to the Tyne and beyond. Those who are our friends will be spared, and their lands

and manors and castles will not suffer the fires of war.
But those who resist us will be devastated utterly, their
houses and fields burned, their crops destroyed, their trees
cut down, their cattle slain, their people annihilated. Even
the elderly and the children shall perish, and we will strip
their land bare and plough their fields with salt so that
nothing may grow or prosper there again. Our enemies and
their families can expect no mercy from us. We will cast our
enemies down into a pit of fire, but to our friends we will
extend the hand of welcome. The choice is upon you now.
Make your allegiance known to the bearer of this letter, so
that we may be clear where you stand.

'When did this arrive?' Lady Mary asked.

'About an hour before you did,' Harry said. 'It is not the first.'

'No,' said Lord Percy. 'We have had other threats. We have also been promised rewards if we do not resist.'

'What rewards?'

Lord Percy was silent. 'Lands in both England and Scotland,' Harry said finally. 'The towns of Berwick and Newcastle to hold as fiefs in our own right. And six thousand marks of silver.'

'Six thousand marks? Ah, now we're getting somewhere. Never mind your cheap talk of duty, *this* is what you mean by realism.'

'Mary, listen to me,' Lord Percy said. 'London cannot defend us, or will not. The Scots have an open door into England. They can walk in, any time they like, and take our lands from us.'

'Whereas if you pledge allegiance to King David, they will pat you on the head and make you rich,' Lady Mary said. 'What answer did you make to the friar?'

'We temporised,' Lord Percy said finally. 'We want guarantees that the Scots will keep their promises.'

She waved the parchment at them. 'They won't. The man who wrote this letter is a Frenchman named Rollond de Brus, and he is a conspirator and traitor even to his own people. He is the kind of man who burns young women to death for sport. He will swear any oath, make any promise in order to bend you to his will, and then betray you. If you join forces with this man, you are as good as dead.'

The men looked at each other. 'How do you know about this Frenchman?' Harry asked.

'Simon Merrivale, the prince's herald, knows all about him. He is part of a plot to bring down the thrones of both England and France, and he is using you as cat's paws to do his work for him. My lord, I beg you, do not give in to this man. No matter how fair his words, he will destroy you, and the country too if he can.'

'Can you prove this?' asked Lord Percy.

'As we speak, the herald is attempting to do exactly that. Give him time, and he will expose whatever treachery Brus is plotting.'

'There isn't much time,' Harry warned.

'No,' said Lord Percy. He looked hard at Lady Mary. 'I appreciate the danger, and I thank you for warning us. We will muster our men and make ready. But for the moment, we must continue to temporise. Let the herald bring proof that Brus intends to betray us. If he does, we will fight. If not...' He spread his hands. 'If not, then we must decide the best course for ourselves.'

'And for your six thousand marks,' she said, her voice sharp with anger. 'Don't forget your pieces of silver.'

There was a long silence. 'Because you are young, and my son's wife, I will overlook your words,' Lord Percy said. 'Do not judge us too harshly, Mary. Try to imagine what you would do, if you were in our shoes.'

The door opened before she could reply and one of Lady Idonia's maids hurried in. Her eyes were wide with alarm. 'The Demoiselle de Tesson!' she said. 'She is gone!'

Mary stared at her. 'What do you mean, *gone*?'

'She went to the garden, but then she disappeared. One of the men-at-arms is missing too, and they have taken two horses.'

'Get after them,' Lord Percy snapped. 'Harry, see to it.'

The younger Percy ran from the hall. A moment later horsemen thundered over the drawbridge, fanning out across the country. But although they searched into the evening, they found no sign of Tiphaine or the man-at-arms.

—

Sunlight shone on the grey stone of the old keep and the green banks of the motte. Tiphaine found the garden and let herself in, walking slowly past the banks of sage and parsley and rue, admiring the pinks and taking a purple damson from the tree as bidden. A stone stair led her up to the battlements and she stood there for a moment, eating the fruit and flicking the stone over the wall into the moat. The east wind was blowing hard; gulls whimpered in the turbulent air and she could hear the distant murmur of the sea. She turned and looked down into the courtyard.

A groom appeared, leading out a horse. Following him came a portly, tonsured man in a black cloak. His face was not fully visible, but there was no mistaking the bandage on his hand.

By the time she reached the courtyard he was already cantering out of the gate and riding away to the west. She had only one thought; to get a horse and go after him. Brus had disappeared, but if she followed Brother Oswald the friar might lead her to him. She hurried into the stables calling for a groom, but a man-at-arms in a mail tunic and helmet with a nose guard stepped out and faced her, hand on the hilt of his sword. 'Who are you?'

The accent was peculiar, with a rough edge but at the same time slightly sibilant. 'My name is Tiphaine de Tesson,' she said quickly. 'I am a companion of Lady Mary. Did you see the man who just departed? I need to follow him.'

'Brother Oswald? Why?'

'Because he is spying for the enemy. I saw him meet a French agent in Newcastle, two days ago. I must go after him.'

The man-at-arms looked at her. 'Are you certain of this?'

'On my life. I need a horse, *now*.'

The man turned to the groom. 'Saddle two horses, at once. It is too dangerous for you to ride alone,' he said to Tiphaine. 'I am coming with you.'

'Are you allowed to leave your duties?'

'I know what my duties are,' the man said cryptically. The two horses were led out and he boosted Tiphaine up into the saddle, mounting his own while she rearranged her skirts. 'You can tell me more as we go. Now, come. I know where Oswald is going.'

'Where?'

'Berwick,' said the man-at-arms. 'He is on his way to meet the Disinherited.'

Newcastle, 24ᵗʰ of September, 1346
Evening

'Welcome,' William Blyth said, smiling. 'I trust your journey was a good one?'

'It had its moments of interest,' said Merrivale. 'May I present Master Peter de Lisle? He has joined my household.'

'Then he is welcome here. You will have learned, I believe, that Lady Mary and the *demoiselle* have departed for Warkworth.'

Merrivale had already read Tiphaine's brief note. 'Yes, thank you. Master Blyth, I need a favour. I'm afraid it is rather complicated, but this is on the queen's service.'

Blyth came alert. 'Tell me what you need.'

'When trading overseas, do you ever do business with a banker from Bruges, Oppicius Adornes?'

'Occasionally, yes. Pretty much anyone trading in Bruges deals with Adornes at some time or other.'

'Gilbert de Tracey claims he deposited his money with Adornes. Is there any way of confirming if this is true?'

Blyth rubbed his chin. 'Adornes won't tell us himself. Bankers tend to be strict about confidentiality, especially where large sums are concerned. But… One of my contacts in Bruges did mention some big transactions, bills of exchange but specie as well. I can ask for more information, but it will take time.'

'I would be grateful if you would. And if you hear anything more, please let me know.'

–

'The fellow who hired the men who attacked us didn't cover his trail very well, sir,' Warin said. 'We asked around the docks, bought a few drinks in taverns, and got the same story every time. Someone recruited men to attack a party on the road between here and Durham. Silver paid in advance. They were to meet at Blackfell, where they would receive their orders.'

'Where is Blackfell?'

'Just outside Washington, sir, not far off the road we travelled. The manor is owned by a man-at-arms named David Harkness. His father was Scottish, a Galwegian, but he himself is in the retinue of Sir Gilbert d'Umfraville.'

'Harkness is one of the Disinherited,' said Merrivale. 'As is Clennell.'

'Yes, sir. We don't know Harkness's colours.'

Merrivale turned to Peter de Lisle, standing bright and eager beside him. 'Two gold chevrons on blue, the lower chevron bearing a red crescent upturned,' he said immediately.

Mauro and Warin looked at each other. 'He was there, *señor*,' Mauro said. 'He was with Sir Thomas Clennell.'

'Yes, I saw him. So it *was* play-acting. Harkness paid those men to attack us, then staged the rescue.'

'There is something else, *señor*,' Mauro said. 'Before she departed, the Demoiselle Tiphaine asked us to find out who the Seigneur de Brus was meeting at the inn. We were unable to do so, but we did discover who owns the inn. It is the same man. David Harkness.'

Merrivale pondered the implications of this. He picked up Tiphaine's letter, and read again what happened at South Shields. 'What about this friar she mentions? Brother Oswald?'

'He is called Oswald of Halton, sir,' said Warin. 'That is about all we have been able to discover.'

Peter looked up. 'Oswald of Halton? From the Dominican order?'

'Yes,' said Merrivale. 'Do you know of him?'

'He has a terrible reputation, sir. He is a very great rogue, who does not obey the rule of his order and ignores the master of his house. Some say he is a thief, and others claim he is a spy. Sir, I hate to say this about a man of God, but he does terrible things to women.'

'He may well be a spy,' Merrivale said. 'The *demoiselle* says he is carrying messages for Rollond de Brus to Lord Percy and the Disinherited.'

He paused for a moment, feeling another wave of weariness wash over him. Reading of Tiphaine's encounter with Brus had left him feeling sick with nerves; a condition to which he was not accustomed. All around him, there was a sense of events spinning out of control. The pieces were all there: Tracey, Brus, the Percys, Harkness and the Disinherited, Agnes of Dunbar. But what pattern linked them? Where was the piece he could take out of the game, to break the pattern and bring the whole plot tumbling down? He didn't know and couldn't see; and meanwhile, the sand in the hourglass was running out.

'What next, sir?' asked Warin.

'Lady Mary has gone to see the Percys. I wish her luck... It is time we tackled the Disinherited, and in particular David Harkness. Let us see what he has to say for himself. Do we know where he is?'

'Yes, *señor*,' said Mauro. 'Sir Gilbert d'Umfraville has called up his men, and Harkness has gone to join him. They are mustering at a place called Harbottle, in Coquetdale.'

'Then that is where we shall go tomorrow. Master Peter, do you know the way?'

'Yes, sir. It is very near the frontier.'

'Then let us hope the truce continues to hold. All of you, get some rest. We shall depart as soon as the town gates open in the morning.'

But the truce did not hold. The messenger who arrived next morning, just as their horses were being saddled, bore no badge and did not give his name. Handing over the letter, he turned his lathered horse and rode away. Merrivale broke the plain blob of wax that sealed the letter and read the neat, light script inside.

> *Brus is schooling the Disinherited, preparing to bend them to his will. Douglas and Carrick are marching to attack them. Their force is already in motion.*

11

The first part of the journey was easy, cantering up the Great North Road with occasional pauses to water and rest the horses. At Felton Bridge they turned and rode west into the hills, and thereafter the track became rougher and in places steep and stony, rutted by the wheels of wagons. Peter led the way, his knowledge of the land as sure as his memory for coats of arms, while Merrivale watched the hillsides for signs of ambush, expecting at any moment to see smoke boiling up to join the thickening clouds.

He hoped he had made the right choice. The note had not said when and where the Scots would attack, only that they would come soon. Chipchase was an obvious target, but from what de Lisle had said, Brus and his allies would probably disregard him on account of his age and infirmity. He suggested this to Peter, and with surprising maturity the boy agreed. 'My father's memory lives in legend, but the true leader now is Sir Gilbert d'Umfraville. He is the one the others follow.' And that meant Harbottle was the enemy's most likely objective.

'Where we are going could be dangerous,' he said. 'If some of the Disinherited are in league with the Scots, they are likely to regard me as an enemy.' He smiled. 'Is this how you imagined a herald's life?'

'I know there is more to it than just coats and armorial bearings, sir,' came the calm reply. 'A herald is an officer of the crown, a messenger and ambassador, and sometimes that service can be dangerous. Had I followed in my father's footsteps, the risks would have been the same.'

Merrivale smiled again. 'True,' he said.

'May I ask a question, sir? Why do heralds not carry weapons, or wear armour? Surely they need protection just like other men.'

The herald touched his embroidered tabard. 'This is your protection,' he said. 'It is the only armour you will ever need. So long as men obey the laws of war, this tabard will be respected.'

The boy glanced at him. 'And what happens when men break those laws?'

'Things become... a bit difficult,' Merrivale said.

The valley narrowed, the hills rising steeply up to harsh stone crags, black silhouettes against the fading light. The clouds were thick overhead now. The air was absolutely still and seemed to crackle with electricity. Thunder grumbled in the distance. Harbottle came into view, a big stone castle on a steep hill overlooking a bend in the river; a small village huddled on the slopes below it, and farms stretched into the distance up the valley. Not for the first time, the herald wondered what possessed people to settle in these desolate places.

The castle gates were open but guarded, and Merrivale saw archers on the wall-walks. The guards saluted his tabard and ushered them into a courtyard busy with men and horses. The castle steward appeared and took them upstairs to the great hall. A matronly woman in a plain brown kirtle met them at the top of the stairs. 'Sir Herald! We were not expecting you!'

'My apologies for arriving unannounced,' Merrivale said, bowing. 'But I have urgent news for Sir Gilbert d'Umfraville.'

'I am Lady Joan, his wife. I shall take you to him.'

A cluster of men around the high table looked up sharply as they entered the hall. They fell silent when they saw the herald's tabard. Merrivale recognised some of them from his time as a King's Messenger; Wake of Liddell, broad-shouldered with a massive, shaggy head, his hair now turning grey; Walter Selby, tall and lantern-jawed; Umfraville himself, face tanned by the summer sun with an aquiline nose and dark hair receding in a widow's peak. Thomas Clennell was there too, and he alone of the group was smiling. 'We meet again, Sir Herald,' he said.

'I will come straight to the point,' said Merrivale. 'The Scots have broken the truce. A force under Douglas of Liddesdale and Bruce of Carrick is on its way to the border. Indeed, they may have crossed by now. I do not know how many men they have, but I believe their destination is Harbottle and the lands around it.'

'How do you know this?' demanded Wake.

'It does not matter. Believe me, my lord, this information is true and genuine. You must act upon it.'

'Why attack Harbottle?' asked Umfraville. His wife's face had gone pale.

'The Scots are sending you a message,' said Merrivale. 'Agree to their demands, or face destruction. This is a demonstration of their power, gentlemen, before the negotiations begin in Berwick.'

Thunder boomed among the hills. The men in the room stared at the herald. Clennell's fists clenched. 'How do you know about Berwick?' he asked.

Wake slammed his fist down on the table. 'For the love of God!' he said violently. 'Are we to stand here asking questions all night? The Scots are on the way, gentlemen. We must *move*!'

They snapped out of their trance then. Lady Joan sent the servants running down to the village to alert the people, while the men mounted their horses and rode out into the valley to bring the farm folk and their livestock to a place of safety. Umfraville and Wake rode up the valley towards the border, the place of greatest danger, and Merrivale rode with them, fitful flashes of lightning flickering off his tabard. Peter de Lisle was behind him and once, turning in the saddle, Merrivale saw the chevrons and crescent of Harkness not far away.

Mercifully, there was as yet no sign of the Scots. Umfraville directed his men, sending them to each farm as they pressed on into the heart of the hills to rouse the people and help them get away, while Wake's men scouted forward, looking for the enemy. Lighting flashed raw around the rugged hilltops and thunder boomed. The Coquet roared, flooding over boulders as it plunged down from the high country by the border. Reaching the tiny hamlet of Barrow Burn, Merrivale rode forward and dismounted, knocking at the door of the first cottage he came to. 'I have come from Harbottle,' he said to the frightened man who opened the door. 'The Scots are on their way. We are here to take you to safety.'

Without waiting for a reply he moved on to the next cottage and the next, and then moved through the crowd while the men armed themselves and the women collected their moveable belongings, some of them wailing with fear, panicky children screaming at the thunder and cattle bellowing in confusion. Quietly, he guided them towards the road that led to Harbottle. When one elderly woman was helped out of her cottage by two men, the herald led his mount forward and helped the men lift her onto the back of the horse. He was pleased to see Peter immediately following his example, giving up his saddle to a man who was struggling to walk.

Gradually the thunder faded, replaced by a cold streaming drizzle. Torches flared in the mist, guiding people and animals through a darkness split by the whinnying of nervous horses and the constant, continuous lowing of cattle. A river of livestock flowed down the valley towards Harbottle, and after it came the people, men on horseback with the jacks and lances that every borderer kept close to hand, the women and children on ponies. Umfraville and Wake and their men came last of all, shielding the people from Scottish attack should it come. At the castle the stream divided, animals flowing into the walled barmekin, people into the courtyard of the castle itself where fires burned to keep them warm and ward off the night terrors. A woman crooned to her restless child, words she had probably heard herself when young,

Hush ye, hush ye, little pet ye
Hush ye, hush ye, do not fret ye
The Black Douglas shall not get ye

Eventually the drizzle stopped. A wind sprang up from the north, fluttering the torches. The barmekin was crammed with livestock now, cattle bellowing in confusion. 'That's the last of them,' called Clennell, riding in through the gate and dismounting. He also had lands nearby, and brought his tenants and their beasts to Harbottle.

'Good,' said Umfraville. 'Close the gates, keep those fires burning and double the watch. Davy,' he said to Harkness, 'you are captain of the guard. If so much as a shadow moves, sound the alarm.'

'You can rely on me,' Harkness said.

Umfraville clapped him on the shoulder. 'Always,' he said.

Wake turned to Merrivale. 'I can guess why you are really here. We need to talk.'

Harbottle, 25ᵗʰ of September, 1346
Midnight

They gathered in the great hall, where the fire had been made up and logs blazed in the hearth. Peter sat beside Merrivale, drooping with fatigue but determined to stay by his master. 'I'm sorry, lad,' Umfraville said to him. 'This is a poor welcome we have shown you. How is your father?'

'As well as can be expected, sir,' said Peter. 'He can no longer ride very far, which makes him unhappy. But his mind is sound and sharp as ever.'

'I can attest to that,' said Clennell, smiling. 'I called on him at Chipchase a month ago, and brought him a book of those *lais* of Marie de France that he admires so much. He read a page once, and then recited every line back to me perfectly. He has the mind of a scholar, and yet what a warrior he once was.'

Walter Selby stood warming his hands by the fire, steam rising from his wet tunic. 'He saved my life once, during that dismal campaign in '28. I owe him a debt greater than I can ever repay.'

'And we could use his wisdom to guide us now,' Wake said heavily. He looked at Merrivale. 'I take it you discussed the present situation with him?'

'I wanted to know where he stood,' Merrivale said. 'I am aware that the name of de Lisle still carries a great deal of weight in the borders. He told me had made his own decision to refuse the offer, but he would not advise others. Each man must make his own decision, he said.'

He paused for a moment, looking at them in turn; Clennell uncomfortable and frowning, Selby staring into the fire, Wake looking at his hands, Umfraville inscrutable. 'It is no secret that David Bruce's agents have offered you restoration of your lost lands and titles in Scotland,' the herald said. 'The court in London knows it, so does Archbishop de la Zouche. What they do not know, not for certain, is that you are considering taking up the offer.'

'What makes you think we are?' asked Wake.

'The fact that you are gathered here, for a start. It is hardly a coincidence that you decided to meet the day before you were summoned to Berwick. You were in the middle of your conference when I arrived, were you not? Trying to decide what answer to give?'

'Yes, of course we were,' Selby said shortly. 'There is no point in denying it.'

'And have you decided on your response?' In the silence that followed, Merrivale said, 'I ask this in the queen's name, gentlemen.'

'I don't believe for a moment that the Scots will keep their promises,' Selby said angrily. 'This meeting in Berwick is a deception, to draw us away so they can raid our lands while our backs are turned.'

Merrivale shook his head. 'The meeting in Berwick is real,' he said. 'You are all commanded to attend. Tonight is a persuader, a demonstration of what they will do if you fail to comply. A foretaste of things to come, if you like.'

He looked around the room again. 'Well? When the raiders come, will you fight them?'

'I will fight anyone who attacks my lands,' said Umfraville. 'I always have done, and I always will.'

Heads nodded. 'I am with Selby on this,' said Clennell. 'The Scots are dangling bait before our eyes. The moment we reach for it, they will snatch it away.' He looked at Merrivale. 'You may assure the queen of my loyalty.'

'And mine,' said Wake.

Umfraville nodded. 'Tell them in London that the Disinherited stand by their allegiance.'

'All of you?' said Merrivale. 'I think there is at least one whose loyalty is doubtful, to say the least. I am speaking, gentlemen, of David Harkness of Blackfell.'

A moment of silence and Clennell exploded. 'Harkness? What in hell's name are you talking about?'

'As you will remember, Sir Thomas, a party of armed men waylaid my servants and myself on our way north. Those men were hired by David Harkness.'

The others stared at him. Even Peter was open-mouthed with surprise. 'Impossible,' Clennell said shortly.

Merrivale looked at Umfraville. 'Tell me about him. When did he come into your service?'

'About two years ago,' Umfraville said. 'Before that he was part of Sir Robert de Lisle's retinue. Robert released him when he retired from active service, and Davy came to join me.'

'What are his antecedents?'

'His father was from Nithsdale in Galloway and was an adherent of the Balliols. He lost his lands when the Bruces conquered the region. His mother was English. He inherited a manor in the County Palatine through her, and a couple of properties in Newcastle.'

'Davy is more than just an ordinary man-at-arms,' Clennell said. 'The king intended to knight him back in '38, but he didn't have enough money to support the dignity. It was a damned shame, though. He's a good soldier and would have made an excellent administrator. He just needs more land.'

The herald nodded. 'Send for him, if you please.'

Harkness was in his forties, about the same age as Umfraville and Clennell. He had that same hard-hewn look that so many border men had, the product of many long and weary weeks in the saddle in all weathers. He bowed to the herald. 'I am glad to see you in good health, sir.'

Merrivale studied him for moment. 'You hired the men who attacked me on the road near Chester-le-Street.'

Harkness looked at Clennell, then back at Merrivale. 'I am sorry, sir, but I don't know what you are talking about.'

'My servants found witnesses in Newcastle who can attest to this,' Merrivale continued. 'Of course, you also gave orders that my servants and I were not to be hurt. The entire affair was staged, including your hunting party galloping to the rescue.'

'What the devil are you talking about?' demanded Clennell. 'I saw them, for God's sake! Those men were about to kill you!'

'No,' said the herald, watching Harkness's face. 'If they had wanted to kill me, I would be dead. The question is, what was Master Harkness hoping to achieve? You all know, I am certain, that attacking a royal herald and envoy is a crime equivalent to treason.'

Harkness stood his ground. 'I know nothing of what you are talking about, sir. We were out hunting when we saw a group of bandits attack you, and we rode to the rescue. That's all there is, sir.'

'And I think you are being damned ungrateful by throwing out accusations like this,' Clennell said sharply. 'Davy Harkness is as true a man as you'll find on the borders. I'd stake my life on it.'

'You own an inn on Pilgrim Street in Newcastle,' Merrivale said to Harkness.

'Yes, sir. What of it?'

'Three days ago, a French spy went to the inn and remained there for some time. It seems likely he was meeting someone. Was it you?'

'I have been at my manor of Blackfell for some time, sir, making everything ready before coming north to join Sir Gilbert, according to the terms of my indenture.'

'He arrived yesterday,' Umfraville confirmed.

'The man of whom I speak is Rollond, Seigneur de Brus,' Merrivale said. 'The same man who is urging you to change your allegiance, and who has instructed you to meet him in Berwick. The same man who has also ordered Douglas and Niall Bruce to raid your lands, Sir Gilbert. So you see, when you say blithely that the Disinherited are loyal, and yet at the same time one of your own retinue stages an attack on me, and offers his property as a safe haven for an enemy spy, I am left with doubts. What should I believe?'

'It's an inn, for Christ's sake,' said Clennell. 'People come and go all the time.'

'It is one of many inns on Pilgrim Street. Why did Brus choose the one owned by a member of the Disinherited?'

'I don't know, sir,' Harkness said helplessly. 'I wasn't there. I have no idea what you are talking about.'

'Let me ask you a question in turn,' Umfraville said to the herald. 'You claim this attack on you was staged. Why? What would Davy, or myself, or any of us have to gain by this?'

'I don't know, yet,' Merrivale said. 'But I intend to find out.'

Lord Wake rose to his feet. 'Enough,' he said. 'Sir Herald, if you find proof against David Harkness, bring it to us and we will consider the matter again. For now, the discussion is closed. Get some rest, all of you. Tomorrow will bring its own trials.'

'Do you think they will fight?' Merrivale asked Peter de Lisle when they were alone.

'I am certain they will, sir. They're proud people, and they don't like invaders on their land.'

Including me, Merrivale thought. He saw Peter hesitate. 'What is it?'

'Davy Harkness, sir. I knew him well when he served my father. When I was small he used to pick me up and give me a lift on his shoulders, and later he made me a wooden sword and taught me to fence with it. My father thought the world of him. Can he really be a traitor, sir?'

Somewhere in the castle a baby was crying, and the unhappy cattle continued their clamour in the barmekin. At least Peter had asked the question, Merrivale thought, rather than denying everything as Umfraville and the others had done.

'For your sake, I hope it isn't him,' he said. 'But someone in that group is, and very possibly more than one.'

He saw the disappointment in the young face. 'My father would never do anything so dishonourable,' the boy said.

'Your father is no ordinary man.' Fighting men who read Cicero and French romantic poetry; he had met some in the past, but they were rare. 'Try to get some sleep, my lad. One way or another, tomorrow is going to be a long day.'

Harbottle, 26th of September, 1346
Morning

At dawn the horns blew the alarm, echoing off the cloud-shrouded hills of Coquetdale. Merrivale rose from his sleepless bed and hurried down to the hall where Umfraville and his men were arming. Harkness was one of them, strapping on his greaves and picking up his sword belt, not meeting Merrivale's eye. 'You were right,' Umfraville said, his voice taut. 'The Scots are over the border. They're burning their way down the valley, and coming straight for us.'

Another man hurried into the hall, mud-splattered and breathing hard. 'They're coming on fast, sir. We spotted the red heart of Douglas, and the red lion.'

'Bruce of Carrick,' said Merrivale. Beside him, Peter nodded. The boy was carrying his unstrung bow and coiled bowstring in one hand and had a quiver of arrows over his shoulder.

'How many?' asked Umfraville.

'Hundreds, sir. They're thick as ants on the hillsides.'

Umfraville's tenants were all armed, and Clennell had brought men from his neighbouring estate. Wake and Selby had only the small escorts they had ridden with from Cumberland. 'What do you intend to do?' Merrivale asked.

'Fight, of course. I told you the queen could depend on our loyalty.' Umfraville picked up his shield, blazoned with a gold cinquefoil on red, and went down the stairs in a clash of articulated metal, followed by Harkness and the rest of his men. A moment later came a clatter of hooves as they rode out of the castle.

'I'll stay with you, sir,' Peter said calmly. 'Just in case.'

It was sometimes hard to remember Peter was only fifteen, but he had grown up on the borders and war was all he had ever known. The castle courtyard was full of frightened people, looking up at the battlements; Lady Joan moved among them, trying to maintain calm. Merrivale spotted the woman he had seen last night, holding her child close to her chest while her lips moved in prayer. He climbed up to the wall-walk, where the garrison stood ready at their posts with spears and bows. Clouds hung in drifts around the crags, and now and then a few drops of rain fell. Peter tucked his bowstring into his pocket, and Merrivale was reminded of the archers putting their strings under their caps during the hailstorm before Crécy. *My God*, he thought, *was that really only a month ago?*

Smoke boiled up over the hills, rising and becoming one with the clouds. Orange flames glittered brilliantly in the dull morning light, and in the distance they could see movement around the burning farms, the black shapes of men and horses, the silver glint of lance points. Umfraville's men had deployed near the river; they had a few archers, Merrivale saw, as well as men-at-arms and light armoured hobelars. Clennell, Wake and Selby had swung left and were positioned further up the hillside. Merrivale was puzzled by this at first, and then he saw that a fold in the ground concealed Clennell and the others from the view of the oncoming Scots.

Down past the burning farms came a solid body of horsemen. Banners waved over their heads, the red heart of Douglas and the red lion of Bruce, two famous blazons that had struck fear along the borders for generations. Peter de Lisle glanced up at the clouds. 'I think the rain has stopped,' he said calmly, and uncoiling his bowstring, he bent his bow and strung it, pulling out an arrow and nocking it.

'They have archers too,' someone said. Merrivale saw them in the same moment, a little company of mounted archers keeping pace with the main body on the flank nearest Clennell's little force. If they spotted Clennell early, they would shoot his men to pieces and leave Umfraville to be overwhelmed by Douglas and Bruce. Merrivale realised he was holding his breath.

The enemy came on, steadily, the horsemen disciplined and keeping ranks. A few were men-at-arms, most were hobelars in leather jacks with long lances. The trampling of hooves could be felt in the stone ramparts. Behind them more farms blossomed with flame, smoke shrouding the valley in haze. Sparks fell across the ramparts. The mounted archers were cantering now, sweeping around the flank of Umfraville's force, moving into position to enfilade them while the Scottish horsemen charged from the front. Merrivale watched Clennell's black lions, standing on the hillside below the dark crags. *Come on*, he said silently. *It's now or never.*

As if in response to his thought, Clennell's men began to move. Down the hill they swept, the black lions flanked by the red and gold bars of Wake and the black and gold of Selby. They hit the Scottish archers before they could turn their horses and smashed through the middle of their formation like a chisel, driving straight on towards the flank of the main body. They hit at almost exactly the same moment as Umfraville charged from the front, and where there had been discipline and order now there was chaos as the old enemies hacked and stabbed at each other, knocking men out of the saddle and spearing them on the ground. Below them, the water of the Coquet began to grow dark with blood.

'Look out!' The Scottish archers had recovered from the shock of Clennell's attack, and instead of joining in the melee along the river they were coming straight for the castle, raising their bows. 'Get down, sir!' Peter cried, and he and Merrivale ducked behind the crenelations as a shower of arrows flew upwards, some bouncing off the stone, others whirring into the courtyard. One of the garrison fell backwards off the wall-walk, an arrow embedded in his neck, and there were screams and cries of pain from the courtyard below. Peter stood up and shot one of the archers out of the saddle, reached for an arrow and shot again, crouching down again as more arrows flew upwards.

Down by the river a horn sounded, and when Merrivale next looked out the archers were retreating. Douglas and Bruce were withdrawing too, their men breaking off the combat and wheeling away from the English horsemen. He saw Umfraville raise a hand, holding his men back at first in case this was a ruse. But the Scots continued to retreat, leaving bodies and riderless horses behind them, pursued cautiously by the English. Within a quarter of an hour both forces had disappeared behind the drifting smoke.

Men began bringing the bodies in soon after. Down in the courtyard, the woman and her child were dead; a single arrow had pierced them both and remained embedded, binding them together. The archer who shot the arrow had been aiming for the battlements; he had been unable to see his victims, and would never know what he had done.

Hush ye, hush ye, little pet ye
Do not fret ye, little pet ye
The Black Douglas shall not get ye

One of the first corpses to be brought back from the field and laid out on the cobbles beside them was David Harkness. He had been shot through the chest, the arrow penetrating his mail coat and the jack beneath, and the blue surcoat with gold chevrons and red crescent was dark with blood. He would have lived for a little while after being shot, Merrivale thought, but not long.

Peter de Lisle knelt beside the man who had once carried him on his shoulders, taking the dead man's hand and bowing his head. 'Did anyone see what happened to him?' Merrivale asked.

'An arrow came out of nowhere, sir, just as they were breaking off,' a hobelar said. 'Davy was right up front, alongside Sir Gilbert. They couldn't hardly miss him.'

'The archers were retreating the castle. How did any of them manage to get off a shot at such distance?'

'The arrow came out of the scrimmage, sir. We think it was one of Carrick's men.'

They were waiting for him, Merrivale thought. *This was not a death in battle but a deliberate killing. And Harkness was right up in the forefront, like Uriah the Hittite. Did Umfraville sacrifice his own man? I will ask him, when he returns.*

But Umfraville did not return, nor did Clennell or Wake or Selby. Everyone had seen them in the middle of the fighting and burning, leading the way up the valley in pursuit of the beaten Scots, but when the smoke began to clear the leaders of the Disinherited had vanished.

12

The man-at-arms was called Murdo, and he knew the country well. He evinced very little interest in who Tiphaine was or how she came here, but he listened intently to her edited version of the meeting at South Shields. He seemed already to know who Rollond de Brus was, which both annoyed her and excited her suspicions, but on the other hand she was alone in a foreign country with war about to break out, and she needed all the friends she could get. Even dubious ones.

They tracked the friar as far as the Great North Road, where they had their first argument. Tiphaine wanted to follow him closely; Murdo insisted they hang back so Oswald didn't spot them. 'We have an advantage,' he said. 'We know where he is going, but he doesn't know we are following him.'

They spent the night in a monastic hospice at Wooler, listening to thunder hammer off the flanks of the Cheviots. Morning brought damp, clammy weather and also the ominous sight of clouds of smoke rising to the south-west. Tiphaine wondered briefly where Simon was, or whether he was still alive, and then pushed the thought firmly from her mind. 'Aye, it's begun,' said Murdo, mounting his horse. 'We'll need to go carefully now. We are only half a dozen miles from the border. Stay close to me.'

Tiphaine had no intention of doing anything else. They rode out of the hospital gates just as its single bell began to ring prime with dull clanging strokes. 'Why are they breaking the truce?' she asked. 'And on a Sunday, too. What about the Truce of God?'

Murdo snorted. 'As if anyone on the Borders gives a damn about God.'

They left the Great North Road and descended to the coast near Lindisfarne, its monastery and church dark in the distance. More smoke boiled up, to the north-west this time. The roads were ominously empty, and despite last night's thunderstorm the air seemed heavy and threatening. After a couple of hours Murdo pointed ahead to a walled town on a steep hill, the silver sheet of a river winding at its feet. 'Berwick,' he said.

The tide was coming in by the time they reached the south bank of the Tweed. A ferry took them across the rushing river, the castle looming high above them and the town falling down the slope towards the water. Murdo appeared to know the ferrymen, and they him. 'Have you seen Brother Oswald recently?' the man-at-arms asked.

'Oswald of Halton? That fat scoundrel. Aye, he came up the south road this morning.'

'Know where I can find him?'

'The stews, of course. He'll be at the whores, as usual.'

Tiphaine could not help herself. 'Even on a Sunday?'

'On the seventh day, God rested,' said the ferryman.

The sentries at the gates were nervous, eyeing the clouds of smoke, but some of them recognised Murdo too and greeted him; they paid no attention to Tiphaine, clad in her dusty gown. Inside the gates the streets were packed with people, many of them country folk from the surrounding villages who had seen the smoke of burning farms and come to seek shelter inside Berwick's walls. Anxious, frightened faces surrounded them. On Castlegate, Murdo dismounted outside an inn and went briefly inside.

'I've taken a room,' he said, coming back out. 'Wait there, and do not go out for any reason.'

'Can't I come with you?'

'Oswald will recognise you, and I don't want him to know you are here. Ask the servants to send up some hot water and a cake of soap. I won't be long.'

Murdo knew Berwick well; better, perhaps, than he should have done. He had served in the garrison once, but he had visited the town before in other guises, and he knew the pattern of its streets and the towers of its churches better than those of his home town, Finlaggan, back in the Sudreyjar, the Southern Isles. Descending Castlegate, he walked down towards the port and came to Sandgate, a narrow cobbled street fronting a row of warehouses and rough stone buildings. He stopped by one of these, looking at a large man in a greasy tunic who stood in the doorway, arms folded across his chest.

'Is Oswald here?' Murdo demanded.

The man said nothing. Murdo flipped a silver penny into the air and the man reached out and caught it, then folded his arms again. 'Room at the back,' he said.

Murdo pushed open the door and went inside. The smells of steam and smoke and sweat mingled in the air. Pink figures moved through the steam, gasping and diving out of the way when they saw Murdo's mail coat and helmet. Ignoring them, Murdo walked through the steam rooms and came to another door, which he flung open without ceremony. 'Brother Oswald,' he said. 'I want a word with you.'

Brother Oswald sat on the edge of a narrow bed, a bandage on one hand and his cassock bunched around his waist. A woman knelt on the floor in front of him, working busily. The friar looked up, his face beet red with tension and outrage. 'How dare you burst in here— Oh, body of Christ. It's you.'

'I want a word,' Murdo repeated. 'Get rid of the bawd.'

'Fuck you,' said the friar. 'I paid for this, and I want my money's worth. Come on, woman! Faster, God damn it!'

The woman complied. She was not young, Murdo thought; her breasts were wrinkled and she was missing several teeth. Oswald must be short of money. The friar leaned forward suddenly, gasping, and then flopped back on the bed, heaving like a stranded whale. Murdo jerked his thumb at the door and the woman scrambled up and out of the room.

'You are a disgrace to your habit and your order,' Murdo said.

'Go to hell. I'm not listening to lectures on morality from Agnes of Dunbar's spy.'

Murdo regarded him. 'You were her spy yourself, once, until you mucked it up. You had one simple task, to bribe the guards at the Cow Port to open up and let our troops into Berwick, and you butchered it. You didn't even have the decency to come back and explain what went wrong, *Muc Sassanach*.'

'No,' growled Oswald. 'I didn't fancy telling Black Agnes I had failed. Would you?'

'I don't fail. Where and when is the meeting?'

Oswald sat up. 'What meeting?'

'Don't be coy with me. You carried a message from the Seigneur de Brus to the Disinherited, telling them to meet him and yourself in Berwick today. Come to the usual place, you said. Where is the usual place?'

'If I tell you, Brus will cut my tongue out.'

'And if you don't, I will cut your balls off,' said Murdo, drawing his sword. 'Where and when is the meeting?'

'Why do you want to know?'

'Because I'm coming too. My mistress doesn't like being shut out of councils. She wants to know what's going on.'

'Jesus,' said Oswald. 'Brus is an evil bastard, you know. If you show up, he's likely to kill us both.'

'I don't frighten easily, Oswald. You ought to know that. I want to see the English traitors for myself, and I want to hear from their own lips what they plan to do. This whole campaign could turn on them. I'll take care of Brus, all you have to do is confirm my story. I'll see you safe too, though Christ knows why.'

'Honour among thieves,' said Oswald. 'How refreshing to see the old values observed.' He looked at the sword blade still pointed at his groin. 'We meet at Saint Leonard's convent in Bondington, an hour after vespers.'

'See? That wasn't so difficult,' said Murdo, sheathing his sword. 'Are you still working for the priory at Durham?'

Oswald said nothing. 'So you are, then,' said Murdo. 'You're spying on Brus for Brother Hugh, aren't you? If Brus finds out, he'll dip your bollocks in silver and wear them as earrings.'

'He won't find out,' said Oswald. 'Or if he does, he'll learn a few things about Black Agnes's spy as well.'

'It's settled then. We keep each other's secrets.' Murdo raised a hand in mock salute. 'Until tonight, brother.'

—

Back at the inn, Murdo took off his helmet and set it down on a table. He had a long straight nose like the prow of a galley and short, roughly cropped brown hair. Steam curled from a jug of water on the table, next to a basin and a cake of yellow soap. 'They meet at Saint Leonard's convent,' he said. 'I know the place. It's a Cistercian house in Bondington, just outside the walls and not far from the castle. The Scots smashed it up in '33 when they were trying to recapture the town, just before the battle at Halidon Hill. Only a handful of nuns still live there, and they mostly keep to the cloister.'

'A perfect place for a rendezvous,' said Tiphaine.

'Aye,' said Murdo, pulling his mail tunic off over his head. It jingled faintly as he dropped it to the floor.

Tiphaine looked around. 'Where is my room?'

'This is your room,' said Murdo, taking off the heavy quilted doublet he wore under the mail. 'They only had one private room left. The refugees from the countryside have taken pretty much every available room in Berwick. It was this, or the common room floor.'

'I see,' said Tiphaine. 'I'm not sure I want to share my room with a man.' She looked again as Murdo unlaced a sweat-stained linen shirt and dropped it on the floor beside the jack. 'Oh,' she said.

'Oh,' mimicked the woman who called herself Murdo. 'Does this make a difference, then?'

'It does. But who on earth are you?'

'I am Lady Mora of Islay, daughter of Aonghais Óg Mac Dhòmhnuill of Islay and sister of Eòin Mac Dhòmhnuill, Lord of the Isles. I am a shieldmaiden in the service of Agnes, Countess of Dunbar.'

It was said with pride. Tiphaine stared at her, intrigued rather than frightened; if this woman had wanted to kill her, she would have done so out in the lonely wastes of Northumberland, not here in the middle of town. 'What was a Scot doing in the garrison at Warkworth?' she asked.

Mora splashed water on her face and body, washing away the sweat. 'Spying on the Percys,' she said calmly. 'My lady wants to know where their true loyalty lies.'

'Why?'

Mora straightened, wiping the water from her strong arms. 'It is no secret that there are factions in the Scottish camp,' she said. 'My lady and her husband are leaders of one such faction. The Seigneur de Brus leads another, along with Niall Bruce of Carrick and William Douglas of Liddesdale. Most of the nobility support them, largely because Brus pays them lavishly in French gold. My lady is suspicious of Brus, and believes he has ulterior motives.'

Tiphaine shivered suddenly. 'He does,' she said, and she told Mora about the conspiracy last summer and Brus's part in it. 'When I last saw him three days ago, the herald was on his way to see your mistress.'

'Was he now?' Mora considered this. 'That is interesting,' she said slowly. 'So, as you can guess, my lady has more than a passing interest in which way the Percys and the Disinherited will jump. If they take up the Scottish offer, Brus and his friends will win. If Ithey stay loyal to England, there is still a chance of preventing disaster. A slim one, but a chance nonetheless.'

'Brus set a trap for the herald. I don't know if he reached your mistress, or even if he is still alive.'

'News about dead heralds travels quickly. I think we would have heard by now. Perhaps Brus will tell me when we meet tonight.'

Tiphaine stared at her. 'You are going to the meeting?'

'Yes.' Mora picked up her shirt and pulled it on, tying up the laces. 'This is what will happen. You will remain in this room and not go out. I will go and reconnoitre the convent, and then find a place to hole up. After this morning's raids, it is not safe for a Scot to be in Berwick any longer than they must. I will attend the meeting and contrive to get word to you. You must then go to Sir Thomas Rokeby, the English commander in Berwick, and tell him what I have told you. Rokeby is a good man. Ask him to take you under his protection.'

Tiphaine's jaw dropped. 'You would betray your own people?'

'The Lords of the Isles are free and independent. My loyalty is to the Countess of Dunbar, not to Scotland. And from what you have said, this man Brus is dangerous and must be stopped.'

Mora pulled on her jack and mail tunic, shrugging the links of the latter into place. She picked up her helmet and set it on her head. 'Stay safe, and wait for my message.'

'Yes,' said Tiphaine.

'Good.' Mora smiled. 'It was a pleasure to know you, *demoiselle*. Perhaps we will meet again one day.'

'Yes,' Tiphaine repeated. 'Perhaps.'

From the window of the room she watched Mora walk away through the teeming, half-panicky turmoil of the street. Away in the distance, smoke hung in shrouds around the flanks of the hills. She waited until Mora was out of sight, then went to the door and called for a servant. A woman in plain kirtle and apron came to the door of the room, dusting her hands.

'I need clothes,' Tiphaine said.

The woman glanced at her travel-stained gown. 'I can send for a tailor, my lady.'

'No. I need a disguise.' Tiphaine lowered her voice. 'I have a rendezvous with a lover. No one must know who I am.'

She handed the woman some coins. 'Find me a white robe with a cowl and hood, like a Cistercian habit,' she said. 'Bring it to me by vespers.'

The fires in the valley were dying out, but smoke still hung thick as a shroud. Some of the refugees sat or stood listless in the castle courtyard, while outside others were burying the dead. There was no point in anyone going home, not when further raids could happen at any time. Lady Joan, a capable woman, was in the kitchen organising food for the exhausted people. 'Do we know what happened?' she asked.

'I have spoken to the men,' Merrivale said. 'All tell the same story. They followed the Scots at a safe distance, with your husband and the other three well out to the front. At Linbriggs, where the valley narrows, they rode through a dense cloud of smoke. When the smoke cleared, there was no sign of Sir Gilbert or his companions. The men at once abandoned the pursuit and searched the area, but no bodies were found.'

'Could they track the horses?'

Merrivale shook his head. 'The ground was badly churned up by the passage of so many animals.'

Lady Joan bit her lip. 'They must have been taken prisoner,' she said.

The herald watched her, wondering how much she knew. 'That is certainly possible,' he said. 'The Scots may have laid an ambush on the far side of the smoke.'

'What is to be done now?'

'Open negotiations,' Merrivale said. He touched his tabard. 'I will find Douglas and Bruce and confirm whether your husband and the others have been captured. If they have, I will bring you the terms of their ransom.'

Her head went down at this; any ransom for a man as important as Umfraville was likely to be costly, more perhaps than his entire estate was worth. *Something is wrong here*, the herald thought. Why would the Scots go to the trouble of bribing the Disinherited and then take them prisoner? Unless they knew already that

Umfraville and the others were going to refuse? And if so, how did they know?

Predictably, Peter wanted to come with him. Mauro and Warin looked unhappy as well. 'No,' said Merrivale. He did not want to take Peter with him, and he could hardly take his two servants and leave Peter behind. 'If there is trouble, it is best I face it alone.'

'I hope there is trouble, sir,' Peter said fiercely. 'I'd like to pay a few of them back, for Davy Harkness.'

Fifteen years old, and yet he had already killed two men in the past few days and was looking forward to killing more. If ever there was a reason why this war had to end, this was it. 'You are thinking like a man-at-arms now, Peter, and not like a herald,' he said. 'You cannot be both. You must choose which course you will follow.'

The boy subsided. Merrivale put a hand on his shoulder. 'Patience is one of the virtues of an ambassador,' he said. 'I will return soon.'

–

Riding up the valley, his herald's tabard a bright splash of colour in the grey and dun landscape, he wondered if he had done the right thing by taking on Peter as an apprentice. *He makes me feel about a hundred years old*, he thought, *acting the role of an ancient sage passing on wisdom to the young. It is a role I do not yet feel ready to play. Tiphaine sometimes makes me feel the same.*

Last night's rain and the passage of hundreds of hooves had churned the ground to mud. He passed farms, the same farms he had helped to evacuate yesterday, now piles of charred timbers still leaking smoke. The hills grew higher and steeper. He came to Linbriggs and paused for a while, surveying the ruins and listening to the roar of the river in its stony bed, and crows cawing around the silent heights. There was no sign of what might have happened to the four men. He nudged the horse with his heels and rode on.

At Barrow Burn, where the hills crowded close and steep, he heard a clink of metal on stone and reined in, looking around and waiting. The crows cawed again, their voices harsh with warning. He heard the clink again and looked up to see a lone horseman riding down the valley, his surcoat and shield bearing the device of a red lion rampant on a field of gold. Merrivale's hands clenched tight on the reins.

He sat motionless on his horse, waiting. Niall Bruce, Lord of Carrick, reined in a dozen paces away and raised the visor of his bascinet. He was a big man, broad-shouldered with dark eyes and a full black beard, armoured in mail and plate with a lance in one hand and a sword at his belt. 'What are you doing here, herald?' he demanded.

'Surprised to see me?' Merrivale asked.

'No. One of the rearguard spotted you following us.'

'And you decided to investigate. Shall we get down to business? Did you take any prisoners during this morning's raid?'

Bruce grinned at him. 'Sir Gilbert d'Umfraville, Sir Thomas Clennell, Sir Walter Selby and Thomas Wake, Lord of Liddell. They are in our hands.' He paused, clearly enjoying himself. 'They will be taken before the king, where they will be tried and executed.'

The herald's eyebrows raised. 'And what would be their crime?'

'They claim lands in Scotland, but refuse to do homage for those lands to King David. They are foresworn, and they must die.'

Merrivale thought for a moment. 'I see. What would persuade your king to change his mind?'

'All four must submit to him, along with all their tenants and their families. They must do homage to him, and fight for him as his loyal retainers.'

'Which is what you asked them to do when you tried to bribe them,' Merrivale said. 'You raided Umfraville's lands to increase the pressure on him, I understand that. But why take them prisoner today?'

The other man grinned again. 'Why not? If we can compel them to our will, we have no need to bribe them. Think of the money we shall save.'

'But it looks uncommonly like bad faith,' the herald said. 'You need them to enter your service willingly, not through force. This all sounds rather clumsy, don't you think? A bit like sending those men to ambush me in Tynedale three days ago.'

Bruce's smile faded. 'Strong words. Killing a herald is a serious offence.'

'Not one I imagine you would shrink from,' Merrivale said. 'Did you not wonder, my lord, when your men never came home?'

'How do you know they were my men?' Bruce demanded.

Too late, the herald realised his mistake. 'One of them told me before he died,' he said.

The lance came down, its point aimed at Merrivale's chest. Shouting with anger, Bruce spurred his horse straight towards Merrivale. A second before the lance point reached him, Merrivale slipped out of the saddle and the lance passed through empty air above him. Bruce hauled on the reins, pulling up his mount, and as he did so Merrivale stepped out from behind his own horse and launched himself at the other man, seizing his arm and dragging him out of the saddle. Bruce hit the ground hard, crashing down on his back with a clash of metal and lying winded. His bascinet fell off, rolling in the mud. Standing over him, Merrivale ripped Bruce's sword out of its scabbard and threw it into the nearby river. The lance lay useless behind him. The herald planted a foot on his chest, pushing him back down as he tried to rise.

'Two things,' he said. 'First, just because heralds are unarmed doesn't mean they can't fight. Remember that. Second, everything you've just told me is a pack of lies. If you'd really taken Sir Gilbert and his friends prisoner, would you really drag them all the way back to Jedburgh? No, you would be outside the walls of Harbottle now, threatening to kill all four of them unless the castle surrendered. Harbottle is the key to Coquetdale, and once you have Coquetdale you can control most of Northumberland. Douglas is smart enough to realise that, even if you are not.'

Bruce tried to push himself up from the ground again, and the herald stamped on his armoured chest, driving him down again. 'You engineered their disappearance,' he said, 'and then tried to sell me this ridiculous story in hopes of throwing me off the scent. When you saw I wasn't buying, you decided to attack me. Tell Brus if he wants to kill me, come and do it himself. Don't send his cousin's second-rate bastard in his place.'

He stepped back. Roaring, Bruce clambered to his feet, but before he could gain his balance, Merrivale hit him on the point of the chin with a force that snapped his head back and sent him tumbling down the bank into the river where he lay, half in and half out of the water. The herald watched him for a moment to endure that he was in no imminent danger of drowning, and mounted his horse and rode away down the devastated valley.

13

Berwick's position as the sole English outpost on the north side of the Tweed meant that its garrisons and citizens lived in a constant state of watchfulness. The gates were closed at sunset, but a nun seeking to return to her convent outside the walls excited no suspicion; at the Saint Mary Gate, the guards opened the postern and let her through.

The castle lay close on her left, and she could see the fluttering of torches on the ramparts and the restless movement of watchmen. She passed a small stream with a millpond and waterwheel and came to the ruins of Bondington, once a prosperous little suburb of the town; now the houses were roofless, and weeds grew in the gardens of the messuages. The clouds were breaking up a little, and stars shone from dark patches of sky. Every so often a half moon peeped through, lighting her way.

The convent church of Saint Leonard's was ruined too, its roof caved in and its tall windows bare of glass. As Mora had said, the cloister still stood and as she crept closer Tiphaine could hear the sound of voices in prayer. Not many; three or four at most.

The moon came out again, and her robe glowed ghostly white. Cursing the nuns for choosing the Cistercian order over the more discreetly black-robed Benedictines, she walked into the ruined church. Weeds were growing out of the walls, and the altar was stained with bird and bat droppings. She looked around for a place to conceal herself. There were several chapels in the apse behind the presbytery, but those were the first places anyone would look; the same was true of the vestry.

In the south transept she found the night stair, leading from the dorter down into the body of the church. In better times, the nuns would formerly have used this stair to come down and celebrate matins. Judging by the amount of rubble and bird shit, she thought, no one had used the stair since the church was ruined. The door at the top of the stair was securely barred, confirming her thought. The stone landing outside the door was in deep shadow. Crouching down and making herself as small as possible, Tiphaine waited, trying to ignore the pounding of her heart.

–

They came on foot, having tethered their horses some distance away, and without torches; the sentries on the castle walls would have seen any glint of light. 'Where are the nuns?' asked Selby.

'Up in the dorter,' said Clennell. 'Did you not hear them singing as we came in?'

'What if they hear us?'

'They won't be stupid enough to come and investigate. Not at night.'

Gilbert d'Umfraville nodded. 'But keep your voices down all the same.'

'How long do we wait?' asked Wake.

'An hour,' said Clennell. 'If he hasn't come by then, that settles it.'

They stood in silence in front of the white-streaked altar. Only a few minutes passed before a shadow moved in the nave, and they turned. 'Who is it?' Umfraville demanded.

'Who were you expecting?' asked Rollond de Brus. He walked forward, still moving stiffly, and threw back the hood of his cloak, letting the moonlight play on his pale face and fair hair. 'You're all here,' he said, his voice deceptively mild. 'Good. Very good.

For a time I wondered if you would come. Have you searched the place?'

'No,' Wake said sharply. 'We assumed you had.'

'For Christ's sake.' Brus walked around the apse end of the church, looking into the chantry chapels and then the vestry. He glanced up at the night stair, but saw nothing in the shadows. Walking back into the transept he stood facing the four men. 'Well? Shall we begin?'

'Why did you attack my lands?' Umfraville demanded harshly. 'You burned good farms and villages, for no reason. My tenants are homeless now, and winter is coming.'

'I burned them, as you know full well, to concentrate your minds and help you focus on making the right decision. Why did you resist? Douglas and Bruce lost good men this morning.'

'For Christ's sake, we had to do something,' Clennell said sharply. 'The herald was there, watching everything. He was already suspicious. Standing by and letting you do your worst would have been an admission of complicity.'

'I don't give a damn about the herald,' Brus said. 'The next time he comes among you, kill him and throw his body to the wolves. Make him disappear from the face of the earth. Is that clear?'

'That seems a little excessive,' said another voice.

Brus wheeled around, pulling his sword out of the scabbard. The other four men drew as well. The man who had spoken, a man-at-arms in a mail tunic and helmet with a nose guard, walked forward, followed by Oswald of Halton carrying a heavy wooden staff. 'What the devil?' demanded Brus. He looked at Oswald. 'Who is this?'

'This is Murdo,' said Oswald. 'I'll let him explain the rest.'

'No more pretence,' said the man-at-arms, pulling off her helmet. 'I am the Lady Mora of Islay, shieldmaiden to the Countess of Dunbar. When her ladyship heard of this meeting, she vowed to be a part of it. Unable to make the journey herself, she sent me as her envoy.'

There was a moment of stunned silence. 'Is she telling the truth?' demanded Rollond.

'Yes,' said the friar.

'How did the countess learn about this meeting?'

'I couldn't exactly say.' Mora's voice was calm. 'But her ladyship approves of your actions. Bringing the Disinherited back into the fold will be a great coup.' Mora smiled at the four men. 'It will be good to welcome you home.'

Still furious, Rollond pointed his sword at the friar. 'You worthless piece of shit. Did *you* tell her?'

'Don't blame him, my lord,' said Mora. 'I already knew the date of the meeting. All I needed was the place. I assumed Oswald would be working for you, because he works for anyone who needs dirty work done in the shadows. I persuaded him to tell me by threatening to enforce his vow of chastity, permanently.'

The Disinherited stared at her. Brus hesitated. What she was saying could be true, or it could be an audacious lie, but at the moment it made little difference. He wanted to kill this woman, but he could not afford to make an enemy of the Countess of Dunbar; not yet. 'Good,' he said finally, sheathing his sword. 'You can bear witness. Your mistress has doubted me in the past. Tonight, I will show her that I keep my promises.'

'And are we one of your promises?' demanded Wake.

Brus turned to face him. 'Of course. I have disciplined you, and now I will bring you to heel.'

'I don't like the sound of your language,' said Clennell.

'I don't care what you *like*,' Brus said viciously. 'What you *like* is of no interest to me. Now listen to me, gentlemen, while I explain what you will *do*.'

They waited.

'The Scottish army is at Edinburgh,' Brus said. 'Tomorrow it will march down the Via Regia towards the borders. Two days later it will reach Jedburgh, where we will celebrate Michaelmas. Thereafter, the war begins in earnest.'

He pointed at Lord Wake. 'You and Sir Walter Selby are responsible for the west. Apart from the usual bastel houses and pele towers, there is only one fortified place of note on the border; Liddel Strength... Lord Wake, you are the owner of Liddel Strength, and Sir Walter, you are the commander of the garrison. You will ensure that the castle surrenders as soon as the Scottish army approaches.'

Wake and Selby looked at each other. Selby's fists clenched, but neither man spoke. 'Sir Gilbert d'Umfraville, Sir Thomas Clennell,' Brus said. 'You will instruct your castellans and tenants to let us pass. There will be no repeat of today, no more brave little shows of defiance. I am the master, and you bow to me.'

'What about Sir Robert de Lisle?' demanded Clennell. 'He is too old and ill to travel. Do you intend to ravage his lands because he has not replied to you?'

'When the time comes, Sir Robert will be given every chance to make his position clear,' Brus said. 'I will make my decision based on what response he gives.'

'Is that everything?' asked Umfraville.

'Not yet. As well as carrying out my orders, you will muster your retinues and as many other men as you can. Don't worry about money, we will see they are paid. When you leave here tonight, you will not return to your homes. Instead you will go to a secret place, a rendezvous that I shall give you. Instruct your men to join you there.'

'Where will you be?' asked Wake.

'With the king in Jedburgh. You will hear from me.'

'And what are we supposed to do when we reach this secret place?' Wake demanded.

'Wait for orders,' Brus said.

Wake's voice growled in his throat. 'And if we refuse to obey them?'

'Then I will crush you,' said Brus. 'Douglas and Bruce of Carrick command the borders, and they are loyal to me. I have only to snap my fingers, and every house and barn and pele on your lands will be burning by day's end, and the crying of children for their mothers will be the loudest sound you will hear.'

'Splendid!' said Lady Mora, clapping her hands. 'A superb performance, my lord. You have us in the palm of your hand. The only thing left now is to tell these gentlemen what they have to gain by acquiescing to your demands.'

'We will keep the promises made earlier,' Brus said. 'All the lands you once claimed in Scotland will be restored, and the titles too. Sir Thomas will become Lord of Selkirk, Sir Gilbert will be Earl of Angus once more.'

'Some of those lands are currently held by other Scottish nobles,' said Lady Mora.

'They will be compensated in other ways,' Brus said.

Mora smiled. 'I am sure they will. Meanwhile, gentlemen, I suggest we cut this meeting short and disperse as swiftly as possible.'

'Why?' demanded Brus.

'Because the castle gate has just opened,' said Mora, 'and a column of men is marching out, heading this way. I think our secret has been discovered.'

They all turned towards the castle, its walls blazing with torch-light now, and saw the armed men running over the drawbridge and spreading out across the fields. 'The south door leads to the cloister,' said Mora. 'From there you can get to the kitchens, and a back door leading out over the fields. I advise you to run. You too,' she said to Oswald.

The Disinherited ran for the door, followed by Rollond clutching at his side. Brother Oswald raced after them. For a big man, Mora thought, he had a surprising turn of speed. She waited until they were gone, then trotted up the night stair and crouched down beside the figure in white, putting an arm around Tiphaine's neck and clamping a hand over her mouth. Tiphaine struggled briefly, and Mora cuffed her. 'Do not move,' she hissed. 'Do not make a sound.'

Tiphaine lay still. Keeping her head down so the light would not shine on her face, Mora heard men running down the nave and around the presbytery. Torchlight flickered off the walls over her head. 'No one here,' a voice said finally. 'Tom, search the cloister. I'll take the outbuildings.'

Footsteps and voices receded and the torchlight faded. They waited, Mora still covering Tiphaine's mouth. Only when the search party began to withdraw towards the castle did she allow them both to sit up. In the cloister one of the nuns was crying out in fear, and they heard a murmur of voices as the others tried to calm her.

'How did you know I was here?' Tiphaine whispered.

'I was watching the place when you arrived, and followed you in. It was very foolish of you to come here, and even more so to send a letter to Sir Thomas Rokeby warning him we were here. You very nearly upset all my plans.'

'I don't care about your plans,' Tiphaine said. 'All I care about is Rollond de Brus. I want to see him captured or dead, preferably the latter.'

'Why? What is Brus to you?'

'I was his lover once, when I was young and stupid. I left him when I realised what kind of man he was. He never forgave me, and last summer he betrayed me to the enemy and tried to have me burned at the stake.' She shivered at the memories. 'I want him dead.'

'I've no doubt you'll get your wish, before too much longer,' Mora said. 'Now, you are going to do what I say. Walk to the castle, announce yourself and see Sir Thomas Rokeby. He will protect you.'

'You sound like the herald,' Tiphaine said. 'I don't want protection. I'm going after Rollond, and you will not stop me. I will find that bastard and I will kill him. Because until I do, Mora, the earth will not be safe for any of us.'

In the darkness Mora sat for a long time, thinking. 'Very well,' she said. 'Come with me.'

'Where are we going?'

'Jedburgh,' said Mora.

It was nearly midnight by the time the herald and his little party arrived at Berwick. The castle gates were closed once more and the drawbridge was up, but at the sight of his tabard the bridge was lowered and they were admitted through a postern. Off to the far south-west, fires flickered on the horizon.

Despite the hour Rokeby was in his office, a big solar with mullioned windows looking over the ramparts and across the dark river towards the distant fires. Four other men were with him, two still fully armed. Rokeby himself looked older than the herald remembered; there were dark circles under his eyes and worry lines on his forehead. 'Simon Merrivale, by all that's holy. Good to see you again, my friend. You could have come at a better time.'

'I fear I have brought trouble with me,' Merrivale said.

'To the borders? No fear of that. This is the land where disasters hatch and calamity spawns. Let me introduce John Stryvelyn, keeper of the castle, and Roger Heron, his deputy.' He turned to the two armoured men. 'This is John Coupland, my right-hand man. And you may remember my nephew Tom.'

Tom Rokeby, one of the armoured men, smiled and bowed. He was a pleasant young man, who bore a strong resemblance to his uncle. Merrivale introduced Peter de Lisle. 'We've not met, but I knew your father well,' Rokeby said kindly. 'Have a seat, lad. The servants will bring us something to drink.'

Peter sat down and promptly fell asleep in his chair, head drooping on his chest. 'What is the situation?' Merrivale asked.

'Douglas of Liddesdale has driven a horse and wagon through the truce. His own men were raiding further south, I hear, but his allies along the borders crossed the Tweed south of Wark and burned everything as far as Doddington. They'll come again tomorrow, I expect, and there's not a damned thing we can do stop them. We don't have enough men.'

'What about the local families?' Merrivale asked. 'Are they loyal?'

Rokeby nodded. 'So far. At the moment they are looking to protect their own homes, but they'll fight if we call on them.'

'They will for the moment,' said Coupland. He was a hard-faced man, probably about thirty but looking older. 'But we can't say the same about Norham.'

Norham was seven miles upriver from Berwick, a key element in the chain of castles guarding the frontier. 'Norham and the lands around it are the property of the Palatine of Durham,' Rokeby said. 'And the priory at Durham has sent word to the castellan at Norham, ordering him not to fight or obstruct the passage of the enemy. Effectively, they have declared themselves neutral.'

'And if Norham avoids the wrath of the enemy, other landowners may decide to do the same,' said Roger Heron. 'It pains me to say this, because I'm a local man myself, but I wouldn't take their loyalty for granted.'

The tide is rising, Merrivale thought, *washing away the sand under our feet.* 'Have you heard any word from Lord Percy?'

'He's calling out his tenants and mustering them at Wark-worth and Alnwick, but he is being bloody slow about it. Which reminds me. I have a letter for you from his daughter-in-law.'

Rokeby handed over a small parchment roll, and Merrivale broke the seal and read it quickly.

> *To Simon Merrivale, heraldus, I give greeting. I have attempted to persuade Lord Percy to declare his allegiance, but I fear I have failed. He is gathering his men, but he will not commit himself to joining the archbishop at Richmond. Sir Herald, it gives me great sorrow also to tell you that the Demoiselle Tiphaine left Warkworth without telling me of her departure or where she intended to go. She may be travelling in company with one of Lord Percy's men-at-arms, a man named Murdo. We have searched for her, but to no avail. I am sorry indeed to give you this news, and*

I have prayed continually for her safety. May God watch
over her, and over you too, my friend.

Merrivale closed his eyes for a moment. 'Bad news?' asked
Rokeby.

'Yes.' He told them the contents of the letter. 'Can you ask
your officers if there has been any sign of the *demoiselle*, or this
man Murdo?'

'I recognise Murdo's name,' said Tom Rokeby. 'He was in
the garrison here last year. A Scots deserter, most probably. I
remember seeing him in company with that fellow Oswald.'

'Oswald of Halton? The Dominican friar?'

'That's the one. The biggest rogue unhung.' Tom turned to
his uncle. 'He was there tonight, too. I caught a glimpse of him,
running like a hare. We went after him, but he disappeared into
the dark before we could catch him.'

Merrivale raised his eyebrows in inquiry.

'We received a message that the leaders of the Disinherited
were coming tonight to meet the Seigneur de Brus,' Rokeby said.
'I sent Tom and John out in hopes of catching Brus, but the whole
lot slipped through our fingers.'

'Body of Christ.' Merrivale did not often show anger, but he
did now. 'I knew they were intending to meet Brus, and I went
to Harbottle to persuade them to remain loyal. They assured me
they would, and then gave me the slip through a ruse so facile
that even a child could have seen through it. Why in God's name
did I believe them?'

The herald shook his head. 'What's done is done. Did you
pursue them?'

'Yes, but not far,' said Rokeby. 'My patrols never venture more
than five miles from Berwick. It's simply too dangerous to go
further.'

'If it can be proven that they met Brus, that is treason.'

'Yes,' said Rokeby. 'On the other hand, if we attempt to arrest
them, that could spark a rebellion by their followers. And if the

Percys and some of the others join in, we could have a civil war on our hands.'

'What about the merchants in the town? Archbishop de la Zouche feared they might be plotting treason as well.'

Rokeby rolled his eyes. 'When aren't they plotting treason? I arrested three of them last year, but I reckon the embers are still burning underground.' He grinned at Merrivale. 'Welcome back to the borders, Simon,' he said. 'Not much has changed since you were last here, has it?'

'No,' said the herald. 'But I have a feeling things are about to get quite a lot worse.'

Servants, one of them carrying the still sleeping Peter, took him to a comfortable room in the Constable Tower. He saw the boy settled on a palliasse and then lay down on the narrow bed, looking up at the shadows on the timber ceiling as the single rushlight flickered to the end of its life.

Once again he felt the weariness in his bones. He had ridden many miles in the past few days, but he had ridden longer journeys as a King's Messenger. *Perhaps I am getting old*, he thought… But the weariness was mental as much as physical, rooted in a sense of dark anticipation. The dread of what was about to come had increased sharply since the news of Tiphaine's disappearance, and for one of the few times in his life Merrivale knew real fear; not for himself, but for her.

He knew how much she hated Rollond de Brus, and why; it was he who had pulled her off the platform at La Roche Guyon with the flames already crackling beneath, and taken her away to safety. He knew, too, that she resented his attempts to keep her safe. His own past failures to protect those he loved was probably warping his judgement. He remembered his mother and sisters, dead in the Great Famine. He remembered Yolande.

Protect those I love… Is love possible between myself and Tiphaine? Or are we too battle-scarred and disillusioned even to make the attempt? Will the shades of past and present always stand in the way?

The rushlight died. Its wick glowed for a few seconds and then went f staring into the blackness and thinking about Tiphaine alone in the night, before exhaustion finally claimed him and he fell asleep.

14

Berwick-upon-Tweed, 27ᵗʰ of September, 1346
Morning

Sitting by the arrow slit in the wall of his room, Merrivale wrote a long overdue report for the queen and council.

> *To her Grace the queen, her humble servant gives greeting. As instructed, I have investigated the loyalties of the northern barons, and I have interviewed Brother Gilbert of Hexham, formerly known to the world as Sir Gilbert de Tracey. I fear I have little that is good to report.*
>
> *Item, concerning the matter of Brother Gilbert's missing fortune. Brother Gilbert insists that the money has been sent to the banker Oppicius Adornes of Bruges, to pay for the support of his late brother's family. I do not believe this to be true. I believe the money is being supplied to the Seigneur de Brus, who is using it to fund the raising of a Scottish army and for several nefarious activities in England.*
>
> *Item, I believe further that this is being done on the instruction of the conspirator known as the man from the north. There is, however, no evidence on any of these points.*
>
> *Item, concerning the Scots. As your Grace will be aware from other sources, the truce, due to expire at Michaelmas, has already been broken, and considerable damage has been done to lands and villages in Tweeddale and Coquetdale. A full invasion of England is imminent.*

Item, concerning the northern barons. The alleged correspondence between Sir Harry Percy and the Scots has been revealed as an informal contact with Agnes Randolph, Countess of Dunbar, who has previously made peace overtures to England. The countess is, I believe, serious about wishing to make peace and is attempting to undermine the more bellicose faction led by the Seigneur de Brus. We must hope that she succeeds.

Item, separately, it has come to my attention that although Lord Percy and Lord Neville are mustering their men as ordered, they are making no great haste to join the Archbishop of York's army. They do not seem to appreciate the urgency of the situation.

And let us leave it at that, the herald thought, dipping his pen in the inkwell. *Give Percy and Neville time to change their minds.*

Item, the leaders of the Disinherited confirmed that they have received offers from Scotland, and assured me of their loyalty to yourself and his Grace the king. Subsequently, however, they met with the Seigneur de Brus near Berwick. The meeting was broken up by Sir Thomas Rokeby's troops but the conspirators escaped, including Brus.

Item, Sir Gilbert d'Umfraville, Sir Thomas Clennell, Sir Walter Selby and Thomas, Lord Wake are now missing, their whereabouts unknown. Sir Thomas Rokeby has advised that further proceedings against them could provoke an insurrection. I agree with this advice.

Item, the priory of Durham has declared its neutrality. The treasurer of the priory, Brother Hugh de Tracey, has declared that Durham will not send men to join the Archbishop of York at Richmond, and the prior has instructed the castellan of Norham not to hinder the Scottish advance.

Item, rumours persist that factions among the merchants of Berwick and Newcastle are disloyal and working to

assist the Scots. Sir Thomas Rokeby and Master Blyth
are investigating these rumours.

Item, in my opinion, all of these manifestations and
events are connected as part of a single plan, and the hands
of the Seigneur de Brus and the man from the north can be
detected behind them. It remains imperative that we discover
the identity of the man from the north. Until then, we shall
be cutting off the branches of treason, rather than pulling it
up by its roots.

Simon Merrivale, heraldus

Sealing the parchment, the herald sent Mauro to find Sir John
Stryvelyn the keeper and ask him to send it to London by the next
courier. Leaving Peter still asleep, he went in search of Rokeby
and found him in his office, conferring with Heron the deputy
keeper about patrols.

'Good morning,' said Rokeby, pointing to a steaming jug of
hippocras on a side table. 'Help yourself.'

'Thank you.' Merrivale poured a small glass, looking through
the windows out over the Tweed and the fields beyond. The
clouds had lifted a little and he could see the high hills of the
Cheviots rising towards the sky. 'Any sign of the Disinherited?'

'None. I'm afraid we have to consider them as fugitives.'

'Yes,' said Merrivale. 'That is what I have just written to her
Grace.'

'They may be making for Jedburgh,' Heron said. 'According
to our spies, the Scottish army will arrive there today.'

'Is it as big as we feared?'

'Not quite. The Lord of the Isles has fallen out with some
of the other barons, and has taken his men back home. But that
still leaves them with about twelve thousand, once you count the
border contingents.'

Something stirred in the herald's mind. 'Isn't there some
connection between the Lord of the Isles and the Countess of
Dunbar?'

Heron looked surprised. 'I don't know, to be honest. Of course, she is the Lady of Mann, and there is an old connection between Mann and the Western Isles. So, yes, it is possible.'

Rokeby looked at the herald. 'Is it important?'

'I don't know,' Merrivale said slowly. 'It might be.'

The sense of futility he had felt last night was growing again. He pushed it away sharply. 'We are sitting here waiting for the axe to fall,' he said. 'We must do something, take some action ourselves.'

'We have too few men,' said Rokeby. 'And the archbishop's army is at Richmond, a hundred miles away.'

'And he doesn't have enough men either,' Heron said gloomily.

'Then if we can't fight, let us try to negotiate,' said the herald. 'Let's send an emissary to David Bruce and see if we can agree an extension of the truce. Even a few weeks would give us more time to prepare.'

'We've had plenty of time,' Rokeby said. 'The problem is, we've nothing to prepare *with*. It's men and money we have lacked, not time.' He paused. 'But I see what you mean. A month or three weeks of grace could be a godsend. Anything can happen in a month.'

'And it would give me a chance to find out more about what plot Rollond de Brus is preparing. If I can do that, I should be able to win the Percys and Nevilles back, and maybe even the Disinherited. The odds will still be against us, but not quite so long.'

He looked at Rokeby. 'I don't have the authority to negotiate on my own. As the king's captain on the borders, you do.'

Rokeby turned to Heron. 'What do you think, Roger?'

Heron looked worried, the herald thought. 'I doubt if they're in any mood to listen. They're just as likely to send back your head in a sack.'

Merrivale smiled. 'That is a hazard of my occupation. We have to trust that the Scots will obey the laws of war.'

Rokeby nodded. 'Very well, I will authorise this. I'll give you safe conducts and provide you with an escort. I will also write to the Scottish captain at Roxburgh, the nearest post to Berwick, and ask him to put you under his protection.'

'I was hoping to start at once,' said Merrivale. In the back of his mind was the thought that if Rollond de Brus had gone to join the Scots army at Jedburgh, Tiphaine might have followed him there.

'No,' said Rokeby. 'You clearly need some rest, and another day won't matter. Remain here until we have a reply from Roxburgh.'

Heron departed to make the arrangements to send a courier under a flag of truce to Roxburgh. 'You spoke to the Disinherited,' said Rokeby. 'What do you think they intend to do?'

'I wish I knew,' said Merrivale. 'They pulled the wool over my eyes, quite thoroughly. But I got the impression that Selby in particular is hostile to any idea of collaboration with the Scots. Reflecting on what he said, I think his anger was genuine.'

'Will he break ranks with the others?' Rokeby asked.

'Possibly. It depends on what pressure is put on him.'

Rokeby watched him for a while. 'You are carrying a great deal of weight on your shoulders, Simon,' he said. 'But then, you always did.'

'It is a habit I seem to have formed,' Merrivale acknowledged.

'Do you ever think about giving it all up? Finding a nice woman to settle down with, buying a manor, keeping chickens, watching the seasons go past?'

'Do you?'

Rokeby laughed. 'It's a fair point. We're two of a kind, you and I.' His smile faded a little. 'At least I wasn't in Savoy.'

'No,' said Merrivale. 'You have that to be thankful for, I think.'

Peter was waiting for him in the courtyard. 'You should have woken me, master,' the boy said reproachfully.

'You needed the rest. Come, walk with me for a while. I need to clear my head.'

They walked towards the keep and the gateway leading to the town. 'I am learning that a herald needs to know about many things,' Peter said. 'Not just armorial devices but also politics and government and diplomacy. There is so much to learn, I don't know where to begin.'

Merrivale began to feel old again. 'Learning takes time,' he said. 'Don't be in too much of a hurry, you have plenty of time ahead of you. How good is your Latin?'

'I read it perfectly,' the boy said proudly. 'You may test me if you wish.'

'There is no need.' Sir Robert de Lisle was an educated man, and would have seen his son educated as well. 'There are some books you need to read, John of Salisbury's *Policraticus*, the *Treasure* of Brunetto Latini, Giles of Rome's *De Regimine Principum*. There are some commentaries on Aristotle that might be helpful too. When we return to London, I will lend them to you.'

They reached the gatehouse and started through the passage under the tower. 'I think you will be a wonderful teacher,' Peter said.

'Don't speak too soon.'

'Oh, sir. You must not make jokes about—'

A sound like wood creaking under strain made them both stop. The noise had come from above. Seizing Peter's arm, Merrivale started to run forward, but he had barely taken a stride when chains overhead rattled and roared through their blocks. The portcullis slammed down onto the cobbles, so close that one of the spikes on the bottom snagged the tail of his cloak and he stumbled and fell headlong. The stones vibrated with force.

For a moment there was a shocked silence. Peter helped Merrivale to his feet. 'Are you all right, sir?'

Merrivale dusted himself down. 'I am in need of a new cloak, but otherwise none the worse.' People were running towards them, attracted by the noise. One of the first to arrive was Roger Heron, pop-eyed with shock. 'What the hell happened?'

'It appears the brake on the portcullis crank has failed,' Merrivale said. 'You might wish to summon your carpenter.'

'Jesus Christ.' Heron looked at the portcullis. 'You could have been killed!'

'I don't think there's any doubt about that.' The portcullis was made of oak and bolted with iron; if it had hit either himself or Peter, it would have broken them like eggshells. Heron snapped orders at his men, and slowly the portcullis was winched back up again. 'I am so sorry,' Heron said. 'This really is a most unfortunate accident.'

'Think nothing of it,' said Merrivale. 'These things happen.'

Brushing another spot of dust off his cloak, he walked out onto the causeway leading across the moat that separated the town from the castle. 'That was very unlucky,' Peter said. 'That we should be walking under the portcullis just as the crank failed.'

'Yes,' said the herald. 'Wasn't it just?'

Jedburgh, 27ᵗʰ of September, 1346
Late afternoon

Tiphaine and Mora had walked along the north bank of the Tweed for a couple of hours until Mora was satisfied they were not being followed. An abandoned barn with a few remnants of last year's straw gave them shelter for the night, and in the morning they walked into the little town of Kelso, a huddle of houses in the shadow of an immense abbey church. Here they found food and a ride on the back of a purveyor's wagon taking the winding road up through Teviotdale towards Jedburgh. There were actually two towns called Jedburgh, Mora said, several miles apart, and to make matters more confusing the locals called both of them Jeddart. Tiphaine was too tired to care.

The town of Jedburgh lay between another big abbey and a rather tumbledown castle. Everywhere Tiphaine looked she saw the scars of war. The monastery showed signs of building, or rebuilding, and most of the roofs in the town looked new. The castle's gatehouse bore the black scorch marks of fire.

All round the town and in the meadows stretching along the river, the Scottish army was making camp. Some contingents were still riding in from the north, but wagons stood parked in the fields and tents and pavilions were going up, the larger ones decorated with bright coats of arms. The army was smaller than the French one she had seen back in the summer, but there was no mistaking its purpose and determination. She had thought the walls of Newcastle and Berwick were strong, but how could they resist a force such as this?

A little dazed with exhaustion, she realised Mora was leading her towards a large pavilion in the abbey park, painted with white lions on a field of red and white borders decorated with red cinquefoils. 'Where are we going?' she asked.

'I am taking you to meet my mistress,' Mora said. 'If anyone can help you, she can.'

A big man-at-arms stood in front of the entrance to the pavilion, in a red surcoat with a strange device of three conjoined legs. Mora raised a hand in greeting. '*Beannachdan, Somairle. A bheil a 'bhan-iarla an seo?*'

'*Fàilte, Mora. Tha ia 'feitheamh riut.*' The big man held the canvas door open and ushered them inside.

Agnes of Dunbar sat before a small table, writing a letter with a wooden pen. The evening sunlight coming through the painted canvas struck red glints off her curling hair and painted her brown skin with ruddy highlights. She looked up and smiled when she saw them. 'Mora. My faithful servant returns. Give me your report.'

Mora told her, ending with the events since she and Tiphaine left Warkworth. 'Brus has done his work thoroughly,' she said. 'The Percys and Nevilles are remaining on their lands, and the Disinherited are bowing to his will. The English are crippled even before the campaign begins.'

'We shall see,' said Agnes. She turned her attention to Tiphaine. 'Why have you brought a nun with you?'

Tiphaine pulled back her hood. 'The Demoiselle Tiphaine de Tesson, daughter of the Sire de la Roche Tesson in Normandy,' Mora intoned. 'I brought her here to keep her out of trouble. She wants to kill Rollond de Brus.'

'Does she now? Why?'

'The feeling is mutual,' Tiphaine said. 'We both want to kill each other.'

'I see.' Agnes considered her for a moment, and Tiphaine realised what a mouse must feel like when a hawk is circling overhead.

'Have the Disinherited come here?' Mora asked.

'No, but Brus has,' the countess said. 'He is at the castle now, closeted with Douglas and Niall Bruce of Carrick. They joined us yesterday, Carrick looking like he had just lost a fight with a gargoyle. I have never seen so many bruises on one man's face. To make it worse, his injuries were inflicted by an unarmed herald.'

Tiphaine's heart jumped in her chest. 'A herald? Simon of Merrivale?'

'The very same. Do you know him? Ah, I see from your eyes that you do. Things begin to make sense now.'

The countess turned to Mora. 'You did well to let Brus think I support his scheme. Send word to him, Mora. Tell him I have heard your story of what happened at Berwick, and wish to congratulate him myself.'

She looked at Tiphaine, pointing to a curtain. 'Remain there in silence, and listen. We will talk again after Brus departs.'

Tiphaine sat behind the curtain. The air in the pavilion was cool; a raw autumn wind was blowing outside, and she drew the heavy woollen habit more closely around her. *Simon is alive*, she thought, and she felt some of her tension drain away. She realised that she had never really believed he was dead, despite Rollond's words at South Shields; if any man knew how to survive an ambush, it was Simon Merrivale. *Besides*, she thought, *if he really was dead, I would have known.*

She checked at this. *Don't be ridiculous*, she told herself sternly. *How would I have known? It's not as if—*

Brus's voice could be heard outside the pavilion. Some of the tension returned, and she hugged herself even more tightly than before, forcing herself to be calm and listen. She heard his footsteps entering the pavilion, followed by someone else whom she guessed was Mora.

'My lord of Brus!' Agnes said. 'Welcome back among us. I hear your journeys have been most fruitful.'

'No more so than expected.'

The sound of his voice made Tiphaine go cold with memories. 'Indeed,' said the countess. 'The captains of the Disinherited are in the hands of Scotland. The king will rejoice when he hears the news.'

'I have already told him,' Brus said. 'How may I serve you, my lady?'

'I wish to talk with you about the Disinherited. Sit down. I see your wound still pains you.'

'It will pass,' Brus said.

'Your courage does you credit. The king has promised that the Disinherited will be given title to all the lands they claim in Scotland, without exception. Of course, as you know this poses a small problem. Many of those lands are already in the hands of someone else. My husband, for example, has possession of the Lordship of Selkirk, which is claimed by Sir Thomas Clennell. If we are expected to give up these lands, what will we receive in return?'

'That is for the king to decide,' said Brus.

'Oh, come now, my lord,' said Agnes. 'We both know the king listens to you in these matters. This entire plan to woo the Disinherited was yours. It must have occurred to you that forcing the king's loyal servants to give up their lands to those who have been regarded as traitors will breed discontent. Victory against England will be meaningless if the king then faces opposition at home.'

To Tiphaine sitting behind her curtain, the silence seemed to go on for a very long time. 'Are you threatening rebellion?' asked Brus.

'You know perfectly well what I am saying,' said the countess. 'We are prepared to back your schemes, but we must also protect our own interests. We will hand over Selkirk to Clennell, but we will have something in exchange.'

'What is it?'

'Berwick,' said Agnes.

Another silence, and Tiphaine could almost see the wheels of Brus's mind turning. 'Very well,' he said eventually. 'You shall have it.'

'Berwick,' Agnes repeated, 'but to hold in our own right, not as a vassal of the king. Berwick shall be a palatine, where we alone are sovereign. That is our condition.'

'The king will never agree.'

'Then we shall not surrender Selkirk,' Agnes said matter-of-factly. 'And when the Disinherited hear you cannot keep your promises, they will betray you. I do not know what role you have planned for them in this campaign but it must be important, given the amount of time and money you have expended on them. It would be a shame if your plan were to go awry at the last minute.'

'The Disinherited will not know any of this until the campaign is over.'

'They will if I tell them.'

'How can you tell them? You don't even know where they are.'

Mora of Islay cleared her throat. 'Do not be too certain of that,' she said.

'We are wasting opportunities,' Agnes said before Brus could speak. 'Each of us desires something, and the other has the power to give it. You have a plan to take Berwick, of course; you would never overlook a town of such strategic importance. Am I right?'

'Yes,' said Brus.

'Of course I am. When you have Berwick in your hands, we will trade it for Selkirk. Everyone will be happy.'

'And why should I wish to see you happy?' asked Brus.

The words were a slap in the face, but Agnes answered calmly. 'Because it will remove an obstacle from your path. It is no secret that I have opposed your plans before now. But your skill and ingenuity have brought us to this point, poised on the brink of a great victory. I cannot deny that. Give us Berwick, my lord, and you shall have not only Selkirk but an end to the discord between us. We will no longer stand in your way.'

'Then Berwick you shall have,' said Brus. 'But do not play me false.'

Tiphaine heard him leave the pavilion. 'You may come out now,' Agnes said quietly.

She rose, and walked out into the main chamber. The countess still sat before her desk; Mora stood to one side, arms crossed over her mail tunic. 'What did you think?' Agnes asked.

'He gave in very quickly,' said Tiphaine.

'Yes. Underneath the arrogance, I think he is nervous. Having come this far, he fears that something will go wrong and his plot will break down. He agreed to my proposal to get me out of the way.'

'You cannot trust him,' Tiphaine said. 'Believe me, my lady. He betrayed me, he betrayed his master the Count of Alençon, he betrayed the king of France to whom he swore fealty. He will betray your king too, and you, and probably the Disinherited as well.'

'I am sure he will,' said Agnes. 'The question is, how?'

She looked at Mora. 'You were bluffing, I assume.'

'Yes,' said Mora, nodding at Tiphaine. 'I could not follow them, as I was too busy looking after this one. My guess is that they will be up in the hills along the border, some wild place where men do not ordinarily go.'

'You could search for them,' said Tiphaine.

Agnes shook her head. 'No. Brus would learn that we were searching, and realise we did not know after all.'

'Watch and wait,' said Mora. 'They will reveal themselves in time.'

Yes, thought Tiphaine, *but by then it might be too late*. 'What about Brother Oswald?' she asked. 'He was at the meeting, he might know.'

'Something tells me Oswald is keen to stay out of Brus's way for a while,' said Mora. 'I expect he has gone back to his other employer at Durham. With luck, we won't see the wretch again.'

'That would be too much to hope for,' said Tiphaine.

A horse pulled up outside the pavilion, the rider's voice asking for the Countess of Dunbar. Somairle entered a moment later, bearing a sealed letter. 'A message from Kelso, my lady.'

Agnes broke the seal and read the letter. 'It is from the Master of Kinross,' she said. She looked at Tiphaine. 'The English want to negotiate. They are sending the herald, Simon Merrivale.'

Mora grinned under her helmet. 'The lord of Carrick will not be pleased to see him.'

'The lord of Carrick needs a muzzle and a leash.' Agnes frowned. 'Somairle, tell the messenger. When the herald arrives, before he sees the king and court, bring him first to me.'

15

Jedburgh, 28th of September, 1346
Evening

Heron had insisted on commanding Merrivale's escort himself, and Stryvelyn the keeper of Berwick agreed he could be released from his duties for a few days. He had intended to use men from his own retinue for the escort, but Rokeby overruled him and hand-picked a troop of twenty from the castle garrison. 'I don't want to face the queen if anything happens to her envoy,' he said.

Heron did secure the services of two of his own hobelars to act as scouts. This pair, Eckies Nickson and Jack Croser, known to his comrades as Kalewater Jack, were seasoned veterans of border warfare. Merrivale was mildly surprised to learn they were both Scots, at least by birth; Croser came from the wild country south of Kelso, and Nickson was a Hawick man who had fled to England after killing a man from another family with whom the Nicksons were at feud. 'The border is a fluid sort of place,' Heron said. 'People move back and forth. It's a different country out here, you see. By and large, the Scottish and English clans have more in common with each other than they do with London or Edinburgh.'

'That doesn't stop them feuding with each other,' Merrivale observed. 'Do the border clans ever stop fighting?'

'No,' was the morose reply. 'We rub along well with the rest of the world. It's ourselves we can't stand.'

Crossing the Tweed, they had ridden down the south bank of the river past the castle of Norham where the bishop's banner, four silver lions on a crossed field of blue, flapped in the wind. The castle itself was silent. The lands around Norham had been left untouched, but soon after they found the first signs of destruction: burned-out houses and barns, a pele tower blackened and roofless. Douglas's raiders had been thorough; even the granaries had been burned. When the people who lived on these farms returned home, they would have little to eat during the coming winter.

Another big castle, Wark, loomed up over the trees and Nickson came cantering back. 'There's a party of Scots waiting for us, sir. The leader's badge is a silver rose on blue.'

'The Master of Kinross,' Heron said. 'The royal captain in Kelso. He has come himself, which is interesting. He's also an ally of Agnes of Dunbar.'

Another coincidence? Merrivale wondered. They found the Scots ten minutes later, a compact, disciplined party of horsemen with lances raised upright. Their leader, immaculate in burnished armour and chainmail, rode forward as Heron's party approached. His visor was raised, revealing a pleasant face with brown eyes and a humorous mouth. 'Well met, Roger. I wasn't expecting you in person.'

'Likewise,' said Heron. 'I think we both have a vested interest in keeping this gentleman safe. James, may I present Simon Merrivale, herald and envoy? Sir Herald, this is the Master of Kinross.'

'I believe I met your father, the Earl of Kinross, when I served in Scotland,' Merrivale said. 'I hope he is well?'

'Sadly, no. He rarely leaves his bed now. A lifetime of fighting his king's wars has taken its toll.'

'As it does on all of us,' said Merrivale, thinking of Sir Robert de Lisle alone at his house at Chipchase.

'Indeed so. Shall we depart, gentlemen?'

They rode on, following the long curving valley of the Tweed, hills rising to their left, the brown grass slopes blistered with purple patches of heather. Here there had been no burning; it had been some time since the English, their forces pared to the bone by the demands of the war with France, had dared to raid across the frontier. Eckies Nickson and Kalewater Jack were recalled to the main party and Kinross put out scouts of his own, which surprised Merrivale, for the Scots were in friendly territory. But Kinross was clearly a man who did not believe in taking chances.

The journey to Kelso and onward to Jedburgh passed without incident. Beside Merrivale, Peter was quivering with excitement; he had never been to Scotland, having been too young to accompany his father to the wars. When the Scottish camp came into sight he stood up in the stirrups, surveying the bright banners and coats of arms displayed on the painted pavilions.

'Blue and white checks, three gold scallops on a bar of black; that's the Earl of Menteith. Two red chevrons on gold, the Earl of Strathearn. Three red diamonds and a red border on gold, the Earl of Moray. Three gold stars on red, the Earl of Sutherland. Three red shields on white, that's the Lord High Constable. White with a red upper band and three gold pallets, the Great Marischal. There's the Douglas heart, and the red lion on gold of Bruce... That red saltire on gold, I don't know that one.'

'That is the Seigneur de Brus,' the herald said quietly.

'And there is another I don't recognise. Three gold diamonds and a gold bar on blue. Is that also a French coat?'

He had seen the coat before, on other journeys and other battlefields, but even so the sight of it was like a punch in the stomach. 'Yes,' said Merrivale. 'That is Guy de Dampierre, the Count of Béthune and Lord of Hamilton.'

They halted outside the Dunbar pavilion, the earl's white lion banner snapping overhead in the wind. Heron looked around in puzzlement. 'Where is your king?'

'At the abbey,' Kinross said. 'He has taken his lodgings there. My lady desires to see the herald first.'

'Did she say why?'

'No,' said Kinross. 'She does not need to. Come this way, Sir Herald, if you please.'

Wrapped in a red robe trimmed with sable, the Countess of Dunbar received Merrivale in her chamber inside the big pavilion. With her were a tall, long-nosed man-at-arms in mail tunic and helmet, and Tiphaine in a white Cistercian habit, which made him blink. 'You're still alive,' she said.

'So far. Aren't you supposed to be in Newcastle with Lady Mary?'

'Yes,' she said. 'But I'm not. Just as you're not dead. The countess wants to talk to you about Brus.'

Kinross, who had ushered Merrivale into the chamber, started to withdraw. Agnes held up a hand. 'Stay, James, if you please. I may have need of you.'

Kinross bowed. The countess looked at Merrivale. 'This is the Lady Mora of Islay, my shieldmaiden,' she said, pointing to the figure in mail.

'Sometimes also known as Murdo,' the herald said.

The woman inclined her head. 'It is a useful alias. I have several others.'

'You may trust Lady Mora and the Master of Kinross as you trust me,' said Agnes. She paused. 'Assuming, of course, that you trust me at all.'

The herald considered this. 'Is there any reason why I should not?'

'I was not as forthcoming as I might have been at our last meeting.'

'No. But then, neither was I. It was only our first chess game, after all.'

'I needed time to think. What you told me about Brus was disquieting, but I confess not wholly unexpected. Your *demoiselle* has given me more details about him.'

'She is not my *demoiselle*,' Merrivale said. Tiphaine rolled her eyes.

'This conspiracy you spoke of. Who was its leader? Brus?'

'No. There were several ringleaders, two of whom were English. One was the knight Sir Edward de Tracey. We do not know the identity of the other, only that he comes from the north of England. Brus was a relatively minor player, or so we thought.'

'What were this conspiracy's aims?'

'Initially, to overthrow the thrones of England and France and to bring about civil war in both realms. But the plot stretched far beyond those kingdoms. Bohemia was involved, as were the papal court and Genoa, and the Knights of Saint John.'

'The Knights of Saint John,' she repeated slowly. 'That interests me... Do you think Brus could be preparing to do the same in Scotland? Bring down the kingdom and start a civil war?'

'He could be,' said Merrivale. 'But he is also still meddling in English affairs as well, and I am convinced that he is using English money to pay for armies and bribes. As I said, the French treasury barely has two écus to rub together. What is not clear to me is whether Brus is acting on orders – and if so, whose orders – or if this is a freelance plot he has dreamed up himself.'

'You mean, the original conspiracy could still be active,' she said. 'Is that why you are here?'

'Yes. If I can persuade your king to extend the truce, I can discover more about what Brus is planning and lay evidence against him.'

The Master of Kinross shook his head. 'The king will never agree. He and my lady's brother and the whole war party are in thrall to the Frenchman.'

'And it is in Brus's interests to prosecute the war swiftly, so he can carry out his designs,' said Lady Mora.

Agnes of Dunbar looked at the herald. 'You did not answer my question. Do you trust me?'

'If you were working with Rollond de Brus, you would not have sent word about Coquetdale. And I would have fulfilled the *demoiselle*'s predictions, and be dead. What are you offering me?'

'Mora is right. This war is not Brus's sole aim. It is a step along the road towards his own ambitions. Do you agree?'

'Yes,' said Merrivale.

'Then I am offering you a pact,' the countess said. 'This man threatens both our kingdoms. Let us put aside our differences, and join forces to make an end to him.'

'How?' asked Kinross. 'Assassination?'

The countess shook her head. 'He is too powerful. We shall have to be more subtle.' She stared at Merrivale. 'That is where you come in.'

'Thank you,' Merrivale said dryly. 'I suspect you are right, and your king will refuse to extend the truce. I shall negotiate anyway. I might learn something useful.'

'It may be too late,' Mora warned. 'The Disinherited have come over to our side, the Percys and their friends are considering whether to follow them. There is very little now to prevent Brus from achieving his ends.'

Merrivale rubbed his chin. 'The Percys,' he said finally. 'I made a mistake there. I thought they could be won around easily, and concentrated on the Disinherited. I was wrong on both counts. I confess I was not expecting Lord Percy to be bribed so easily.'

'What was he offered?' asked the countess.

'Berwick,' said Merrivale. 'And Newcastle, both to be held as their personal property.'

Tiphaine's breath hissed. Agnes and Mora looked at each other. 'Now that *is* intriguing,' said the countess. 'Because twenty-four hours ago, he promised Berwick to me.'

From outside came the sound of a man's voice, harshly ordering people out of his way. Tiphaine ducked behind a curtain at the back of the chamber, and a moment later Rollond de Brus pushed his way into the room. 'Sir Herald,' he said in a voice full of venom. 'You are late. The king is calling for you. You will accompany me into his presence at once, or your embassy will be terminated. You too, my lady,' he said to the countess. 'You also are summoned.'

—

The abbey church of Saint Mary the Virgin was a massive building, a deliberate statement of power by an earlier king of Scotland. Time and war had left their marks; the timber roof was new, and the glass in the three high storeys was plain and clear, filling the nave with pale evening light.

David Bruce sat on a high-backed wooden chair in front of the rood screen, wrapped in a yellow robe decorated with red lions. The herald saw a man in his early twenties, with a narrow face, sharp nose and slightly receding chin. Rings decorated his long fingers, which tapped restlessly on the arm of his chair as he watched the herald walk towards him.

A crowd stood around him, men in coats bright with heraldry, women in silk kirtles and sleeveless surcoats, a few black-robed canons from the abbey; the grey-bearded man was probably the abbot, John of Eskdale. Niall Brus of Carrick stood beside his half-brother, his face dark with bruises and his eyes narrowed. *Those bruises are spectacular*, Merrivale thought. *I only hit him once. He must have got the rest falling into the river...* William Douglas of Liddesdale stood just behind him.

Agnes of Dunbar moved forward to join a handsome, silver-haired man who Merrivale guessed was her husband. Kinross followed her. The red diamonds of the Earl of Moray were visible on the far side of the nave; John Randolph had fairer skin than his sister, but the same curling dark hair. A man in a tabard like his own, gold with a single embroidered red lion rampant, stood beside the king; Archibald Graham, Lyon Herald, the royal herald of Scotland. Behind Graham was a tall man wearing the red cloak and white eight-pointed cross of the Knights of Saint John, and a finger of unease drifted down the herald's spine; he remembered the last time he had seen that cross, on bodies riddled with arrows in the streets of Saint-Riquier.

Brus bowed to the king and went to stand beside another man, dark-haired, wearing the device of gold diamonds and bar on blue; Guy of Béthune. He saw the anger in the other man's eyes and gazed back at him, his own eyes blank. Then he saw the woman standing beside Béthune. The shock was like walking into a wall. He took an iron grip on his will and looked away from her, gazing steadily at the king as he walked up the nave. Stopping the prescribed three paces away, he bowed deeply, quelling the sick churning sensation in his stomach.

'In the name of Queen Philippa of England,' he said formally, 'I give your Grace greeting.'

David looked both surprised and amused. 'Your Grace? King Edward still refuses to recognise me as the rightful king of Scotland. Does his wife take a different view?'

Merrivale could feel her gaze burning into his skin. He forced himself to concentrate. 'To be honest, I never asked,' he said. 'But I was taught to be polite to my hosts.'

The king laughed. 'Simon Merrivale. I have heard of you. They did not tell me you had a sense of humour. Very well, state your business.'

'As you know, sire, the truce between England and Scotland expires at sundown tomorrow. I have come to request an extension for another month, to All Saints' Day.'

'You are right, your Grace,' said Niall Bruce of Carrick. 'He has a sense of humour.'

Laughter rippled around the nave, echoing in the timber vault. Merrivale did not move. 'My embassy is to the king, not his fool,' he said. 'Your Grace, we stand poised on the brink of war, but there is still time to step back. Another month gives us time to agree terms for a lasting peace.'

'Only a beaten foe asks for peace,' said Rollond de Brus. 'All we have to do is walk into England and collect the spoils.'

His eyes were malevolent, but Merrivale saw the confidence and arrogance there too. *All his plans are in place*, the herald thought. *He is sure he has won.*

He looked back at the king. 'England is hardly beaten, your Grace. The Seigneur de Brus saw the power of England firsthand at Crécy. Trial by combat is risky, and no one can foresee its outcome. Should we not decide our destinies for ourselves, rather than leaving it to fortune?'

David pursed his lips. 'You are asking us to abandon all our endeavours, disband our troops and send them home? This army was assembled and equipped at vast expense, herald. It would be a shame for it to all go to waste.'

'Even more of a waste to see all your fine army stretched dead on the battlefield,' the herald said. 'Ask the Seigneur de Brus. He can tell you what that looks like.'

Brus started to speak, but the Earl of Moray stepped forward, pointing a finger at Merrivale. 'Why are we listening to this?' he demanded. 'England has no intention of making peace, it never has and it never will. This is just an attempt to delay us. And this man is no true ambassador. He should be whipped as an impostor and sent bleeding back to his masters.'

'Cut his tongue out first,' someone else suggested.

'Hold fast,' said Agnes of Dunbar. 'This man is a royal herald. By all our laws, you may not harm him.'

Moray turned on her. 'Do not lecture us on laws, bitch! Keep your foul mouth shut, or by Christ I'll cut your tongue out as well!'

The Earl of Dunbar clenched his fists, but his wife put a hand on his shoulder. Merrivale looked at the king, raising his eyebrows. 'Are things always like this?' he asked.

He saw the glimmer of amusement in the king's eyes, but Niall Bruce stepped forward, bruised face darker than ever with anger. 'You will show respect,' he said harshly. 'Or by God, herald or no, we will teach you manners.'

The herald turned to him. 'And who is going to teach me, my lord? Certainly not you. From my experience, you fight like a child.'

Bruce of Carrick reached for his sword. 'Hold him,' the king commanded, and Douglas of Liddesdale grabbed Carrick's arms, pinning them behind his back.

'Why stop him?' Rollond de Brus asked. 'Kill him, now. It will send a signal to the English.'

'May I remind you all that this is a house of God?' the abbot said sharply. 'And the Countess of Dunbar is right. This man is a herald, and protected.'

Carrick twisted, trying to get free, but Douglas held him still. 'Enough,' said the king, rising to his feet. 'Father abbot is right. My lord of Carrick, you will stand fast. Release him, Douglas.'

The king turned back to Merrivale. 'I like you,' he said. 'You amuse me, and I had not expected that. I like things that are unexpected. Therefore, I shall give you a hearing. I shall take council with my advisors, and tomorrow morning we will meet before the Michaelmas feast. And of course, you shall be our guest at the feast.'

Merrivale bowed. 'Your Grace is wise and just,' he said. 'I look forward to continuing our discussions.'

'Lodgings have been prepared for you,' said the king. 'Go to them now and remain there. When the time comes, we will summon you.'

16

Jedburgh, 28ᵗʰ of September, 1346
Night

Kinross escorted the herald to the pavilion that had been set aside for his use, a plain canvas tent in the abbey park not far from the river. Peter, Mauro and Warin were already there along with Heron and his men. After a brief discussion Heron and Kinross posted their guards in pairs, one Englishman and one Scot. 'Thank you,' said Merrivale. 'That should make Sir Roger's men feel much safer. As we have seen, feelings are running high.'

Kinross looked around to see if Heron was within earshot. 'This is for your safety, not Sir Roger's,' he said. 'I'm not sure who is the greater danger to you, herald. Friend or foe.'

'What do you mean?'

'I recognise two of Heron's men, Nickson and Croser. Did you know they are renegade Scots?'

'Yes. I understand Nickson killed a man in a feud with another clan.'

'Like hell he did. He killed his own brother because he wanted his brother's wife. Croser has killed at least three men because someone paid him to, but he also murdered a monk from Kelso who owed him threepence. Because these two are part of your escort, they have the same protection as you do. Believe me, if they didn't, I would hale them out and hang them in the morning.'

'There are plenty of violent men on the borders,' Merrivale said. 'What makes you think these two might be a threat to me?'

'I'll answer a question with a question. Who picked your escort?'

'Rokeby selected the men. Sir Roger asked for these two as scouts.'

'And why did he choose these two cut-throats in particular? You might want to ask him.'

The herald regarded him. 'I thought you seemed friendly with him.'

'I know him well, especially since he became deputy keeper last year. That doesn't mean I trust him, or any Englishman. Come to that, I don't trust most Scots, either.'

Merrivale nodded. 'May I ask a question? Why does the Earl of Moray hate Countess Agnes so much?'

'Ah, you don't know the story. Moray was captured by your lot about ten years ago. When Lord Salisbury was laying siege to Dunbar, he sent for Moray and led him out in front of the castle walls with a rope around his neck, threatening to execute him unless Lady Agnes surrendered. She told Salisbury to go ahead and hang him; if he died, his lands and title would all come to her. Salisbury backed down, but my lord of Moray has never forgiven his sister.'

'And so, when she opposed Brus and his friends, Moray joined them to spite her.'

'Something like that.' Kinross nodded. 'I wish you a pleasant evening, herald.'

—

Food was brought from the royal kitchen, roast venison and quails in honey, a fish pie, stuffed eggs and an apple tart, along with a jug of wine. The kitchen servants who brought the food insisted on tasting it to show it was safe, which made Merrivale uncomfortable. Mauro and Warin helped themselves and withdrew, and Merrivale sat down to eat with Peter. The boy had quick ears; he had already heard what happened at the church. 'Do you think the Scots will make peace, sir?'

'I very much doubt it,' Merrivale said. 'If there is a chance, of course, we must grasp at it. But David was right. Having made such elaborate preparations for war, why should they lay down their arms?'

Wiping his fingers, Peter considered the question. 'They have the upper hand, therefore there is no reason for them to make peace.'

'Exactly. The secret to diplomacy is making the opposition want something they do not already have. To do so, that other thing has to be in your gift. At the moment, I have nothing to offer. I am going into these talks empty-handed, which is the worst possible position.'

'But at least they have agreed to talk,' said Peter.

'Yes. But I suspect that is David's whim. And perhaps...' Merrivale paused for a moment, considering. 'And perhaps Brus's hold over David is not as secure as we imagined it to be,' he said. 'Perhaps this is David's way of showing Brus and his friends that he can make decisions for himself. I wonder if something can be made of that.'

'Well, if there is,' Peter said confidently, 'I am sure you will find a way, sir.'

Few things irritated Merrivale, but flattery was one of them. He opened his mouth to say so, and stopped when Mauro came into the pavilion. 'Pardon me, *señor*. A lady wishes to speak to you.'

Merrivale was surprised. 'A lady? The countess?'

'No, *señor*. Another lady. She is alone.'

He knew who it was, then, and the sick feeling came back to his stomach. 'Show her in,' he said abruptly. 'Peter, leave us, if you please. Make sure we are not overheard.'

'Yes, sir,' the boy said, wide-eyed. He departed and Merrivale stood, hands clenched behind his back, facing the door.

She looked older than he remembered; but of course, so did he. There were lines at the corners of her eyes, and her mouth, imperfections in that once flawless face. Her eyes, which had once been so bright with hope, were full of shadow now, a deep-grained sadness drawn like a veil across her soul. The incandescence of youth had faded from her face; and yet, to his eyes, she had never been more beautiful.

'Simon,' she said softly, holding out her hands.

Merrivale did not move, and after a moment her hands fell slowly to her sides. 'What are you doing here?' he asked.

'Here in this pavilion? Or here in Scotland?'

'An answer to either would be helpful.'

'Guy has lands in Scotland. He has come to support the king.'

'Guy? Of course, you call him Guy. Why not?'

'He is my husband, Simon.'

'You cannot expect me to recognise that fact, or accept it.'

'Simon, please.' There were tears in the corners of her eyes, and he bowed his head.

'I am sorry. Please go on.'

'Guy is lord of Hamilton in Scotland, as you may know. You must also know that his brother, the Count of Flanders, was killed last month at Crécy.'

'Yes. I watched it happen.'

'He is eager to avenge his brother. He gathered some of his retinue and came to Scotland, where he joined forces with an old friend, the Seigneur de Brus.'

'So, Guy is here, and you decided to come with him, presumably because the autumn weather in Scotland is always so fine. Why did you come here tonight?'

The tears welled again. 'Because I had to see you again,' she said. 'I could not bear the thought that you might hate me.'

'Hate you?' Merrivale stared at her. 'No, I have never hated you. I have tried, desperately, to forget you.'

Her voice was low. 'And have you succeeded?'

'No.'

They faced each other in silence for a long time, her eyes wet. The oil lamp flickered a little in the draught from the door. 'I loved you,' Merrivale said finally.

'I know.' She smiled a little through the tears. 'Do you still?'

'I no longer know. It is so hard to say, after everything... It might help if I understood what happened.'

'What do you mean?'

'Please don't pretend you don't know what I am talking about. We were one being, one passion, one soul. We were ready to run together, to defy everyone, to spend our lives together.' He raised his hands suddenly to his head. '*We were ready to die together.*'

'I couldn't,' she said.

'Couldn't what?'

'Couldn't go with you. Couldn't die with you.'

Premonition chilled him to the bone. 'Why not?'

'You've guessed, haven't you? You were always so good at guessing.' Tears fell down her face now, a silent waterfall on each cheek. 'I was with child,' she said.

The silence that followed seemed to go on forever. Merrivale lowered his hands, clenching his fists so hard that his nails bit painfully into the palm of his hand. 'Mary, mother of God,' he said finally. 'What have I done to you, Yolande?'

'It is good to hear my name on your lips again,' she said, wiping her face. 'You must not blame yourself. I took everything you offered and demanded more, and I was ready to see it through to the end. I was happy to put myself in danger for you, in order to defy my father. But I could not risk my unborn child.'

'Of course not,' he said softly. 'Did you tell them? About us?'

'No, but they knew anyway. And then my father ordered you to be killed. I married Guy at my father's command, and I bore my son. For a long time, for many years, I thought you were dead. I gave up mourning for you and tried to make a new life.'

'A son.' Merrivale paused for a moment. 'Is he well?'

'Healthy and thriving. We did one thing well, at least.'

'Oh, Christ,' said Merrivale in sudden agony, and he reached for her hands but she drew back.

'No,' she said. 'You were right. I am not sure I could bear your touch. The sight and sound of you are torture enough. I must go.'

'I am... so desperately sorry.'

'Do not be. The torment lies in my regret for what we lost, what might have been. I shall not see you again.'

'Of course you will. We both have to be at this wretched feast tomorrow.'

'I shall be diplomatically ill. I shall also ask my husband to send me back to Flanders. I do not want to know what happens to you.' She shivered suddenly. 'No. That last sentence is a lie. I shall always want to know.'

'Is there any way,' he asked, 'any way at all that I can reach you? That I can at least write to you from time to time?'

She shook her head. 'It is too dangerous,' she said. 'I don't care what happens to me. But they might harm my son.'

'Yes,' he said quietly. 'Of course. It was selfish of me to think of it... What is his name?'

'Jean,' she said. 'After my father. It seemed a... politic name to give him.'

She turned and walked out of the tent. Slowly the herald sat down, resting his elbows on the edge of the table and staring at the lamp flame without seeing it.

She was the fire and the flame. She was the lily, and the rose.

Beauty, he said, if it please you
and this great joy should be mine,
that you give me your love,
I shall listen always to you and your call
and fulfil your every wish and desire.
You are my only lord and sovereign.
All others, I have abandoned for you.
Let me never part with you again.
This is the hope that burns in my heart.

He became aware of someone standing beside him; Mauro, looking anxiously down at him. 'May I clear away the supper, *señor?*'

'Please do.' The smell of the food, the venison fat, the sickly sweet quails, was making him feel ill. Mauro began piling dishes onto a platter. 'And there is a man to see you now, *señor*, a *hospitaliero*. Señor Kinross wants to know if you wish to see him.'

At first he thought Mauro was talking about a doctor, but then he realised his servant was referring to the Hospitallers, the Knights of Saint John. He stood up quickly, pushing Yolande out of his mind. 'Show him in,' he said.

The man who entered the chamber a moment later was the one he had seen in the church; tall, long-limbed, with dark hair and skin leathered from many years' exposure to the sun. He wore a plain black cloak with a hood covering the robes of his order. 'Forgive me for disturbing you at this late hour,' he said. 'My name is Brother Alexander Seton, and I am the preceptor of the Order of Saint John in Scotland.'

Merrivale bowed. 'How may I serve you, brother?'

'I shall have to explain my own presence first.' Seton glanced at the wine jug, which Mauro had left behind, and Merrivale poured two glasses. He took his own unwatered, needing to scrape off the ragged edges of his nerves.

'As you may know, when the Scottish wars began, the Order in Scotland foolishly became involved in secular politics,' Seton said. 'They supported Edward of England, your king's grandfather, against the Scottish faction led by Robert Bruce. When Bruce triumphed, the Scottish members of our Order fled to England or took service in the Levant. Bruce allowed his supporters to take over most of the Order's lands in Scotland.'

'Those lands would have been extensive,' said Merrivale.

Seton sipped his wine. 'Very. As well as our own estates, we were given custody of all the lands of the Knights Templar after their suppression. We are, or were, a power in the land.'

Merrivale tried to work out where this was going. 'Did the Order not try to recover its lands?'

'Not at first, no. We were too busy establishing ourselves in our new home on Rhodes. But a few years ago, the grand master summoned me and gave me a commission to return to Scotland and begin recovering our property. I have fought a number of court cases, and I am pleased to say I have won most of them. However, more recently I have run into an obstacle.'

The herald waited. 'The cases I won were small ones against local landowners,' Seton said. 'A house here, a messuage there. Now I am up against more powerful men, magnates who have deeper pockets and so can afford to buy better lawyers and more competent forgers of documents. One of them is the Lord of Hamilton, who is also the Count of Béthune.'

'Go on,' Merrivale said.

'Last week, while I was in the midst of presenting a case against Béthune and his family for wrongful seizure and occupation of our estates, he sold his entire claim to the Seigneur de Brus. I have since learned that Brus has bought the title to more than two dozen other manors that once belonged to us, some of them very large and wealthy.'

'He is building an estate for himself in Scotland,' Merrivale said. 'Why?'

'I was hoping you might know the answer.' Seton finished his wine and set the cup down. 'I have a bargain for you,' he said. 'I believe you have information that will be useful to us, and I am fairly certain I know things that will be helpful to you. Shall we exchange?'

The secret to diplomacy is making the opposition want something they don't already have. It was difficult to tell how much Seton knew about the herald's mission, or even indeed whether Seton was telling the truth; as usual, there was only one way to find out. 'You go first,' said Merrivale.

'Earlier this year I received a letter from my grand master, informing me that the high council of the Order had grave doubts about the loyalty of Jean de Nanteuil, the Grand Prior of France. I was instructed to look into the matter, but before I could do so, Nanteuil was killed. As you of course know, Sir Edward de Tracey, who had recently joined the Order, died along with him.'

Merrivale nodded. 'Here is the thing that interests me,' said Seton. 'And I think it will interest you too, Sir Herald. When Sir Gilbert de Tracey, Sir Edward's brother, decided to wind up his business and withdraw from the world, pressure was put on him to join the Order too.'

There was a moment of silence. 'From where did this pressure come?' the herald asked. 'Inside the Order?'

'No, from the English court. I am told the suggestion came from one of King Edward's councillors, who urged the chancellor to take up the matter with our prior in London. The prior, needless to say, would have been quite happy to receive Sir Gilbert, and his money, but Sir Gilbert chose another path.'

The hair on Merrivale's neck was standing up again, for a different reason. 'Do you know which councillor?'

'No. I don't think my informants knew either. The suggestion was made anonymously. But it definitely came from the king's inner circle.'

Christ, thought Merrivale. If Seton was right – if he was telling the truth – the conspiracy was still very much alive. The man from the north was rebuilding his scheme with new allies. 'What do you want to know?' he asked.

'Whether this affair has anything to do with Scotland,' said Seton.

'Yes,' Merrivale said quietly. 'It does. Nanteuil and Tracey were part of a wide-ranging conspiracy spanning half of Europe, to overthrow established kingdoms and create a new order. From what you have said, I suspect someone within your own Order is also working with the conspirators. Rollond de Brus was, and I believe still is, one of this group.'

'What do you think he intends to do?'

'I don't yet know. At the moment, it is clear that he intends to cause as much havoc and chaos in England as he can. But from what you have said, it seems he also wants to establish himself as a power in Scotland, and that is a concern. Can you stop him from taking control of your lands?'

'I am trying,' Seton said. 'I came to plead my case with the king. He has told me to continue through the courts, but no judge will hear a case against Brus. They are too afraid of him. Meanwhile, rumours are spreading that I, like my predecessors, am in league with England.' He spread his hands. 'I have no interest in secular politics. The Order has one aim only, to return Jerusalem to Christian hands. But that does not stop the whispering in the corners.'

'No,' said Merrivale. 'And for what it is worth, brother, I suspect that traitors like Nanteuil intend to harm your Order as well. Perhaps even bring it down, just as they brought down the Knights Templar.'

'That is what the grand master fears also,' said Seton. 'Thank you, Sir Herald, for seeing me.' He paused for a moment. 'If I learn anything useful, where should I send word?'

'There are two men I trust,' Merrivale said. 'Sir Thomas Rokeby in Berwick, and William Blyth of Newcastle. Send word to either of them, and I will do likewise to your priory.'

Seton sketched a cross in the air between them. 'May God watch over us both,' he said.

17

Michaelmas. The last day of peace; unless, somehow, he could work a miracle.

'Good day to you, Sir Herald,' said Guy of Dampierre, Count of Béthune.

Merrivale looked at the other man. His voice was genial, but his face was full of malice. 'It is a fine morning,' the count said.

It was; earlier the valley had been full of fog, but that was clearing and the sun shone on the hills overlooking the town and abbey. 'How may I be of service, my lord?' the herald asked, his voice neutral. His head ached from the tension of the previous night and he had not slept for more than a few minutes at a time, but his manner was calm.

'Oh, I merely called to pay my respects. Are you going to the abbey? Yes, the king has summoned you to discuss the truce. Allow me to walk with you.'

'Of course, my lord.'

They walked across the pavilions in the park towards the abbey, the last skeins of mist drifting around its towers. 'You had a visitor last night,' Béthune said.

Merrivale's pace did not falter. 'Yes,' he said.

'A touching reunion, I have no doubt.'

'Not particularly,' said Merrivale. 'Your lady wife assured herself that I was well, and I did likewise. After that, she took her leave.' He glanced at the other man. 'You may rest assured that nothing improper passed between us, if that is what's troubling you.'

'*Nothing* is troubling me,' said Béthune. 'I trust Yolande, she is a dutiful wife who knows her place. I am more interested in you. Was it very painful, seeing her again after all these years?'

'No,' said Merrivale.

'Oh, come now. You had high aspirations once, didn't you? She was a king's daughter, you were a base-born rogue who charmed his way into royal service. You were never destined to succeed, but you knew that all along.'

'Allow me to correct you, my lord. I am not base-born. My father's family were gentlemen, who owned lands on Dartmoor for centuries.'

'Ah, but then your father lost them. I seem to recall some story about his wife and daughters starving to death because he was too poor and base to feed them. And you became Simon Lack-lands. To tilt your lance at a king's daughter...' Béthune shook his head. 'I suppose I should admire your audacity, but I can't bring myself to do so. Still, it all ended well. You were taught your place.'

'I have always known my place,' Merrivale said.

'Oh! Do I detect an edge in your voice? Is the weasel daring to show its teeth? I do find it amusing when the lower orders attempt to show spirit. They do it so *badly*.' Béthune draped an arm around the herald's neck. 'It gives me such pleasure to know that I have won,' he said. 'And to know that I have bested *you*, and that you are still suffering and in pain because of my victory; that makes the dish taste even sweeter.'

Merrivale took the other man's arm and flung it off with a force that made Béthune wince. 'Enjoy your triumph,' the herald said in a voice taut with anger. 'Long may it continue to satisfy you.'

'Oh, it will,' said Béthune, rubbing his wrist. 'I wish you good fortune with your negotiations, Sir Herald. Somehow, though, I do not think they will go well.'

The negotiations did not go well.

Waiting with the king in the abbey's painted chapter house were the senior nobles, the constable and marshal and the earls. Dunbar was among them, silver-haired and patrician; until seeing him at close range, Merrivale had not realised how much older Patrick of Dunbar was than his wife. Inevitably, Bruce of Carrick, Douglas of Liddesdale and Rollond de Brus were beside the king; the herald's opposite number, Archibald Graham the Lyon Herald, stood to one side. He smiled in greeting when Merrivale entered. 'Welcome among us, sir. Will you take a glass of wine?'

'Thank you, sir, but no.'

The king poured himself a healthy measure and downed it at a gulp. 'Right,' he said. 'Let's get this over with.'

Calmly, Merrivale repeated his request; that the truce should be extended by a month to All Saints' Day, to allow time for a formal peace treaty to be drafted and discussed. The others listened in silence. Bruce of Carrick's bruised face was flushed with anger, but he kept his peace. Rollond de Brus did not look at the herald at all, but kept his eyes fixed on the king.

'And what is England willing to offer to secure such a peace?' the king asked.

'I have no authority to make a formal offer at this time,' Merrivale said. 'I propose that each side appoints negotiators to discuss the matter further over the coming month.'

'I am puzzled by one thing,' said the king. 'Why now? Why not offer a permanent peace back in the summer, when this truce was first arranged, or even a few weeks ago when we were mustering at Perth. Why wait until the last moment, when your backs are against the wall?'

'Because the English know they are weak,' said Brus. 'They cannot trust their own nobles. The Disinherited have deserted and others are preparing to follow suit. We can march into northern England virtually without opposition. This is just a desperate attempt to postpone the inevitable.'

'I agree the offer should have been made earlier,' said Merrivale. 'But please believe me, your Grace, that late though the offer is, it is absolutely genuine.'

He looked around the room. 'It is fifty years since this war began,' he said. 'In those fifty years, how many lives have been lost? How much treasure has been expended? And for what, my lords? All that has changed is that Berwick is in the hands of the English. Otherwise, the border is exactly as it was at the start of this conflict. The Scottish crown has never been more secure; oh, London plays lip service to the notion that Balliol is king, but they will abandon him in a heartbeat if it suits them to do so. Balliol's own closest followers have rejected and abandoned him. He is a spent force.

'So then, what do we do, my lords? Do we carry on fighting for another fifty years, or a hundred, until no one can remember why the war began? Why? Why persist? England and Scotland are locked in an eternal wheel of violence, *but it makes no sense*. As nations, we have our differences, but those things we have in common – our trade, our language, our heritage – these are far greater than the things that divide us.'

Merrivale looked at the king. 'Peace is in your gift, sire. You can bring this to an end, you can halt this wheel. In times to come, the chroniclers will praise you as the man who brought peace between nations. You have but to say the word, now, and it is done.'

Silence fell. Patrick of Dunbar leaned back in his chair. 'He speaks fairly, sire.'

'Yes,' said the Earl of Menteith, frowning. 'But how do we know the English will keep their word? They have broken it often enough in the past.'

'So, in fairness, have we Scots,' said the Earl of Sutherland. 'At some point, if we are to bring this war to an end, we shall all have to start trusting each other.'

'I would sooner trust a pig,' the Earl of Moray said violently. 'There is only one way to have peace with the English. Smash them on the battlefield, rip their northern counties away, burn and pillage everything as far south as the Humber, and *then* dictate peace terms at the point of a sword.'

'We tried that, back in the reign of the first King David,' Dunbar said. 'We failed, and nearly wrecked our own kingdom in the process.'

'But this time, we will not fail,' said Brus. 'This time we will make a new kingdom, stronger than ever. Scotland will reign supreme in these islands now, not England.'

Rising from his seat, Brus walked around to stand in front of the king. 'Complete the work of your father, sire, and make Scotland a great nation once more. That is the task you were born for. That is your destiny.'

David looked at the herald. 'You have surprised me once more. You spoke with an eloquence and a passion I had not expected. I admire your words and the manner in which you have delivered them. But I have spent much of my life in exile, unable to return home while the English ravaged my country. Now, it is time to redress the balance. My army awaits. I have not come this far to turn back.'

'You would rather seek battle,' said Merrivale. 'And roll the dice.'

'Say rather that we will seek battle and trust in God,' said the king. He smiled. 'And in any case, the Seigneur de Brus assures me that the dice are loaded in our favour. This is a game of hazard that I fancy we will win. Thank you for your embassy, Sir Herald, and you shall continue to enjoy our protection. But at sunset today the truce will expire, and the war will begin.'

–

Smoke rose from a hundred fires in the park and fields around the town as the army prepared its Michaelmas feast. Inside the abbey the king and his nobles gathered, brilliantly robed and glittering with jewels. Merrivale watched them, seeing some faces anxious, others exuberant. He wondered how many would still be alive by the time this campaign was over.

Lyon Herald clapped him on the shoulder. 'Good to see you again, Sim. A herald, now! Congratulations on your promotion.'

'Thank you, Archie. You're looking well. The years have been kind to you.'

'Oh, aye. My hair's a wee bit thinner and there's a bit of lard around my waist, but I get by. How is Andrew Clarenceux? The clack is you'll take over his job when he retires.'

Clarenceux was the king's herald, the man who had trained Merrivale. 'He doesn't appear ready to retire just yet,' Merrivale said smiling.

'Give him my warm regards. Come and eat, laddie. It's the last decent meal we'll see for a while, so let's make the most of it. We'll be on salt cod and pottage once the campaign starts.'

The invitation to the feast had extended to himself only; Peter, despite being the son of a knight, had been left to eat with the servants. The boy had made no complaint; he never did. He had taken a shine to Mauro, and spent much of his time asking about life in Spain and how many Spanish coats of arms the latter could remember. Tables ran down the length of the nave, and Merrivale and Graham took seats on a bench with one of the black-robed canons, a cheerful red-cheeked man with a shock of grey hair and a barely perceptible tonsure who introduced himself as the almoner of the abbey. 'You made a brave attempt at peace, Sir Herald. I salute you.'

'Nevertheless, I failed,' Merrivale said.

'You're not to blame for that,' said Graham. 'The king gave you a hearing, which is more than I expected he'd do, but his mind was already made up. Or rather, Brus and Carrick had made it up for him.'

Rather undiplomatic language for a herald, Merrivale thought, or perhaps Archie Graham was just trying to make him feel better. They had both been messengers for their respective kings when Merrivale first served on the Scottish frontier, and had collided as often as they had collaborated, but respect and friendship had developed between them.

The almoner looked around to see if anyone was listening to their conversation. 'I confess to some disappointment that the king would not listen,' he said quietly. 'He is young, and wishes to prove his worth in the eyes of his nobles. But he has no experience of leading men into battle.'

'He thinks he doesn't need it,' said Merrivale. 'He is putting his trust in God.'

Lyon Herald snorted. 'Good luck to him. In my experience, God doesn't much like battlefields. He steers well clear of them, and lets the hand of man do its work.'

'Or the hand of the devil,' suggested the almoner.

'The devil would make a better job of it,' said Graham. 'Battles are fractured, broken, chaotic things that usually leave matters unfinished. The devil likes things tidy, and wraps up his loose ends.' He winked at Merrivale. 'Or so I'm told.'

Lamps and candles flamed in the painted nave of the church. Servants brought in platters of food, roast venison, salmon pie with sage and ginger, eels in parsley sauce, pigeons stewed with garlic and saffron, sausages with fennel, stuffed capons, tarts with plums, cloves and cinnamon, and a pickled cabbage the king was particularly fond of. Merrivale ate without appetite. He glanced around the church, but could see no sign of Yolande. She had been as good as her word.

The brutal shock of seeing her in the flesh, and speaking to her for the first time in eight years, had been hard enough. Coming on top of that was Seton's news, and the more he thought about it, the more convinced he was that Seton was genuine. It was entirely possible that Nanteuil and his companions had been plotting against the Order of Saint John, and that the grand master had got wind of this and asked one of his officers to investigate.

Why he had asked Seton and not Philip de Thame, the prior of the Order in England, was also a question. Someone close to the king had tried to persuade Gilbert de Tracey to join the

Knights of Saint John. Was this the man from the north? He thought about the northerners whom the king trusted most. Lord Rowton, the king's councillor, held lands in Cheshire and Lancashire; Michael Northburgh the royal secretary was also a Lancashire man; Thomas Hatfield, the bishop of Durham, hailed from Yorkshire. But Rowton was one of the king's most trusted friends, at his side that wild night back in 1330 when the king stormed through Nottingham castle to arrest his mother and her lover and seize control of England for himself. His loyalty was absolute. Northburgh was an old friend of Merrivale, who owed his position to the king's patronage and had never shown even a hint of disloyalty. Hatfield...

Hatfield, now. He was an ambitious man, who had entered royal service in his mid-twenties and risen like a comet to become bishop of Durham at the age of thirty-five. Unlike Zouche, who was most comfortable in the council chambers and law courts, Hatfield fancied himself as a warrior bishop; during the campaign last summer he had commanded the rearguard of the English army, albeit with a group of seasoned professional captains to hold his hand. Was it possible that he desired more?

Another thought occurred. Was it also possible that he had mended fences with the all-powerful priory of Durham? Was he the recipient of the wealth that the treasurer, Hugh de Tracey, was so carefully amassing?

God knows, Merrivale thought, *and I can't find out while I am sitting here, watching the King of Scotland get drunk and gloat with his friends over the victories he is about to win. It was a fool's errand coming here*... But he knew that was not true. He had two allies now, both sitting far up the table and ignoring his presence; the Countess of Dunbar and the preceptor of the Knights of Saint John. Only two, and neither of them in favour at the moment, but it was better than nothing.

Seton was talking with Guy of Béthune. The count looked up once and met Merrivale's gaze, his eyes cold. Merrivale bowed a little and turned away.

He realised he had drifted away from the conversation. The almoner was speaking of the lands Jedburgh Abbey still owned in Northumberland. 'Several fine manors north of Newcastle, along the coast. They produce coal and salt and fish as well as corn. Father Abbot has been pleading his case ever since the king arrived.'

'His case?' Merrivale asked.

'There's a rumour that when the king takes Northumberland he intends to seize all church lands, whether held by English houses or Scottish ones.' The almoner nodded towards the high table, where Brus sat next to the king. 'Yon Norman wants the estates, it seems. He's grabbing lands wherever he can get them.'

'I expect he wants them so he can reward his followers,' Lyon Herald suggested.

'I don't care why he wants them, but he needs to keep his grubby hands off the church lands. We've warned our friends at Lanercost and Hexham.'

Lanercost Priory in Cumberland, like Hexham and Jedburgh, was an Augustinian house. For the religious orders, the border between England and Scotland barely existed; their estates on either side of the border were sacrosanct, or were supposed to be. Now, under threat, they were uniting against a common enemy. 'Father Abbot and the English priors have all signed a letter to King David and another to King Edward, asking that our lands be respected,' the almoner said. 'We asked the priory at Durham to join us, but they refused.'

'Let me guess,' said Merrivale. 'They won't get involved in secular affairs.'

'That's their excuse, anyway,' said the almoner. 'Aye, well, what can you expect from Benedictines? They've no sense of solidarity with their fellow religious houses, never have had. Conceited bastards.'

'You're letting your prejudices show, Willie,' Lyon Herald reproved. 'Have you had a response to your letters?'

'Nothing from London, yet. King David's secretary wrote to say the king had promised to think about it. Father Abbot chewed his ear again this morning, but got no further. Our English friends are just as worried as we are. One of the brothers at Hexham has offered to intercede personally with King Edward.'

'Who was that?' Merrivale asked. 'Father John, the prior?'

'No,' said the almoner. 'A new man, Brother Gilbert. You may have heard of him, he used to be the king's banker. Then there was some sort of family trouble.'

Merrivale laid down his eating knife. 'Brother Gilbert offered to contact the king to help preserve the priory's lands?'

'Aye,' said the almoner. 'It was generous of him. Let's hope your king remembers his friends.'

The board was cleared. Musicians came and bowed to the king and played, one of them singing in a fine silvery voice. The song was one Merrivale recognised; it was a song of the crusades, long ago, and he wondered who had chosen it. Guy of Béthune was watching him again, and this time he was smiling. Of course; Yolande's father had been fond of this song.

> *Knights, you are the ones who have been chosen,*
> *For it was to you that God first turned*
> *When the Turks and Almoravids*
> *Shamed Him so greatly by seizing Jerusalem.*
> *And for this wrong, we now suffer*
> *For this is the land where God was first served*
> *And recognised as our Lord.*
>
> *Those who journey now with King Louis*
> *Will never fear hell again*
> *Because their souls will ascend to Heaven*
> *And dwell with the angels of our Lord.*
>
> *Rohais is taken, hear now the sad news,*
> *And the Christians there are in turmoil.*

Monasteries burn and are deserted,
God is no longer celebrated there.
Oh knights, go forth from your homes and your loved ones,
You who are praised for your feats of arms,
Offer up your bodies to the One
Who gave his life for you on the cross.

High overhead a bell rang, tolling vespers; the end of Michaelmas. Out in the fields around the town a trumpet called, followed by the raw skirl of a bagpipe. A roar went up in the church, rebounding and echoing in the vaults. The king rose unsteadily to his feet, raising his wine goblet. His nobles and knights answered him, draining their cups and pounding their fists on the tables as they chanted. In the midst of the turmoil, Merrivale looked up and saw Rollond de Brus watching him too. The other man bowed, mocking him. The truce was over. The war had begun.

III

18

Berwick-upon-Tweed, 30th of September, 1346
Evening

'I failed.'

'At least you got out alive,' said Rokeby. 'That's something.'

They were in Rokeby's office once more, looking out over the dark river towards the flickering orange light on the horizon. All day the raiders had been at work, scorching the districts south of the Tweed, and the air during the ride back from Jedburgh had been full of ash and smoke.

He had not seen Yolande again. Nor had he seen Tiphaine. Instead, the Master of Kinross had entered his pavilion just before they departed. 'I would like a word with you, Sir Herald. Alone, if I may.'

Merrivale nodded to Peter, who bowed and went out. 'We don't have much time,' Kinross said. 'Sir Roger is busy elsewhere in the camp, but he could return at any moment. My lady of Dunbar sends word. She will not see you again; she does not want to draw attention to any connection with you. But my lady bids me tell you that she is keeping the Demoiselle de Tesson by her side.'

Merrivale blinked. 'Did she say why?'

'The *demoiselle* knows the mind of the Seigneur de Brus better than anyone. The countess wants her advice on how to deal with him. Also, the *demoiselle* herself believes she can help gather more information about Brus's intentions.'

'For God's sake,' Merrivale said sharply. 'That will put her in danger.'

'It will. But you can count on my lady to protect her as far as she can.'

'Really? If Brus spots Tiphaine and exposes her as a spy, will the Countess of Dunbar protect her?'

Kinross was silent. 'Of course she won't,' Merrivale said. 'She cannot risk exposure. Tiphaine will be thrown to the wolves, there will be no choice. The countess has no right to put this young woman in danger.'

'I don't think that's how Agnes sees it,' said Kinross. 'As one proud, courageous woman who is ready to take risks for her country, she recognises a kindred spirit in the *demoiselle*.'

'Body of Christ,' the herald said in sudden anger. He looked at Kinross. 'Is she genuine? The countess? Does she really want to undermine Brus?'

'She is already doing so,' said Kinross. 'Through Mora of Islay's influence, she has already persuaded Mac Dhòmhnuill, the Lord of the Isles, to withdraw his retainers, robbing the army of two thousand prime fighting men. She will do more if she can.'

Roger Heron had returned; his voice could be heard outside, marshalling his men. Kinross turned away abruptly. 'Time to go,' he said.

—

'Did you see any sign of the Disinherited?' Rokeby asked.

'No,' said Merrivale. 'I was half-expecting them to ride into the Scottish camp as soon as the truce expired. Have you heard no word?'

'Not of the leaders, but their retainers are on the move. Five hundred men rode out of Coquetdale yesterday, and as many more from Redesdale and Tynedale. They were heading west.'

'Heading towards this secret meeting place,' Merrivale said. 'Where is it, do you think?'

'God knows. You've seen that country, Simon. From Kielder Moor to the Bewcastle Wastes, it's nothing but hills and crags and broken ground. They could be hiding an army there.'

'That's almost certainly what they are doing,' Merrivale agreed. 'What about the Percys, and the Nevilles?'

'Mustering their men,' Rokeby said. 'But doing it slowly. They're waiting to see which way the cat will jump.'

'And the plotters here in Berwick?'

'Still plotting,' Rokeby said tiredly. 'And there's not a lot I can do about it. The Scots have been prowling around outside the walls all day. After fending them off and strengthening the guard on the gates, I don't have enough men left over to search the town for traitors.'

His eyes searched the herald's face. 'What are your intentions?'

'I think I can win the Percys around,' Merrivale said slowly. 'But there's something I need to do in Berwick first. Have I your permission to remain for a couple of days?'

Rokeby smiled through the exhaustion in his face. 'You're the queen's envoy,' he said. 'I can hardly throw you out. Do what you need to do, Simon. You have my blessing.'

—

Tired, the herald thought, *we're all tired, and we are only at the beginning of the war.*

Kinross was suspicious of Heron, and it was more than just a Scot's dislike of an Englishman. It wasn't much, but it was a start.

In his chamber in the Constable Tower, he called for Mauro and Warin. 'Tomorrow, I want you to keep watch on Heron's men, Nickson and Croser. If they leave the castle, follow them and tell me where they go.'

'I can help too, sir,' said Peter.

Merrivale looked doubtful.

'I've tracked deer and wolves across the moor, sir,' the boy persisted. 'I know what to do.'

'Very well,' said the herald. 'Consider it part of your training.'

Warin grinned at the boy. 'We'll look after him, sir.'

They departed. *Peter is doing well, for one so young*, the herald reflected. *He has a talent for making people feel at ease around him, no matter what their station. My master the Prince of Wales is learning how to do this, but to Peter it comes naturally. Yes, he will do well.*

He sat on his bed, listening to the restless tramp of sentries along the ramparts outside. *So many pieces*, he thought, *like a broken mosaic, and I don't know how to put them together. The Disinherited, the Percys, the plotters working in secret in Newcastle and Berwick. Agnes of Dunbar, the Knights of Saint John, the Augustinians. Rollond de Brus... Everything comes back to Brus; or does it? Where is the man from the north? Is he Brus's master, or is there some other game in play?*

Why did Gilbert de Tracey offer to intercede with King Edward? And why did his uncle Hugh at Durham refuse to join with the Augustinians? What game was *he* playing?

What was Guy of Béthune doing here, and why particularly had he brought his wife?

Merrivale stood up suddenly, his heart racing. *He came to support the king*, Yolande had said, and she had mentioned the death of his brother the Count of Flanders at Crécy. Louis of Flanders had been an ally and friend of John of Hainault, who in turn was a close friend and councillor of Philip of France. But Merrivale knew that Hainault was also a senior member of the conspiracy, and in league with the man from the north.

Which meant that Béthune was as well. Did he know Yolande had come to see him last night? Did he send her deliberately, to unsettle the herald, as he himself had tried to do next morning?

He remembered the sheet of tears on Yolande's face. *I cannot trust her*, he thought. *I cannot believe a word she says. And that is the hardest pain of all.*

Berwick-upon-Tweed, 1ˢᵗ of October, 1346
Morning

'They called on two merchants of the town, *señor*,' Mauro said. 'Nickson went to the house of a man named John Brotherton, and Croser called at another house not far away, owned by Henry Cheswick.'

'Both are members of the Guild Merchant,' said Peter. 'Brotherton deals mostly in timber and corn, and is less important. Cheswick imports pepper and spices from Flanders. He is a leading member of the guild.'

'What did they do next?' asked Merrivale.

'They returned to the castle, sir. We're not sure what Nickson did next, but I saw Croser speaking to Sir Roger Heron just a few moments ago.'

'We must talk to these merchants,' Merrivale said. 'Immediately.'

Down in the courtyard men were in motion, stepping into the saddle, grasping their lances and riding out with a clatter of iron-shod hooves. From the ramparts came the twanging thud of a ballista launching an iron bolt. The herald saw John Coupland and waved a hand. 'What is happening?'

'The Scots are getting a little too close. We're going out to make sure they keep their distance.'

'Have they come in force?'

'No, only a couple of hundred, so far. There's no sign of the main army. This lot are here to tweak our noses and keep us busy.'

'Either that, or they are waiting for something,' Merrivale said.

'Could be.' Coupland closed his visor and rode away after his men, horseshoes striking sparks from the cobbles. Merrivale followed him, his three attendants at his heels, passing through the gatehouse and crossing the drawbridge. On the far side of the fosse they met young Tom Rokeby, fully armed and headed the other way. Merrivale hailed him.

'Tom, I need your help.' He explained briefly what had happened, and the younger man frowned.

'The Scots are very close to the walls, sir.'

'Coupland has just ridden out to drive them off. This won't take long, Tom.'

'All right. I can spare a few minutes.'

It had rained overnight, and the cobbled streets of the town were slippery. Cheswick's house on Marygate was a fine one, with ornamental foliage carved around its windows and doors. A terrified maidservant admitted them and pointed in the direction of the master's solar. Tom Rokeby charged upstairs, followed by Merrivale, but they were too late; one of the solar windows was open and they could see footprints in the muddy lane beneath. Merrivale scooped up a handful of parchment sheets and rolls, handing them to Peter. 'We'll go through these later,' he said. 'Let's find Brotherton.'

John Brotherton's house was on Ravensden in the east side of the town. 'There's no rear exit,' Rokeby said. 'If he comes out, it will be through the main door or the kitchen entrance.'

'Mauro and Warin will watch the kitchen,' said Merrivale. 'Let's go.'

Forewarned by whatever means, Brotherton was already trying to make his escape. Rokeby, Merrivale and Peter had barely set foot in the hall when they heard shouting in the courtyard and ran outside to find the merchant struggling while Warin pinned his arms behind his back. The herald stopped in front of him.

'I do not have time to waste,' he said. 'Tell me everything about the conspiracy, and I will spare your life. If not, you will be drawn and quartered before this day is over. Make your choice, now.'

–

After a short violent fight through the ruins of Bondington, the Scots had retreated over the horizon, leaving only a few scouts. Coupland's men came trotting back to the castle, waving bloody lances in the air. Merrivale found Roger Heron up on the battlements, watching them. 'We have won the day, it seems,' the herald observed.

'Temporarily,' Heron said. 'They'll be back, you can depend on it.'

'But this victory will lift the men's spirits and give them heart. Is there any word of the main army?'

'They're shifting south-west, towards Hawick. Rokeby reckons their first target is Carlisle. This lot are here to pin us down and keep us from sending men to join the archbishop's army.'

'Possibly,' said Merrivale. 'Sir Roger, might I have a word in private?'

Heron looked at him. 'Of course.'

They walked around the walls to the southern rampart, overlooking the steep bank down to the river. The guards were fewer in number here and they found a quiet place on the wall-walk between two strong towers. Little pools of water stood here and there from last night's rain. Smoke hung in the air, and fires flickered on the horizon.

'John Brotherton has made a full confession,' Merrivale said. 'He is in the town gaol at the moment. Henry Cheswick has escaped, but we have seized his account rolls. There is clear evidence of treason. It is equally clear that both men are connected to you.'

He saw Heron's face turn pale. 'You disappeared for a while yesterday morning, before we left Jedburgh,' said Merrivale. 'I presume you were meeting with the Seigneur de Brus, to receive your final instructions. This morning, you sent Nickson and Croser to pass on those instructions to your confederates. The Scots are here, Sir Roger, because they are waiting for you, Brotherton and Cheswick to open the gates for them.'

Heron opened his mouth to speak. 'Don't,' said Merrivale, raising a hand. 'Don't tell me this is all a mistake, or that you can explain everything, or that Brotherton must be lying. I have all the evidence I need to send you to the scaffold. I will extend mercy to you, but only if you cooperate. Brus intends to seize both Berwick and Newcastle by stealth. He has promised them both to Lord Percy, but he has also promised Berwick to the Countess of Dunbar. What is his real intention?'

'Go to the devil,' Heron said, drawing his sword, and he swung the gleaming blade with all his force at Merrivale's head.

But the herald had already read the intention in the other man's eyes, and he ducked under the whistling blow and then slammed hard into Heron, throwing him back against the stone rampart and pinning him there. His hand closed on Heron's wrist and twisted it savagely. Heron yelped with pain and dropped the sword with a clatter. His other hand was already reaching for his dagger but Merrivale plucked it out of his grasp and threw it over the wall, and then transferred his hands to Heron's neck in a throttling grip, bending him back through an embrasure in the rampart until the upper half of his body was over the edge, suspended in space above the drop towards the river. Heron clutched at his arms, but off-balance he did not have enough strength to break the grip. He tried to kick Merrivale but his boots slipped, scrabbling on the wet stone, and he nearly went over the edge.

'Brus intends to keep both towns for himself, doesn't he?' the herald said. 'Along with the church lands he wants to seize, and the estates of the Knights of Saint John he is buying up. Brus is building an empire.'

'God damn you,' Heron gasped.

Merrivale tightened his grip. The other man's face turned red and he started to choke. 'Brus intends to betray the Percys. How?'

There was no answer. 'I can save you,' Merrivale said. 'I, and I alone, can ensure you do not go to the scaffold. But you must tell me.'

'Lord Percy... and his son will be invited to Berwick... to receive the keys of the city,' Heron said, gagging. 'Once inside the walls... they will be trapped and killed.'

'By you,' the herald said.

'Those are my orders.'

Merrivale pushed harder, forcing more of the other man's weight over the rampart. 'You also had orders to kill me. You would have done so on the ride to Jedburgh, but Rokeby fore-stalled you by picking the escort himself. Kinross was suspicious of you too. He thought you had planted Nickson and Croser to assassinate me.'

'Yes,' Heron said. 'For God's sake... let me up. My back is breaking.'

'One more question. What was your reward to be? What did Brus promise you?'

'Land. Money, lots of money. Anything I wanted.'

'He lied to you, like he lied to the Percys,' Merrivale said. 'Once you had served your purpose, you would be killed and your body left for the crows. You will come with me to Sir Thomas Rokeby, where you will make a full and formal confession. Do you understand?'

Half-strangled though he was, Roger Heron had not lost his spirit. He nodded in agreement, and in the same moment with a superhuman effort managed to tear one of Merrivale's hands from his neck. His knee came up, driving towards the herald's groin, but his other foot slipped again and his body tipped over the edge of the rampart. Letting go of his throat, Merrivale grabbed instead for his sword belt, trying to haul him back, but the buckle snapped and the belt came away in Merrivale's hands. Silently, Heron's body fell thirty feet to the ground and then tumbled loose-limbed and broken down the bank, finally coming to rest at the water's edge.

'That wasn't supposed to happen,' the herald said under his breath.

Men were running towards him, eyes wide with astonishment under the rims of their helmets. Merrivale turned to them. 'Fetch Sir Roger. If he is still alive, treat his wounds and then put him in the gaol. If he is dead, call a priest.'

Berwick-upon-Tweed, 1ˢᵗ of October, 1346
Evening

'He died an hour ago without regaining consciousness,' Merrivale said. 'I am sorry. I should have ensured he made a full confession.'

'For God's sake,' Rokeby said impatiently. 'You were an unarmed man, against an armoured knight. You're damned lucky he didn't kill you.'

'He did try,' Merrivale said dryly. 'I heard there was fighting on the other side of town.'

'Yes. The Scots came back and made a dart at the Magdalene Gate. I sent Coupland and Tom to outflank them, and they sheered off and rode away over the hills. It's been quiet ever since.'

'They were expecting Heron's men to open the gate for them,' Merrivale said. 'They may leave you in peace now, for a little while, at least. I tried to arrest Nickson and Croser, but I suspect they have already deserted. I also went through Heron's strongbox this afternoon. I'm sorry, Thomas, but there are letters and receipts for money dating back years. God knows how long he has been in Scottish pay.'

'And he wasn't even smart enough to destroy the evidence,' Rokeby said. 'I hope the bastard roasts slowly in hell. I'll find out who else may have been working with Brotherton and Cheswick. What guarantees did you give Brotherton?'

'I promised his life would be spared,' Merrivale said. 'Nothing else. I shall depart in the morning, Thomas. I need to see Lord Percy before it is too late.'

19

Durham, 2ⁿᵈ of October, 1346
Afternoon

'Brother Oswald,' said Hugh de Tracey. 'You took your time.'

They were standing in the cloister of Durham cathedral, listening to rain drip from the eaves. 'I ran into Brus,' said Oswald of Halton. 'He asked me to carry some letters for him. I thought it would be a chance to find out what he is doing.'

'And?'

'He has the Disinherited by the balls, I don't know how or why. Brus's friends raided their lands to put pressure on them. When they fought back, he rebuked them, and they cringed like little girls. I saw it myself.'

'Where are they now?'

'Vanished. But here's the important bit. Brus is grabbing land, from the Knights of Saint John and from the church. And according to a rumour I picked up in Newcastle, he is making a play for the town as well.'

'*Newcastle!*' Hugh had kept his voice low, but his tone was vehement. 'What do you mean, making a play?'

'Exactly what I said. Some of the merchants are planning to open the gates when the Scottish army comes. They're already bribing officers of the garrison. I heard something similar in Berwick too, but in Newcastle they were definite. Brus is planning to take the town for his own.'

'Then he is exceeding orders,' Brother Hugh said.

'He damned well is. The instructions were clear. We parcel out the spoils at the end, to make sure everyone gets their fair share.'

Hugh made an impatient gesture. 'What about the herald?'

'I lost him for a while when Brus got his hooks into me. He had some rendezvous out beyond Hexham, I don't know who with. Then he tried to win over the Disinherited, and failed. Last I heard he was riding off to Jedburgh to try and persuade the Scots to extend the truce. Oh, and Brus is trying to kill him, too.'

'That's not in the plan either,' Hugh said sharply.

'What about your nephew, Gilbert? The word among the religious houses is that he is trying to curry favour with the king. Does that mean he wants out?'

'That is what I am trying to discover.' Hugh looked at the friar. 'Who do you work for now? Myself, or Brus?'

'Brus pays better.'

'I'll double whatever he paid you. Now listen.' Hugh leaned forward until his voice was next to the other man's ear. 'This is what I want you to do,' he said.

Hawick, 2nd of October, 1346
Evening

It was raining north of the border too, the hills above Teviotdale shrouded in silver mist, the burns rushing and roaring with water pouring down the slopes towards the dark river. 'And so, after one day, the glorious campaign of 1346 judders to a halt,' said Sir William Douglas of Liddesdale.

Brus turned on him. 'Don't be ridiculous. You know we can't get the army over the hills in this weather.'

Douglas shifted a little. Like Brus he was in near constant pain, from a wound taken during the attack on Carlisle the previous year. The pain did nothing to sweeten his temper. 'You mean, we can't get the king's baggage over the hills, or the ladies and their pretty gowns. My hobelars travel in worse weather than this.'

Rain pattered steadily on the roof of the pavilion, painted with Brus's red and gold saltire. 'Then get them out into the field,'

Brus snapped. 'The eastern march of England is already reduced to ashes. Let's burn the west next.'

'Patience,' said Niall Bruce of Carrick. The bruises on his face were turning dull red and yellow, matching the colours on the canvas. 'Nothing will burn in this weather. A day or two's delay won't kill us.'

'Since when have you been the voice of reason?' Douglas demanded.

'He's right,' Brus said. 'For God's sake, Douglas, the archbishop's force is a hundred miles away. Shorn of the Disinherited, and of the Percys and their friends, he will be lucky to raise three thousand men. We have four times that. All the nobles are falling into line now, even the Dunbars.'

'Why?' asked Guy of Béthune, the fourth man in the room. 'What did you offer them?'

'Something they couldn't refuse. We'll take Northumberland and Cumberland without a fight. We'll have Durham too, unless the priory cooperates with us. It's all turning out exactly as we planned.'

'Exactly as we planned?' Douglas said sharply. 'We were supposed to seize Berwick yesterday, and that failed. We still don't know why. This is not exactly an auspicious start, Brus.'

'Berwick was one element in the larger plan,' Brus said. 'Give it time. When the rest of Northumberland falls into our hands, Berwick will fall too. We have come too far, gentlemen. Let's not start doubting each other now.'

'It's not each other we're doubting,' Douglas said, still with an edge to his voice. 'I want what I was promised, Brus. And if you fuck this up, it's you I'll be coming after.'

Béthune held up a hand for silence. Walking to the pavilion door, he looked out into the rain but saw nothing apart from a female camp servant carrying a pail of milk from the dairy. Closing the canvas sheet, he turned back to the others.

'This is no time for disunity,' he said. 'We took oaths that we would make this happen. When England is destroyed we will refashion Scotland. That is what we promised, remember?'

Douglas said nothing. Béthune nodded. 'Good,' he said. 'Now, let's go over the plan one more time.'

–

'I could not hear everything,' Tiphaine said. She had shed her nun's habit and wore a shapeless brown kirtle with her hair tucked up in a scarf. 'But they were falling out among themselves. Douglas is unhappy.'

Agnes of Dunbar nodded. 'Nothing new there,' she said. 'But this could prove useful. Go on.'

'I thought they were just discussing the army's strategy. But then they checked to see if anyone was listening and closed the door. I dared not linger long after that, but I heard Béthune refer to an oath the three of them had sworn. To destroy England, which I understand, but also to refashion Scotland. I don't know what that means.'

There was a long silence, broken only by the steady drumming of the rain. 'Brus has some vision for making Scotland into a great power,' Agnes said finally. 'That is the notion he has put into the king's head, that the country can be restored to the same position it occupied in its years of glory. Except those years never existed. Two hundred years ago, when England was racked by civil war, David I tried to seize and hold the north of England, but he failed. We tried again thirty years ago in the aftermath of Middleton's rebellion, and seized part of Northumberland, but again we failed.'

She stirred a little, thinking. Black corkscrew curls of hair framed her face. 'But this may be what Brus is imagining,' she said. 'These events may be his inspiration.'

'But if so, why the secrecy?' Tiphaine asked. 'As you said, the king himself must be aware of Brus's plan.'

'Perhaps,' said the countess. 'But perhaps not all of it.' She turned to Mora of Islay, standing by. 'There is more to learn here, I think.'

Mora nodded. 'We will keep working on it,' she said.

The rain had churned the roads to mud and the going south from Berwick was slow. It took two days for Merrivale and his companions to reach Warkworth, and by the time they arrived the wind had come up, blowing rain horizontally across the road. They could hear the surf booming on the bar at the mouth of the Coquet.

There were tents and pavilions in the fields around the castle, and lines of horses wrapped in blankets standing miserably in the rain. Merrivale looked around, doing a quick calculation of numbers. Riding beside him, Peter said quietly, 'There's Yorkshire coats here, sir, as well as Northumbrians.'

Merrivale nodded. The Percys had lands further south in Yorkshire too, and judging by the evidence they had stripped their estates of men. They were determined to fight, he thought. The question is, for whom?

He answered his own silent question. *For us, of course. And it is my task to ensure that they do.*

Lord Percy received them in his solar, granite-faced and silent. Dull light shone through the red and white diamond panes of the windows. A servant brought a jug of warm hippocras and Merrivale stood by the fire, his clothes steaming as he sipped his drink. 'You have mustered a strong force,' he said. 'What about the other northern lords? Has Lord Neville called up his men as well?'

'So I understand,' Percy said.

Merrivale took another sip. 'This must be costing you a great deal, to raise so large a retinue. The crown will reimburse you, of course, but you will have needed a lot of money up front. Even more difficult, now that Gilbert de Tracey is no longer your banker.'

Percy waited; by his face, he knew what was coming. 'But of course, I am forgetting,' Merrivale said. 'Your new banker is the

Seigneur de Brus. How much money have you had from him already?'

'Damn you!' Lord Percy said angrily. 'I have never taken a penny from the French, or the Scots!'

'I could order an inquisition to see if that is true,' Merrivale said. 'However, we are short of time. You were promised even more money if you joined the Scots, and more estates too. The towns of Berwick and Newcastle would be handed over to you.'

'Mary told you.' Percy stared at him, eyes still hard with anger. 'I presume she also told you we rejected the offer. Turned it down out of hand.'

'Ah,' the herald said. 'But did you?'

Percy said nothing. Merrivale banged his cup down hard on the table. 'Because if you did, my *lord*, why is your army sitting here at Warkworth rather than marching to join the archbishop at Richmond? Because as I distinctly recall, those were your orders!'

'Because it's no good going to Richmond,' Percy said. 'It's too far south, you know it yourself. Zouche has bungled it. He should have called the muster at Barnard Castle, or even further north. By the time we march all the way to Richmond and back again, it will be too damned late.'

'So you're going to stay here and protect your own lands,' Merrivale said. 'And if things go badly wrong, you can always take up Brus's offer.'

'That will never happen,' said Percy.

'Never is a long time, my lord. Incidentally, Brus has also promised Berwick to the Count and Countess of Dunbar, but I rather suspect he intends to keep it for himself. Berwick was bait. Once it was safely in his hands, Brus intended to invite you and your son to join him. Once you were inside the trap, you would be killed.'

'How do you know this?' demanded Percy.

'One of the plotters confessed to me, just before he died. And after *you* were dead, I believe, Brus intended to seize *your* lands as well. The name and estates of Percy would be snuffed out. He will betray you, my lord, utterly and finally.'

The herald waited for this to sink in. He saw Lord Percy's face change, and knew he had won. 'You knew all along that this was a possibility,' he said.

'Yes,' Lord Percy said finally. 'Yes, I did. But I don't trust Zouche to run a Whitsun fair, let alone command an army in the field. And after the last eight years of bungling and neglect, I am not even certain I trust the king. I decided to put my own interests first and yes, I believed what I wanted to believe. What man wouldn't, in my position?'

'The Wardenship of the March should belong to you and Lord Neville,' the herald said. 'I shall recommend this to the king. I believe the archbishop will be grateful to lay down this burden. Send word to his Grace that you will wait for him at Barnard Castle.'

'I will need to leave some men to guard Alnwick and Warkworth. I cannot leave them unprotected.'

Inwardly, Merrivale sighed with relief. 'Of course,' he said. 'That is understood.'

Silence fell. 'How much does London know?' Percy asked finally.

'You may expect a rebuke for not mustering your men quickly enough,' said the herald. 'Otherwise, there will be no further consequences. You have my word on it.'

'Thank you.' Lord Percy regarded him. 'You're a clever fellow. Perhaps the king should make you Warden.'

Merrivale smiled a little. 'No,' he said. 'I'm only a herald.'

20

Newcastle-upon-Tyne, 4th of October, 1346
Afternoon

The rain had stopped but the wind was raw with sea damp when Merrivale rode up to Newgate in the north wall of Newcastle and demanded entrance. The guards saw his tabard and admitted him and his followers, all splashed and splattered with mud.

At Blyth's house they were given hot water and clean clothes, and then Merrivale and Peter joined Blyth in the solar. To the herald's surprise, Lady Mary was there too. 'Where is Tiphaine?' she demanded as soon as he entered.

'She is well,' Merrivale said, looking hard at Mary and hoping she would take the hint. 'I have some other news for you, too. When we left Warkworth this morning, Lord Percy and Sir Harry were preparing to march. They are on their way to join the army.'

Lady Mary closed her eyes with relief. 'Thank God,' Blyth said. He held out a handful of birdseed and the linnets fluttered down and began to eat from his hand. 'It is hard to doubt the loyalty of a man like Lord Percy, who has given so many years of service to the crown but… I had begun to wonder.'

'It turned out that he was simply making a point. He is not happy that Archbishop de la Zouche was appointed Warden instead of himself. Dragging his heels was a way of showing London his displeasure.'

Lady Mary looked at him. He ignored her. 'Not all the news is good,' he said. 'The Scottish army is on the march and has now crossed over the hills into Liddesdale. They are now within striking distance of Carlisle, and the only fortification between them and the city is Liddel Strength. And Liddel Strength's captain is one of the Disinherited.'

Peter sat listening in silence. His home valley of Tynedale had not yet been raided, but it was only a matter of time. 'They are going down the west side,' said Blyth. 'They will attack Cumberland and Lancashire next.'

'Possibly. They could just as easily turn east from Carlisle down the valley of the South Tyne and attack us here. I have had further confirmation of a plot to seize Newcastle. Rollond de Brus intends to have the town for himself.'

'Does he, by God?' said Blyth. 'If he tries, he'll have a fight on his hands.'

'It is difficult to fight against treason from within,' Merrivale said. 'Master Blyth, you volunteered to look at your fellow merchants and determine which, if any, might be in league with the Scots. I hate to press you, but time is growing short. Have you heard anything that might be useful?'

Blyth shook his hand gently and the birds flew away, trilling. He turned, dusting his hands. 'I have investigated all of my colleagues in the Guild Merchant, discreetly of course. I would stake my life on the fact that none of them is in contact with the Scots. However, I was reminded of your interest in Bruges. There has not been time, yet, to find any evidence of large transactions between England and Flanders. But increasingly, I suspect that some of the foreign merchants may not be entirely loyal.'

'Are there many of them in the town?'

'A dozen or more, trading under licence, plus some tradesmen and craftsmen. The most prominent is a cloth merchant named Kristoffer Tielt. He does business with a wide range of merchants and bankers in Bruges, including the man we mentioned earlier, Oppicius Adornes.'

'And does he have contacts in Scotland?' demanded Lady Mary.

'I don't know. But there is a large colony of Scottish merchants in Bruges, and it is entirely possible that he has business dealings with some of them. In fact, it would be surprising if he did not. I have written to my friends in Bruges to ask for more information.' Blyth looked unhappy. 'Unfortunately, this too takes time.'

'I understand,' Merrivale said. 'I appreciate everything you are doing for us.'

Blyth smiled. 'I have done precious little to deserve thanks. And of course, it is an honour to serve my king and queen.' A bell sounded from the hall below. 'Shall we go down and dine? It might be our last peaceful meal for some time.'

—

After dinner Blyth left them, pleading the necessity of work. 'A banker's day is never done,' he said. 'And war of course brings its own problems.'

Logs crackled in the fireplace, suffusing the room with welcome warmth. Outside, sunset was a wet pink glow over the western hills. Lady Mary looked at the herald. 'Where is she?'

Merrivale glanced around the room. 'I am sorry,' he said. 'But walls have ears. All I can say is she was well when I left her.'

'Oh, God,' said Mary in despair. 'I should never have let her out of my sight.'

'You must not blame yourself.'

'Of course I blame myself. I promised to look after her. Well, I'm not going back south again until I know she is safe and sound.'

He knew better by now than to argue with her. She leaned forward a little, her white wimple reflecting the firelight. 'Master Blyth said he had done precious little,' she said, her voice quiet. 'From what I have seen over the past few days, I would agree with him.'

'What do you mean?'

'I mean, for all his protestations of devoted service to the crown, he spends most of every day in his office, going through his account rolls. He hardly ever goes out.'

'Account rolls can be an excellent source of intelligence,' Merrivale said. 'I learned as much from the Chancery clerks in

London. They can follow a trail for miles through the parchments, checking and matching numbers.'

'I expect you are right. I just prefer more direct methods. What do you think about this man Tielt?'

'He is a possibility. I will call on him myself tomorrow.'

'Let me come with you. I can help.'

The herald shook his head. 'Thank you. But it is better I do this alone.'

Her lips compressed a little. 'That's your motto, isn't it? *It is better I do this alone.* No wonder Tiphaine gets angry with you.'

'Does she? Why?'

'Because you shut her out. You keep her at arm's length, even when you are... never mind,' she said hastily, seeing Peter listening with rapt attention. 'You wear that tabard like a suit of armour. Take off your harness sometimes, let your guard down, show her you are human.'

'She knows I am human,' the herald said. 'What is this about, my lady?'

'Honestly, men are so blind sometimes... Look, I know this is none of my business. I only met her a few weeks ago, but now that I know her, and know something of her history, I have come to care for her. I want to see her happy.'

'Yes,' said the herald. 'Believe me, my lady, that is my devout wish also.'

—

Later that night Peter knocked at the door of the herald's chamber. 'I hope I am not disturbing you, sir.'

'Of course not. Come in.'

Peter entered the room, closing the door behind him. 'Will the *demoiselle* be safe, sir?'

'As safe as any of us can be,' Merrivale said.

As a statement, it existed somewhere in the half-realm between truth and lies, and he suspected Peter knew it. The boy nodded. 'I am beginning to realise what a complex profession this is, sir.'

'It could be worse. I am protected by the laws of war, and I am paid well enough to afford servants and good wine. It is a better living than salt-panning, or raking coal from the sea.'

Peter smiled. 'I do enjoy your jests, sir. May I ask a question? What drew you down this path? Why did you become a herald?'

Merrivale paused for a moment. 'I never intended it,' he said. 'My family had lands on Dartmoor, but they lost them after the Great Famine. My mother and my sisters died then, and my father was left a broken man. A family friend took me into his household and managed to procure me a post at court. I became a King's Messenger, and served in that role for ten years.'

'That sounds exciting,' the boy said.

'A bit too exciting at times,' Merrivale said dryly. 'Unlike heralds, messengers aren't protected. The enemy regard us as fair game. I'd probably have continued as a messenger, but the Earl of Lancaster was going on a mission to Spain and asked if I would serve as his herald. Unlike you, I hadn't studied heraldry properly, so I had to learn quickly. Then, back at the start of the year, the king decided to appoint a herald to his son's household, and I was chosen.'

He looked at the boy. 'Now that you've seen what the job entails, do you still want it?'

'More than ever,' the boy said soberly. 'I'll be honest with you, sir, when I joined I thought being a herald was just a matter of knowing about coats and badges. I didn't realise what a service it was, nor what an honour it is to serve.'

'It is not always an honour,' Merrivale said.

Peter shook his head. 'I cannot agree with that, sir. To serve you will always be an honour, and a pleasure.'

Merrivale looked at his hands. 'I don't know what to say,' he said finally.

'You don't have to say anything, sir. I like to think I'm doing what my father would have done, had his health remained. I don't mean he would have become a herald, but he would have served, like I'm doing now. I want to make him proud of me, and I want to make you proud of me. That's all I ask.'

Merrivale smiled. 'I am proud of you,' he said. 'I owe you my life. And I'm damned sure your father is proud of you too. Go to bed, lad. Get some rest. God only knows what tomorrow will bring.'

Saughtree, 4ᵗʰ of October, 1346
Night

The rain had stopped in Liddesdale too, and a waning moon shone fitfully through gaps in the cloud, lighting the barren hills above the valley. Watchfires flickered along the banks of Liddel Water where the Scottish army lay camped. Lamps glowed in the pavilions of the nobles. Wrapped in a dark cloak with a hood covering her hair, Tiphaine crouched in the shadows behind a wagon, listening to the conversation in the nearest pavilion.

'The patrols have returned,' Brus was saying. 'Apart from Liddel Strength, which is defended, there is no other English force in sight. And Sir Walter Selby has orders to surrender Liddel Strength. The way to Carlisle is open.'

'Do we burn the town?' asked Douglas. They were speaking in French, the Scots with burred accents that would not have sounded out of place in Normandy.

Brus laughed. 'You did that last year, remember? They haven't even finished rebuilding yet. Let the townspeople pay a ransom and we will leave them in peace... for now. You'll have plenty of chances to squeeze them dry later, when you are lord of Cumberland.'

A third voice spoke, and she recognised Niall Bruce of Carrick. 'What about the Disinherited? Where are they now?'

'Safely hidden away where no one will find them. They're the surprise we'll spring later, when we confront Zouche and his little army.'

'Are you certain you can trust them? I'm still dubious about Umfraville and Wake. They have always been loyal to their king.'

'They won't have a king for much longer,' Brus said. 'My friends will see to that.'

'Your friends tried before and failed, you recall. I'll ask the question again. Can we trust Umfraville and Wake?'

'Body of Christ,' Brus said impatiently. 'Haven't you been listening, Carrick? One of the leaders of the Disinherited is also one of us. He's been at the centre of the plot, right from the beginning. He'll bring the others along.'

In the shadows, Tiphaine felt her heart beat a little more quickly. The herald had said there were five leaders of the Disinherited: Umfraville, Wake, Selby, Clennell and de Lisle. Robert de Lisle was infirm, and besides he had sent his son to join Merrivale. But one of the other four was part of the larger conspiracy, and was in league with the man from the north. And Walter Selby had promised to betray an English castle to the Scots; at least, she had heard Brus demand it of him, that night at Berwick, and he had not refused.

She had to get away and report this. She rose to her feet and turned, and almost collided with another woman walking past the wagon. In the wash of moonlight she caught a glimpse of a pale face framed by the hood of a fur-trimmed cloak, and she turned to run. She was too late; the other woman caught her by the wrist and held her. 'You, girl! What are you doing here?'

'Let me go,' Tiphaine hissed and she tried to pull free but another woman, a tirewoman, hurried up and seized her other arm. Grimly, Tiphaine prepared to fight them, but then to her horror she heard Brus's voice close at hand. 'What is going on here?'

'This servant girl was loitering outside your pavilion, my lord,' said the first woman.

'Was she, by God?' Brus took a long step towards Tiphaine and ripped the hood back from her face. She looked up, and saw the moonlit face of her former lover and betrayer.

The next moment she doubled up in agony as Brus's fist slammed into the pit of her stomach. Dropping to her knees, she barely felt the blow to her head that knocked her sprawling to the ground. 'Treason!' Bruce snarled, and he kicked her where she lay. Fresh pain washed through her body. She lay still, unable to move or even think.

'Who is this girl?' Douglas demanded.

'I recognise her,' said the woman. 'She is one of the Countess of Dunbar's servants.'

'She is no servant,' Brus said. 'She is a traitorous whore and an English spy. Burn her.'

Panic stronger than pain seized Tiphaine. She tried to struggle up and Brus knocked her down again. 'Hold fast, my lord!' the woman said sharply. 'I do not know what this girl was doing, but let her explain herself! Or let her mistress the countess explain for her. You cannot simply execute her out of hand.'

'I can, and I damned well will,' Brus said.

Swiftly the woman stepped across Tiphaine's body. 'You cannot touch her without laying a hand on me. And you know who I am.'

Shivering, Tiphaine lay on the ground, listening. 'I know who you are, Madame de Béthune,' Brus said grimly. 'I shall be interested to hear what your husband makes of your behaviour, when he learns of it.'

'What passes between my husband and me is no concern of yours,' the woman said coolly. 'May I suggest you send for the Countess of Dunbar?'

'She is here,' said Agnes, coming out of the darkness. 'What have you done to my servant? Rise, girl.'

Painfully, Tiphaine rose to her feet. A small crowd had gathered, attracted by the noise, and she saw the bright tabard of Lyon Herald. Robert Keith the Marischal was there too, along with the countess's brother, Moray. 'I have done nothing wrong, my lady,' she said.

Brus sneered at her. 'Explain who this girl is and how she came into your service,' he demanded.

'Her name is Flora,' the countess said calmly. 'She was formerly in service to the nuns of the priory at Eccles, which is in the patronage of my husband. While we were camped at Jedburgh, I sent to the prioress and asked her to find me another servant.'

'Lies,' Brus said. 'Her name is Tiphaine de Tesson, she is from Normandy, and her father is an executed traitor. And she is the whore of the English herald, Merrivale.'

Tiphaine spat him. 'I was your whore once, Brus. Since then, I have belonged to no man.'

'Face me,' Agnes said.

Tiphaine turned and looked into her eyes. She saw nothing there; no pity, no emotion at all. The countess could not save her. She had made the ultimate mistake of getting caught, and now she would pay the price alone.

'Is this true?' the countess said, her voice level. 'Are you who the Seigneur de Brus says you are?'

'I am,' Tiphaine said steadily.

Brus nodded. 'You heard my order. Make a pyre and burn her.'

'No!' said the Countess of Béthune sharply. 'She is only a girl! For God's sake, have pity on her!'

You should have thought of that before you exposed me, Tiphaine thought darkly, but Lyon Herald was stepping forward. 'We must have due process of law,' he said.

'I agree,' said the Marischal. 'The girl has admitted her identity, but there is no proof yet of her treason. Confine her, keep her safe, and when there is time there will be a proper trial.'

He turned to Douglas. 'Your castle of the Hermitage is not far from here. We will send her there for safekeeping, and summon her when we are ready. My lord of Brus, have you any objection?'

'No,' Brus said. He looked at Douglas. The latter winked.

'Allow me to add a further suggestion, my lord,' said Moray. 'The Countess of Dunbar employed this woman, and brought her into our midst. When she is tried, let the countess her mistress be put on trial along with her. And if it transpires that the countess knew of her treason and consented to it, then let them both burn together.'

Agnes turned on him, dark eyes spitting fire. 'Next time someone threatens to hang you, *brother*, I will pay them to finish the job.'

'Enough!' commanded the Marischal. 'You will show unity in the face of the enemy, my lords, or the king will know the reason why. Take this woman to the Hermitage. Make it so.'

Two of Douglas's hobelars bound her hands in front of her and lifted her roughly into the saddle of a horse. One took the reins and led her mount, the other followed behind. They splashed across the shallow river and up the far bank, Tiphaine clinging to the pommel and feeling the leather thong around her wrists already rubbing raw. West of the river the ground rose steeply into hills cut with deep valleys, down which burns bubbled and flowed. Hurrying clouds scudded across the moon, plunging the hills into sudden shadow.

She knew there would be no trial. Douglas's wink had told her as much. She would go to this place called the Hermitage, and she would die there. Her body ached from where Brus had beaten her, but she barely noticed. All her mind was running on one thing; how to escape before she and her escort reached their destination. She thought of simply kicking the horse and riding hard away, but the leading rider still held her reins, and the one behind would run her through with his lance before she could escape.

The moon was still obscured. She saw the hills above her, autumn grass pale in the moonlight, and realised they were near the summit. Beside her the ground dropped steeply away towards a burn bubbling invisible at the bottom; how deep or how steep the slope was she could not tell, for all was in shadow. She had only a limited idea of where she was. Even if she could escape, the Scots would hunt her down.

Maybe. But better that than whatever fate Brus and Douglas intended for her. She took a deep breath, expecting to feel a lance point in her back at any moment, and then twisted her body and fell sideways out of the saddle and down the slope.

Her shoulders hit the ground first with a shock that drove the air out of her lungs, and then she was tumbling over and over, trying desperately to use her bound hands to shield her head. The burn came up sooner than expected; she landed half in water and half on a muddy bank and lay gasping, trying to decide if any important bones were broken. From above she could hear shouting. 'Get after her, Tam!'

'What do you think I'm doing? Christ, it's black as the pit down here.' She heard boots on the slope above her, sliding on scree, and kept her head down as far as possible, praying the moon would remain hidden. Her prayer was answered; the little valley remained inky black. Her pursuer passed a few yards away without seeing the body huddled on the edge of the burn.

'She's probably broken her neck!' Tam called over the noise of water.

'Don't bet on it. Come on, let's look downstream.'

She heard Tam move away, swearing as he slipped on wet rocks. The other man, still mounted, was riding along the top of the slope; she saw him once, silhouetted dim against the clouds as he peered over the bank. Hoping the water in the burn would cover any noises she made, Tiphaine struggled to her feet. Every part of her body hurt, except where the icy water had numbed her. On all fours, struggling with the bonds on her wrists, she climbed slowly back up the slope. After what seemed like hours of pain, she reached the top just as the moon slid out from behind the cloud wrack.

The moon showed her the hobelar, still on horseback, a quarter of a mile away down the hill. It also showed her own mount, standing nearby and cropping grass. The horse raised its head as she approached, but did not stir. With the last of her strength she raised her bound hands to grasp the pommel and drag herself into the saddle. There she leaned forward, resting for a moment with the horse's mane in her face, struggling to stay conscious.

The inner steel that had kept her alive for two years in solitary confinement came to her rescue. She raised her head, looking at the moon and the surrounding hills and valleys. The river where the army lay camped, she knew, was Liddel Water, and Agnes had told her it ran south-west towards the English border. Once over the border, if she could find a farm or a bastel house she could rest for a while and find a fresh horse, and perhaps also directions to Newcastle. What she had learned must not be lost. Simon had to know.

Tiphaine kicked the horse and it moved, reluctantly at first; kicking it harder eventually roused it to a canter. Riding south-west across the hills, keeping the river to her left, she looked around for Scottish patrols but saw nothing. Behind her, torches flickered like tiny points of light; the enemy had discovered that her horse was missing and were searching for her in strength. She kicked the horse again, clinging to its mane with all her strength. If she fell now and the horse went on without her, she was dead.

Time passed. She slowed the horse a little to let it rest, which was a mistake because the animal stopped altogether and stubbornly refused to go on. It took her several minutes of kicking and prodding to get it moving again. The hills were growing lower, and now a flat plain opened out in front of her with another river winding down from the west.

She pushed the horse on, determined to get across the border at all costs. The moon passed its zenith and sank in the west. Once the clouds cleared the night air grew cold, and she was glad of the warmth of the horse. Her body ached, her bound wrists were burning and raw, and her brain felt numb. Once she fell asleep and nearly dropped from the saddle; panicked, she clung on again and kicked the horse back into a canter. She searched the country ahead of her, looking for any form of shelter.

Lights ahead, a yellow flicker on the edge of vision. Had she imagined it? No, there it was again; more of them, lights twinkling like a vision of hope. She turned the horse towards them, seeing a high bank on the south side of Liddel Water and a tower on top of that, surrounded by walls. Torches burned along the ramparts. The south side of the river; that meant the castle was English. They would give her shelter; they had to.

The horse was stumbling with weariness, but she urged it carefully across the stony bed of the river and up to the castle gates, hearing men calling from the ramparts overhead as she crossed the drawbridge. Somehow she managed to climb down from the horse without falling, and stood looking up at the faces of the watchmen. 'Please,' she said. 'Help me. I am the Demoiselle de Tesson from Normandy, and my father served your king. The Scots are pursuing me. For the love of God, give me shelter.'

A postern in the main gate opened. A man-at-arms, clad in armour and mail with a surcoat decorated with black and gold bars, stepped out. She looked into his face and froze with horror. She had seen that face before, in the ruined church outside Berwick. It was Sir Walter Selby, one of the leaders of the Disinherited, and his sword was pointed directly at her heart.

21

Liddel Strength, 5ᵗʰ of October, 1346
Early morning

'Where did you come from?' Selby demanded. 'How did you get here?'

'The Scottish camp. I escaped.' She waited for his reaction.

Selby sheathed his sword. 'Inside, quickly.' He took Tiphaine's arm and she stumbled and started to fall. The knight caught her before she hit the ground, scooping her up in his arms and carrying her through the postern, shouting at his men to fetch the horse inside. The next few minutes were a semi-conscious blur, and by the time she came to she was sitting in a chair in a small stone hall, next to a fire. Someone was untying the filthy leather strap around her wrist and applying salve to the raw wounds beneath. Selby poured wine into a wooden cup and handed it to her. 'Drink this. Slowly.'

She sipped the wine and felt warmth begin to return to her body; and with it, the aches and pains and bruises. 'You are Sir Walter Selby,' she said.

'How do you know my name?'

She did not answer. 'The Scottish army is coming,' she said. 'They think you will open the gates to them.'

'They are wrong,' Selby said abruptly. 'If the Scots come here, I will fight them to the bitter end.'

'Your comrades, the Disinherited. Where are they?'

Selby made an impatient gesture. 'I do not know,' he said. 'Why do you ask?'

Tiphaine knew she had to trust him; there was no choice. 'I must send a letter to Simon Merrivale, the herald. I have urgent information for him. Can you help me?'

'Bring her what she needs, Will,' Selby said to the young man who had been salving her wrists. 'Fetch a candle too.'

Will smiled and rose to his feet, unlocking a wooden chest and bringing out a writing set, placing it on a small table before her while Selby watched. She wrote, her head swimming and the letters on the parchment blurring together. She could have given a verbal message, but until a few minutes ago she had thought Selby was the man involved in the conspiracy; for all she knew he might still be, and this was some sort of elaborate trap. If it was, she could not think of a way out of it.

When she had finished writing, the young man called Will dusted the parchment to dry the ink and then folded it and placed a blob of candlewax on the edge. He guided her hand while she sealed it. 'Where is the herald?' Selby asked.

'Newcastle,' she said, feeling the world spin. 'At the house of a merchant named Blyth.'

'I know him. Will,' he said to the young man, 'ride hard. Return here as soon as you are done.'

Will left the hall. 'He is my son,' Selby said. 'He will see your message gets through.' Then his voice faded away and Tiphaine lost consciousness.

Newcastle-upon-Tyne, 5th of October, 1346
Evening

Kristoffer Tielt, merchant of Bruges based in Newcastle, was a tall thin man with long arms and legs who reminded Merrivale of a spider. His expensive black clothes emphasised the likeness still further. 'I fear I cannot tell you anything of importance,' he said.

'Cannot, or will not?' Merrivale asked.

'I cannot tell what I do not know. One hears rumours, of course. They might be true, they might not.'

'Tell me what they are, and I will decide.'

Tielt looked unhappy. 'It is said that some of the merchants have banded together and bribed officers of the garrison. When the Scots come, these officers will open the gates and admit them. The property of the merchants will be protected, while the rest of the town is pillaged.'

'Are you one of those whose property will be safe?'

Tielt gazed at him. 'What do you think? Whenever there is trouble or unrest, the mobs turn against the foreign merchants. No, my property is not protected, and I would not expect it to be. I can tell you further that whenever any town or city is threatened by the enemy, these same rumours always emerge. When in doubt, blame the foreign merchants.'

It was true, of course; Merrivale had heard the same rumour in other times and other places. He had been hearing it again all day from Mauro, Warin and Peter who had gone out to listen to the gossip in the marketplace and taverns, and from the captain of the guard and his officers and the other leaders of the Guild Merchant. He had come to see Tielt last of all because, like Blyth, the other merchants had been keen to point the finger at the foreigners. Everything he had heard could be true, he thought, or it could be fiction; or dust, thrown in his eyes to distract him from some other plot.

'You are a merchant of Bruges, Heer Tielt,' the herald said. 'Have you ever done business with Oppicius Adornes?'

Tielt smiled briefly. 'I have dealt with representatives of his house, yes. Never the man himself.'

'Why not?'

'You mistake both my importance and my wealth, Sir Herald. Adornes only deals with the biggest names, the richest bankers and the international traders who buy and sell in bulk. I am a humble importer of spices. I doubt if Adornes even knows of my existence.'

Merrivale nodded. 'Do you have business interests in Scotland?'

'Yes, I have partners in Leith and Dunfermline. I can supply you with their names if you wish.'

'Thank you. Does that not put you at risk? If the populace knew you were trading with the enemy, they would not be happy.'

'That is because they are ignorant. A few bales of pepper or casks of alum will not help Scotland win the war. Nor am I alone. Ask the members of the Guild Merchant the same question. They will say no, of course, but they will be lying. Newcastle thrives on the Scottish trade. Without it, the town would wither away.'

'Which gives the merchants plenty of motive for opening the gates,' Merrivale said.

Tielt nodded. 'You understand.'

On my list of potential traitors, the herald thought, *I shall place Tielt's name near the bottom.* Of all the people he had spoken to today, Tielt was the one most likely to be telling the truth, or at least part of it. Deep in thought, he walked back through the streets to Marygate, seeing the flare of torches on the walls and hearing the tramp of sentries along the stone ramparts. *Newcastle sleeps uneasily*, he thought.

At the Blyth house, Lady Mary and Peter de Lisle were waiting for him in the hall. Both were wide-eyed with alarm. With them was a young man in a mail coat and surcoat splattered with mud. 'Sir Herald? My name is Will Selby, and I am sent by my father from Liddel Strength.'

Merrivale checked. 'Sir Walter Selby is at Liddel Strength?'

'Yes, sir. The Demoiselle de Tesson is there too. I bring you a letter from her.'

Merrivale tensed. Taking the letter, he broke the seal and read the weak, faint writing. 'She has discovered something about the Disinherited,' he said. 'Something she was too worried or too frightened to write down. She needs to see me.'

'Is she well?' asked Peter.

'She is exhausted and suffering from cuts and bruises,' said Selby. 'The Scots were not kind to her, but they did her no grave injury.'

'How far is it to Liddel Strength?'

'Sixty miles, sir. We can change horses along the way.'

'No, you've done enough. Stay here and rest.'

The young man shook his head. 'You'll need a guide, sir. It's rough country out west, and the Scottish army is in Liddesdale, not far away.' He smiled. 'Honestly sir, I'm fresh as a flower.'

He had ridden sixty miles, and was preparing to ride sixty more. *They breed them tough on the borders*, Merrivale thought. 'All right. Peter, find Mauro and Warin and tell them we are riding. Lady Mary, if you are determined to remain, can I ask you to keep watch on the merchants?'

'Isn't that Master Blyth's job?'

'It is. Master Blyth is a generous host and an excellent merchant and banker, but I have some doubts about his skills as an investigator. Don't go out of your way, but if you do learn anything I would be grateful.'

'He spends too much time feeding those blasted birds,' she said. 'Tell Tiphaine I want to see her again as soon as possible. And if she promises to behave in future, I *may* decide not to turn her over my knee and spank her.'

The herald smiled a little. 'I will give her your love.'

Liddel Strength, 6ᵗʰ of October, 1346
Dawn

They had followed the Carlisle road through the cold moonlight, but in the small hours they had veered off to the north-west, passing Lanercost Priory and climbing up over the shoulder of the Bewcastle Wastes. Here Merrivale was glad of a guide, for even with the moon it would have been easy to get lost amid those harsh hills and fells. First light found them descending towards the coastal plain, the waters of Solway Firth gleaming in the far distance.

The Scots caught them a mile from the castle. There were about a dozen of them, reavers come in advance of the main army to burn and plunder, and they came racing across the field with lowered lances, yelling with glee. 'Ride hard,' Will Selby said, and he touched spurs to his tired horse, the others following suit. They fled over the fields towards the castle, its torches pale sparks in the growing light, but halfway there Selby's horse stumbled and went down in a thrashing kicking heap, throwing its rider clear.

'Ride on!' Merrivale shouted at Peter and the others, and he turned his horse, seeing Selby's mount struggling to its feet and Will Selby himself on all fours, dragging his leg at an awkward angle. The young man saw him turn, and gestured towards the castle. 'Get out of it!' he screamed. 'Go! Quickly!'

The reavers were racing towards him. Even if Merrivale could drag a man with a broken leg over the back of his horse, they would never outrun the pursuit. Selby was still down on all fours, hanging his head in pain, but then he looked up again. 'Find the demoiselle, sir,' he said. 'That's all that matters. Tell my father I did my duty.'

Lashing his horse with his riding crop, Merrivale turned again and galloped towards the distant castle. Glancing back he saw Selby surrounded by a little group of horsemen. Two had broken away from the rest and were pursuing him, lances lowered. Border reavers lived on the edge of the law and beyond it; if they caught him, his herald's tabard would mean nothing. Up ahead he saw the gates of the castle swing open and the drawbridge come down. Mauro and Warin rode into the castle but Peter halted his horse at the end of the drawbridge, jumping down from the saddle and stringing his bow. He could hear the hooves of the pursuing horsemen now; they had stopped shouting and were grimly silent, intent on riding him down.

He saw Peter raise his bow. There were archers on the ramparts too, and arrows whickered in the air. He heard the thud of one striking home, and when he looked back he saw a body on the ground; the other pursuer was wheeling and riding back out of range. In the far distance the rest of the Scots were still clustered around Will Selby; it was impossible to tell if he was dead or alive. Merrivale slapped his horse on the neck and the exhausted animal cantered over the drawbridge and stopped dead in the courtyard, covered in lather and head hanging down. Merrivale dismounted, stumbling a little with weariness himself, and someone threw a bucket of water over the horse to cool it down. The drawbridge rose, groaning, and the gates slammed shut.

Walter Selby came down from the ramparts, mail coat and the bars on his surcoat gleaming in the morning light. 'What happened?'

Merrivale told him. 'I don't think it was an ambush, just a chance encounter with a raiding party. Pure bad fortune. Sir Walter, I am deeply grieved about your son.'

'He's still alive,' Selby said abruptly. 'I saw them just now, putting him on the back of a horse. Perhaps he'll turn out to be the fortunate one. I'll take you to the lady.'

Tiphaine was sitting before the fire in the hall, wrapped in blankets. She was still white with exhaustion, her skin almost translucent apart from the livid bruises and the raw red chafing on her wrists. 'Here I am,' she said, looking up at the herald. 'In trouble again.'

'We'll get you out of it,' Merrivale said. Peter had come in behind him, still carrying his bow. 'How are you?'

'I feel like I have been crushed by a millstone. I slept all day yesterday, but I can still barely move.'

'Then don't move,' the herald said smiling. 'Now, what is this news you have for me?'

'I overheard Brus talking about the Disinherited. One of their leaders is part of the conspiracy, and has been from the beginning. Simon... we have talked about the man from the north. Could this be him?'

In spite of his weariness and lack of sleep, Merrivale could feel his nerves tingling. 'Possibly. But there are strong indications that the man from the north is someone close to the king, which doesn't sound like any of the Disinherited.' He paused. 'Did Brus say who it was?'

'The others have doubts about Umfraville and Wake. That doesn't mean it's not them, of course, but it sounded like either Clennell or Sir Walter Selby. But Sir Walter gave me shelter, and helped me send a message to you. He sent his own son.'

'Yes.' Merrivale did not tell her what had happened to Will Selby. 'How did they discover you?'

'I was careless,' Tiphaine said. 'The countess could do nothing to save me.' Briefly, she told him the story of her escape. 'Brus wanted to burn me. Again.'

Merrivale bent and kissed her gently on the forehead. 'You are safe now,' he said. 'Rest, and recoup your strength. I will talk to Selby.'

He found Selby in the inner bailey overseeing his men as they laid out weapons and bundles of arrows, drew buckets of water from the well for fighting fires and carried up baskets of stone shot for the castle's single catapult. 'Sir Walter, I am deeply grateful to you for everything you have done. As soon as the *demoiselle* is able to travel, we will depart.'

'I can spare you no men for an escort,' Selby said. 'With Will gone, I now have forty-one men to defend this place, including myself.'

The herald nodded. 'Of course, I would not ask it of you. Sir Walter... might I speak with you a moment?'

They walked away from the others, past the little stone chapel huddled in the shadow of the castle keep. 'You and the other Disinherited met the Seigneur de Brus at Berwick,' Merrivale said. 'Did he instruct you to surrender Liddel Strength to the enemy?'

'He did. This castle bars the way to Carlisle. It must be reduced or taken before the Scots can advance.'

Merrivale glanced around. 'But I see you are preparing to fight.'

'Yes,' Selby said curtly. 'Let me spare you the trouble of asking more questions. I was never comfortable with what Brus proposed, nor was I certain we could trust him. His behaviour during the meeting at Berwick increased my suspicions. After the meeting broke up, I told the others I was going my own way.'

'What did they say?'

'Clennell begged me to change my mind. He even offered to go back to Brus and see if they could pay me more money, or give me some additional lands. I said no, I was done with the whole thing.'

'Why was Clennell so adamant, do you think?'

'God knows. He kept repeating that we all had to stick together. I got the feeling he has more to lose than the others, but I don't know what.'

A voice from the top of the keep shouted, '*My lord! They are coming!*'

–

By the time Selby and the herald climbed to the top of the keep, the plain north of the river was alive with colour and motion. Columns of mounted men-at-arms were coming over the fields, armour and mail sparkling in the sun, their coats and banners of red and blue, black and white and gold all gleaming in the strong light. Behind them came wedges of foot soldiers, spearmen from Galloway, archers from Lothian and Fife, highlanders with heavy swords and shields strapped to their backs. Clouds of border hobelars and other light cavalry streamed out from the flanks of the approaching army; the nearest, half a mile away, were already fording the river and racing down to cut the castle off from the south.

In a few more minutes, the castle would be surrounded.

Merrivale turned to Selby, who was staring grimly at the oncoming army. 'I shall postpone my departure,' he said quietly. 'I believe, Sir Walter, that you may need the services of a herald.'

22

Liddel Strength, 6ᵗʰ of October, 1346
Late morning

Given a larger garrison, Merrivale thought, Liddel Strength could have held out for several weeks. The centre of the position was the keep, a square tower built on an earth motte and protected on the north by a precipitous drop into the river. Below it was the inner bailey, containing the hall and chapel and protected by high stone ramparts with another tower over the gatehouse leading to the outer bailey; the catapult was located on its roof platform. The outer bailey was enclosed by a wooden palisade with a broad wall-walk and yet another stone tower protecting the main gate. Both inner wall and palisade were protected by deep fosses.

The problem was that with forty-two men Selby did not have enough strength to man all the walls and towers. Forty-two, because Peter de Lisle had insisted on joining the defenders. 'I have a bow, sir, and I'm a good shot.'

'I know you are,' said Merrivale. 'But you are also training to be a herald.'

'Yes, sir. With your permission, I should like to take leave of my post for a short time.'

Why do I surround myself with stubborn people? Merrivale wondered. Tiphaine was just the same. Despite instructions to rest, she had struggled up onto the wall-walk to watch the approaching army. She saw Brus's red saltire among the coats of arms, but did not flinch. 'Why haven't you gone?' she asked. 'Your herald's tabard is your passport, you say it all the time.'

'And usually I am right,' Merrivale said. 'But Brus wants to kill both of us. When we go, we will go under a proper flag of truce, with an escort I trust.'

Most of the Scottish army was over the river by now, with only a few companies left on the north bank in case the garrison should try to break out that way. Slowly, jostling for position, the men-at-arms and spearmen and archers closed in on the castle, advancing with deliberate calm under bright banners flapping in the sunlight.

A trumpet sounded. The advancing ranks shuffled to a halt. From the direction of the king's standard came a single man on foot, unarmed, with a wooden staff in his hand and wearing a brilliant glittering tabard with the red lion of Scotland on a field of gold. 'My old friend Lyon Herald,' Merrivale said. 'With your permission, Sir Walter, I shall go to meet him.'

He turned to Selby. 'You are forty men against twelve thousand. No one would think it dishonourable if you surrendered.'

Selby rubbed his long chin. 'You're right, of course. I want a safe-conduct for myself and my men to Carlisle. And I want my son back.'

Merrivale waited while the drawbridge was lowered, and then stepped out through the postern and walked across the bridge towards his opposite number, waiting on the other side.

Lyon Herald's eyes opened in surprise. 'Sim! What the devil are you doing here?'

'Running an errand,' Merrivale said pleasantly. 'How are you, Archie? How is the campaign going so far?'

'A lot of floundering around in the rain up until now.' The other man glanced up at the sky. 'We might see some action now the weather's improved.'

'What have you come to tell me?'

Lyon Herald cleared his throat. He seemed uncomfortable, Merrivale thought. 'His Grace demands that Liddel Strength be surrendered to him immediately, with all its weapons and goods. The surrender must be unconditional.'

Merrivale shook his head. 'Sir Walter Selby demands that his men be allowed to withdraw to Carlisle, with all their weapons and accoutrements. He also asks that his son, who was taken prisoner earlier this morning, be returned to him.'

'Sorry, Sim. The king won't have it, and neither will the Seigneur de Brus. I can offer a safe-conduct for you and your attendants, but that is all.'

In the distance behind Lyon Herald a wagon had drawn up and two men were unloading a long bundle wrapped in canvas. 'That is against the rules of war,' Merrivale said. 'If a garrison surrenders before the fighting starts, they must be allowed to withdraw safely. Come on, Archie, you know that.'

'Aye,' said Graham unhappily. 'But that's what the king is saying, Sim, and that's what Brus is saying. They're accusing Selby of being a traitor. They want him dead.'

'And they want a fight,' Merrivale said. 'They want to blood the army, give them a victory to lift spirits. If I take up your safe-conduct, the Demoiselle de Tesson comes with me.'

Graham looked even more unhappy. 'Sorry, Sim. There's another condition to the safe conduct. You must surrender the *demoiselle* to us.'

The two men carrying the bundle were drawing closer. Both had white kerchiefs, flags of truce, wrapped around their arms. 'Surrender her? Really? Do the laws of war in Scotland now approve of murdering young women out of hand?'

Graham said nothing, but he looked deeply unhappy. 'There are no circumstances under which I am prepared to hand her over,' Merrivale said. 'I will not send this woman to her death.'

Lyon Herald spread his hands. 'That's it. It's the safe-conduct for you alone, or nothing. Sorry, Sim.'

'On your heads be it,' said Merrivale. 'The walls are strong, and the garrison is large and well-armed. Taking this place will not be easy. If your king changes his mind and wants to offer new terms, I will be waiting.'

'I'll bear it in mind,' said Graham.

'What about Sir Walter's son? Do you have any news of him?'

Lyon Herald was not listening. The other two men had halted at the edge of the fosse. Unwrapping the canvas, they lifted something heavy and threw it into the mud at the bottom of the ditch. It was a man's corpse, stripped of the armour he had once worn, his shirt stained deep red where the sword blades had bitten into his flesh over and over again. He had been slashed across the head too, and his face was caked with dried blood, but it was still possible to recognise Will Selby, the captain's son.

The silence seemed to go on forever. 'I knew nothing of this,' Graham said.

Merrivale turned on him. 'Then you should have known, Archie,' he said violently. 'One of the duties of a herald is to intercede for unarmed prisoners, to make sure they are treated well. You failed. You allowed that boy to be murdered, when he had a broken leg and was in no condition to harm anyone. Brus uses you like a tool, just like he uses the king.'

He pointed to the red lion rampant. 'You are a disgrace to that tabard and the office you hold. I had thought better of you, Archie. I really had.'

Silently, Graham bowed and turned away. The two men who had carried the corpse followed him. Merrivale turned to the horrified Englishmen looking down from the ramparts. 'Fetch the body in,' he said. 'We can at least lay him to rest.'

Liddel Strength, 6th of October, 1346
Evening

They laid out the body of Will Selby in the little chapel before the altar. There was no priest to say prayers for him but Selby knelt by the body, closing his eyes and gripping his son's hand silently for a moment. Then he rose, and when he opened his eyes they were bright and hard.

'Come,' he said. 'We have work to do.'

Despite their overwhelming numbers the Scots did not attack immediately; perhaps, Merrivale thought, Lyon Herald had believed him about the garrison. As the day wore on the enemy made camp and parties of men began scouring the countryside; not burning this time but wrecking, tearing down houses and barns, byres and walls and dragging loads of timber and stone back to their lines.

Inside the castle Selby's men were equally busy. The armoury had plenty of breastplates and helmets, far more than the garrison needed. It was Mauro who showed them how to make mannekins of straw and dress them in armour, posting them in embrasures around the ramparts. Peter cut the captain's bedsheets into the shapes of banners, painted them with the arms of several prominent Cumberland families and paraded them gleefully around the walls. Tiphaine helped him, limping a little. 'I have to do something,' she said.

The rest of the garrison polished their weapons, checked the fletchings of their arrows and honed their sword blades to razor sharpness on the grindstone. They brought out jars of oil and struck rags in them for wicks, and carried more stones up onto the ramparts and piled them in heaps. Then they waited.

As the sun sank over the Solway Firth, Selby went into the chapel and sat for a few minutes, alone with the body of his son. Then he called his men together in the inner bailey. The herald and Tiphaine stood to one side, watching.

'There is one thing we can be certain of,' Selby said. 'We are going to die here.'

The grief for his son was plain in his face, but he stood straight and tall, hand on the hilt of his sword. 'The enemy have made it clear, through the herald, that they intend to show us no mercy. These are the last days, possibly the last hours, of our lives. Understand that, and know what it means. We have no priest to shrive us but we can at least pray, and hope God listens.'

The men watched him in silence. 'But we will not die easily,' Selby said. 'The Scots cannot advance on Carlisle until they have taken this castle, and they cannot advance further until Carlisle falls or surrenders. Every hour of resistance gives Archbishop de la Zouche more time to gather his army and march north. Every hour we fight increases the chance of victory. So, let us sell our lives dearly.

'One day they will sing songs about the defence of Liddel Strength, and the forty-two heroes who defended it to the end. Let's make those songs damned good ones.'

'We will, my lord,' an archer said quietly. 'For you, and for your son.'

After a moment of silence, Selby nodded. 'Good. Now, light the kitchen fires and get some food. It's going to be a long night.'

Newcastle-upon-Tyne, 6th of October, 1346
Evening

Lady Mary had been afflicted with a touch of rheum for the last couple of days, which she thought was probably quite useful. No one ever suspected the motives of a woman with a pink nose.

After dinner she put on a cloak, summoned her maidservant and went out. The cool evening air made her eyes water and her nose stream, and she wondered briefly if this was a good idea. After all, the herald had said she should not go out of her way, whatever that meant. But he had also asked her to keep watch on the merchants, without actually saying what he wanted her to do. Typically vague male instructions, she thought.

Blyth had told her the names of all the members of the Guild Merchant, and assured her once again that they were innocent. *That could be true*, she thought, *or else they are all bound up in the plot together; either way, I will get nothing out of them.* The only other name she had was that of Kristoffer Tielt, the merchant from Bruges.

'I don't think Tielt is involved,' the herald had said before he rode away. 'But that doesn't mean none of the foreign merchants are.' She had thought of asking Blyth for more details about the

237

foreign merchants, but wondered how reliable his information would be if it came through the Guild Merchant. Instead, she decided to go and see Tielt herself and ask him.

The merchant received her in his solar, a bright painted room with a coal fire burning on the brick hearth. 'It is an honour to welcome you to my home,' he said, bowing. 'How may I serve you, my lady?'

'I would like to buy a pot of saffron, please,' Lady Mary said brightly.

'You could have sent your servant to do that,' Tielt said.

The shutters had come down behind his eyes. *So much for my theory about women with pink noses*, Lady Mary thought. 'I also wanted to talk to you. The herald, Simon Merrivale, came to see you yesterday. He said he had a very interesting conversation with you.'

'I told him everything I know.'

She gazed at him, feeling her sinuses filling up. This was not going at all well, she thought.

'I understand your feelings, Heer Tielt. It cannot be easy for you as a foreign merchant – ah-*choo!*' She paused, taking a square of linen from her reticule and blowing her nose. 'I do beg your pardon,' she said. 'It cannot be easy for you. Distrusted by the populace, disliked by your rival merchants from the town, aware that any moment a stroke of the royal pen could expel you from the kingdom. I think it is quite wrong that you should have so few rights or liberties.'

Tielt crossed his long arms over his chest. 'What is your point, my lady?'

'My point is that, given the situation, you are unlikely to say everything you know to a royal official,' she said. 'To a herald, for example.'

'I can assure you I gave him my full cooperation,' Tielt said.

'I'm sure you answered every question he asked you, yes. You would have been unwise not to. But knowledge is power, Heer Tielt. Knowing things other people don't know gives you a shield, a defence. And that is why I am here,' she said, fighting back another sneeze. 'I have come to find out what you are holding back.'

Tielt looked at her. 'If I didn't tell the herald everything I know, what makes you think I will tell you? You are his friend.'

'I'm not, really,' she said. 'I met him by chance last month, and saw him again when he came to Newcastle. I don't know him at all well.'

'You don't know him well, yet you reside under the same roof as him, in the house of William Blyth.'

'Yes.' She caught something in the tone of his voice, and her fuddled brain cleared for a moment. 'It's not the herald, is it? It's Master Blyth. You don't trust him, and you think he might have sent me to spy on you.'

Tielt pursed his lips. 'Did he?'

'May I tell you a secret, Heer Tielt? I don't like people who keep birds indoors, as pets. They should be allowed to fly free. Don't you think?'

'Blyth is a wealthy man. He can do what he wants.'

'Yes, bankers usually do… As a matter of curiosity, do you know how he made his money? Was he always a moneylender, or did he start off as a general merchant, like so many do?'

'I regret to say I don't know,' Tielt said. 'Beyond Master Blyth himself, I doubt if anyone does. All I know is that he rose very far, very quickly. It is strange, is it not, how fast these men rise? De la Pole, Pulteney, Blyth, Gilbert de Tracey; one moment they are down in the mud with the rest of us, the next they are among the mighty, bankers to the king, royal councillors, knights. Fortune's wheel is kind to them, I think.'

'It hasn't been kind to Tracey,' Lady Mary said. 'Are you jealous of Blyth? Do you envy him his fortune?'

'If I am honest, yes,' Tielt said after a moment. 'But you were right, my lady. I don't trust him. You see, his antecedents are not so different from my own. And I don't know what happened to make him into the man he is now.'

'Tell me,' Lady Mary said gently.

'Blyth is twenty years younger than me. He does not know it, I think, but we were born in the same street in Bruges. His mother was a woman of the city, and his father was an English trader who had settled there. I was already living here in Newcastle, my business well established, when Blyth senior and his son returned from Bruges and started a new venture here. The father died not long after, and his son took over his business.'

'Did he inherit a fortune?'

'No, not at all. The business was no larger than my own. But somehow, in the space of a few fortunate years, Blyth secured royal patronage and became the most powerful and wealthy banker in the north of England.'

'You think there was corruption involved,' Lady Mary said.

'It is not for me to say.'

'Well, it would hardly be surprising. I doubt very much if any of the men you mentioned climbed to the top of the greasy pole without doing some underhanded things along the way. It's pretty much the same in every walk of life. The greedy prosper, while the honest watch their children starve.'

'Of course,' said Tielt. 'But this gets us no closer to understanding who is plotting against the town.'

She asked the question directly. 'Could it be any of the foreign merchants?'

'They have very little to gain and everything to lose, including their lives. If even a whiff of treason reaches the streets, the mob will set upon them. I believe this plot exists, my lady, but you will find it among the merchants of the town, not the outlanders.'

'I see,' said Lady Mary. 'The Guild Merchant says it is the foreigners, and the foreigners say it is the Guild Merchant.'

'Yes,' said Tielt. 'And someone, somewhere, is lying.'

'Where have you been, my lady?' Blyth asked when she returned. 'It is not safe for a woman to be out at this hour, not with soldiers patrolling the streets.'

'Oh, I was safe enough,' Lady Mary said. 'I went to see Tielt, the spice merchant.'

'May I be permitted to ask why?'

'I wanted to buy a pot of saffron, as a gift for my mother,' she said. She held up the pot. 'He gave me a cure for my rheum, too.'

Blyth looked disappointed. 'If there is anything you need, my lady, I would be only too happy to procure it for you. Just say the word.'

'Thank you, but I always prefer to see spices for myself when I buy them. They are so often adulterated, don't you think?'

'Can your mother not get saffron in Kent?'

'Not at these prices. No wonder the local merchants hate him, if he is undercutting them like this. I think you must be paying your shipmasters too much.'

Blyth smiled. 'Perhaps we are,' he said. 'I shall have to look into it. Will you join me in a glass of wine, my lady?'

Lady Mary sneezed again. 'Thank you,' she said. 'But I am going to take my cure and withdraw to my bed. Good night, Master Blyth.'

23

Liddel Strength, 7th of October, 1346
Midday

'Here they come, my lord!' called an archer from the inner gatehouse.

'About time,' Selby said sharply. 'What have they been waiting for, a fucking invitation?' He ran up the stair to the roof of the tower, plate armour clanking. Merrivale followed him. On the roof platform the catapult stood, mounted on a turntable with a pile of stone shot beside it. The day was hazy with smoke; away in the distance towards the sea they could see the orange flicker of farms and hamlets burning. The Scottish army lay camped in a great circle around them, bisected by the river. Nearer at hand, a cluster of armoured men-at-arms was riding towards the gates, the red and gold banner of the Marischal flying overhead.

'Reconnaissance party,' Selby said. He called to the men in the outer bailey. 'Shoot when they come within range. Make sure they keep their distance.' Turning to the men by the catapult he said, 'Wind her up.'

At two hundred yards the archers on the outer wall-walk began to shoot. Peter de Lisle was one of them. Selby nodded to the crew of the catapult, and the arm sprang into the air, hitting the crossbar with a hard thud. The stone shot flew straight into the middle of the oncoming horsemen, plucking one from his saddle and smashing him to the ground. The garrison shouted with delight, men punching the air, and Selby smiled grimly. 'First blood,' he said.

The archers were shooting well too, and several horses were down. The Marischal pulled his men back out of range and commenced a slow, deliberate circuit of the southern walls, right around to the river on the east side. They could see the enemy turning in their saddles to study the ramparts. 'I didn't think they would be this cautious,' Selby said.

'They're not yet sure what strength we have,' said Merrivale. 'A bloody nose now could lower the spirits of the army, and make it less fit to fight.'

'Let's hope so,' said Selby.

The reconnaissance party withdrew towards the Scottish lines. More smoke billowed to the east and south. The sky turned grey, deep orange sunlight falling across the plain. Little companies of light horse came sweeping past the castle, kicking up dust, darting at the walls from time to time in order to test the defences. The defenders ran along the wall-walk to keep pace with them, leaving the armoured dummies in place. The catapult wheeled on its turntable, trying to track the fast-moving horsemen. 'They're trying to tempt you into a sortie,' Merrivale said quietly.

'I know. I've played this game before.'

Archers came running behind the horsemen, using them and their dust as cover, halting and shooting at the walls. The defenders ducked for cover and shot back, and the catapult banged again, sending stone shot bouncing lethally through their ranks. In response came fire arrows, orange streaks hissing through the air and thumping into the outer palisade. Flames licked up the wooden wall, and men leaned out to pour buckets of water over them. One man dropped his bucket and fell back with an arrow in his chest, the first of the defenders to die.

The afternoon wore on. Slowly at first but then more thickly as the Scots pressed forward, bodies began to litter the ground outside the palisade. Showers of arrows flew into the outer bailey until they littered the ground like kindling wood, some still smouldering. The ramparts of the palisade were full of impaled arrows, standing out like a hedgehog's quills. The defenders shot

243

back, ducking in and out of cover, and more Scots fell, but still they came on. The palisade was burning in half a dozen places, and another man leaning out to douse the flames was killed. His comrades dragged his body back to the rampart, leaning it up in an embrasure along with the dummies. Even the dead were defending Liddel Strength now.

Late in the day came a pause, time for the defenders to rest their aching arms and backs and for waterskins to be passed along the ramparts. The catapult crew lowered a sling and began winching more stones up to the top of the tower. Merrivale went down to the chapel where Tiphaine had taken refuge. The chapel was, he reasoned, the safest place in the castle and she had Mauro and Warin to guard her. She was still exhausted and the sound of the fighting outside had torn at her nerves, but she still managed a smile when he entered. 'Are we winning?'

'We are holding our own,' said Merrivale, 'which is all that can be expected. Mauro, Warin, there is bread and cold meat in the kitchen. Take some food to the defenders.'

'I will help,' Tiphaine said, standing up with an effort. She held up a hand when he started to speak. 'No, Simon, let me do this. Anything is better than sitting here, waiting.'

Liddel Strength, 7th of October, 1346
Evening

Two were dead; forty defenders still remained.

As the sun set bloody red beyond Solway Firth, the Scots returned to the attack. Waves of men came forward, Galwegians and highlanders, dragging stones and beams and the trunks of trees. Others carried bundles of wooden faggots. Men-at-arms on foot covered them, using their shields and armour to ward off the arrows flying from the palisade. Stone shot from the catapult cut bloody furrows through the ranks, but the Scots did not hesitate. Reaching the fosse, they threw their burdens into the ditch, trampling them down and piling more on top.

The defenders were ready. At Selby's orders torches had been placed along the ramparts, and now men lit the wicks in jars of oil and threw them down onto the Scots. Heavy stones and more arrows followed. Men reeled back burned and bleeding, armour crushed and scorched, paint peeling from their shields. Some fell into the fosse and died, their bodies quickly covered by more stones and wood. On the ramparts men died too, three more killed by Scottish arrows hissing through the embrasures in the fading light.

The Scots had taken heavy losses, but they had achieved their object; the fosse had been filled in several places, broad enough for a storming party to cross. As night fell the enemy lit torches too, and Merrivale could still see the devices of the enemy, Brus's red saltire, Carrick's lion, Douglas's heart, the red diamonds of Moray coming to the fore. He watched Peter tracking Brus, and knew he was shooting for Tiphaine's sake; twice when the Norman came too close to the walls the boy raised his bow, and twice arrows thudded into Brus's shield.

Selby ran down into the outer bailey, sword in hand. 'This is it, lads. They're coming.'

Fire arrows streaked through the air, and more flames licked up the face of the blackened palisade. Out of the fireshot dark came three storming columns, men-at-arms in testudo formation, holding their shields locked together over their heads like the shell of a tortoise. Stones rained down on them, burning oil made rivers of fire, but through the howling chaos they came, stumbling over the debris-filled fosse and hacking at the wooden palisade with axes and picks or digging away the foundations to undermine them. Men went down dead and wounded, but the rest stuck to their task.

The drawbridge slammed down. The postern gate opened. Selby ran through it, followed by a handful of his men-at-arms. Running full tilt, they slammed into the rear of the nearest testudo, hacking wildly with their swords. The Scots, not knowing how many men assailed them, broke and ran for safety. Hearing their shouts of alarm, the other two testudos fell back quickly as well. Selby and his men ran for the shelter of the postern; halfway across the drawbridge a flying arrow hit one of his men in the leg and brought him down. Shouting at the others to go on, Selby turned and dragged the wounded man to safety. The drawbridge rose, groaning and rattling. Slowly the flames on the palisade died away. Silence fell over Liddel Strength, washed in the bitter light of the rising moon.

Liddel Strength, 8th of October, 1346
Morning

Six dead; in addition to the three killed yesterday evening, another man had died in the night. Wounded in the neck, he had bled to death at his post. They propped him up in an embrasure alongside his comrades. There were thirty-six defenders left, at least half of them wounded to some degree.

The Scots had been quiet during the rest of the night, probing towards the palisade from time to time, just often enough to make sure the defenders were robbed of sleep. In the morning, Tiphaine and the two servants made porridge and carried bowls up to the men on the ramparts while Merrivale washed and bandaged their wounds as best he could. One man had been badly burned when an oil bottle had been smashed by a flying arrow. 'I have some salve that will cool the skin a little,' the herald said. 'But there is not much left.'

'Save it for the others, sir,' the burned man said through clenched teeth. 'God will ease my pain soon enough.'

'They're making ready again,' said another man, his voice taut with strain. His face and hands were blackened with smoke, his breastplate dented where an arrow had struck him.

Merrivale looked over the ramparts. The testudos were forming up again, solid walls of men-at-arms with painted shields, and behind each testudo was a forest of spears, blue and white banners waving above them. 'Those are Galloway colours,' Peter said.

'Shit,' someone muttered. 'Fucking Galwegians.'

The Galloway spearmen, descendants of Norwegian *vikingr* from long ago, were among the toughest and most feared troops in the Scottish army. Fiercely independent, they fought against Scotland as often as for her, but there was no mistaking their intent today. Trumpets blared and they heard the long moans of pipes inflating. Selby came along the wall-walk, the blade of his sword still crusted with dried blood. 'Stand to. Make ready.'

The trumpets sounded again. Shouting, the Scottish men-at-arms ran forward, raising their shields above their heads to ward off the arrows and stones from the palisade. Some stumbled and fell but the rest ran on, crossing the filled-in fosse and hacking at the palisades again. The burned man collapsed with an arrow through his neck; Merrivale hauled him upright again, leaning the body against the ramparts. He saw Peter shooting fast and accurately, bringing down three of the enemy, others shooting as well, Scottish arrows thudding into the palisades or cutting the air around their heads. Another defender was down, then another.

A section of the palisade heaved; the Scots had cut through the foundations. Another minute and the timbers came crashing down, throwing two men into the courtyard just as the Galwegian spearmen came pouring through. Both staggered up, but were stabbed before they could run. 'Get back!' Selby shouted, and all the defenders who could move ran from the rampart and back to the gatehouse leading into the inner bailey. Merrivale held the gate, ushering the rest inside; Selby ran through last of all and he and Merrivale slammed the heavy gate and dropped the bars just as the first spearpoints thudded into the wood outside. The gate shuddered as the Scots hammered at it, shouting in anger, and then the shouts changed to screams as the defenders on the gatehouse roof threw stone shot down on their heads. They heard the Scots retreating.

Selby opened his visor and wiped the sweat from his face. 'That was too damned close,' he said.

They had lost six more men in the defence of the palisade; thirty were left.

The outer bailey was a no man's land, with the English defending the inner wall and the Scots sheltering behind the smouldering, splintered remains of the palisade. Any Scot who tried to cross the bailey was quickly shot down; anytime a defender showed his head above the parapet, a stream of arrows arched towards him. Three more English archers were killed in these cat-and-mouse duels, but the defenders had the advantage of height and the Scottish archers suffered heavily; man after man was killed or wounded as he raised up to shoot. 'They're losing men a damned sight faster than we are,' Selby said with satisfaction.

No one bothered to point out the obvious; they could afford to.

After an hour or so the Scots went quiet, some retreating to their camp, only a few still clinging on behind the palisade to prevent the English retaking it. Selby briefly considered a sortie to dislodge them, but decided against it; the palisade was too damaged now to be defendable, and he would suffer casualties he could not afford to lose. Silence fell, broken only by the buzz of flies feasting on the blood and the groans of wounded men. Once again Merrivale went around the ramparts with a pot of water and strips of linen, washing and binding wounds that would never have time to heal.

When he had finished he found Tiphaine in the stable, feeding the horses. The animals were uneasy, shifting in their stalls; they could smell the blood, he thought. She looked at him, bruises dark against her pale skin. 'What will happen now?'

'They will wait until darkness,' Merrivale said. He pointed to the curtain wall around the inner bailey. 'If that position falls, go to the chapel and stay there. I will join you if I can.'

'I am sorry,' she said. 'If I had not been caught, we would neither of us be here.'

Merrivale smiled briefly. 'In war, nothing ever turns out as expected,' he said. 'You have nothing for which to blame yourself.'

'Yet I do blame myself,' she said abruptly. 'If we are about to die, I would like to know one thing before I go. The lady you once loved was called Yolande. That is also the name of the Countess of Béthune.'

'Your guess is correct,' he said. 'She was the one.'

Tiphaine shivered suddenly. 'She betrayed me to Brus,' she said. 'But I think it was inadvertent. I do not believe she meant me any harm. When she realised what she had done, she tried to protect me.'

'Then I owe her my thanks,' Merrivale said.

'Do you? For what?'

'For trying to protect you.'

They looked at each other in the strong light. Behind them the horses munched uneasily on straw. 'Who is she?' Tiphaine asked. 'Besides the Countess of Béthune, I mean.'

'She is called Yolande of Bohemia. She is the illegitimate daughter of Lady Yolanda of Mazara, a Sicilian noblewoman, and King Jean of Bohemia.'

Her eyes flew open. 'King Jean, who was killed at Crécy? The one who threw you into a river, tied in a sack?'

'The very same.'

'You aimed high,' she said after a moment.

'I aimed for the stars,' said Merrivale. 'And the stars came down and crushed me.'

'And Béthune? Why did she marry him?'

'Having got me out of the way, her father was anxious to see her wed and forced her into the first suitable marriage he could find. Or so I have always thought. I could be wrong, of course.'

'Don't you care? Don't you want to find out?'

'Why? So I could steal her away from her husband and elope with her, as we once planned to do? That seems unlikely now,

I think.' He thought of her son back in Flanders; he would be about eight years old now. 'She has too much to lose,' he said.

Tiphaine looked out into the courtyard. Men were dragging tables and benches out of the hall, building a barricade around the entrance to the tower. 'And now, we will never know,' she said. 'It is a pity. I would have liked to see the two of you resolve things, one way or another.'

Merrivale shook his head. 'I don't think that is a good idea,' he said. 'I see Mauro and Warin going to the kitchen to prepare more delicious porridge. Shall we go and assist them?'

—

The orange ball of the sun slid down to the horizon and vanished. Night rolled across the plain and engulfed the castle, lit with torches burning along its ramparts. The twenty-seven defenders made ready. They had a shorter perimeter to defend now, and they still had a few inflammables and plenty of stone shot and arrows. The torches illuminated the inner bailey and dimly showed the first Scots gathering outside the walls. The ground trembled to the sound of marching feet, company after company massing for the assault.

First came the fire arrows, blazing like comets in the night. The walls of the inner bailey were of stone, not wood, but the fire arrows dazzled the defenders and forced them to take cover while the first storming parties ran through the gaps in the palisade. The catapult launched stone shot into their midst, knocking men over like skittles, but the rest charged on. At the bottom of the wall the testudos formed again, men at arms holding their shields over their heads while others burrowed at the foundations of the wall, holding on as long as they could until the deluge of burning oil and stones and arrows forced them back. Beyond the palisade they regrouped and came again, and again, until the cobbles of the courtyard were dark and greasy with blood.

The defenders suffered. Three more were shot and killed on the ramparts, and on the gatehouse roof two of the catapult's crew were killed too, so there were not enough men to work the machine and the rest began throwing stone shot down onto the heads of the men who hacked at the gate and tried to force it open. Nearly all of the remainder were wounded now; Selby, always in the thick of the action, had half a dozen arrows protruding from his mail coat. Peter de Lisle was one of the few who remained miraculously uninjured, dodging along the ramparts, sniping at the enemy below, encouraging his older comrades to keep fighting. *This is no herald*, Merrivale thought, watching him, *this is his father's son. This is a captain of men in the making.*

Around midnight the Scots drew back to rest. The Galwegians, who had borne the brunt of the fighting, had left more than thirty of their number dead in the outer bailey. Stones had been hacked out of the bottom of the wall and lay strewn around the courtyard, but the foundations were still sound. The wooden gate was badly damaged, however, and Selby's face was grim as he examined the splintered wood. 'This won't hold for long,' he said, hobbling back into the inner bailey, and he gave orders to pack the base of the tower with wood and straw and soak the lot in oil. He grinned at Merrivale, his face streaked with blood. 'We'll roast the bastards,' he said. 'Give them an early foretaste of hell.'

Merrivale glanced at his leg. 'Sit down and let me take a look at you.'

Selby's boot, when he pulled it off, was full of blood. He bandaged the arrow wounds in the other man's leg and eased the boot back on again, and looked at the commander's other wounds. 'Never mind,' Selby said. 'There's others worse hurt than me. Look after them.' Stiffly, he climbed back up to the ramparts and looked down at the bodies dark in the torchlight. One of the Scots was still alive, crying of thirst and calling out for water. 'Drink your blood!' Selby shouted down, mocking him. 'Your thirst will soon pass!'

Five more defenders had died; twenty-two men remained.

The cold silence of night draped around the castle. Merrivale could feel the dew falling on his face, and taste it on his lips. The man who had cried for water had gone silent.

Out of the darkness came the drums, thundering, shaking the air, and through the din came the ear-splitting scream of pipes, shredding the nerves. Fire arrows, flaming death, flew over the ramparts in clouds. Men flooded into the outer bailey, Moray's highlanders now, charging towards the walls with their heavy swords and shields in hand. Flinging themselves against the walls they began to prise more stones away, heedless of the missiles falling on their heads. Men screamed and fell writhing, covered in flames, or collapsed streaming with blood where the stones and arrows hit them. In the gatehouse, the gate shattered with a crash of timber and the Scots poured through the passageway, trapping the men of the garrison who were still on the roof. Some raced up the stair; others ran into the inner bailey, screaming their war cries, swords raised ready for the kill.

Selby led the counter-attack. The men behind him were battered and bleeding and Selby himself could barely walk, but they stopped the highlanders in their tracks while Peter de Lisle and two other archers on the ramparts shot down their flankers, and together they drove the rest of the Scots back inside the gatehouse. 'Light the fire!' Selby shouted, and Peter picked up a torch and ran into the bloody shambles in the gatehouse. Within minutes the tower was well alight, wooden floors and ceilings boiling with flame and smoke.

Selby and his remaining men hurried back out into the court-yard, coughing the smoke out of their lungs. Inside the tower they could hear men screaming as they tried to get out, and as the flames burst through the roof two of the Scots jumped, their clothes already on fire, trailing flames as they fell. One landed in the river outside the walls; the other crashed down on the cobbles of the courtyard where he lay without moving, his coat still smouldering.

Once again the attackers fell back. The tower burned like a gigantic torch, vomiting smoke and sparks into the sky. The roof caved in with a crash, taking with it the floors below and choking the passageway behind the gate with burning timbers. A last few vengeful fire arrows flew into the courtyard and lay smoking on the cobbles. In the silence that followed a sickle moon rose over the eastern hills, hanging in the sky like an omen of death. Merrivale looked at Peter, leaning exhausted on his bow; at Tiphaine, silent, her eyes haunted by what she had seen; at Mauro and Warin. *How can I protect them? How can I save them when the time comes?*

Liddel Strength, 9th of October, 1346
Dawn

Seven more had died in the night assault, most of them in the grim fighting around the gatehouse. Fifteen defenders were still standing.

The end was swift. There were too few men on the wall-walks now to stop the undermining, and as the Scots attacked the wall once more the stone rampart began to crack and bulge. Merrivale placed a hand on Peter's shoulder. 'Lay down your bow,' he said.

The boy gazed at him, dazed. 'Lay down your bow,' Merrivale repeated. 'Return to your post with me, now.'

Taking Peter's arm, the herald guided him towards the chapel. Tiphaine and Mauro and Warin ran to join them. Just as they reached the door a ten-foot section of wall cracked and fell with a roar, stones scattering across the courtyard. A roar of triumph went up and the Scots poured through the gap. Selby shouted to his men to make a run for the keep. Two of them made it, along with Selby himself. The rest were hacked down in the courtyard.

The herald closed the chapel door and led the way to the altar. Will Selby's body still lay stretched out on the floor before it. 'Stand behind me,' Merrivale instructed the others, and they obeyed, Tiphaine putting an arm around Peter's shoulders to keep the exhausted boy upright. Heavy blows hammered on the door, which splintered and swung open. Armed men entered the chapel, weapons raised.

Merrivale raised his voice. 'I am a herald,' he said. 'Under the laws of war, you may not harm me. And these people are under my protection.'

'We know,' said Lady Mora of Islay, striding up the aisle. The big man Somairle was behind her along with three more of his Manx companions, triskeles still gleaming on their dusty surcoats. 'We have come to take you out of here. Quickly now.'

They walked out into the courtyard, and Mora and the Manxmen guided them towards the gap in the wall. Just as they reached it, Merrivale turned. Up on the motte, Sir Walter Selby came hobbling out of the keep and down the slope towards the Scots waiting below. Two of his men followed him, the last survivors of the garrison.

A man stepped out of the Scottish ranks, armoured, with a red saltire on his surcoat. Merrivale heard Tiphaine's breath hiss, but Brus, intent on his prey, had probably not even seen them. 'Selby,' he said. 'You betrayed me.'

'I betrayed no one,' Selby said. 'I served my king to the end.'

'You are foresworn!' Brus shouted at him. 'And now, you will pay the penalty!'

Selby raised his head. 'I am ready. But save the lives of my men.'

Brus made a gesture with his hand. Two of his men-at-arms stepped forward, drew their swords and stabbed both men through the body. One screamed as he fell; the other collapsed in silence.

'Lay him on the ground,' Brus said. The two men seized Selby and threw him down on the cobbles on his face, pulling off his bascinet. Someone handed Brus an axe. Tiphaine turned her face away. Brus walked forward, standing over Selby and raising the weapon. 'Hold him still,' he commanded as the knight struggled.

'You are the one who is foresworn, Brus,' Selby gasped. 'You are the traitor here, not me.'

'Burn in hell, you bastard,' Brus said, and he brought the axe down hard across Selby's neck.

24

Newcastle-upon-Tyne, 10th of October, 1346
Late morning

Egidia Murton was a rose-cheeked woman in her mid-twenties, who wore clusters of rings on her fingers and fur-trimmed gowns that tested the sumptuary laws to the limit. She clasped the hands of her new friend Lady Mary Grey with delight, drawing her into a pretty parlour just off the great hall of her home on Newgate. Sunlight shone through red and green glass windows, lighting walls painted with flowers and wild beasts, some real and some clearly made up by the artist.

'My husband will join us shortly,' she said, summoning a servant. 'I fear he had to go out early on business. Poor Adam, he is so busy, and of course the war has added greatly to his cares and concerns.'

'I'm sure it has,' said Lady Mary, smiling. 'But I didn't come to see your husband, you goose, I came to see you. We have become such marvellous friends in so short a space of time, and I shall truly miss you when I go south.'

'When will you go?'

'As soon as it is safe to travel. I have been away for long enough already, and with my father in poor health I really cannot linger for too long.'

Apart from the aches and pains that a gentleman of fifty was likely to acquire from spending too long in the saddle in all weathers, there was absolutely nothing wrong with Lord Grey's health. Mary felt an unaccustomed pang of guilt. She did quite like Egidia Murton, but it was not really Egidia she had come to see. It had taken her some time to negotiate the labyrinthine paths of borough and guild politics in Newcastle, but she had finally identified the alderman of the town, Adam Murton, as the man who could tell her what she wanted to know, preferably without realising he was doing so.

And so, she had engineered a casual meeting with Murton's wife, striking up a conversation that led to her being invited to see the latter's home and then sit down with a glass of posset and a good long gossip. The house was delightful, with not a captive bird in sight; Mistress Murton's children were charming and Egidia herself was always as cheerful as a bed of daisies even with war clouds boiling up on the horizon.

They sat in the coloured sunlight and talked about children. Egidia had two so far, and was confident of more. Realising suddenly that she was talking to a childless woman, she blushed. 'I am sure you will have many children when your husband returns.'

'Whenever that is,' Mary said glumly. 'I've just had a letter from him. He and my brother have got into a fight with the king, and have left the army in France. They're on their way east, to Prussia.'

'Prussia is not so far away,' Egidia said consolingly. 'My husband has trade connections in Danzig. There are very fine people in Prussia. Oh; I hear the door. That will be Adam now. Dearest! We are in the parlour! Do come and meet my friend Lady Mary.'

Murton was about twenty years older than his wife and a contrast in almost every way; tall, sober and dressed in dark coat and hose without adornment. He was respectful and polite, but he kept glancing at Lady Mary as if trying to figure out why a knight's lady should be keeping company with the wife of a merchant. Mary smiled at him and turned to Egidia. 'My dear, I keep forgetting. You said you had a receipt for chicken mawmeny. My mother is so fond of it; do you think it might be possible to have a copy?'

'Why, of course!' said Egidia, rising. 'I will write it out for you now.'

'There is no need—'

'No, please, I insist. It would be my pleasure.'

Egidia left the room with an expensive swish of skirts. Lady Mary smiled at her husband. 'Your wife is the kindest woman in the world. I have been so lonely in Newcastle. I would have gone back to my mother-in-law at Warkworth, only it really isn't safe to travel now. But I am so glad to have made a friend here.'

'We are honoured to have your company, my lady.'

She smiled again. 'It is good to meet you, too. Lord Percy speaks highly of you. You act for him in certain matters of business, I gather. He says he can always trust you. Do you see him often?'

Murton looked gratified. 'I had the pleasure of his lordship's company a few days ago, when he passed through Newcastle with his troops.'

'Such a brave array they made, too. I am quite confident we shall repel the Scots. My host, Master Blyth, is very worried about what Durham will do, but I'm sure it doesn't matter. They are only monks.'

'Very wealthy monks,' Murton said dryly. 'They control much of the new industry in the Palatine, and beyond. Their estates are vast.' He paused. 'But I am sure your ladyship is not interested in such things.'

'I somehow feel I ought to be,' Mary said thoughtfully. 'These things do matter, don't they? I wonder why Master Blyth is so concerned about Durham.'

'Surely it would be best to ask him, my lady. He knows Durham well and has done business there for years.'

'He has?'

'Oh, yes. He invests in their mining ventures, and helps arrange shipping and insurance. The priory relies on him for arbitrage.'

Mary smiled again. 'You see? I don't even know what that is. I will ask Master Blyth, but I don't expect for a moment I will understand the answer. Oh, Egidia; is this the receipt? You are a darling. It looks delicious, and I have already bought some fresh saffron for mother.'

'Congratulations,' said Oswald of Halton. 'I hear Carlisle has surrendered.'

Rollond de Brus poured a cup of wine and drained it down, then filled the glass again. He did not offer wine to the friar. 'Yes. They paid a ransom,' he said.

Oswald glanced at Guy of Béthune, sitting on a bench and watching. 'How much?'

'A thousand pounds.'

'You should have asked for more.'

Brus turned, wincing at the pain of his broken ribs. 'Don't tell me my business. What is the news from Durham?'

'The priory still intends to remain neutral. They're waiting to see how things turn out.'

'Then tell them everything is going according to plan. Liddel Strength has been reduced, Carlisle has fallen, and now we march east. We will sweep the Tyne valley, take Newcastle, and then turn south. Durham will have to make up its mind then.'

Oswald raised his eyebrows. 'I reckon you're behind schedule, and I hear you took losses at Liddel Strength. I thought the castle was supposed to open its gates.'

'Our losses were minor,' Brus snapped. It was true, although the Galwegians had lost some of their best men, and the bowmen had suffered too; Scotland was not a nation of archers, and they would be hard to replace. He brushed the thought aside. 'Anything else?'

'Yes. Gilbert de Tracey wants out.'

Béthune looked up. 'What do you mean, he wants out?'

'He has written to King Edward. Ostensibly to ask him to respect church property during the war, but actually to ask if he can return to court and resume his life as the king's banker.'

'God's blood!' Brus slammed his cup down on the table, spilling wine across it. 'Selby learned what happens to men who betray me, and Tracey will learn it too.' He thought for a moment. 'Find Douglas. Tell him I need the services of two of his hobelars, Nickson and Croser, the two who were in Heron's service. Tell them to set a watch on Hexham, and if Tracey leaves, send word immediately to me. I'll hunt that bastard to the end of the earth if I must.'

'It shall be done,' said Oswald. 'For your usual fee, of course.'

Brus opened his purse and slapped some coins on the table. Gold glinted in the sunlight. 'I also hear you have captured the herald,' said Oswald, counting the coins. 'What do you intend to do?'

'Kill him,' said Brus.

'Really? He is under Agnes of Dunbar's protection.'

'I don't give a damn about Agnes.'

Oswald looked sceptical. 'If you alienate her, she and her husband will leave the army and take their troops with them, like the Lord of the Isles did. Theirs isn't the largest contingent in the army but it has some of the best fighters, including the Galloway men. Can you really do without them?'

'God damn it, Oswald! I don't need you to tell me what to do! You have your orders; carry them out.'

'Well, you need someone,' the friar said. 'Between your ribs and the wine, you're not thinking straight. Find out her price, and give her whatever she wants. You haven't won yet, my lord, and there is still a long road to go.'

After Oswald had gone, Guy of Béthune rose to his feet. 'He's right,' said the count, running his hand through his thinning black hair. 'You should talk to her.'

'Jesus Christ on the cross. Not you too.'

'Talk to her,' Béthune repeated. 'Nothing says you have to keep your promises, Rollond. Just make it sound convincing.'

–

Somairle of Mann escorted Brus into the red and white painted pavilion of the Dunbars. The countess sat in a wooden chair; her husband stood beside her, still in mail and armour, his bascinet resting on a table beside him. 'My lord of Brus,' Agnes said calmly. 'To what do we owe the pleasure?'

'I have come to negotiate,' Brus said.

'For what? You have already promised us Berwick, which is all we asked for.'

'Then perhaps you need to be more ambitious,' said Brus. 'I can offer you an earldom.'

Patrick of Dunbar stirred a little. Steel to his wife's quicksilver, he was a veteran of four decades of war and knew every twist and turn in the road of diplomacy. Men sometimes underestimated him, but never more than once.

'I already have two of them,' he said. 'I am Earl of March as well as Dunbar, remember.'

'Then make it a trinity. I can offer you Northumberland as well.'

Dunbar glanced at his wife. She sat calmly, twisting a curl of black hair around her finger. 'Go on,' said the earl.

'You will have Berwick, and Newcastle, and all the lands I shall seize from the church. The Percys have thrown in their lot with King Edward, so I shall take their lands too and give them to you. Once the English are defeated, you will control everything from the Tyne to the walls of Edinburgh, plus my lady's lands in Galloway and Mann. Yours will be the most powerful polity in these islands.'

'Tempting,' said Agnes. 'What is it that you want in exchange?'

'Loyalty,' said Brus.

'To whom?' the earl asked sharply. 'To yourself?'

'To the king of Scotland. Whoever that may be.'

He had their attention now. Dunbar had stiffened a little; the countess was sitting forward in her chair. 'Leave us,' she said to Somairle, and the Manxman bowed and left the pavilion. There was no sign of Mora, her other usual companion.

'Now speak plainly,' Agnes said.

'The king still hopes to sire an heir to continue his line. However, as you are well aware, many years of marriage have yet to produce any children. The kingdom needs an end to the uncertainty over the succession.'

'Go on.'

'The king tells me that after the English are defeated, he will nominate an heir. One of his closest friends and supporters will be named.'

'You?' demanded Dunbar.

Brus spread his hands. 'He has not confided in me, and I do not know his mind. But… it is possible. I am his cousin, after all, and he does rely on me.'

'And if he makes the offer, will you accept?'

Brus bowed. 'With great humility and love for my adopted country, I would dedicate my life to the service of Scotland.'

'There are others with better claims than you,' Agnes said. 'Carrick is the king's half-brother. Robert Stewart is his cousin. My brother is the son of the last regent, and respected among the nobles.'

'If Carrick took the throne, there would be civil war,' said Brus. 'He knows the fate of Manfred of Sicily, and all the other bastards who tried to seize thrones before him. Stewart is a dull ass whom no one respects.'

He paused. 'And if John Randolph should ever become king, my lady, I do not think you would live very long thereafter. Your best chance is to support me. I can make you rich, and you can put the crown on my head. It seems a perfect arrangement.'

The Dunbars glanced at each other again. 'I agree,' the earl said.

'So do I,' said Agnes, and she smiled. 'You have played the game well, my lord. I did not expect this of you.'

'There is one more thing,' Brus said. 'The herald, and the Demoiselle de Tesson. You took them under your protection at Liddel Strength. Why?'

'To stop you from slaughtering them out of hand,' Agnes said. 'Murdering a herald is both a crime and a mortal sin. And you have already agreed that the girl should be put on trial. If they are to be put to death, let it be done properly, according to law.'

She rose to her feet. 'Do you doubt me still, my lord? My Galwegians broke the back of the English resistance at Liddel Strength. The blood they shed there is proof of my loyalty.'

Brus said nothing. 'Tomorrow, the army marches to Lanercost,' Agnes said. 'There, I will surrender Merrivale and the girl to the king's officers and they will be put on trial for spying and treason. If found guilty, the herald's protection will be stripped from him and they will both be put to death in a lawful manner.'

Brus stood for a long time, looking from one to the other. 'Then I hold you responsible for them until then,' he said. 'If they escape, the offer I have just made you is null and void. If you try to help them in any way, you will gamble your future away. Am I clear?'

'Completely clear,' said March.

After Brus had gone, Agnes sat down slowly. Mora of Islay walked out from behind the curtain where she had been listening, mail coat rustling a little. 'This is a coup,' she said.

'Yes,' said Dunbar. 'He will persuade the king to nominate him as heir. And then he will kill the king.'

'Obviously,' said Agnes. She rested her chin on her hand. 'I wonder who will *really* get Northumberland? Not us. He'll parcel up the kingdom to reward his favourites; Carrick, Douglas, Béthune. My brother, perhaps. The rest of the old nobility, like Strathearn and Menteith and ourselves, will be swept aside.'

She paused for a moment. 'There is more to this. The herald spoke of a wider conspiracy, embracing England and France too. How does Brus's coup fit into that? Who are these conspirators, and what do they want?'

'The only man who knows is the herald,' said Dunbar. 'And he cannot tell us if he's dead. We need to protect him, Agnes, at all costs.'

'The longer we keep him under our protection, the more our own danger grows,' she warned.

'I know.' Dunbar tapped his fingers on the pommel of his sword. 'We must think of something.'

Once again the sky was full of smoke and ash, and the air reeked of burning. Not far from the camp was a small stone church, and next to it the burned-out ruins of a village. In the far distance more smoke rose in towering columns as the reavers scorched their way down the dales south of Carlisle. Fortified towns like Carlisle could escape burning by handing over their silver. Poor country villages and farms did not have that luxury.

Guards surrounded the pavilion where Merrivale and the others were being held. They were Kinross's men, not the countess's Manx bodyguard; Kinross, it seemed, was someone she trusted like few others. The rest of the Scottish camp lay stretched around him; he could see the white cross on red of the Knights of Saint John, and remembered his conversation with Brother Alexander Seton.

Inside the pavilion itself, Peter and Tiphaine were sleeping. Both were at the last limits of exhaustion, and had been half asleep in the saddle when the army moved south yesterday, leaving the ruins of Liddel Strength behind. Her capture and escape and the horrors she had seen at Liddel Strength had etched lines into Tiphaine's face. *How can a merciful God allow anyone so young to endure so much?* the herald wondered.

And Peter, too; but no, Peter was different. For him, the siege had been a coming of age. *I shall have to speak to him*, the herald thought. *For all his love of pageantry and the bright blazons of heraldry, this is not his calling. He will be a man-at-arms and captain of men, admired and respected as his father was before him. That is the path he will follow.*

A pity, he thought. *I've got used to the idea of having an apprentice. I shall him miss him, when we finally go our separate ways...*

He looked again at the church. Supposedly, the church at Arthuret had been founded on the site where King Arthur was buried, but Merrivale knew of several other places that made the same claim. *It's a bit like the True Cross*, he thought. *Add up all the relics and myths and burial places of Arthur, and you would have enough to make several kings...*

He knew his mind was wandering. He forced himself to concentrate. The more he thought about Thomas Hatfield, the Bishop of Durham, the more possible it seemed that he could be the man from the north. He was a Yorkshireman who, like so many administrators and royal officials, had risen without a trace. He had attended Exeter College, the smallest and poorest of the Oxford colleges, and somehow made his way into royal service around the time the French war began, nine years ago. As Receiver of the Chamber he had been highly efficient at ensuring the king and queen always had enough money to pay their gambling debts, which were often considerable, and to maintain their high style of living. His reward had been an appointment as Lord Privy Seal two years ago, and Bishop of Durham last year.

The herald recalled the latter appointment. The priory of Durham had a history of objecting to and even blocking royal nominees for the bishopric, but in Hatfield's case they had accepted without a murmur. Was this because they knew the bishop intended to remain at court, to further his ambitions and advance his career? Or had Hatfield and the priory – including the powerful treasurer, Brother Hugh – some joint enterprise in mind?

He smelled her scent, even before he heard the rustle of her skirts on the grass, and the sensation was a like a blow between the eyes. He stood motionless for a moment, composing his tired mind and soul, and turned to face her.

Her skin was pale in the hazy sunlight, and the lines inscribed at the corners of her eyes were deeper than before. She looked at the guards. 'I wish to speak to this man in private,' she said. 'Leave us, please.'

The guards looked at her. 'I have no intention of escaping,' Merrivale said. 'Nor will I do harm to this lady. Summon your master, if you doubt me.' The guards moved some distance away.

'I thought you were going home,' said the herald.

'My husband does not wish it,' Yolande of Bohemia said quietly. 'I think he wants me to remain, as a witness to your death. It will close the circle.'

Merrivale raised his eyebrows. 'Am I going to die?'

'Tomorrow they will put you and the girl on trial. Lyon Herald insists this is illegal, but the king has overruled him. The verdict, I think, is beyond doubt. I do not believe Guy and Rollond de Brus intend to let you live.'

'Why does Guy hate me so much?'

'Because he knows you were first,' Yolande said. 'Every time he touches me, he knows you were there before him. He cannot bear that.'

'He must be a man of very simple imagination,' the herald said tartly. 'Does he think eradicating me from the face of the earth will change that?'

'He hopes it,' said Yolande.

'I think there is more to it than that. Guy's brother was close to Jean of Hainault, yes? What about Guy himself?'

'They know each other well. Hainault came to stay with us at Béthune sometimes. I don't like him. He is the sort of man who would stab you in the back if he thought there was a penny in profit for him.'

Merrivale shook his head. 'Hainault would want more than a penny. His ambitions are broader than that. Has Guy ever mentioned Gilbert de Tracey?'

'Yes, he spoke of him this afternoon. He and his brother used to be associates of Hainault. Guy said Hainault won't be happy about something Tracey has done.'

The herald looked up at the sky. 'What about the Bishop of Durham, Thomas Hatfield?'

'I've heard of him. He is one of King Edward's councillors, with the army in France. Simon, why are you asking these questions?'

Again Merrivale shook his head. 'I can't tell you. If you knew the truth, you would be in danger.'

'Do you think I care? I faced danger many times, to be with you.'

'Yes,' said Merrivale. 'But you said in Jedburgh that they might harm your son, and you were right. If you cross John of Hainault, there is absolutely no doubt he will harm the boy in order to punish you. That is the kind of man he is. You were right, you must keep him safe.'

'And so, I am powerless,' she said bitterly. 'I can do nothing except watch you die.'

'Yes,' said the herald. 'I'm afraid so.'

She made a sudden violent gesture with her hand. 'No. I will take the risk, any risk, to save you. You can escape, now. I will help you.'

Merrivale did not move. 'No,' he said.

'We can save the boy. If we are quick we can get to him before Guy's men, or Hainault's. He's your son too, Simon. Don't you want to see him?'

'Not at this price,' said Merrivale.

She stared at him, her eyes wet with tears again, but he thought they were tears of anger this time. 'Why not? Is it the girl? Is she yours?'

'She belongs to no one,' said the herald. 'Certainly not to me.'

'I don't believe you. I should have let them burn her,' she said bitterly.

'So you could have me to yourself?' he exclaimed. 'Is this who you are now, Yolande? You will sacrifice anyone, Tiphaine, your son, to be with me? That is not a price I will pay, not now, not ever. And I am horrified that you would dream of doing so.'

'I would sacrifice anything for you,' she said, and now her eyes spilled over, the tears on her cheeks glittering in the sunlight. 'I thought you felt the same. Or do you not remember?'

'I remember everything,' the herald said. 'I remember every line of your body, every coil of your hair, the smell of your skin, how the sweat of passion used to shine like diamonds on your skin. Even now I am drawn to you, like opium. You once held my soul in the palm of your hands.'

'Then run with me,' she said through her tears. 'Run with me, like we promised we would do. Or else I will die with you tomorrow.'

'No,' said the herald. 'I cannot. And neither can you. You must live, Yolande, for the boy's sake.'

'Is that all?' she said bitterly. 'Is that all that remains to me on this wretched earth?'

For the second time she turned and walked away weeping. The herald watched her go, feeling his heart bleed even while he wondered why she had come and what the real purpose of her visit was. He did not know, but where John of Hainault and the man from the north were concerned, anything was possible.

The guards watched him curiously, wondering what he had said to upset the lady. Merrivale took one last look at the smoke gushing into the southern sky, and went back into the pavilion.

Lanercost, 11th of October, 1346
Evening

There were men in the army old enough to remember the last time the Scots had visited Lanercost, in the deadly summer after the great victory at Bannockburn when Scottish raiders had ravaged the north of England without resistance. Now, having scorched their way across the Cumberland countryside, burning every building in sight, the army descended into the deep valley of the River Irthing and surrounded the priory. The inhabitants, a handful of Augustinian canons and their servants, made no resistance.

Lyon Herald was waiting for Merrivale and his party as they rode into the park around the priory, his face full of sympathy and gloom. 'You're to come with me,' he said. He led the way into the cloister and up the stair to the dorter, and ushered them into a cell. A chill ran down Merrivale's spine. The two guards at the door were no longer Kinross's men, but members of the royal bodyguard blazoned in red and yellow.

'When will the trial take place?' he asked.

'After dinner,' said Lyon Herald. 'I'm sorry about this, Sim. It shouldn't be happening.'

'I assume you have made your objections known.'

'I have argued until I was hoarse. For God's sake, you can't arbitrarily strip a royal herald of his privileges! Only your king can do that, and he's away in France.'

'Brus does not care about rules,' said Tiphaine. 'He makes his own.'

Peter de Lisle looked up. The boy was still in a fog of fatigue, and had spent most of the journey cross-country from Arthuret dozing in the saddle. 'What are you talking about?' he asked. 'What trial?'

The herald told him. Peter stood petrified with shock. 'Why didn't you tell me?'

'Because we thought you would do something stupid,' Tiphaine said tartly. She was afraid, of course, but her chin was up and her eyes were bright and clear. Merrivale turned back to Lyon Herald.

'Thank you, Archie. We won't detain you further.'

Unhappily, Lyon Herald departed. One of the guards looked in the door, grinning. 'They're building a pyre and a scaffold facing each other,' he said. 'You'll be able to watch each other die.'

'Already?' said Merrivale sharply. 'In advance of the verdict?'

'We all know the verdict, spy.' The grin broadened. 'There's no minstrelsy tonight, so you're the show instead. Make it a good one, will you?'

The door slammed shut. Merrivale turned to Peter and the two servants, dropping his voice to a whisper. 'Listen to me. One of two things will happen. One is that our allies will find a way to release us. The other, more likely, is that we will be tried and executed. That means drawing and quartering for me and burning for Tiphaine. You may be forced to watch this. Prepare yourselves.'

There were tears in Peter's eyes. He turned his head away. 'Your duty is clear,' Merrivale said. 'You must contrive to escape, all three of you, and find the English army and tell Archbishop de la Zouche what we have learned. Now, listen closely.'

Still whispering, he told them what he knew and what he suspected. 'Do this for both of us,' the herald murmured. 'For myself and Tiphaine. Do not let us down.'

Peter wiped his eyes. 'No, sir.'

The smells of cooking drifted up the stairs into the dorter. 'Now, get some rest,' Merrivale said. 'Whatever happens, we're going to need it.'

—

Time passed. The light outside began to fade; through the tiny window in the cell, Merrivale could see sunset light still brushing the high ground, but the valley was falling into shadow. The Irthing burbled in its bed. In the distance he could hear men talking and laughing. Someone brought the guards their dinner and they ate, one of them slurping broth from a bowl. The food smelled good, and Peter rubbed his stomach. None of them had eaten anything apart from a few pieces of bread that morning.

'Good evening,' said a pleasant voice outside the door. 'I wish to see the prisoners.'

'Why?' demanded the guard. 'Who are you?'

'I am the prior, John of Bothcastle. I wish to pray with them, and to hear their last confessions. Allow me to do God's work, gentlemen, if you please.'

Muttering, one of the guards opened the door. A black-robed Augustinian canon, an elderly man with white hair, entered the room, his hands folded in prayer. 'My children,' he said softly. 'I have come to console you in your hour of need.'

'It is kind of you to do so,' Merrivale said. There would be no rescue; he knew that, and he had only mentioned it to keep up the spirits of Peter and the two servants. Agnes of Dunbar would not risk her own position; to do so would bring about her own downfall. He had faced death many times before and had no fear of it, or the pain and humiliation that would accompany it. But he feared, terribly, for Tiphaine.

'You are well in body?' the prior asked. 'You have not been harmed?'

'Not yet,' said Tiphaine.

'Good, good. These are terrible days, my children, terrible days. My own canons and servants are safe and well, but the spoliation and destruction of this priory has been dreadful to see.'

Merrivale looked at him. The prior appeared to be in no hurry to start praying or hearing confessions. 'I assume they have plundered your treasury,' he said, wondering why they were having this conversation.

'The treasury is only the beginning. They have taken everything, the altar dishes, the table silver, the holy relics. Ah, we had such a fine collection of relics, Sir Herald, a delight to the eye and a refreshment to the soul. We had bones of all the great northern saints, Cuthbert, Kentigern, Ceolwulf, Chad. We had the tibia of Saint Godric, did you know that? All gone now, vanished into the hands of the plundering hordes. It will cost a fortune to replace them.'

Out in the corridor came the sounds of retching and vomiting, followed by the thump of a body hitting the floor. The prior held up a finger for silence, waiting. Another body fell with a clank of armour, and Father John nodded with satisfaction.

'Belladonna,' he said. 'Now, we must move quickly.'

In the corridor they stepped around the bodies and pools of sour vomit and hurried down the night stair, the prior leading the way. At the foot of the stair he stopped and looked into the church. The nave was nearly dark now, with only a little dim light coming from the high windows; outside, torches and lanterns flickered. The prior motioned with his hand and they slipped through the cloister, past smashed furniture and torn books and scrolls. 'That passage leads to the latrines,' he whispered. 'Your friends will be waiting there.'

'What about you and your people?' Merrivale asked. 'The Scots will take vengeance on you.'

'Only if they find us,' murmured the prior. 'Do not fear, the rest are already safely away. They await only me to follow them.' He sketched a cross in the air. 'God go with you.'

They ran down the passage to the latrines. A back door stood open, leading towards the river. Two silhouettes stood waiting for them; Mora of Islay, and Brother Alexander Seton, preceptor of the Knights of Saint John. 'In the name of Jesus Christ and Odin the Victorious, don't just stand there!' Mora hissed. 'Come on!'

25

They followed the line of the river, using the trees along its bank as cover, until they were a safe distance from the camp, and then Mora led them up a steep wooded hill, following the line of a small burn splashing down from the moors above. Merrivale listened for sounds of Scots patrols, but there were none. The Scots had taken few precautions; the nearest English force was many miles away.

Behind them the Scottish camp was a patchwork of torches and fires in the fields and park around the priory. A trumpet sounded, harsh and urgent. 'That's the alarm,' Mora hissed. 'Quickly now! If they catch us, we're raven's meat.'

They fled up the hill, stumbling over stones invisible in the dark and sliding on the dew-damp grass. At the crest of the hill was a long line of stones half-embedded in the ground, the remains of the old Roman wall. Further along was an ancient tower, a black crumbling silhouette against the stars, and they heard the whicker of horses.

Agnes of Dunbar walked out of the tower, followed by her Manx bodyguards. She too was wearing mail, a coif pinning back her black curls and framing her face. 'Thank you,' the herald said. 'I know what risks you have taken. I hope you do not end up sacrificing yourself for us.'

'So do I,' the countess said dryly. 'Actually, it was the Countess of Béthune's idea.'

'Oh?'

'Yes. The prospect of your death had reduced her to tears. Mind you, so do most things. That woman dwells in a house of melancholy, with grief for a foundation and sorrow etched into its rooftrees. I thought this was likely to be a trap and refused to help, but my husband and Mora both said I was wrong.'

'I knew Brother Alexander would be willing to help us,' said Mora.

Horses were led up, and Merrivale helped Tiphaine into the saddle. 'I am grateful,' he said to the Knight of Saint John. 'May I ask why?'

'The king informed me yesterday that he was awarding all the confiscated lands of my Order to the Seigneur de Brus,' Seton said bitterly. 'Not just the ones where Brus has purchased the title, but all of them, dozens of manors, thousands of acres. My years of work have been wasted, and I have been told to leave Scotland. So, having nothing to lose, I went to her ladyship and volunteered my services.'

'Nevertheless, you too are taking a great risk,' Merrivale said. 'But I am profoundly grateful to you.'

'As am I,' said Tiphaine, and she looked at the countess and Mora.

They mounted their horses. 'There is one more thing you need to know,' Agnes said. 'Brus intends to assassinate the king and take the throne for himself. He told me so, though not in so many words. Does this fit into the larger conspiracy you mentioned?'

Scotland in the control of the man from the north and his allies would be far more dangerous than Scotland ruled by David Bruce. 'Yes,' said the herald quietly. 'It does. Thank you.'

'What will you do?'

'Try to cut Brus off from his co-conspirators. That is about all I can do.'

'Time is short,' Agnes warned.

'There is never enough time, but I will do my best. Farewell, my lady. I do not know when we will meet again.'

'At a conference to discuss peace, I hope,' said the countess. 'Stick to the high ground, away from the river. Follow the line of the wall east, and eventually it will take you to the Tyne. From there you can descend to Hexham. May God watch over you.'

Lanercost, 11ᵗʰ of October, 1346
Night

In the corridor of the monks' dorter, Brus raged over the bodies of the drugged guards. 'When these two wake up, I want them whipped until their backbones show.' He looked at the men around him. 'Well? Does anyone know where they went?'

'The scouts found tracks further upriver,' said Béthune.

Douglas nodded. 'They'll go east towards Hexham and Newcastle, looking for safety.'

'Then we must stop them. That damned herald knows too much. Did you say he was asking about Gilbert de Tracey?'

'Yolande was quite definite,' said Béthune. 'He asked her whether I knew Hainault, and about Tracey and the Bishop of Durham.'

'Christ,' Brus said bitterly. 'He really is getting close. No more mistakes, gentlemen.'

'I'm not aware that any of *us* made mistakes,' Douglas said cuttingly.

Brus looked at him. Béthune held up a hand. 'This is not the time,' he said. 'What are your orders, *seigneur*?'

Brus rubbed his ribs again. 'Carrick, you're with me. We'll push on up the road towards Hexham. Put out a cordon, search every cottage and barn and byre we come to. Béthune, Douglas, take the high ground along the wall. I don't care what you have to do or how far you have to go, but find them.'

Another man ran up the stairs. 'The preceptor of the Knights is missing, my lord. His servants say he left a couple of hours ago. No one knows where he went.'

Béthune snapped his fingers. 'That solves the mystery of who helped them. Very well, my friends, to horse. We have a long night ahead of us.'

Roman wall, 12th of October, 1346
Early morning

They rode in near silence at first, Merrivale leading the way and Seton bringing up the rear. The pace was slow. In some places there were tracks paralleling the stumps of the wall protruding from the earth, but elsewhere there was only rough open ground, cut by burns and sikes running across their path, tumbling down-hill to join the river below. Overhead the cold stars turned on their slow wheels, marking the passage of time.

After a couple of hours they halted to rest. 'We are about to cross the watershed,' Seton said. 'From here the streams run down into Tynedale, and the waters flow east.'

'Can we reach Hexham by morning?' Merrivale asked.

'Not unless we go down into the valley,' said Seton. 'But I think that is too dangerous. The countess is right, we should stick to the high ground.'

'We could go to Chipchase,' Peter volunteered. 'My father will give us shelter.'

Merrivale started to say he did not want to draw trouble down on Sir Robert's head, but stopped. Faint to his ears, almost imperceptible in the night air, came the clop and thump of hooves.

Swiftly, the herald slid out of the saddle to the ground. 'Give me your knife,' he said to Seton. The knight passed it over and Merrivale rammed it point-first into the bole of an ash tree and closed his hand around the hilt, feeling the vibration.

'How many?' asked Seton.

'Too many to count. Thirty at least, probably more. I reckon they're about a mile behind us.'

He handed back the knife and climbed into the saddle. 'Come on,' he said.

Thereafter Peter led the way and both Merrivale and Seton rode rearguard. 'That was a neat trick with the knife,' Seton said. 'Where did you learn it?'

'I used to be a King's Messenger,' the herald said, listening to the distant murmur. 'Have you given any more thought to what I said? That Brus and the conspirators may have designs on the Knights of Saint John?'

'I have thought of little else,' said Seton. Like Merrivale, he was listening to the horsemen behind them. 'The Order has been the target of plots before. Like the Knights Templar, our lands and estates make us tempting prey for greedy men. Indeed, when the Templars fell, we were nearly dragged down with them. How widespread is this conspiracy?'

'In the summer it embraced Bohemia, Genoa and the papacy as well as France and England. Now we see Scotland dragged in. God knows how far the net has been spread.'

'Then we are all in danger,' Seton said quietly. 'My Order included.'

'Yes.' Merrivale spurred his horse, calling to the others in front. 'Pick up the pace, my friends. They are getting closer.'

Torches flickered like stars behind them. 'They're lighting the ground,' Seton said, cantering beside Merrivale. 'They must have picked up our trail.'

'It's going to be damned hard to throw them off,' said Merrivale. The ground was growing rougher; the river valley was a deep pit of darkness to the right, while to the left lay high moors broken by bogs and crags. The broken stumps of the wall remained beside them, punctuated from time to time by ruined turrets and the vestigial remains of castles. They slithered down the banks of another deep burn and climbed back up a slope so steep they had to dismount and lead their horses. The ground hampered the enemy too, of course, but somehow they were edging closer. At the top of the next hill Merrivale and his party were silhouetted against the starlight, and a shout from behind told him they had been spotted.

Now they were in a race, and with the pursuit both fresher and more numerous, there could only be one winner. Galloping across a broad expanse of moorland, Seton drew level with Merrivale. 'It is about three hours until dawn. If they catch us out in the open in daylight, they'll finish us.'

'What do you have in mind?'

Seton pointed towards the deep valley. 'I'll ride downhill. Try to draw them off.'

Merrivale looked at him. 'Do you know what you are doing, brother?'

Seton smiled in the starlight. 'My soul is already safe. You know more than anyone about these men, who they are and what they intend.'

The herald said nothing. 'Go,' said Seton. 'Find safety. Then write to my grand master, and tell him what you told me. Do this, so that my Order may survive.'

Merrivale closed his eyes for a moment. 'May God receive you in glory,' he said quietly.

Seton raised a hand. Pulling up his horse, he turned back to face the pursuit while the others raced on. Out of the shadows came the pursuing pack, forty horsemen with two armoured men-at-arms in the lead; it was too dark to see clearly, but he thought he recognised the diamonds and bar of Béthune.

Seton let the pursuit get to almost within bowshot, and then spurred his horse to a full gallop. Leaping over the remains of the wall he rode down the dark hillside towards the invisible river below, his pace reckless, daring the Scots to follow him. Most of them did. Two horses slipped and fell almost at once, throwing their riders; the rest crashed after Seton, yelling with fury, quickly lost to view with only the shouts and clatter of hooves telling that the pursuit continued. There came a sudden clash of metal, sword blades clattering on armour, and a piercing scream of agony followed by another. The swords clattered for a little longer, and then stopped.

The others rode on, leaning forward in the saddle, urging their mounts to the utmost speed. Tiphaine had tears on her face. 'Are they still following us?'

Merrivale glanced behind. Not all of the riders had followed Seton; a solid group of six or seven horsemen led by Béthune was still coming after them, though they had dropped back a little. 'Yes,' he said. 'As long as we stick to the wall, they will continue to follow us. We need to go out into the wild lands. Peter, can you guide us?'

'I've hunted over this ground since I was old enough to ride,' Peter said. 'Follow me, sir. I'll see us safely through.'

Wark Moor, 12th of August, 1346
Early morning

There followed a nightmare scramble through a wasteland of hills and crags and moors. No one lived here; the only signs of human life were occasional circles of stone, planted by people far older than the Romans. Sometimes they splashed through burns thick with boulders, soaking themselves and their mounts; sometimes they skirted treacherous bogs, slipping and skidding in the oozing black mud. Without the stars, Merrivale would soon have lost all sense of direction.

Peter guided them. As he had said, he knew this moor well. He pointed out the patches of dark grass that showed where the ground was wettest, and the pale screes of stones that would clink against horseshoes and betray their presence. He kept them off the high hills where they would be easily spotted and down in the shadows along the burns. They could hear Béthune's men following them but rarely saw them, and when they did there was always another hill to duck behind, hiding them from view again. Gradually, as they twisted and turned among the hills, the pursuit fell further and further behind.

Dawn found them deep in the heart of the moor. Peter called a halt, dismounted and ran up the nearest hill where he lay flat on his belly for a while, scanning the horizon. Eventually he slithered back down again. 'I think we've lost them, sir.'

It was three hours since Seton had been killed, and they had been riding without a pause for longer than that. The horses were drooping with exhaustion. They had nothing to feed the animals, but they found a deep burn where they could water them and drank a little water themselves. No one had eaten since the previous morning. Merrivale instructed the others to get some sleep and stood guard while they did so, acutely aware that the only weapons they had were a few knives; Peter's bow had been left behind at Liddel Strength. The past few days had shown that his herald's tabard offered no protection, not against enemies like Brus and his allies.

He grieved for Seton, who had been so willing to sacrifice his life to save them. The Knights of Saint John he had known in the past had rarely been so selfless; at worst, like Jean de Nanteuil, they were ruthless political creatures who would do anything to serve their own ends. But Seton had been a decent and honest man who, in dying, had passed his burden on to Merrivale. His own duty was clear; if he survived, he must get word to the grand master and do whatever he could to unravel the conspiracy that threatened the Knights. Seton was owed that much.

After a couple of hours, Peter woke and came to relieve him. 'You should get some rest too, sir.'

The sky had clouded over, and a north wind was rising. 'Where are we?' Merrivale asked.

'That hill is called Black Law,' Peter said, pointing. 'Go over that and you come down to another burn, bigger than the others in a deep valley. There's a place there called Stonehaugh that has good grass all year around. We can graze the horses there, and then follow the burn down to the North Tyne. Once we reach the river, my father's house at Chipchase is not far away.'

'I do not wish to endanger your father,' Merrivale said.

'Don't worry, sir. I'll ride ahead to the house alone, and see if it is safe. If nothing else, I can take some food from the kitchen and ride back to join you. I'm in need of a good feed,' the boy said, rubbing his stomach.

There it was again, Merrivale thought, that quick assumption of authority. Smiling a little, he lay down on the grass and fell immediately asleep.

When he woke it was around midday, though again it was hard to tell; the cloud ceiling had lowered, obscuring the sun. The wind hissed in the dry grasses around them. 'No sign of the Scots, sir,' said Peter.

'Good.' Mauro and Warin were already awake, and he shook Tiphaine gently. Her eyes opened and he saw a moment of fear in them. 'Where are we?'

'The middle of nowhere,' Merrivale said. 'But Béthune and his men have gone. We're safe, at least for the moment.'

They watered the horses again and then mounted and rode on. Peter remained cautious, keeping to the valleys and skirting around Black Law rather than going over it, never moving at faster than a walking pace so he and Merrivale could listen to the air around them. Gradually the deep valley Peter had spoken of began to open out ahead of them.

The clink of metal on stone behind them was the first warning. Merrivale looked back and saw horsemen coming over the skyline, spears upright and dark against the clouds, and heard the shout as they were spotted. More horsemen appeared on the right. 'Ride downhill,' he said to the others. 'As hard and fast as you can.' If they could reach the burn and follow it down to the Tyne they stood a chance, even if only a faint one.

They kicked their horses and rode down the steep slope, slipping and sliding, hearing the pursuit coming after them. For a moment Merrivale thought they would get away with it; their mounts were rested, if hungry, and had recovered some of their vigour. For a quarter of a mile they fled downhill, turning past a spur of rock that they hoped might hide them from the view of the enemy. Warin, who was up front, shouted in alarm. Merrivale looked up and suddenly he felt sick again.

An entire company of horsemen faced them, sixty or seventy men easily, far larger than the force that had pursued them last night. They were border hobelars, armoured in boiled leather and carrying long lances, with faces like slabs of stone under the brims of their helmets. Merrivale reined in, the others alongside him, hearing the pursuing parties coming down from behind to hem them in. The chase was over.

One of the horsemen rode forward, staring at Peter. 'Are you Master de Lisle?' he demanded. 'Sir Robert's son?'

'I am,' Peter said sharply. 'And who might you be?'

'I'm Jamie Hall from Redesdale, sir. You won't remember me, but I saw you at Bellingham horse fair a couple of years ago; you were younger then, of course. What are you doing out here, master?'

'I can't see that is any of your business,' Peter said. 'This is Simon Merrivale, herald to the prince of Wales, and he is on the queen's service. Stand aside, if you please.'

Hall shook his head. 'I'm afraid we can't do that, sir. We'll have to ask you to come with us. Our lord gave particular instructions that any persons found in this area were to be detained and brought to him.'

'And who might your lord be?' demanded Peter.

'He is Sir Gilbert d'Umfraville, Lord of Redesdale. He'll remember you too, no doubt. Now, sir, and you too, Sir Herald, come along please. Sir Gilbert's camp is not far away.'

Out of the pan and straight into the fire this time, Merrivale thought. They had evaded the Scots, but unless he could talk his way out of this, the end was likely to be the same. They were in the hands of the Disinherited.

26

By sheer bad luck, the place where Peter had intended to take them was also where the Disinherited had made their camp. Or perhaps not luck, the herald thought. Stonehaugh had water and grazing and it was hidden in the heart of the moor; the perfect place for an army to assemble in secret. Looking at the tents and horse lines, Merrivale thought there must be a thousand men assembled here, perhaps more.

There was no pageantry, no bright banners to betray who these men were from a distance. Umfraville, Wake and Clennell, who stood waiting in front of one of the larger pavilions, wore plain surcoats over their armour. Merrivale challenged them even before he dismounted from his horse. 'As you are foresworn, I see you have laid aside your coats of arms. Have you abandoned your families and your names as well? Instead of the Disinherited, shall we now call you the Nameless Ones?'

Clennell's face was grim. 'Have a care, herald. Your authority does not run here.'

'You are wrong.' Peter de Lisle's clear young voice picked up the attack. 'The herald's authority runs the length and breadth of the kingdom, that is the law. If my father were here, he would remind you of your duty to your king and his officers. Lay a hand on us, and you will suffer for it.'

Clennell stared at the boy. 'No one will lay a hand on anyone,' said Umfraville, his voice placating. 'You are safe among us. But we have a right to know what you are doing here.'

'We came to tell you of the death of Sir Walter Selby,' said Merrivale. 'Or perhaps you have heard already?'

The three men looked at each other. Other men crowded in, listening and staring. 'No,' Wake said quietly. 'This is grievous news. Walter was a brother-in-arms and a friend.'

'Did he tell you where he was going when you parted company at Berwick?'

'He said he didn't trust Brus, and didn't want to accept his offer. Then he left. What happened?'

'He returned to his post at Liddel Strength,' said Merrivale. 'When summoned to surrender, he refused. With little more than forty men, he held off the entire Scottish army for two days. Only on the morning of the third day did the castle fall.'

He paused for a moment. 'Selby was grievously wounded and had laid down his arms,' he said. 'An honourable foe would have allowed him to surrender. Brus ordered the remaining defenders to be slaughtered, and beheaded Selby himself. He died without dignity, unshriven.'

'But he was a hero,' said Peter, 'and will be remembered as such for evermore. How will you be remembered, my lords?'

The three men said nothing. Wake was still horrified by the news of Selby's death; Umfraville's face was wooden. Clennell shifted a little. 'Selby knew the risks of not joining us,' he said. 'All the more reason why we stick with the plan, or we will face the same fate.'

'Plan?' said Merrivale. 'You have received your final instructions from Brus?'

'No,' said Wake after a moment. 'Nor have we yet decided whether we will obey them, when they do come.'

Clennell turned on him. 'Jesus Christ. Haven't you just heard what happens to people who cross Brus? It'll be our heads on spikes next time. We don't have a choice now. We made our decision at Berwick.'

'Whatever Brus has promised, you will never receive it,' Merrivale said. 'He will betray you, as he betrays everyone around him. Did you know he intends to murder David and take the throne of Scotland for himself? By your faces, I see you did not. And he has already decided to hand over the lands he seizes in England to a new Scottish earl of Northumberland. I don't know who this man will be; one of his trusted allies perhaps, Bruce of Carrick or Douglas of Liddesdale. I strongly suspect your own lands will be among those seized and confiscated, once you are dead.'

'Have you evidence of any of this?' demanded Clennell.

'Yes,' said the herald. 'I have the statements of witnesses who have spoken to Brus, and I have the evidence of his actions. I know also that one of you is his agent, working on his behalf.'

'What are you talking about?' demanded Wake.

'Brus's venture in Scotland is part of a much larger design. Others are working in England and on the continent, and they give Brus his orders.'

He looked at Tiphaine. 'I heard Brus say it himself,' she said. 'One of the leaders of the Disinherited has been part of the conspiracy since the beginning. It cannot be Sir Robert de Lisle, and it cannot be Sir Walter Selby. Therefore it must be one of you three.'

Merrivale waited for this to sink in. He was positive that he knew who it was, but an open accusation would be risky. At the moment they would not dare to harm him, not with the son of their revered former leader looking on. But if they were goaded too far, that might change.

Clennell slapped his armoured thigh with one hand. 'This woman has taken leave of her senses. I've never heard of this conspiracy, and doubt if it even exists.'

'It sounds plausible to me,' Umfraville said.

'Oh, for God's sake, Gilbert! Can't you see they're trying to turn us against each other? Walter would still be alive if he had stayed with us.' Clennell gestured towards Merrivale and the others. 'We should get rid of them,' he said.

'What do you mean, get rid of them?' Umfraville's voice was sharp. 'Are you suggesting we kill a royal herald? And Robert de Lisle's son?'

Clennell raised his hands. 'Just keep them out of sight and out of trouble, that's all I ask. Lock them up somewhere secure until this is over.'

'I can't see my old friend Robert would be happy with that either,' Wake said dryly. 'Let them go, Gilbert.'

'Are you mad?' demanded Clennell. 'Let them go, so they can tell everyone where we are?'

'What does it matter?' asked Peter. He gestured around the camp. 'You have hundreds of men here. My father has fourteen men-at-arms at Chipchase; they are no threat to you. The monks at Hexham are unarmed. The nearest English army is forty miles away.' He glanced at the herald for approval. 'We can shout your location from the rooftops, but it will make no difference. You are perfectly safe.'

'They're your prisoners, Gilbert,' Wake said. 'It's your decision.'

'I need to think about this,' Umfraville said finally. He nodded to his men. 'Put them in my pavilion and see they are comfortable.'

'And while we are waiting, bring us some food,' Peter said imperiously. 'It's been a bloody long time since we've eaten, and we're famished. Bread and beef, if you please, and a capon wouldn't go amiss either.'

A smile twitched the corner of Umfraville's mouth. 'We'll see what we can do,' he said.

Hautwistle, 12ᵗʰ of October, 1346
Afternoon

Béthune and Douglas found Rollond de Brus in the middle of the Scottish army as it made camp on the banks of the South Tyne.

'They gave us the slip, but it doesn't matter,' Douglas said. 'They walked straight into the camp of the Disinherited.'

'Then we can leave it to Clennell to finish them off,' Brus said. 'We have bigger game now. The English army has moved up to Barnard Castle, in Teesdale. Percy and Neville have both joined them with their retainers, so they have a larger force than we planned, somewhere between four and five thousand.'

'Do we know their intentions?' asked Niall Bruce of Carrick. The bruises on his face were finally fading.

'They're waiting to see what we do. The initiative rests with us, gentlemen. We shall proceed east down the Tyne valley, taking Hexham and Corbridge. Newcastle will open its gates, and we will mop up the rest of Northumberland before we turn south.'

'And the English?' asked Béthune. 'Won't they try to interfere?'

'That's where the Disinherited come in. We send them south to block the English advance. There aren't enough of them to defeat Zouche's army, but they will slow them down. And also, their appearance out of nowhere will come as a surprise. That too will make Zouche and his captains hesitate. Zouche is inexperienced. It won't take much to stop him in his tracks.'

'Clever,' Douglas said. 'When they do fight, of course, Zouche will have superior numbers. The Disinherited will be ground to pieces. Or most of them will.'

Brus nodded. 'But they will have served their purpose,' he said. 'The orders go out in the morning. Be ready, gentlemen. Our time is coming.'

Stonehaugh, 12th of October, 1346
Evening

'How certain are you?' asked Umfraville.

The clouds still hung low over the moors and an early dusk was falling. At Umfraville's request – an instruction thinly veiled as a request, the herald thought – they had walked out to the edge of the camp where they could talk in private.

'We became aware of this conspiracy in the summer,' Merrivale said. 'A number of its members were killed at Crécy, but others survived. Brus was one of them. He did not come to Scotland as an emissary of the King of France, as everyone believed, but as an agent of the conspirators.'

'And you believe one of us is part of this plot.'

'You heard the *demoiselle*,' Merrivale said.

'Who do you think it is?' demanded Umfraville. 'Myself?'

'No. My lord, you must have worked it out by now. You must know who it is.'

'Yes,' Umfraville said finally. 'What led you to him?'

'Do you recall the staged attack on myself, at Chester-le-Street? It was arranged by David Harkness on the orders of Clennell, who was also present. When he realised I knew Harkness was involved, Clennell had him killed to prevent him from confessing. Whether the arrow that killed Harkness came from the Scottish ranks or our own, I will never know. But it was shot deliberately, with Harkness as the target.'

A long silence fell. 'You say Clennell is in league with Brus and the Scots,' Umfraville said finally. 'Very well, we're on the verge of going over to the Scots ourselves. The Rubicon beckons, and we must make our final decision very soon. Once we do, there is no returning to the past.'

He looked at Merrivale. 'Clennell could be our best hope of safety. If he is deep in the conspiracy, he can protect us.'

'But he won't,' Merrivale said. 'I think they are already planning to sacrifice you and Lord Wake and your men. This is only a guess, but I suspect the new Earl of Northumberland will be Thomas Clennell.'

Umfraville paused again, taking this in. 'Very well. You have told me the truth as you see it, and I respect you for that. For Peter's sake, and his father's, I will ensure no harm comes to you. Just in case you are right, I will post a strong guard around you tonight. In the morning, you may depart.'

'What will you do?' the herald asked.

'Think,' said Umfraville. He smiled, without much humour. 'It turns out the Rubicon is a damned big river.'

Newcastle-upon-Tyne, 12th of October, 1346
Evening

'Good evening, my lady,' said William Blyth. 'I trust you are well and recovered from your rheum?'

'Master Tielt's remedy has done its work,' said Lady Mary. 'I feel entirely restored. Is there any news of the Scots?'

Lamplight shone on the room's treasures, the glowing carpets and ikons, sparkling off the glass-framed mirrors. Blyth held out a hand full of birdseed and the linnets came obediently to feed. 'They are reported to be at Hautwistle, a day's march west of Hexham,' the banker said soberly. 'That means they are only about two days from here.'

Lady Mary gasped a little. 'Oh, my. So close... The people plotting to open the gates will be making ready. Have you found out any more about who they might be?'

Blyth shook his head. 'I am confident that no member of the Guild Merchant is involved, and the herald was equally confident that the foreign merchants are innocent. That means we are stymied, I am afraid.'

'So what do we do now?'

'Nothing. To be honest, Lady Mary, there are always rumours of plots like this, especially in time of war, but they rarely come to anything. I think we are starting at shadows.'

'Do you?' said Lady Mary. 'How unfortunate. Because you may not have found any evidence, Master Blyth, but I have.'

Blyth shook his hand and the birds flew away. 'Have you?' he said mildly. 'That is interesting. To whom have you spoken?'

'Some of the merchants. Tielt, of course, and Master Murton the alderman. But mostly, I read these.'

She reached under the table beside her and pulled out a heavy parchment roll. 'Your accounts,' she said. 'Not the public ones, but the secret ones you keep behind the panels in your office. They made very interesting reading. Particularly the items concerning your dealings with Gilbert de Tracey and his uncle, the treasurer of Durham.'

Blyth looked at her calmly. 'I have made no secret of my dealings with Tracey before his disgrace. And there is nothing unlawful about my business with Durham.'

'No, although the size of these deals is quite breathtaking. But your even larger transactions with the banker from Bruges, Oppicius Adornes, will require some investigation, I feel. As will the payments you made to Thomas Clennell of the Disinherited. You have sent a lot of money to Sir Thomas, haven't you? Enough to pay for an army.'

Blyth nodded. 'An interesting conjecture. But if you go back further through the accounts, you will find that I have been Clennell's banker for years.'

'Hmm. I thought you might say that,' Lady Mary said. 'I checked, and you have not. Your connection with Clennell only began last year. I am only a woman, Master Blyth, and I have no head for figures. But if I have been able to learn so much from your accounts, imagine what the sleuths at the Chancery will uncover once they get their hands on them.'

Blyth raised a hand. 'Enough. You have been very clever, my lady, but you have overreached yourself.' He raised his voice. 'Woodburn! Come up to the solar, immediately.'

Barely a second passed before the man-at-arms knocked and entered the room. Blyth pointed at Lady Mary. 'Her ladyship is overwrought and has become hysterical. Take her to her room and confine her there until I give further orders.'

'I am sorry, sir,' Woodburn said helplessly. His hands were spread, and there was no sword in his scabbard. Entering the room behind him came two more men-at-arms in the red and white livery of the town, weapons pointed at Woodburn's back. Behind them came the tall black-clad figure of Alderman Murton, chain of office glinting around his neck. More men-at-arms followed.

'Blyth, I am arresting you in the king's name,' Murton said. He sounded nervous but also, Mary thought, rather excited. 'I am seizing your papers and accounts until an inquisition can examine them. You will come with me.'

Blyth smiled ruefully at Lady Mary. 'I underestimated you,' he said, and before anyone could move he ran straight at the solar windows and crashed through them with a shower of splintering glass. Lady Mary and Murton ran to the window in time to see Blyth pick himself up in the courtyard and run like a hare towards the gates. 'Damn!' Murton said. 'I should have left a guard in the street. Never mind, he won't get far. We'll have him in custody soon.'

'I wouldn't bet on it,' said Lady Mary. 'He'll have anticipated this, and had a bolthole prepared. Never mind. We have his papers, and that's the main thing.'

Wings fluttered over her head. The linnets, scenting fresh air, flew out through the broken window and soared away into the night sky. She heard one last trill of song, and they were gone.

27

Hexham, 13ᵗʰ of October, 1346
Morning

Umfraville was as good as his word. He put them in a pavilion for the night with a strong guard of his own men, and in the morning came to see them. 'I can't do anything until I speak to Clennell. I want to hear the truth from his own lips.'

'Where is Clennell?' Merrivale asked.

'He rode out this morning. Said he's worried that someone might have followed your trail and discovered our location. I repeated what the boy said, but he is obsessed with secrecy.'

'Does that itself not make you suspicious?' Merrivale asked.

'I want to speak to him myself,' Umfraville repeated. 'You and your party are free to go.'

They rode through a misty morning down to the North Tyne and picked up the Hexham road north of Chipchase. 'We must hurry,' Merrivale said. 'The Scots may well arrive at Hexham later today. We must be gone before they do.'

There was, Peter agreed, no time to call on his father. 'What is your business at Hexham, sir?'

'I need to speak to Brother Gilbert again. The almoner at Jedburgh said he had written to the king. I want to know why, and what he really said.'

He turned to the others. 'Let us take no more risks than we must. I am going to the priory alone. As soon as we reach the main road, I want you to ride straight to Newcastle, as quickly as you can. I will follow you.'

He faced the predictable mutiny, not from Peter or Tiphaine, but from his servants. 'I have said this before, many times,' said Mauro. '*Señor*, one day you will go too far. Let us come with you.'

'You have endured enough danger on my behalf,' Merrivale said. 'And if things go wrong, I can escape more easily on my own.'

Tiphaine turned up her nose. 'He thinks we are baggage, encumbering him.'

'I will not argue about this,' Merrivale said. 'You will ride to Newcastle, and I will meet you there.'

'We will do as you say, sir,' said Peter. 'May I ask one favour? When you reach Hexham, will you give money to have a mass said for Brother Alexander?'

'I shall do so on behalf of us all,' said Merrivale.

–

By the time they reached Hexham they could see the smoke clouds in the distance, marking the advance of the Scottish army. The nearest fires were only three or four miles away. Silently, Tiphaine, Peter and the two servants turned their horses towards Newcastle, and Merrivale rode into the town.

Hexham town was even more silent than before. The priory grounds were full of people and cattle who had taken refuge there, the latter lowing in distress.

'You will make no defence?' asked Merrivale, looking at the newly repaired walls.

John of Bridekirk, the prior, spread his hands. 'We can keep out raiding parties, but not the entire Scottish army. If we resist they will kill everyone, like they did at Liddel Strength. All we can do now is trust in God.'

God hadn't intervened to help the garrison of Liddel Strength, Merrivale thought, or Alexander Seton. He glanced at the smoke clouds in the west, drawing nearer. 'Father, I wish to speak to Brother Gilbert. It is urgent.'

'He is in the church. Come, I will take you to him.'

Inside the church and cloister the canons were hard at work removing items of value, reliquaries, altars, cups and pyxes, manuscripts and vestments, taking them away to hide them. They found Brother Gilbert in the presbytery carrying a wooden processional staff with a gilded crucifix mounted on top. His dark eyes widened at the sight of Merrivale. 'What are you doing here?'

'We need to talk,' Merrivale said abruptly. He led the way into the south transept, where the night stair ran up to a covered passage at the top. 'You wrote to the king just before the war started,' he said. 'You asked him to protect the lands of the church in Northumberland, especially those of your order. Am I correct?'

'Yes, though God knows how you found about it.'

'What else did you say? Did you ask him to restore your position? To allow you to resume your business and become one of his bankers again?'

Shouting and turmoil outside the church, the sudden clatter of iron-shod hooves. Gilbert glanced towards the church door. 'Yes. I asked him to grant me this favour in exchange for information I could give him.'

Merrivale tensed. 'What information?'

Gilbert hesitated. The shouting outside had increased in volume. A woman screamed. 'We don't have much time,' Merrivale said.

'I lied when I said I had no contact with my brother. We worked closely together, and did so for years. Our uncle Hugh became involved too. It was he who suggested I retire to Hexham.'

'What information?' Merrivale repeated.

'My brother was betrayed by his fellow conspirators. Brus was one of them. He urged that my brother be killed, and Nanteuil the Grand Prior, too. The conspirators wanted to get their hands on the lands of the Knights of Saint John, but Nanteuil wouldn't agree. He had other plans for the Order, he said.'

The door of the church slammed open, echoes reverberating in the high wooden ceiling. Merrivale heard Father John protesting, and another voice ordering him roughly out of the way. He seized Gilbert by the collar of his cassock, half choking him. 'What information?' he asked through gritted teeth.

'Brus is a rogue. He disobeyed orders. He has taken our money and made his own plans. God knows what they are.'

'Whose orders did he disobey? Who is your leader? *Who is the man from the north?*'

Gilbert struggled. 'I'll tell you, but you'll have to protect me. If they find out I have told you, they will kill me.'

'Yes,' said Rollond de Brus. 'They will.'

He stood ten feet away in the crossing, the saltire on his surcoat stained with ash and dust, a drawn sword in his hand. He had raised the visor of his bascinet, and his face was red with anger. 'You fucking traitor,' he said to Gilbert. 'Just like your brother.'

Gilbert had gone pale. He backed towards the night stair, still holding the wooden staff and crucifix. 'I have told them nothing,' he said.

'And you never will,' said Brus, and he strode forward, raising his sword. Gilbert screamed and turned to run up the stair, but tripped over the cross and fell forward onto his knees. The armoured man stooped over him. 'This is how traitors die,' he hissed, and drove his sword straight into Gilbert's back. The canon screamed again and slumped down on the stairs. Blood spread along his back, turning his black cassock crimson red.

Before Brus had withdrawn his sword from the body, Merrivale had picked up the processional cross. Brus wheeled on him, the dripping blade pointing at Merrivale's chest. 'The devil has given you many lives, herald,' he said, breathing hard. 'But today, they run out.'

'You sent Carrick and Heron and they both failed,' said Merrivale. 'Are you hoping for better luck?'

Brus lunged at him. Merrivale stepped to one side and swung the cross like a quarterstaff, slamming the crucifix into the side of Brus's bascinet, then reversing his grip to rap the butt across the wrist of the other man's sword hand. The sword fell clattering to the floor. Brus reached for his dagger, but Merrivale hit him twice more on the bascinet and then smashed the butt into his breastplate with the force of a battering ram, directly over his broken ribs. Brus screamed and staggered back, doubling up in pain.

Merrivale stepped forward, intending to finish his work, but more boots were pounding up the nave. He turned instead, stepping over Gilbert's body and running up the night stair. The covered passage at the top led to another door and an external stair leading out of the church. He opened the door and started down the steps. Two more men came around the corner of the church and stood looking up at him, grinning. They were border reavers, in leather armour and open-faced helmets, and they had swords in their hands. He recognised them without difficulty; Heron's tame killers, Eckies Nickson and Kalewater Jack Croser.

'You thinking of going somewhere, herald?' asked Nickson.

Croser chuckled. 'Only place he's going is down—'

He didn't get a chance to finish the sentence because the herald launched himself down the stair with the cross levelled like a lance and hit Croser full in the mouth. The crucifix broke, taking several of Croser's teeth with it. Nickson slashed at him, but Merrivale ducked under the blow and hit Nickson on the kneecap with the butt of the cross, followed by a second blow into his groin. Nickson went down, gasping with pain, and a whirling circular blow caught Croser on the side of the head just below his helmet and knocked him unconscious on his back.

Picking up the broken crucifix once more, Merrivale ran back up the stair and rammed it under the door, wedging it. By the time he reached the ground again, men were pounding on the door from inside. He hit Nickson again with the remains of the cross to knock him out and then ran across the park, seeing panicky people trying to flee while the first flames lifted from the rooftops of Hexham. Smoke boiled in clouds across the park, full of ash and sparks. He ran on, clutching the broken staff of the cross. There was a postern gate in the wall around the park, he remembered, and if he could reach that and get away from the priory, he might be able to find a horse and escape. He had done this sort of thing before, as a King's Messenger; he was good at it.

, A man came out of the smoke, another armoured man-at-arms with a plain surcoat and no badge, a sword in his right hand. *The devil walks in Hexham today*, Merrivale thought savagely, *and God is in heaven, fast asleep.* He stopped, leaning on the staff and catching his breath. 'I told Umfraville who you are,' he said.

'It doesn't matter,' said Sir Thomas Clennell, walking towards him. 'Gilbert is a good fighting man, but he is easily gulled. I can explain everything away when I return, and make him trust me once more. It will be quite easy.'

More smoke boiled around them. Merrivale nodded. 'I assume you intend to kill me,' he said. 'Before you do, satisfy my curiosity. Why did you instruct Harkness to stage an attack on me?'

'To draw attention away from myself,' Clennell said, coming closer. 'I knew you would be looking at the Disinherited, and I wanted to turn your gaze away from me. Unfortunately, it didn't work.'

'Yes. That was your first mistake. Not your worst, by any means, but certainly the first.'

'Enough talking,' Clennell said, and he strode forward, raising his sword.

Someone came running out of the smoke behind Clennell and jumped on him, grabbing his sword arm and dragging it down, trying to twist the weapon free. Instinctively, Clennell pulled his dagger from his belt with his left hand and turned, stabbing hard. Merrivale heard the blade rasp against bone, and the other man staggered back, dropping to his knees with blood pouring out of a wound in his belly. Clennell took a step forward, and then saw the face of the man he had stabbed and stopped.

'Jesus Christ!' he said sharply.

Merrivale hit him a two-handed blow with the staff across the back of the neck. The staff snapped, one end cartwheeling across the ground. Clennell went down in a clatter of metal and lay without moving, and Merrivale ran to the other man.

Peter de Lisle had fallen forward onto his face. Gently, Merrivale turned him over and saw the wound gushing blood. The boy was conscious, moving feebly, his lips moving but no sound emerging. Merrivale picked him up and carried him the short distance to the postern gate. Tiphaine, Mauro and Warin were waiting with the horses, and Tiphaine looked at Peter and covered her face suddenly with her hands.

'Clennell may have had men with him,' Merrivale said harshly. 'Have you seen them?'

'No, sir,' said Warin. 'In this smoke they could be anywhere.'

Merrivale laid Peter's body down. The boy was unconscious now. 'I need a bandage.'

They had no baggage; everything had been lost at Liddel Strength. Tiphaine tore a strip off the hem of her travel-stained kirtle and Merrivale bound it tightly around the boy's midriff, hoping to put pressure on the wound, but blood stained the cloth almost immediately. Tiphaine's face was wet with tears. 'Is he going to die?'

'Yes,' said the herald, 'and very soon. Mauro, Warin, help me.'

He stepped into the saddle and the two servants handed the limp body up to sit before him. Merrivale wrapped one arm tightly around him to hold him in place, heedless of the blood gushing from the wound. The smoke was thicker than ever now, and they walked their horses quietly away from the abbey. Only when he was certain the Scots were not following did Merrivale call a halt outside the burning town.

'Help me,' he said to the servants, and together they lifted Peter down to the ground once more. 'Is he dead?' asked Tiphaine. She was still crying.

'Yes,' said Merrivale. Kneeling beside the body, he took Peter's hand and held it in his own, just as Peter had done with his dead friend David Harkness weeks ago. He felt no pain, no sorrow, not yet; those would come later, he knew. At the moment, he felt only a dark emptiness in his soul. Something bright and beautiful had gone out of the world.

'We have no tools to bury him, *señor*,' said Mauro, who had seen enough death to be pragmatic about it. 'What do you wish to do?'

'We're going to Chipchase,' said the herald. 'We're going to take him home.'

Chipchase, 13th of October, 1346
Afternoon

Chipchase had its own chapel, and a resident priest. Ashen-faced, for he had known Peter de Lisle since he was a boy, the priest took charge of laying out the body and saying prayers for his soul. Sir Robert de Lisle came in, leaning on his stick, and sat down by the bier, holding his son's cold hand clasped in his. Merrivale nodded to the others and they retreated to the hall. A fire burned on the hearth. *The Dream of Scipio* lay on the table, abandoned when they had arrived.

An hour passed before the old man hobbled back into the hall. 'Tell me again what happened,' he said, sitting down heavily.

'I ordered Peter and the *demoiselle* to ride to Newcastle while I went to Hexham,' Merrivale said. 'He decided to turn back.'

'He said you were in danger,' Tiphaine said. She was weeping again. 'He said he had to help you. He could not leave you behind.'

'And it was Clennell who killed him? You're certain of that?'

Merrivale nodded. 'Clennell is a traitor twice over,' he said. 'To his country, and to his brothers in the Disinherited.'

'And he killed my last remaining child,' de Lisle said. He looked around the hall. 'It will all end with me now; this house, this estate, everything. It will pass into the hands of strangers, and our name and lineage will be forgotten.'

He looked at Merrivale. The herald saw the agony and grief in his eyes. The end of his line did not matter. He had loved his son, loved him for his courage and his selflessness, for the very qualities that had brought him to his death.

'Peter had your courage,' Merrivale said. 'He saved my life twice. And young though he was, he was wise beyond his years. You say your name will be forgotten, but we who knew him will never forget.'

De Lisle nodded slowly. 'Thank you. I am glad that others knew his worth. He was better than me, better than all of us. It breaks my heart to know he has gone, and the world is a darker place without him.'

They sat in silence for a while, each with their own memories. The fire crackled. 'Peter is in God's hands,' Merrivale said finally. 'But for his sake, I can undo some of the evil that Clennell has done. The Disinherited and their men are camped at Stonehaugh. I intend to go back there, and persuade them to their true loyalty.'

'How will you do that?'

'By telling them the truth,' the herald said.

De Lisle looked sceptical. 'The truth won't be enough. It never is. I'm coming with you.'

Merrivale looked at him. 'Are you able to ride, my lord?'

'I can ride as far as Stonehaugh.' The old man banged on the table, shouting for a servant. A pale-looking man appeared, bowing. 'Send to the stables,' said de Lisle. 'Tell them to saddle a horse, and tell the men to make ready to ride.' He looked back at Merrivale. 'Do you mind acting as my esquire? I'll need help to arm.'

'It would be my honour,' Merrivale said.

Tiphaine wiped her face with the sleeve of her kirtle. 'How can I help?'

'Mauro and Warin will take you to Newcastle,' he said gently. 'Wait for me there.'

She nodded. For once, she did not resist. 'We will go now. If we hurry we can reach the gates before dark.'

Their eyes met for a moment. 'May God watch over you,' Merrivale said softly.

Her voice echoed his own thoughts in Hexham. 'I don't think God is interested in us anymore,' she said. 'I think we need to start watching over ourselves.'

Late afternoon

The meadows along the little burn were full of activity in the fading light. Pavilions and tents were being struck, horses saddled and men were arming. The need for secrecy was past; the bright colours and heraldry were back now, Wake's red and gold bars, Umfraville's gold cinquefoil, Clennell's black and white lions. Merrivale's lips tightened at the sight of the latter.

'They're preparing to march,' he said.

The man beside him said nothing. Sir Robert had not spoken during the ride from Chipchase, and Merrivale could only guess at the pain he was in. Outriders from the camp spotted the little party of Merrivale, de Lisle and his handful of men-at-arms, and galloped to investigate; they pulled up and saluted respectfully when they saw the de Lisle's coat of arms. Hall, the Redesdale hobelar, was one of them. 'Come, my lord. I will take you to Sir Gilbert.'

They found the three captains in the centre of the camp. Clennell was talking quickly and urgently, gesturing with his hands. He must have regained consciousness quite quickly, Merrivale thought, and come galloping back to camp in hopes of getting the others moving before the herald could reach them. He looked up and saw Merrivale, and his hand went to the hilt of his sword. Then he saw Sir Robert de Lisle and froze, the blood draining from his face.

'Gentlemen,' said Sir Robert. 'I am surprised to see you here. Why are you not with the archbishop and his army, where your duty lies?'

No one answered. With immense effort the old man slid off his horse and walked forward. Hundreds of men stood around them, watching in awestruck silence as a legend strode into their midst.

'What are you doing here, Robert?' Wake asked quietly. 'We heard you were ill.'

'I am ill,' said de Lisle. 'Ill and near my death. But I will not go to my grave until I have justice for my son.'

Umfraville tensed. 'Peter? What happened to him?'

Merrivale looked at Clennell. 'Tell them,' he said.

Clennell stood still. His mouth opened but no sound came out. De Lisle ripped his sword from his scabbard and advanced towards him. '*Tell them!*' he screamed.

'It was an accident,' Clennell said. His nerves collapsed and he fell to his knees, raising his hands in supplication. 'I didn't know who it was. Sir Robert, I beg you, for the love of God. I would never hurt your son.'

'But you killed him,' Merrivale said. 'I saw you do it; I am the witness. And now, the hand of every man on the borders will be against you. Your own retinue will desert you. Why did you come back, Clennell? Why not run and join Brus and his friends? You might have been safe there.'

The men around Clennell turned towards him. Umfraville and Wake drew their swords, as did Hall and some of the others. 'It was an accident,' Clennell repeated. 'God help me, I never meant to harm him.'

De Lisle raised his sword. With a force born of anger and despair, he drove the point through Clennell's throat, snapping the mail links that protected it and stabbing through jugular and windpipe and spinal column. Clennell slid slowly off the blade and fell onto his side. His hands clawed feebly at the grass for a moment, and then went still.

Merrivale ignored the body. He looked at Umfraville and Wake. 'You are preparing to march. What orders have you been given?'

'It no longer matters,' Umfraville said. 'Whatever they were, we no longer intend to obey them. Clennell is dead, but Peter de Lisle has still to be avenged.'

De Lisle turned. 'You accepted me as your commander once,' he said. 'Will you do so again?'

There was a moment of silence. No one remembered his illness now; all they saw was a proud old veteran standing before them. Umfraville knelt, and so did Wake, and after them every man of the hundreds gathered around. De Lisle held up his bloody sword, the hilts and guards like a cross against the dark sky. 'We ride to join the archbishop,' he said. 'To horse, gentlemen. We are almost out of time.'

Newcastle-upon-Tyne, 13ᵗʰ of October, 1346
Evening

The gates were closing when Tiphaine, Mauro and Warin reached Newcastle, but they used the herald's name to talk their way past the guards. The Blyth house was dark and silent, and a frightened servant told them Lady Mary had gone to stay with Alderman Murton at his house on Newgate. Puzzled, Tiphaine and the others made their way there.

Tiphaine was still wearing the servant's gown in which she had escaped nine days ago – *God*, she thought, *was it only nine days?* – filthy with mud and with the hem torn off, and the doorkeeper at Murton's house refused to admit her. Shivering with exhaustion and grief and cold, she stood in the street and screamed Mary's name, and after a moment Lady Mary herself came hurrying out, scooping her into a tight embrace while the doorkeeper stared in astonishment. 'Come in, come in,' she said quickly. 'Mauro, Warin, come with me.'

In the hall, before Mary could speak, Tiphaine poured out her story, Murton and his wife listening in wide-eyed silence. Only at the end did Tiphaine recollect herself and become aware of her surroundings. 'Why are you here, Mary? Where is Master Blyth?'

'Gone,' said Lady Mary. She related her own story. 'As I suspected, he had a route of escape already planned. We think he got away downriver by boat, and picked up a larger ship there. My guess is that he has gone to Bruges.'

'His treachery is clear from his account books,' said Murton. 'He has been planning and preparing for at least a decade. Unfortunately, we don't know the names of his confederates.'

'We can guess at some of them,' said Mary. 'Hugh de Tracey and the late unlamented Gilbert, for a start. And Rollond de Brus, of course. That takes us to John of Hainault and the mysterious man from the north.'

'But what do they want?' asked Egidia. 'Who are they conspiring against, and why?'

'All of us,' said Tiphaine. 'The kings and queens and popes and bishops, of course, but ultimately they want power over all of us. Why? To show that they can. Brus is preparing to seize power in Scotland, not because he wants to be king, but to show the rest of Europe how much power he has. He and the man from the north want to attract others like themselves as allies, to replace those that were killed last summer and to extend their reach across Europe, perhaps even beyond.'

She looked down at her dirty hands. 'The preceptor of the Knights of Saint John is dead. The king of Scotland is to be assassinated. According to Brus, there is a new plot to kill the king of England. No one is safe from these men.'

'Unless we stop them,' said Lady Mary.

'Yes.' Tiphaine raised her head again. 'I must see this through, Mary. I'm going to join the English army.'

Lady Mary nodded. 'We shall ride in the morning,' she said.

28

Stonehaugh, 14th of October, 1346
Early morning

The march of the Disinherited from Stonehaugh never became part of the folklore of the borders, because no man who made that journey ever spoke of it again. But the survivors lived with its memory etched on their hearts.

They had made their preparations well. Along with weapons and armour they had provisions, bags of oats for the horses, water bottles, packs of bread and dried beef for the men, and these hung from the pommels of every man's saddle. Packhorses carried more supplies. They could march and fight for several days, Merrivale reckoned.

Far to the south the sky glowed red as Hexham and the surrounding villages burned. De Lisle, Umfraville, Wake and the herald gathered around a map lit by torches held overhead. 'It's a waiting game now,' de Lisle said. 'The Scots could advance on either Newcastle or Durham, but if they move too far, Zouche could come up from Barnard Castle to hit them in the flank or rear. If Zouche moves up too quickly, the Scots could get past him and strike into Teesdale, like old Bruce did back in '28. Both sides will sit where they are and see who moves first.'

He looked at the others. 'And that gives us our opportunity. If we ride hard, we can be at Barnard Castle before the Scots can overtake us. Our first step is to reach Corbridge. We'll seize the bridge there and cross the Tyne.'

'The whole Scottish army is now at Hexham,' Umfraville warned. 'That's very close to Corbridge. We could well meet with opposition.'

De Lisle shook his head. 'Speed and surprise, gentlemen. We'll hit them hard, cross the bridge and over the river before they can recover. The bridge is narrow and we can only cross it in column. Wake, you're first; Umfraville will cover you and follow. I'll bring up the rear with my own men and Clennell's. They have something to prove, I think.'

'I'll ride with you, Sir Robert,' the herald said.

The old man looked at him for a moment. 'I'd be glad of that.'

–

They waited until after midnight to begin their ride; de Lisle wanted to reach Corbridge at dawn. There were no trumpets or fanfares, just a single word passed in the dark. There was no moon now, only the sheen of starlight to show them the way. They rode down the burn in a long jingling column, fording the North Tyne and climbing up onto the desolate moors beyond. The night wind had a cold edge to it, a reminder that autumn was not far away.

High on the moors they came to the Via Regia, the old royal road that connected England and Scotland, built a thousand years ago by the Romans and traversed by armies ever since. Turning south, they rode in column over the hills and down the long slope towards the valley of the Tyne. De Lisle rode beside Merrivale, never slackening his pace. Only once did he speak, his voice taut with pain.

'Did my boy serve you well?'

Merrivale thought again about Liddel Strength. All the high hopes, he thought again, all the bright promise; all the wit and intelligence and selfless courage, gone. But he would not share his own pain with the boy's father, not now.

'He was everything I hoped he would be, and more,' the herald said. 'He did you great credit, sir. You raised him well.'

'Aye,' said de Lisle. He did not speak again.

Dawn bloomed coldly over the hills. Away to the west, Hexham was still an inferno. More fires glowed closer at hand as farms and byres burned. They saw the gleam of the river in the pale light, and then the houses and towers of Corbridge, the long span of the bridge beyond. Fires were breaking out in that town as well, smoke and sparks rising.

A messenger rode back from Wake's company in the vanguard. 'The enemy hold the town, my lord.'

'Tell Lord Wake to go in hard and fast,' de Lisle said. 'He is to stop for nothing until he reaches the bridge. Instruct Sir Gilbert to protect his company while they cross the river. Make it so.'

They urged their horses to a gallop, flying down the long road towards the town. Wake's men disappeared into the smoke. Merrivale heard the first shouts and the clatter of weapons breaking out, but the column did not slacken speed. Beside him de Lisle rode grimly, reins clenched in hands bent like claws. 'You should draw your sword, Sir Robert,' the herald said.

'Later,' said de Lisle.

Umfraville's company were into the town now, and de Lisle and Merrivale followed them. Houses burned everywhere, flames roaring upwards, spooking the horses. Bodies lay in the streets, English and Scots, killed in the fighting as the earlier companies passed through. From ahead came the continuous din of swords smashing on metal, men shouting and screaming.

They reached the town square. A pele tower next to the church was still holding out, its garrison shooting at the Scots and throwing stones down on their heads. De Lisle waved a hand and his men closed up around him, driving into the Scots and spearing some, throwing others bodily from their horses. Scottish lances stabbed back, and the man next to Merrivale screamed, holding his neck, and then rolled out of the saddle. Another lance point hit de Lisle's breastplate and broke into splinters. The Disinherited pressed on, a solid wedge of horsemen driving the Scots out of the square and into the burning lanes beyond.

More fighting here; Merrivale saw the red heart banner of Douglas of Liddesdale through the smoke. Where there was pillage and burning, Liddesdale would not be far away... More bodies in the streets, some of them townsmen and women who had not reached the shelter of the pele, and Merrivale had a flash of memory, the dead woman and her child at Harbottle. *Hush ye, hush ye, do not fret ye, the Black Douglas shall not get ye...* Now Douglas had seen them and turned his horse towards them, charging through a street turned into a tunnel of flame, raising his sword, and now finally de Lisle drew his own sword and spurred to meet him. Merrivale held his breath; Douglas's first blow fell on de Lisle's shield, and de Lisle calmly leaned down and stabbed Douglas's horse. The animal reared up in pain, Douglas cursing and fighting to stay in the saddle, and then the rest of de Lisle's men came shouting behind him, driving Douglas back through the flames.

A curtain of sparks drifted glowing across the road, the dark silhouette of another armoured man coming through them; Umfraville. 'Wake is across the river, Sir Robert.'

'Get your own men over the bridge. We'll hold Douglas back.'

They held, against a series of darting, vicious, disorganised attacks, little parties of hobelars charging through the smoke and smashing against the iron wall of de Lisle's men. Merrivale watched them closely, but Clennell's former retainers never wavered; men fell dead and wounded from the saddle, but the line held. Jamie Hall rode up, his jack and face stained with smoke and blood. 'Sir Gilbert's men have crossed, my lord.'

'Good.' De Lisle turned to his own company. 'Every second man, ride to the bridge. The rest of you, hold the line.'

Half the company turned and rode for the bridge. The rest stood their ground, coughing and spluttering in the smoke, trying to calm their horses. They could see the Scots dimly, holding back now. 'They've lost their appetite, by God,' said a hobelar.

'They're under orders,' de Lisle said. 'Douglas can't stop us now, and he doesn't want to lose any more men. They'll regroup and come after us, never fear.'

He looked along the line. 'Cross the bridge in file. Slowly, now. We don't want to tire the horses.'

They crossed the bridge at a walking pace in the light of the rising sun, watched by the Scots and the defenders of the pele tower. The latter would have to be left behind, but from what Merrivale had seen they appeared to be putting up a good resistance. And de Lisle was right; Douglas would almost certainly abandon the town to pursue them, once he had reorganised his men.

They crossed the southern floodplain of the Tyne and rode up the steep hills behind, reaching the high moors again. Here they left the old road and turned due south, riding on through the windswept morning. Some of the men were burned and bleeding; one fell unconscious from his horse, hitting the ground with a hard thud. Two of his fellows lifted him and tied him across his saddle, and they rode on. De Lisle turned from time to time, watching the horizon. Wake had posted scouts and flank guards, but the old man was still uneasy.

He was right. An hour after leaving Corbridge the Scots struck again. De Lisle's men could see them coming from a long way off, light armoured hobelars and heavy men-at-arms with painted shields under the banner of Bruce of Carrick. 'Now we push hard,' said de Lisle, and they picked up speed to a canter, Wake swinging right and Umfraville veering left while the Scots closed on de Lisle's rearguard… and de Lisle waved his hand in a circular motion, and Wake's and Umfraville's companies wheeled like birds of prey and came sweeping back, attacking the Scots from either flank. The manoeuvre almost worked, but Carrick had seen the danger and was turning away; a few of his men, slow to move, were caught and killed but the rest fell back. Wake and Umfraville turned too and the march continued, the Scots trailing them at a distance with more companies coming up from behind.

In late morning under a hazy sun the Disinherited rode down into the valley of the Derwent. Here the Scots attacked again, Carrick's men stiffened with more men-at-arms under the Earl of Moray. They had fewer men than de Lisle, but they saw their advantage as the English forded the river and charged home, screaming their battle cries. Moray was in their midst, standing up in his stirrups and slashing around him with his sword, and the waters of the Derwent turned red as horses and men fell in the shallows. Once again Wake and Umfraville turned and launched their men into the fighting, and sheer weight of numbers pushed Carrick and Moray out of the river and back up the slope. Raging and cursing, Moray dismounted and hurled his sword to the ground while the battered companies of the Disinherited assembled once more and rode away up the far side of the valley.

'Are they following?' de Lisle asked.

Merrivale shook his head. 'They're turning back.'

The old man's voice creaked with exhaustion and pain. 'Robert Keith, the Marischal, has called them back. Keith understands tactics. He won't want his men scattered across the north of England.'

'Then we could halt and rest,' Merrivale said.

'No,' said de Lisle. 'No rest. We'll water the horses when we reach the Wear, and move on. If the men are hungry, they can eat in the saddle.'

The sun passed its zenith. They rode on through the bleak, empty hills, the wind whistling around them, passing occasional tumbledown farms and barns abandoned after the Great Famine twenty years before. Sometimes the wounded men groaned with pain, but after a while even they fell silent, too weak and exhausted to make a sound. Birds circled overhead, buzzards and hobbies drifting on the currents of air.

Another deep valley lay ahead, the Wear. Scouts rode back to give the all-clear. Exhausted men and horses rode down the slope to the river bubbling in its stony bed. They let the horses drink, but sparingly, and gave them a few handfuls of oats before they mounted, forded the river and rode on up another long slope to the high moors. The mountains of the Pennines were blue to the west, under the enormous dome of the sky. 'How much further?' Merrivale asked.

'Twenty miles,' said de Lisle, and he closed his eyes. Merrivale watched him, knowing what was going through his mind.

I should have said no, he thought. *I should never have accepted him into my service.*

'You couldn't know,' de Lisle said, as if he was reading Merrivale's mind. His eyes were still closed. 'You are not to blame.'

'But I am responsible,' Merrivale said. 'I chose to accept him into my service. If I had not, he would still be alive today.'

'Perhaps. Or perhaps he would have had an accident out hunting, or caught the flux and died. God chooses who he calls, and there's not a damned thing we can do about it.'

'I wish I had your philosophy,' Merrivale said.

'Comes with age,' the old man said. There was a long pause. 'I regret nothing. But he was the light of my soul. And now, there is only darkness.'

They rode on across the moor, the rattle of harness the loudest sound. De Lisle reeled a little, and Merrivale reached over and caught his arm. 'Sir Robert, you should rest,' he said gently.

'No rest,' de Lisle said again. 'The only rest I desire now is the sleep of the grave. It will come to me, presently. But first, there is work to be done.'

–

The sun was a burning ember on the horizon when they started down the last long slope into the valley of the River Tees. Gilbert d'Umfraville dropped back along the column and motioned to Merrivale. The herald left de Lisle under the watchful gaze of his men and trotted out to join him. 'Wake and I have been talking,' Umfraville said. 'What reception can we expect at Barnard Castle?'

'I expect you will be welcomed with open arms,' said the herald.

'Everyone will know we failed to join the muster. How much else is known?'

'The queen has known from the beginning that you were considering throwing in your lot with Scotland. You, and most of the rest of the nobles of the north. When you left Berwick, I reported that you had disappeared.'

'You believed we had defected.'

'I did. Now, I shall tell the archbishop I was mistaken, and report that also to the king. You and Lord Wake became aware of the treachery of Sir Thomas Clennell. When he invited you to join him, you played along in order to learn more about his plans. Once he was exposed and killed, you marched immediately to join the army.'

Umfraville watched him. 'Will the king and queen believe this?'

'They will if I tell them,' the herald said. 'And they will know that for the good of the kingdom, they should not want to believe anything else.'

—

In the farms and villages along the Tees, people ran for cover when they saw the column of battered, bloodied men ride down off the moor, not knowing if they were English or Scots. Ignoring them, the Disinherited pressed on down the river. Lights came into view ahead, the watchfires of the English army camped in the meadows. Barnard Castle, high on its bluff, sparkled with torches. Men turned out to watch them, mouths agape with astonishment, turning to shout the news. 'The Disinherited! They are here!' Someone cheered, and in a moment the cheering spread, up and down both banks of the river and along the ramparts of the castle. Merrivale smiled at Umfraville. 'There is your welcome,' he said.

Marshals showed the men where to make camp and find hot food. De Lisle, Umfraville, Wake and Merrivale rode across the bridge over the Tees and up to the castle gate. Banners hung from the towers, and he saw the archbishop's crossed keys and the blue lion of Percy and white saltire of Lord Neville of Raby alongside many others. The northern lords had assembled, and now their numbers were complete. For the first time since he rode north,

Merrivale felt a sense of hope. *Possibly*, he thought, *just possibly, we can pull this off.*

Gently, he helped Sir Robert down from his horse. He had left his stick behind at home, and now he used his sword as a prop, leaning on Merrivale's arm as he hobbled up the steps into the hall. The others followed. The hall was full of people, staring at them in astonishment: Zouche, Lord Percy with his granite face, Harry his son, a big broad-shouldered man who must be Lord Neville. Then he blinked with astonishment. Lady Mary was there, standing with her brother-in-law, and next to her was Tiphaine. She wore a green gown that did not fit her very well and was probably someone else's but was, he thought, an improvement on her tattered servant's kirtle.

De Lisle inclined his head towards the archbishop. 'I give you greeting, your Grace,' he said, his voice hoarse. 'And I give you apologies also for our lateness. I trust we have arrived in time.'

'You have, and you are welcome,' Zouche said, his face full of relief. 'I had begun to wonder if you would come at all.'

'Have no fear,' said de Lisle. 'The Disinherited know their duty. And they will do it to the end.'

Barnard Castle, 14th of October, 1346
Night

Being a royal herald had its privileges; the rest of the army was under canvas or sleeping in the open along the banks of the Tees, but a room was found for Merrivale in the castle, a small chamber in one of the towers overlooking the river. Mauro and Warin were waiting for him, their faces full of relief. 'We are glad to see you, *señor*,' said Mauro. 'We were not certain if we would.'

'You should have more faith,' Merrivale said. His writing case was on a table and he knew he should write a report for the archbishop and the queen, but he could not face the task. He was weary to the bone, exhausted from strain and tension and endless hours in the saddle. Then he was briefly ashamed; what he felt was nothing compared to the pain Sir Robert de Lisle was enduring.

He heard footsteps and a swish of skirts on the stair outside his room, and smelled an unfamiliar scent. Tiphaine stood in the doorway, Lady Mary behind her. 'I thought I had better bring her myself,' Mary said. 'She tends to get lost.'

'She does,' Merrivale acknowledged. Her hair had grown again. 'Was Newcastle no longer safe?'

'Newcastle is safe as the Tower of London,' Lady Mary said. 'I found out who the traitor was. It was Blyth.'

'The queen will not be pleased,' Merrivale said after a moment. 'She trusted him.'

'A lot of people did,' said Mary. 'We think he may have fled to Bruges. He has family there, and his accounts showed payments to people there.'

'You saw his accounts? Was John of Hainault among those mentioned? Or Guy of Béthune?'

Lady Mary nodded. 'Both of them, frequently. I found the entire affair deeply disturbing, if I am honest. If people so close to the king and queen are traitors, what hope is there for us? Still, at least the birds are free.'

'There is that,' Merrivale acknowledged. 'The answer, my lady, is that none of us is safe, or will be safe until the man from the north and his allies are exterminated from this earth. We are fighting a hydra. We cut off one head at Crécy, we have cut off another in Blyth, but new heads still keep sprouting.'

'Are you any closer to knowing who it is?' Tiphaine asked.

'A little, possibly. Gilbert de Tracey knew who it is, but he decided to bargain with me. That cost him his life. If he had told me sooner, I might have been able to save him.'

'That is the least of my regrets,' Tiphaine said quietly.

'Mine also.' Their eyes met. 'I will find him,' Merrivale said. 'For Peter's sake, if nothing else.'

They continued to look at each other. 'I will leave you two alone,' said Lady Mary, and she turned and went down the stair.

Mauro and Warin followed her. Merrivale and Tiphaine looked at each other in silence for some time.

'I know how much you thought of him,' she said.

'He would never have made a herald. But he would have been a very good leader of men.'

'And what about her? Yolande?'

'What about her?' the herald repeated.

'Is she still the only woman in the world for you?'

'I don't know.'

'That is not a very satisfactory answer,' she said after a while.

'I know it isn't. The only thing I have learned is that a window separates us from the past. We can see it through the glass, admire it, remember its glow and even feel the warmth of the sun shining through. But we can never touch it again.'

'You can shatter glass,' she said. 'When the window is broken, you can walk through it.'

'But when you do, everything changes,' said the herald.

She laid a hand on his arm, and reached up and kissed him softly on the cheek. 'You are grieving,' she said. 'And you are white with exhaustion. I will leave you now to rest. Simon?'

'Yes?'

'It is good to see you again,' she said softly, and she turned and went down the stair.

Hexham, 14ᵗʰ of October, 1346
Night

'Things aren't going well,' said Brother Oswald. 'Are they?'

They were standing in Brus's pavilion in the camp near the ashes of Hexham. 'Go to hell,' Brus said.

He looks tired, the friar thought. *Perhaps his wound is paining him.* He tried to feel sympathy, and failed.

'Blyth has been exposed, and your plan to seize Newcastle has collapsed,' he said. 'Percy and Neville have joined the English army, and now the Disinherited are on their way as well. Your men were unable to stop them. And you've lost Clennell, I hear.'

Brus turned on him. 'Kindly refrain from pointing out the obvious. What is the situation in Durham?'

'Hugh de Tracey has broken with you. He wants nothing more to do with you. You have disobeyed orders, he says, and broken your promises.' Oswald paused. 'You're in shit now, aren't you? Your allies are disappearing one by one. What are you going to do?'

'I don't need allies. I can do this myself.'

'Oh, I don't think so. You need Douglas and Carrick, and Béthune; and me. If we all desert you, you're finished. And that damned herald is still interfering. Well? What are you going to do?' Oswald repeated.

'For Christ's sake, stop jabbering like a fishwife and let me think!' Brus pressed his hand to his forehead, and looked at the friar. 'Oswald, how would you like to earn more money than you have ever dreamed of?'

'I have quite big dreams,' Oswald warned.

'Believe me, what I pay you will satisfy even your greed. Douglas has lent me two of his men, Nickson and Croser. They're border men and don't know the country down there, so I want you to guide them to the English army. Take them to the camp and leave the rest to them.'

'Is that it?'

'No,' Brus said. 'I told you once that if Durham resisted me, I would burn the cathedral and slaughter every monk in the priory.'

'I told Hugh what you said. He thinks the priory is strong enough to defy you.'

'Then he has made his last mistake. I was intending to move against Newcastle next, but I have changed my mind. The army marches on Durham tomorrow. You will return there as quickly as you can.'

'You want me to warn Hugh you are coming?'

'No,' said Brus. 'I want you to kill him. Hugh de Tracey is the one man capable of organising resistance against me. Once he is dead, the cathedral and priory will fall into my hands.'

Oswald cleared his throat. 'I will need a down payment,' he said.

29

Barnard Castle, 15ᵗʰ of October, 1346
Morning

'It is a pleasure to see you again, Sir Harry,' Merrivale said with gentle irony. 'I trust your journey down from Warkworth was uneventful.'

Around them the army was breaking camp, men-at-arms riding across the bridge under the frowning walls of the castle, followed by hard-marching companies of archers. Percy pulled on his gloves while his esquire held the reins of his horse. 'It wasn't the happiest of occasions,' he said. 'The old man was furious that Brus had tricked him. I tried to warn him, after Mary came to Warkworth and bearded him in his den, but he wouldn't listen. He hates it when I'm right,' Sir Harry said with satisfaction. 'What is our situation?'

'The Scots have been kept out of Berwick and Newcastle hasn't been threatened, so far. But Hexham and Corbridge have been destroyed, and much of the Tyne valley with them. Even with the losses they took at Liddel Strength and yesterday, the Scots must still have well over eleven thousand men.'

'And even with de Lisle's men, we have half that,' said Percy. His face, framed by mail coif and bascinet, looked glum. 'I know we won against greater odds at Crécy, but the Scots will use different tactics, won't they? And we don't have enough men-at-arms, or enough archers.' He paused. 'What game is Brus playing? Is he trying to take over Scotland?'

'Yes,' said Merrivale. 'But I assume this is also part of some larger plan.'

'You mean the man from the north. I know all about him, Mary had it from Tiphaine and she told me. She said that last summer Brus was a minor player, nothing more than the Count of Alençon's lackey. Now he has plenty of money, and power and influence too. How did he get them, do you think?'

Merrivale paused for a moment, thinking. It struck him once again that Harry Percy was rather more acute than he at first appeared. 'David Bruce trusts him,' he said finally. 'He relies on his cousin for advice, and Brus has used his connections with the king to enrich himself.'

Percy looked at him sceptically. 'But how did he get to that position in the first place? This is the man from the north's doing, isn't it? When Alençon was killed, did he call up Brus to take his place?'

'That is certainly possible,' Merrivale said slowly. The plan, back in the summer, had been to dethrone King Philip of France and replace him with his brother, the Count of Alençon. Brus couldn't replace King Philip, but he *could* replace his cousin David Bruce. Was this an expedient, dreamed up after Alençon's death at Crécy had halted the plan in France? Or had the man from the north intended all along to send Brus to Scotland?

Because if the latter was true, if this was all part of some long-ordained strategy, then it was quite possible that another plot against France was underway as well; and against England too. What had Tiphaine overheard Brus say? *They won't have a king for much longer. My friends will see to that.*

Another company of men-at-arms rode past, harness and armour clinking. The red and white banner of Mowbray floated over their heads. 'How well do you know Thomas Hatfield?' Merrivale asked.

Percy looked startled by the change of subject. 'The Bishop of Durham? Well, you saw him last summer. Typical ambitious clerk, although he fancies himself as a war leader as well. He's very much in favour at the moment. I expect he'll be Lord Chancellor one day soon. Why do you ask?'

Merrivale did not answer directly. 'Are you aware of any friction between him and the priory?'

'No, they seem to get along pretty well together. For a wonder, the bishop keeps his nose out of priory business, which is all they seem to want.' Glancing around, Percy lowered his voice. 'But if you wanted to hatch a conspiracy, Durham would be the place to do it. The whole of the County Palatine is cloaked in secrecy. Within its borders, the bishop and prior and their officials can do whatever they want.'

'Mm. Yes,' said Merrivale.

'Is that it? Do you think Hatfield might be the man from the north?'

'It is someone close to the king. That is all I know.'

'You must tell me if I can help,' Percy said.

–

A messenger in the archbishop's livery ran up, saluting. 'Sir Herald, his Grace commands you to his presence. You too, Sir Harry.'

Zouche was in the great hall of the castle, leaning over a parchment map spread out on a table. He wore a mail coat and breastplate, and looked almost warlike. His senior captains were gathered around him. 'A message has arrived from Sir Thomas Rokeby,' the archbishop said, his voice tense. 'He has come south from Berwick, and is shadowing the Scottish army around Hexham. Last night he observed that the Scots are preparing to march.'

'In what direction?' demanded Lord Percy. 'Newcastle?'

'No. Sir Thomas says they sent out scouts towards Ebchester, to the south-east. He thinks they are preparing to move towards Durham.'

'Durham has declared its neutrality,' said Lord Neville.

'Rollond de Brus will not respect that neutrality,' said Merrivale. 'Nor will he respect the sanctity of church property. He has already stripped Lanercost to the walls, and I assume he did the same at Hexham. Now he wants Durham and its treasury for himself.'

'Then we must stop him,' said Robert de Lisle. He was leaning on his sword again, his face sunken with weariness, but his eyes were bright. He pointed at the map. 'We know where the Scots are going. We're twenty-five miles from Durham, and the Scots at Hexham are only a little further distant. It's a race now, gentlemen.'

Ebchester, 15th of October, 1346
Night

'The English have left Barnard Castle,' Douglas reported. 'Our scouts report they are at Auckland, about ten miles from Durham, roughly the same distance as ourselves.'

'Then we shall meet them outside the walls of Durham,' said Brus. 'After we destroy their army, we shall seize and sack the city.'

'When do we fight?' asked Carrick. 'Tomorrow?'

Patrick of Dunbar shook his head. 'The men won't be fit, ours or theirs. The English will pause to give their men a chance to rest and be ready for the following day. Sire, I recommend we do the same.'

'That is wise advice, sire,' said the Marischal.

King David looked around at his councillors. 'Then we are agreed. We will camp tomorrow night at Beaurepaire, north-west of the city, and meet the enemy the following day. Make it so, gentlemen.'

They bowed and departed, Douglas, Carrick, Brus and Béthune all together, talking in low voices. Dunbar lingered for a moment, looking at the king. 'Victory awaits us, sire,' he said.

The king nodded. 'This is our hour,' he said. 'I want to thank you, Dunbar, for your loyal service on this campaign. I confess that I had doubts about you at first, you and your wife, but you have both served me well.'

'It is our honour to do so, sire.'

'When we meet the English, I shall place you in command of a division of the army. Moray shall have the vanguard, and I shall lead the main body myself. To you I shall give command of the rearguard.'

The smallest of the three divisions, Dunbar thought, *but it proves we are trusted. For the moment, at least...* He bowed. 'This is an honour, sire. I shall try to prove worthy of it.'

The king smiled and took a gulp of wine. 'Shall I let you in on a secret, Dunbar? It is my great sadness that my lady wife has yet to produce an heir.'

'I have no doubt that your Grace will sire many sons in the years to come.'

'Of course. But in the meantime, the people need to know that the kingdom is safe, that there will be a king on the throne no matter what happens. Therefore, I intend to appoint an heir. A temporary measure only, of course, until my own son is born.'

'May I ask who will receive this honour?'

'I thought about one of our own nobles, of course, but if I name one of them it is bound to provoke the jealousy of others. Better an outsider, who has no loyalty other than to me. Who better than my kinsman and faithful servant, the Seigneur de Brus?'

'A wise choice, sire,' Dunbar said quietly. 'When will you make the announcement?'

'The day after tomorrow, when we have vanquished the English army and taken Durham into our hands. A historic day, Dunbar. I cannot imagine a more auspicious moment.'

Dunbar bowed. 'I shall be the first to pledge my loyalty,' he said. 'With your Grace's permission, I shall withdraw. I need to make sure my men are ready for the morning.'

Outside the royal pavilion the earl took a deep breath. Grimly, he started to walk towards his own lodgings, but he had not gone more than a few paces before he heard men speaking, and stopped. He recognised the voices at once. One was Rollond de Brus, the other was the renegade friar, Oswald of Halton.

'Is Tracey dead?' Brus was asking.

'Not yet. He knows what happened to his nephew, and he is alert. He is never alone, and someone tastes his food. But I have learned something that may help.'

'Spit it out,' Brus commanded.

'He has written to Sir Harry Percy, asking to meet him secretly outside the city. I know where they are going. I think I can get close enough for a crossbow shot, but I might need help getting away.'

There was a long silence, during which Dunbar fancied he could hear the wheels of Brus's mind turning. 'You still need me,' Oswald said. 'I'm one of the few left who is loyal to you.'

The silence lasted a little longer. 'I'll see to it,' Brus said. 'Once you have shot Tracey, Douglas and a party of light horse will be there to pull your fat out of the fire. What about those two reavers? Did you send them into the English camp?'

'Yes.' Oswald chuckled. 'They should have done their job by now. Croser wants additional payment for his missing teeth.'

'To hell with his teeth. He shouldn't have been so careless in the first place. Very well, Hound of God. You can be on your way now. Report to me when you have completed your task.'

In their pavilion a few minutes later, Dunbar related what he had heard to his wife. Agnes ran her hand through her black curls. 'Once the king names him as heir, Brus will not linger. David will die very soon, and Brus will take revenge on everyone who has ever crossed him in the past, starting with us. Our lives and those of our followers hang by a thread, my lord.'

'Yes,' Dunbar said. 'Our only chance is to thwart him. Why do you think Tracey wants to meet young Percy?'

'At a guess, he has found out about our communication and intends to use it to his advantage.'

'Possibly,' said the earl. 'But Brus wants to kill Tracey, and is going to considerable lengths to do so. If he is Brus's enemy, then he is also our friend. We need to keep him alive, at least until we can find out more.'

The countess turned to Mora of Islay, standing by. 'Can you get a message to the herald? By the end of tomorrow?'

'If you command it, my lady, it shall be done,' said the shield-maiden. 'Do you wish me to remain with the herald, or return to you?'

'Stay with him,' Agnes said. 'He may need you before all is done.'

Auckland, 15ᵗʰ of October, 1346
Night

Merrivale was dining on bread and mutton with a glass of well-watered wine, listening to the patter of rain on the canvas roof of his tent, when the door flap opened and Harry Percy walked in. 'I need a word, Sir Herald. In private.'

Merrivale gestured to Mauro and Warin, but Percy shook his head. 'We need to get away from the camp. Too many listening ears.'

The herald rose and Mauro brought him a cloak, draping it over his shoulders. '*Qué está pasando, señor?*' the servant murmured.

'*No sé. Síganos.*'

Outside the night was dark apart from the flare of torches in the wind and rain. Trees stood like spectral shapes in the misty light. The army lay camped around them in the park of Auckland, the Bishop of Durham's palace and preferred residence a comfortable distance from his cathedral and priory. Mauro and Warin followed them at a discreet distance; if Percy was aware of their presence, he gave no sign. 'Did you know Lady Mary and Tiphaine are still with the army?' he asked.

'No, I didn't.'

'I suggested they remain at Barnard Castle, but they didn't listen, of course. The archbishop has taken them under his protection.'

That won't mean much if we are defeated and Brus captures them, Merrivale thought. Passing the palace they walked down towards the River Wear. Bits of broken wall stood up from the ground, the ruins of an ancient watchtower. The night was almost completely dark.

Percy stopped in the shadow of the wall. 'I've had a letter,' he said quietly. 'I need your advice on what to do about it.'

'A letter from whom? The Countess of Dunbar?'

'No, I've heard nothing further from her. Perhaps she has given up on the idea of peace. She's with her husband and the Scottish army, I hear.'

Merrivale shook his head. 'The Dunbars will make peace when the time comes. For the moment, they are concentrating on staying alive. Who is the letter from?'

'Brother Hugh de Tracey, the treasurer of Durham Priory. He wants to meet with me.'

'I see,' said Merrivale after a moment. 'When and where?'

'Dawn, the day after tomorrow, at Ferryhill. It's just south of Durham. I am to come alone, he said.'

'Did he say why?'

Percy shook his head. 'Then I am not sure what you need from me,' Merrivale said.

Even in the darkness he could tell the young knight was annoyed. 'I need information,' he said. 'One of Tracey's nephews was our family banker, until he took holy orders. The other was a traitor working with the man from the north. Is Hugh de Tracey one of the conspirators?'

Sudden suspicion filled Merrivale's mind. *Play along*, he thought. *If he is innocent, it won't matter what I tell him; if he is guilty, then he already knows.*

'Yes,' he said. 'So was Gilbert, until he was killed.'

Percy stared at him. 'When did that happen?'

'Two days ago, at Hexham. Brus killed him.'

'So why would Hugh want to meet with me?'

'Perhaps he thinks you are also one of the conspirators,' Merrivale suggested.

He waited for a reaction. Percy merely looked irritated again. 'The Traceys have fallen out with Brus,' Merrivale said. 'It is possible that Hugh wants your protection.'

'But why would he send for me?' Percy asked. 'Why not you?'

'Because I am only a herald. You, on the other hand, are a knight with a retinue of men-at-arms at your back—'

Just in time he saw the blur of movement in the shadows, a dim flash of reflected torchlight on steel. He dodged sideways, and the blade meant for his chest ripped through the sleeve of his cloak. Pain stabbed up his arm. He grabbed the other man's sword arm, but the man cursed and wrenched his arm free. He raised his sword for another blow; Merrivale seized him and threw him bodily backwards against the ruined stone wall of the tower, but the other man simply bounced off the wall and came straight back at him. Merrivale dodged the swinging sword but not the hard left fist that followed it, smashing into his midriff.

He doubled up in pain, bracing for the blow that must surely come, but nothing happened. Raising his head he saw the man fighting with someone else, a knife flashing in the shadows and then a gasp and a sound of snapping bone. The man fell, sword clattering on the ground, and the other man bent and stabbed him hard, administering the *coup de grâce*. The newcomer raised his head, and Merrivale saw it was Mauro.

Harry Percy was on the ground, wrestling desperately with another attacker. Out of the darkness Warin appeared, dragging the man off and holding his head back before drawing his knife across his throat. There was a gagging noise and the other man slumped to the ground.

'Are you all right, *señor*?' Mauro asked, his voice full of concern.

'Cuts and bruises, nothing more.' He could feel blood trickling down inside his sleeve, but he had taken worse wounds in the past. 'Sir Harry, are you hurt?'

'Apart from my pride, no,' Percy said ruefully. He climbed to his feet. 'Your servants saved our necks.'

Merrivale looked down at the man Mauro had killed. The light was faint, but he saw the bruised mouth and missing teeth and recognised the hobelar Kalewater Jack Croser. At a gesture from the herald, Warin turned the other man over. It was Eckies Nickson.

'Brus's hired killers,' Merrivale said, his fingers searching inside his sleeve for the gash on his arm. 'He certainly has enough of them at his disposal. I wonder how long they have been tracking me.'

Percy's voice was wry. 'What makes you think they were after you?' he asked. 'I've just thought of another possible reason for this meeting, herald. They want to grab me and use me as a hostage. They'll threaten to hang me unless my father withdraws his men from the army. It won't work, of course, the old bastard won't give an inch and besides, he has plenty of other sons. But Brus and his friends won't know that.'

Merrivale pressed the edges of the wound together. *That will need stitches*, he thought; *I shall have to call on Mauro's skills with a needle.* 'Then you won't go to the meeting.'

Percy sounded vexed again. 'Of course I'll go,' he said. 'How else will I find out what is going on?'

Merrington, 16ᵗʰ of October, 1346
Evening

A column of horsemen came sweeping down from the north, riding hard across the moor. A trumpet sounded the alarm, but Merrivale held up a hand; he had seen their banner, a black chevron and three ravens. 'It is Sir Thomas Rokeby,' he said.

They waited. In Merrington church, a single, cracked bell rang vespers, harsh notes thudding into the damp air. The rain had stopped, though the sky was still full of cloud, and men were down in the open coal pits around the village, bailing them out with buckets. Black water stained the streams running down to the Wear, meandering through meadows to the left of the line of march. Mist was already rising from the river.

Rokeby arrived a few minutes later, accompanied by about fifty men; young Tom Rokeby and John Coupland were among them. 'Once I heard the Scots were advancing down the Tyne, I stripped every spare man from the garrison at Berwick and came south,' Rokeby said to the archbishop. 'I thought if I cut across their line of march, I might pick up some intelligence about their movements.'

'What can you tell us?' Zouche asked.

'The Scots are at Beaurepaire, the prior of Durham's hunting lodge, about two miles from the city. They've made camp for the night.'

'By God, they've made good time,' exclaimed de Lisle. He stood hunched over, utterly exhausted and leaning on his sword again, but his eyes were as hard and determined as ever.

'They are energetic and very well led,' Rokeby said. 'They intend to challenge us outside Durham, your Grace. My scouts had a good look at their camp from the high ground near the city. They are preparing for battle.'

'Then we must do likewise,' said the archbishop. He looked at Merrivale. 'You've seen their full strength. Can we prevail against them?'

'They have eleven thousand men to our six,' the herald said. He had just spotted a familiar figure in the ranks of Rokeby's men-at-arms. 'They have some of the finest fighting men in the world, Moray's highlanders and the Galwegians. But the latter and their archers were mauled at Liddel Strength, and the captains are not united. Brus has secret enemies, some at the highest level. And if David Bruce finds out that his cousin intends to kill him, who knows what might happen? There is hope, my lords.'

Rokeby smiled. 'There is always hope,' he said. 'Well, gentlemen? The southrons are still crowing about their victory at Crécy. Let's show them what the men of the north country can do.'

The baggage wagons arrived, toiling up the road from Auckland, and tents and pavilions went up across the moor. Merrivale walked to his own quarters and found, as expected, Lady Mora of Islay waiting for him. 'Have you become Murdo again?' he inquired.

'For a time,' she said. 'I joined Rokeby's men this morning, pretending to be a defector from the Scottish camp.'

'Pretending?'

'Let's not get tangled up in words,' she said impatiently. 'My lady has news for you.'

Swiftly she told him about the plot against David Bruce, and Oswald's plan to kill Hugh de Tracey. 'My orders are to assist you,' she said. 'Command me.'

Much depended on whether Harry Percy was genuine. 'You were in the garrison at Warkworth,' he said. 'Will Sir Harry recognise you?'

'Not if I keep my distance.'

'Good. Keep watch on him. If he leaves the camp, come and find me at once.'

After Mora had gone, the herald put on his cloak and went out. Mauro had mended the rent in the sleeve; his arm, heavily bandaged, throbbed a little as he walked. He thought of calling on Tiphaine to tell her what was happening, but decided against it; Tiphaine was a complication, and he could not think of her without confusing his mind still further.

He found Sir Thomas Rokeby's quarters. Rokeby was still in full armour, talking with Coupland and young Tom; all three turned as the herald entered the tent. 'Good evening, Simon. Still alive, I see.'

'For the moment,' Merrivale said. 'Thomas, I need a favour. Quite a big one, as it happens.'

30

A hand touched Merrivale's shoulder; Mauro, waking him gently. 'The lady is here, *señor*. The *dama del escudo.*'

Merrivale sat up quickly, reaching for his tabard. 'Run to Sir Thomas Rokeby. Tell him I need his services as requested.'

Outside the fog was thick, particles of water swirling in the air. Silver-grey light seeped through it. Mora stood waiting, her mail coat and helmet glittering with damp. 'He rode out alone just now, going east.'

'Well done,' said the herald. 'Warin, bring my horse around.'

'Shall I come with you?' Mora asked.

'You have done more than enough already. I have another favour to ask of you. Go to Tiphaine and Lady Mary. If there is fighting today, keep them safe.'

'I am a shieldmaiden, not a lady's tirewoman,' grumbled Mora, but she saluted and departed. Rokeby's men were already forming up, his own company from Berwick with John Coupland in command and a hundred or so hobelars from other retinues, dark shapes with upright lances moving through the mist. 'He has gone east towards Ferryhill,' the herald said.

'Tracking him in this fog will be the devil's work.' They rode past the sentries and east across the moor, passing clumps of gorse and threading their way around the dark coal pits that yawned suddenly under their feet. Gradually the fog cleared a little as they rode further away from the valley of the Wear, climbing up onto high ground, but visibility was still not much more than a long bowshot.

'I hear something,' Coupland said.

Rokeby held up his hand and the column jingled to a halt. They all heard it then, the drumming of massed hooves coming at speed across the moor from the north. Rokeby looked at Merrivale. 'Is this what you thought might happen?'

'Yes. Can you hold them off?'

'We'll do better than that.' Rokeby waved his hand. 'Let's go.'

Wheeling left, the horsemen charged away across the moor just as the first Scots rode out of the fog. Merrivale saw the red heart of Douglas, pulling up in astonishment. Yelling like fiends, Rokeby's men charged home, and the crash of breaking lances and clatter of swords erupted through the morning. Spurring his horse, Merrivale rode east alone, quickly swallowed up by the fog.

He came to the Great North Road and reined in, listening. The wind whistled around him. Otherwise, apart from the sounds of combat fading away to the north, all was silent.

The fog swirled and parted a little. He saw the hamlet of Ferryhill away to the right, and nearer at hand a series of coal pits following a seam. Two horses stood near one of the pits. Beside them, two men stood talking. One was Harry Percy. The other wore a black Benedictine habit. A shaft of sunlight pierced the fog and illuminated both men, and Merrivale saw the face of Hugh de Tracey.

'My nephew always spoke well of you and your family,' Tracey said.

Harry Percy looked disbelieving. 'I've never heard a banker speak well of anyone.'

Tracey's voice was sharp in response. 'I'll come straight to the point. I know about your correspondence with Agnes of Dunbar.'

Percy's hand went to the hilt of his sword. 'Are you blackmailing me?'

'No, of course not. I want your help. And I want the countess's help too.'

They heard the eruption of combat in the distance, a dim clamour muffled by the fog. 'If you have played me false,' Percy said grimly.

Brother Hugh raised his hands. 'I swear before God I have not.' Both men waited for a few minutes, tensed and listening. 'The sound is moving away,' Hugh said. 'Perhaps a Scottish foraging party ran into one of your patrols.'

It was possible. Percy listened for a few more moments as the sound faded, and lifted his hand from his hilt. 'You were saying.'

'Rollond de Brus intends to kill his cousin David and proclaim himself king of Scotland.'

'I know all about that. I know all about your conspiracy, too. The herald told me.'

'That goddamned herald.' Tracey's voice was bitter. 'None of this would have happened without that interfering bastard. Brus has broken ranks. He wants to seize control of Scotland and make the country his personal base of power. He tried to drag Gilbert and myself into his scheme. When we refused, he killed Gilbert. Now he is coming for me.'

'Where does the Countess of Dunbar come in? Come to that, where do I come in?'

'I know Brus and the countess hate each other. If he becomes king, she and her husband will soon be dead. I need her to kill Brus, and I need you to help me make contact with her.'

Percy considered this for a moment. 'And just why should I help you?'

'Because I can make you rich,' said Tracey.

'I'm already rich. Or will be, when the old man goes to his rest.'

'Come on, Percy. You're young and ambitious. Are you really content with your present estate? I can give you all of Northumberland, if you want it, and more besides.'

'Really? How much more?'

Tracey said nothing. Instead there came the dull thud of a missile striking flesh and bone. The monk's knees buckled and he fell heavily onto his face, his arms and legs twitching a little and his fingers clawing at the grass. A black crossbow bolt protruded from between his shoulder blades, buried up to the vanes. Percy looked up and saw another horseman standing just on the edge of the fog bank. The rider wore the white robe and black cloak of the Dominican friars, and he held a crossbow in his hands.

The herald turned towards Oswald, spurring his horse. The Dominican saw him coming, and hesitated. It would take him fifteen seconds to load and wind the crossbow, and by that time Merrivale would be on top of him. Cursing, he dropped the weapon and galloped hard away to the north with the herald pursuing him. More hoofbeats drummed in the heavy air; Harry Percy had mounted his horse and was following too.

Off to the left the fighting continued, invisible in the fog. They raced across the moor through patches of drifting mist, Oswald heading steadily north towards the Scottish army and safety. But the River Wear was about to cut across their path, and the only way over the Wear was the bridge on the Great North Road, not far from where Rokeby and Douglas were still hammering each other. Merrivale spurred his horse again. He wanted to catch Oswald before they became entangled in the fighting.

Up ahead was another hamlet on a low hill, the ground beyond sloping down towards the river. The hamlet, he remembered, was called Hett. A large wooden shed stood at the foot of the hill, black heaps of coal around it. The grass dipped and became uneven. Oswald's horse stumbled, whinnying, and then went down in a tangle of thrashing legs, throwing the friar clear. He staggered to his feet, looking back to see the two horsemen bearing down on him, and turned and ran into the shed.

Merrivale pulled his lathered horse to a halt beside the building and slid from the saddle. Percy galloped up a few seconds later, dismounting and drawing his sword.

'What are you doing here?' he demanded.

'Covering your back. You said yourself that this might be a trap.'

'For me, yes. Not for Tracey. I didn't see that coming.'

'What did Tracey want with you?'

'He thought Brus wanted to kill him,' Percy said, 'and he wanted to get his retaliation in first. But he wasn't fast enough.'

'Oswald is a rogue who will do anything for money. If we find him, we can persuade him to talk.'

Percy nodded towards the shed. 'Let's go fetch him, shall we?'

–

Unlike the shallow pits in many fields, the miners at Hett had dug underground, following a rich seam of coal. The shed covered the entrance, keeping out rainwater which would otherwise have filled the tunnels. They descended a short wooden ladder and found several torches leaning against the wall with a tinderbox on a shelf above them. Merrivale lit one of the torches and held it up. Flickering light showed them a low, rough black tunnel with wooden props holding up the weight of the stones and earth above.

'Come out, Oswald,' he shouted into the tunnel. 'If you do, we will spare your life. You have my word of honour.'

The words echoed down the tunnel and died away. There was no response. 'We'll have to drag him out,' Percy said, drawing his sword. 'I'll go first. You light the way.'

Bending low, Percy entered the tunnel. Merrivale followed him, holding up the torch. Broken stone crunched under their feet. One of the pit props shifted alarmingly as they passed, sending little showers of earth and dust down from the ceiling. The mine was deserted; knowing of the armies nearby, the miners had either hidden themselves and their families or fled. Once Percy stopped, pointing to a sandalled footprint in the dust. 'He's here.'

After twenty yards the tunnel branched. They halted, listening. Both tunnels were dark but there was a sense of a presence, someone watching and listening, in the tunnel to the right.

Merrivale pointed and they moved on, treading slowly and carefully, trying to ignore the little stones that fell from the ceiling and pinged off Percy's armour. If the roof caved in now, all three of them would be trapped here forever.

They passed a cluster of tools leaning against the wall, picks and spades and baskets; they must be nearing the end. The tunnel curved around to the left and widened a little. They found themselves in a broader chamber cut out of the earth and rock. The black face of the coal seam glistened like ebony in the torchlight.

Oswald stood with his back to the coal face, holding a knife in one hand. His face was streaked with black dust and covered in sweat. He smiled a little. 'Very clever of you to bring a torch. I fear I was in too much of a hurry.'

'If you come with us, we will spare your life,' said Merrivale.

'Will you? What guarantees can you offer? Your word of honour isn't good enough, I'm afraid. Having no honour myself, I don't trust those who claim they do.'

'We can give you protection,' said Percy, 'and an easy path out of the kingdom.'

Oswald smiled again, beads of sweat rolling down his broad face. 'Protection? Can you keep me safe for the rest of my life? Can you save my immortal soul?'

No one answered. Oswald laughed. 'Don't worry, I won't ask for miracles. I know they're keeping a seat warm for me in hell. In exchange for this *protection*, what do you want?'

'Did Brus pay you to kill Tracey?' the herald asked.

'Oh, for God's sake. You didn't need to chase me through the underworld like Orpheus looking for Eurydice to learn that. Ask me a question where you don't already know the answer.'

'Is Brus acting alone? Or is he following his master's orders?'

Oswald smiled again. 'That's more like it. Alone, of course. He has shaken off his master's halter and is determined to set up a kingdom of his own, supported by his creatures. Carrick, Douglas, Béthune, Clennell.'

'And the Traceys also turned against him,' said Percy.

'More correctly, they never joined him in the first place. They stayed true to their oath. That annoyed Brus. He wanted their loyalty, but even more than that, he wanted their money. That's why he has brought the army to Durham now, to pillage the place and seize its treasury.'

Torchlight flickered off the black stone walls of the chamber. 'You say the Traceys were true to their oath,' the herald said. 'Their oath to whom? Who is their master?'

The friar looked at him. 'I'll have that protection you promised me. Now, if you please.'

Percy nodded. 'Let's take him up,' he said to Merrivale. 'Go ahead with the torch. Friar, clasp your hands on top of your head and follow the herald. I'll bring up the rear with my sword at your back. One false move, Oswald, and I'll bleed you like a pig. Move.'

They retraced their steps, reaching the branch in the tunnels. Merrivale heard the sudden scrabbling behind him and tensed, but he was too late. Oswald slammed into him, pressing him hard against the wall of the tunnel. The torch fell from his hand, rolling onto the floor where it still flickered and flamed. Merrivale felt the sting of a knife blade against his throat.

'Don't move!' Oswald snarled.

'Don't be a fool,' the herald said quietly. 'Drop the knife.'

'Put up your sword, Percy, or I'll cut his throat, by God I will.'

Out of the corner of his eye Merrivale saw Harry Percy hesitate, sword in hand. Raising his free hand, the herald stabbed his fingers back into Oswald's face, seeking the other man's eyes. Cursing, Oswald pulled his head back and the pressure of the knife relaxed for a second. Before the friar could move again, Percy took a long stride forward and ran his sword through the Dominican's midriff. Oswald fell to the floor, blood pouring from his stomach. He screamed once with pain and Percy stabbed him again, this time through the heart. He shuddered convulsively and then went limp.

Merrivale stared at Percy. 'We needed him alive,' he said.

'On the whole, herald, I think you are rather more valuable.' Percy gestured with his sword. 'Leave this carrion where he lies. The miners will find him when they next come down. Let's go.'

As promised, Rokeby had done more than just hold the Scots at bay. Not expecting opposition, Douglas's men had been caught off guard by the sudden charge through the fog. After a brief fight they turned and fled towards the bridge over the Wear, pursued by Rokeby's hobelars who caught them just as they reached the bridge. Here, the fight turned into a slaughter. Hemmed in against the river and the stone parapets of the bridge the Scots could not fight back and the Northumbrians killed them one by one. By the time Merrivale and Percy arrived, Douglas and the survivors had fled across the bridge and up the hill beyond and Rokeby's men were dragging up bodies and piling them in rows. Coils of blood stained the waters of the Wear.

'Douglas escaped, I am sorry to say,' Rokeby said. 'That man has the luck of the devil. John Grey ran him through with a sword last year, and he still got away.'

He looked at Merrivale. 'Did you do what you needed to do?'

'Yes, and no,' said Merrivale. 'We will need to send word to the priory at Durham. Their treasurer is dead. His body is in a field up near Ferryhill.'

Rokeby looked surprised. 'We'll send a party to fetch it back to the priory once the fighting is over,' he said. 'What happened?'

Merrivale told him. He was still angry with Percy, and the latter knew it. 'I knew Oswald was a spy,' Rokeby said at the end. 'I never thought of him as a killer.'

'He was,' Merrivale said. 'Just not a very efficient one. Like so many, he was seduced by the money Brus paid him.' The jangle of harness and rattle of horseshoes echoed down the road from the south. 'Here comes the army. All we can do now is go forward, and discover what destiny awaits us.'

31

Neville's Cross, 17th of October, 1346
Afternoon

They could hear the Scots army even before they saw it, the sounds of men chanting and singing, the blare of trumpets and hammer of drums, the wailing of pipes drifting out over the moor. Passing Neville's Cross with the cathedral on the far side of the river, Merrivale realised it was less than a month since he had last ridden this way. It felt like an entire age of humanity had gone by.

Ahead lay another moor, open grassland clumped with heather and gorse, swept by a cold north wind. The first companies of the vanguard were already deploying into line of battle, men-at-arms under the blue lion banner of Percy and the white saltire of Lord Neville dismounting and forming long lines brilliant with metal and colour. Wedges of green and russet-clad archers formed up on each flank; the same formation as at Crécy but with fewer men, far fewer.

The archbishop's division pulled into line alongside the vanguard, the men-at-arms sending their horses back to the rear. Merrivale dismounted too, handing over his horse to Warin and sending him to join Mauro with the baggage train. There was no sign of Mary or Tiphaine, which was good; he could trust Mora of Islay to protect them. The archbishop, sweating under the unaccustomed weight of his armour, was directing his men into position; fairly competently, Merrivale thought, although his experienced Yorkshire knights knew their business and needed little in the way of orders. The third division under Rokeby's command had halted further back by the pilgrim cross; they were the army's reserve. The Disinherited took up their position in the centre of the line, making a tight formation around the white lion of de Lisle. Merrivale thought of the boy they had buried at Chipchase, and wondered if that pain would ever fade.

Up ahead the Scottish scouts were falling back towards the clamorous main body. Like the English the Scots had dismounted, all except for one company behind the main line under the banner of the Earl of Menteith. Unlike the English men-at-arms who were standing in lines, the Scots had formed up into tight wedges known as schiltrons, with the most heavily armoured men at the front. The royal standard, the red lion rampant on yellow, fluttered on the right of the Scottish line, facing the archbishop's men. He could see the king too, up front where his men could see him; David Bruce lacked many things, the herald thought, but courage was not one of them. Other familiar devices could be seen around him, the red saltire of Brus, the gold and blue of Béthune, the lion of Bruce of Carrick, the red heart of Douglas. The herald's eyes narrowed a little. The inner circle, the trusted conspirators were all gathered near the king.

Over on the left were the red diamonds of Moray, his highland men chanting and slamming their swords against their shields. Further back, on a little rise in the ground, Merrivale saw the colours of Dunbar. He wondered what was going through the minds of Agnes and her husband. *We tried to prevent this moment, and we failed*, he thought. *Now, everything is in the hands of God*.

Zouche was looking at the enemy lines too. His face was pale beneath the visor of his bascinet. 'Trust in your captains, your Grace,' Merrivale said quietly. 'They are men of great experience. They will not let you down.'

The archbishop gestured towards the enemy. 'Their captains are experienced too. And they have numbers.'

'But the ground is not in their favour,' Sir Robert de Lisle said. 'Whoever chose this battlefield chose unwisely. There is no room for manoeuvre. Their only choice is a frontal attack.'

It was true, Merrivale saw. To the east the ground fell away steeply towards the Wear, with Durham's towers rising on the far side; the bells of the cathedral were tolling nones. To the west was a slightly less steep incline down to another river, the Browney. The spine of high moorland between them was further narrowed by deep valleys of tributary streams running down to the rivers, and sandstone quarries above the banks of the Browney presented sheer cliffs. There was absolutely no chance of a flank attack, by either side.

Zouche hesitated for a moment. 'What do you advise we do, Sir Robert?'

'Stand and wait,' said de Lisle.

'Wait? For how long?'

'For as long as it takes,' the old man said, his voice hoarse with exhaustion. 'Time is one thing we have plenty of.'

They waited. Across the moor the Scots waited too, drums still hammering, pipes wailing. Merrivale saw the familiar gold and red colours of Lyon Herald making his way towards the English lines, and he called to the archbishop. 'The enemy wish to parley, your Grace.'

'We must observe the conventions,' Zouche said. 'Go and speak to them, Sir Herald.'

'What terms may I offer?'

Zouche glanced at de Lisle. 'Tell them to lay down their arms,' the old man said. 'If they do, we will allow them to return unmolested to Scotland.'

The men around them murmured a little. They knew there was no chance the Scots would agree, and they were glad. *They don't care about the numbers against them*, Merrivale thought. *Some have already lost their homes in Northumberland and the west, and now they want blood.*

He walked forward, seeing at once what de Lisle meant. The ground was rough and undulating, and the thorny spines of gorse and tangled roots of heather presented obstacles to both sides. The enemy had the wind at their backs, which would assist their archers, but they had very few of these left now; too many had been killed or wounded at Liddel Strength. Lyon Herald had stopped halfway between the two armies, and he waited for Merrivale to reach him.

'What do you think?' he asked, looking up at the skies. 'Is it going to rain again?'

'This moorland will turn into a bog if it does,' Merrivale said. 'The soil here is even worse than Dartmoor. What do you have for me, Archie?'

'You can probably guess. Lay down your arms, withdraw south of the Tees, swear an oath not to take up arms against Scotland for a year.'

Merrivale looked surprised. 'A year? That's asking a lot. All we demand is that you return to Scotland.'

'I thought our proposal was more imaginative. I take it the answer is no?'

Merrivale nodded. 'Likewise,' said Lyon Herald. 'What are your lot planning to do, Sim?'

'Stand fast, and hold their position until you attack.'

'Unsurprisingly, our side are doing the same. Aye, it's a staring contest,' said Graham. He looked around. 'I don't like this field. The ground is too rough and too narrow. I thought Brus was supposed to know his business.'

'He's a better plotter than he is a soldier, I reckon. Still, you have the numbers.'

Graham shook his head. 'Ground is more important than numbers, Sim. You know that. I'd say it's an even contest.' He looked up at the sky again. 'We'd better get back.'

'Good luck, Archie.'

'You too, lad.'

Back at the archbishop's post in the second line, Merrivale made his report. 'They're waiting for us to make the first move, your Grace.'

De Lisle leaned on his sword. 'Hold your position, your Grace. Make them come to us. Let them make the first mistake.'

Across the moor, the pipes and drums had fallen silent. The cathedral bells had stopped too. Silence fell over the battlefield.

–

Armoured like the men around her, Agnes of Dunbar moved up to stand beside her husband at the head of the rearguard. 'Will the king hold his nerve?' she asked.

Dunbar looked at her. 'You know as well as I do that it isn't the king we need to worry about,' he said. 'It is the men around him.' He paused. 'When he appointed me commander of a division, I thought he had begun to trust me. Instead here I am, stuck far behind the line of battle.'

'He does trust you,' Agnes said. 'As commander of the reserves, you will know when to intervene, and how.'

Dunbar shook his head. 'I received an order this morning, from Brus. Once battle is joined, we are not to advance without a direct order from the king himself.'

The Master of Kinross turned his head. 'Brus gave this order? In the king's name?'

'Yes. Brus thinks he can win the battle himself, and we are to have no share in the glory.'

'Then he is a fool,' said Kinross.

Dunbar said nothing more. Silence fell once again. Both sides waited, the wind whipping at the bright standards and banners. In the trees down by the Browney the crows cawed, waiting for their feast.

–

With dreamlike slowness, the passion play of battle began to unfold.

The first move came from the English side. Three hundred archers detached themselves from Lord Percy's division, moving cautiously forward towards the wedges of Scottish spearmen. Zouche stiffened. 'What are they doing? The orders were to hold fast.'

342

'Trust Lord Percy, your Grace,' said de Lisle. 'He is trying to tempt them to attack.'

At two hundred and fifty yards the archers raised their bows and began to shoot. Even at a distance the men around the archbishop could hear the clatter of arrowheads striking metal. The Scottish schiltrons huddled together, men raising their shields to ward off the arrows. The archers were shooting at long range and into a stiff wind, meaning that by the time the arrows arrived at their target they had lost much of their penetrative force; but even so, a Scot fell, then another, and another. More men staggered back wounded, and the schiltrons began to lose their tight formation.

From the Scottish lines a trumpet sounded and Menteith's company of horsemen began to move, sweeping forward and spurring to a gallop. The archers turned to face them and for a moment Merrivale was reminded of Crécy, armoured men-at-arms charging, the archers standing their ground and shooting fifteen arrows a minute in hypnotic, repetitive motions, *nock-draw-release, nock-draw-release, nock-draw-release*, over and over as horses and men crashed to the ground. Shattered, most of the Scots turned and fell back out of arrow range. Menteith charged on alone; a hailstorm of arrows converged on him, but he seemed impregnable. A murmur ran through the watching English ranks as the lone horseman bore down on the archers, lance levelled, and just when it seemed that nothing could touch him, his horse was shot and fell, throwing the earl to the ground. Some of the archers ran forward and seized him, dragging him back to their lines.

Harsh and raw, its notes cracking in the wind, a trumpet sounded. Another answered, and another, and the pipes began to wail their war songs, and with a clash of metal that rose to the clouds the Scottish army stirred into motion.

–

Moray led his men from the front, as he always did. The schiltron behind him was like the blade of a spear, and he and the heavily armoured men-at-arms around him were its steel tip. Arrows hissed around them as they tramped forward, clattering off armour, thudding into upraised shields; Moray's own shield was hit three times in less than a minute and another arrow hit his bascinet and ricochetted away, leaving a dent the size of an egg behind it. A fifth found a gap in his plate armour and punched through the mail beneath; the wound was not deep, but he felt the blood began to flow. But Moray never wavered, and the men behind him did not waver either; each time a man fell, another ran forward to take his place.

The English line drew closer. Strathearn's schiltron was close beside his own, the men of Fife on his other flank. *This is our moment*, Moray exulted; *this is the day we pay the English back for the last fifty years*. He thought of the rewards that had been promised him, the lands and titles and power that would come to him in the aftermath of victory; he imagined, as he had imagined many times before, presiding over the execution of his sister, the bitch who had abandoned him to his death... He heard a sudden scream of pain and looked over to see Strathearn staggering; an arrow had smashed through his visor and hit him in one eye. Two men were alongside him, shielding him as more arrows rattled off their armour, but Strathearn raised his head and motioned with one hand; forward.

The English lines were just ahead, gorse bushes a dense obstacle in front of them. Moray hacked at these with his sword, feeling another arrow bite into his leg, but the pain merely spurred him on. 'Come on!' he shouted to his men, and the schiltron burst through the last of the gorse and slammed into the English line.

–

Harry Percy was waiting for them. As the Scottish schiltrons began to move he left his post beside his father and ran to the forward line. The men around him cheered when they saw the blue lion, men of the Northumbrian dales and the high hills of the Cheviots, fighting for their kin and their homes. Anger surged in Harry's mind as he watched the Scots coming; anger at his father for having considered treason, anger at himself for having listened to the old man in the first place. He knew the herald still distrusted him too, and that angered him still further.

Mary was right, he thought, watching the red diamonds of Moray come closer and closer, the scream of the pipes shredding the air; *we should have done our duty. Well, we're doing it now.*

The Scots were coming on fast now, the gleaming wedges of the schiltrons tearing through gaps in the gorse bushes, and after them poured Moray's highlanders, swords and axes aloft. They smashed like a battering ram into the wall of English men-at-arms. Under their impact, the wall buckled. 'Stand fast!' Percy shouted, and he ran down the line, warding off blows with his shield and dragging his own men back into the line again.

Arrows, dark furies hissing in the air, clawed and tore at the Scots. Percy found Moray in the middle of the fighting, swinging his sword around him, armour and surcoat stained with blood, shield riddled with arrows, and ran straight at him. They clashed swords, again and again, and sharp rapid blows drew blood on Percy's leg and neck, but he had hit Moray again too, and the Scottish earl stumbled. Slowly, step by step, Harry Percy drove Moray back and his men retreated with him.

–

As Moray's men fell back, fresh schiltrons from the king's division came crashing into the attack. Niall Bruce of Carrick led one of these, holding his sword aloft to guide his men. The English archers saw him and a cloud of arrows converged on him; shot twice, he stumbled but came up again, roaring like a bull, and led his men straight at the solid shield wall of the Disinherited.

Raging, Carrick threw himself at the enemy. The Disinherited had promised to serve Scotland, and had broken their promise; therefore, they must die. He hacked down two men, breaching the shield wall, and drove forward, his men crowding behind him and stabbing at the English with their long spears. Sword blades hammered at his shield; he stabbed back, feeling the point of his weapon burst through mail and leather and slash deep into flesh and bone. His battered lion shield was splattered with blood.

More and more Scots came piling in. Douglas was there too, moving towards the heart of the fighting; Sutherland was not far away. The air reverberated to the clash of metal, punctuated by the screams of wounded men. Carrick spotted the cinque-foil of Umfraville and slashed through the press until they were face to face. He raised his shield, and Umfraville's sword split the shield vertically and banged off the Scot's vambrace. But Umfraville stumbled on rough ground, and a back-handed blow from Carrick knocked his bascinet off and threw him onto his back. Carrick stood over the dazed man, sword raised for the kill.

Another sword smashed into his shoulder, ringing off his pauldron. He turned to face his assailant, a man in gleaming armour with white hair flowing out from beneath his bascinet. 'Sir Robert de Lisle,' he snarled. 'It will be a pleasure to kill you, old man.'

De Lisle said nothing. For a moment they faced each other, red lion and white; then de Lisle circled, clashing his blade against Carrick's, and stabbed low, sword point gliding beneath the bottom of Carrick's breastplate and punching through the mail links beneath.

Disbelieving, Carrick felt the blood start to flow. How could this old man hit him so hard? Roaring again, he attacked with a flurry of cutting and slashing strokes, but de Lisle's shield and blade blocked every blow; and when Carrick halted, gasping for breath, de Lisle advanced, stabbing and cutting through weak spots in his armour time and time again. Staggering, faint now with loss of blood, the Scot reeled back. *God damn it*, he thought, *this wasn't supposed to happen*. Rollond had promised that they would roll straight over the English, grind them into dust. He wondered if Douglas was right, if Rollond really couldn't be trusted, and then another blow hit Carrick on the head and the world around him went black.

—

Carrick was down, but the enemy were still pouring forward, the schiltrons of Douglas and Sutherland hacking their way through the English line and ignoring the hail of arrows around them. David Bruce's men were coming forward too, ready to administer the final blow. Off to the left, the archbishop's standard was almost entirely surrounded. De Lisle leaned on his sword, gasping for breath and feeling a sharp pain spreading through his chest. *Rokeby*, he thought, *now is the time to commit the reserves. Do not wait for orders, old friend. Throw your men in, now.*

He raised his sword again. A Scot came at him with upraised axe; de Lisle ran him through, pulled his sword clear of the body and pressed on towards the red heart of Douglas, shouting at his men to follow. Wake was alongside him. 'We can't hold on much longer, Robert.'

'We'll hold until the end,' said de Lisle. The pain in his chest was stronger now, and speaking was a great effort. 'Our honour demands nothing less.'

Behind the visor of his battered bascinet, Wake grinned at him. 'I knew you would say that. Let me lead the way.'

De Lisle opened his mouth to object, but this time no words would come. The pain was spreading, swelling, roaring in his ears. He looked up suddenly and saw that the clouds had parted, and in a patch of pale sunlight he saw suddenly the faces of his family; Eleanor his beloved wife, Robert his son who had been killed at Annan, Richard who had died on pilgrimage far away and dearest of all, Peter, the sweet, eager boy who had wanted so much to be a herald. All of them were smiling at him, and suddenly the pain in his body was gone, and the sounds of combat disappeared too, replaced with music like an eruption of joy. Light as a cloud, he rose through the air to join his family, and the knowledge came in a flash of light; *we will be together now, for all eternity.*

Standing on the base of the pilgrim's cross, Rokeby surveyed the scene. 'Percy's men and the Disinherited are still holding firm, but the archbishop's men are almost done.'

John Coupland grunted. 'Time we saved their arses, then.'

'My thoughts precisely.' Rokeby jumped down and turned to the captains of the rearguard, Coupland and his nephew Tom among them. 'Archers on the flanks, men-at-arms up the middle, hobelars behind them. Run fast, hit hard and do not stop for anything. After that, you know what to do.'

He slammed down the visor of his bascinet. Young Tom grinned at him. 'I can imagine old Charlemagne giving just such a speech, before leading his army against the Saracens.'

'If we survive this, you can set it to music,' Rokeby said. 'Trumpeter! Sound the advance!'

They ran, the men-at-arms and hobelars raising swords and lances, the archers on the wings nocking arrows. Ahead Rokeby could see Zouche standing with a heavy mace in his hand, and Merrivale beside him holding a wooden staff – *damned heralds*, he thought with a flash of irritation, *why should they get to avoid the fighting*, but he knew Merrivale had already survived more brushes with death than most men – and beyond them a wedge of Douglas of Liddesdale's men cutting its way through the English line. Already one gap had opened up and the Scots were breaking through. Following his own instructions Rokeby ran straight into them, knocking two men off their feet, punching a third with his shield, slashing at a fourth, and then Coupland and Tom were alongside him forcibly heaving the Scots back. Through the bars of his visor Rokeby saw Douglas coming at him with upraised sword and he ducked under the blow; before the Scot could strike another, Tom Rokeby had smashed the sword out of his hand and knocked Douglas down. 'Do you yield?' the young man asked.

Rokeby didn't hear his response because the rest of the rearguard slammed home around him, hitting the struggling, shouting, screaming mass of men with a shock that could be felt in the air. Cohesion began to vanish and formations broke up; men fought blindly, hacking and slashing at other men around them until they crashed down among the gorse bushes, and the clatter of weapons on armour and the deadly hiss of arrows went on and on, and on. There was little movement; men occupied their own yard of ground where they stood, fought and died. But the English had no more reserves left now, and a few hundred yards away stood the third Scottish division, wedges of men-at-arms and the feared spearmen from Galloway and the few remaining archers, gathered under the white lion banner of Dunbar.

Gradually, the pace of the fighting fell away. Men-at-arms and hobelars on both sides began to stumble, exhausted. Many of the English archers were out of arrows and had thrown themselves into the hand-to-hand fighting, which they were not used to or trained for, and they too were staggering with weariness. Little scattered combats broke out between men barely able to lift their weapons, and died down again.

–

Merrivale ran forward, pushing his way between groups of men. 'My lords, withdraw your men!' he commanded. 'Make a truce while you treat your wounded! Put twenty yards between your lines, now!' He began shoving bewildered Englishmen away from their enemies; Lyon Herald arrived on the scene a moment later and began pushing the Scots away as well. Slowly, raggedly, the men of both sides began to rejoin their formations, bringing their wounded with them. The smell of blood was harsh and hot in the air.

Sir Robert de Lisle lay on his back. They had taken off his bascinet and his white hair stirred a little in the wind, his sightless eyes staring up at the sky. Gilbert d'Umfraville knelt beside him. 'What happened?' Merrivale asked.

'He is unwounded,' Umfraville said, and the hard border man had tears in his eyes. 'His gallant old heart has given out. It is a miracle that it sustained him for so long.'

'A miracle that saved us,' said Wake, wiping his eyes. 'God sent him for a purpose, to recall us to our duty. Now God has taken him for his own.'

Merrivale gazed down at the old man's face, peaceful at last in death. It happened, sometimes; in the heat of battle, burdened with armour, a man's heart would fail. He had seen it before, but that did not make this loss any less painful.

Come! How long will your mind be chained to the earth? Do you not see into what regions you have come? The herald thought of *The Dream of Scipio*, and wondered if it was still lying on the table in the hall at Chipchase. It would lie there for a long time now, until the king's escheators came to take the estate into their hands and, no doubt, sell off the contents of the estate to help fill the Treasury's coffers. There would be no monument in Chipchase chapel to mark Peter's grave.

He looked around at the others. 'God has taken him,' he repeated. 'But if Sir Robert were still here, he would remind you that the work is not over. Honour his memory, gentlemen.'

Wake nodded. 'You may be sure that we will,' he said.

–

Water bearers were coming forward on both sides. An Englishman struggled to rise to his feet and one of the Scots stepped out of the line and helped him up, patting him on the back as he hobbled away. Guy of Béthune leaned on his sword, sucking in air. He and Brus were so far unwounded, but the same could not be said of many others. Moray was down on his knees with his eyes closed, his armour stained with blood; Strathearn's face was a gory mess, one eye gone. Niall Bruce of Carrick lay on the grass, eyes closed and breathing shallowly while blood poured from his wounds; he would be dead within a few minutes. The king's own schiltron had disintegrated under a hail of arrows before it could reach the English line; David himself had an arrow embedded in his body and another in his head, punched through the visor of his bascinet. Douglas had disappeared, God knew where.

The king spoke, his voice taut with pain. 'Send for Dunbar and the reserves. We need them.'

'No!' Brus said violently. 'We are on the verge of victory, sire. We can win this battle without Dunbar's help.'

Guy of Béthune stared at him. 'On the verge of victory? For Christ's sake, man, look around you!'

'Damn you, Béthune, are you questioning me? If Dunbar advances now, he will claim all the credit and the glory. Let him stay where is.'

'You have taken leave of your senses. I'll send a messenger.'

Brus drew his sword. 'If you do, I'll kill him myself. This is *my* victory, Béthune. No one will take it away from me, not you, not anyone.'

He nodded towards the English lines. The herald, the hated Merrivale, was conferring with his Scottish opposite number. He imagined briefly the fate he would finally mete out to Merrivale once the battle was over, but tore his mind away. There was other, more important business to do first.

'Get ready,' he said. 'We are about to resume.'

Merrivale met Archie Graham in the bloody space between the armies. 'You've taken one hell of a hammering,' Lyon Herald said quietly. 'There's no need for more bloodshed. Any chance you could persuade your side to withdraw?'

'And leave Durham to its fate?' Merrivale shook his head. 'The commanders will never agree. Your fellows are pretty beaten up as well, you know.'

'We've taken losses,' Lyon Herald acknowledged. 'But I'm afraid it's a foregone conclusion, Sim.'

'Perhaps,' said Merrivale. 'All right, Archie. One way or another, let's get this over with.'

They walked to one side of the battlefield, turning to stand on top of a hill looking down to the Wear. The sound of chanting drifted up from the river; the monks had come down to the bridge and were praying for an English victory. *I don't suppose it can hurt*, Merrivale thought. He wondered what would happen in the priory now that Hugh de Tracey was dead, and realised that if England lost this battle, it would not matter; within days, there would no longer be a priory.

He turned towards the two armies. He saw the banners waving in the wind, the lions rampant and roaring, the red of Scotland, the blue of the Percys, the white of de Lisle which his men had raised once more. 'My lords!' he shouted. 'Are your men refreshed?'

'They are,' said Lord Percy, and the Marischal of Scotland nodded.

'Then you may resume,' said the herald.

—

Like the fighting lions on their banners, the two armies launched themselves at each other. Men shouted and stabbed with sword or spear or knife, or when weapons broke, grappling with one another and falling down to wrestle on the bloody grass. Arrows still flew, but fewer now, and once again the archers ran in among the fighting men, groups of three or four surrounding Scottish men-at-arms and dragging them down to kill them. That was how Strathearn finally died, stabbed over and over by English daggers as he lay helpless on the grass.

The Disinherited still stood in the middle of the English line, and in blind fury the Scots threw in their battered schiltrons in hopes of breaking them. Moray's men led the first wave, shouting their war cries while the pipes screamed and moaned. Umfraville was still groggy from his head wound, and into his place stepped Lord Wake. His armour dented, his shield split, his sword crusted with blood, he turned to his men. 'Honour Sir Robert's memory!' he commanded. 'Do not yield an inch of ground!' They hammered their sword hilts against their shields and crouched, intent on the oncoming Scots.

Wake remembered his dead friends, Selby and de Lisle, and Clennell who he had counted a friend too, until he betrayed them. He gripped his sword hard, watching the Scottish spear-heads race across the moor, and waited for the moment of impact.

It came, harder and more violent than he had been expecting. For a moment it was all he could do to stay on his feet, leaning into his broken shield and pushing hard, his own men packed tight and straining behind him while the Scottish spears stabbed at them. An axe blade hammered against his helm and his ears rang for a moment, but then the weight of men behind him began to slowly drive the Scots back. He freed his sword arm in the press and slashed at the axeman, knocking the weapon out of his hands. More Scots fell and then the first wave gave way, leaving a heap of bodies on the ground. Some of the English started to pursue and Wake snarled at them, telling them to stand their ground. His ears were still ringing and his limbs ached. *My God, how much longer can we keep doing this?* Already the Scots were reforming, and out on the moor Moray himself was coming forward, leading a second wave of schiltrons.

–

Dizzy with loss of blood, Moray stumbled forward past the bodies of men fallen in earlier attacks, his men pressing close behind him. He barely heard the sound of the pipes or the shouts of men on both sides. All he could think about was getting to the English line, cutting a way through it and breaking the enemy. He knew he was growing weak, but the enemy were weak too. One more blow would smash them.

They reached the enemy line. Summoning the last of his strength he raised his sword, cutting down the first two men who barred his way, but more stepped in to replace them. His own men piled in behind him, pressing forward, trying to drive the Disinherited back or knock them off their feet. They failed. The enemy were like a rock, and his own men like the sea breaking against it. Already some of the highlanders were falling back, unable to find a way through the shieldwall in front of them.

Moray shouted at them, ordering them to stand fast, but the trickle of men retreating became a flood.

He turned. A man-at-arms with a broken shield and bloody surcoat with red and gold bars barred his way; Wake, who had been one of the commanders at Dupplin Moor where his brother had died. Moray hated Wake as he hated all the English, as he hated his sister who had abandoned him to captivity and death among them. He raised his sword and swung it blindly at Wake's head, and Wake dodged the sweeping blade and hit him a two-handed blow that shattered his right arm. His sword fell to the ground. Bloody and weak he stood swaying, confronting the Englishman.

'Yield,' said Wake.

'Fuck you,' said Moray, and he bent to reach left-handed for his sword. He never saw the blow that killed him, only felt the shock as the sword blade hit his neck. In one last brief flash of fury he cursed his sister and wished for her death, and then fell heavily to the ground.

–

'Moray's men are breaking,' Guy of Béthune said. His voice was full of disbelief. 'Blood of Christ, they're breaking! They're running away!'

It had happened in the blink of an eye; one moment the Scots were raging forward, the next their formations had collapsed. Men fled across the moor, some throwing away weapons and armour so they could run more quickly. Already the English were breaking ranks, starting the pursuit. 'Where is Moray?' Brus demanded.

'Dead, I think. Strathearn too. Douglas has been taken. They're finished, Brus. The whole division is running.'

The king's division wavered. Most of the men were still holding fast, but out on the flanks a few were turning to join the fugitives. Brus began to run towards the king, shoving tired, wounded men out of his way. Béthune caught up with him after a few paces. 'Where are you going?'

'I'm going to kill that bastard. Then I'm going to proclaim myself king. I'll rally the men and we'll fight back. Are you with me?'

Béthune caught the other man by the shoulder and spun him around violently. 'Are you mad? This battle is lost! Do you not hear me? All your plans are in ruins, Brus. Everything you have worked for has come undone.'

'To hell with you.' Brus's face was dark with rage. 'Will you betray me too? Must I win this battle by myself?'

Béthune hesitated. *He is on the edge of insanity*, he thought. *Why did we ever trust him?*

'Look out!' someone shouted. 'Ware the left!' The English were advancing fast now, Percy's division pouring through the gap where Moray's men had stood. Harry Percy led them, running out in front with the blue lion banner following him, wrapping around the flank of the king's division and threatening to surround it. The Marischal waved his sword, trying to rally men for a counter-attack, but a shower of English arrows cut him down. For a moment the blue lion of Percy confronted the red lion of Scotland; and then the king's division broke too, and the whole of the moor was covered with fleeing men, with the English running in among them and cutting them down.

Béthune seized Brus's arm. 'Come on. We must get out of here, or we're dead. Find the horses.'

Panicked men flooded around them, jostling them. 'It's all that goddamned herald's fault. I should have killed him. I *will* kill him.'

'Don't just stand here talking about it!' Béthune shouted. Rokeby's banner was coming towards them, Wake and Neville too, hacking their way through the tide of fugitives. 'Here come the English, you fool! *Run!*'

Far to the rear, Dunbar's division watched the rest of the army disintegrate. Agnes turned in the saddle and touched her husband's arm. 'Turn the men away, my lord,' she said.

The earl looked at her. 'Turn them away,' she said. 'The rest of the army is wrecked, and the battle is lost. Once again, our country stands on the brink. It will need us, and our men, if it is to survive at all.'

'Her ladyship is right, my lord,' said the Master of Kinross. 'The English have the upper hand. Even if we attack now, we will not prevail. We will sacrifice ourselves to no end.'

Dunbar nodded. There were tears in his eyes as he turned to his captains. 'We will withdraw to Ebchester,' he said. 'We will rally the survivors there.' He took one last look at the fleeing mass of men. 'May God help Scotland,' he said quietly.

32

Lyon Herald wept too as he watched them go. Merrivale put an arm around his shoulders. 'I'm sorry, my friend.'

'Why are you sorry? It is the fortune of war.' A group of men gathered around the wounded King David, half carrying him from the field, fighting off the English who raged around them. 'When in the name of God are we going to learn?' Graham asked. 'How many have we lost today, how many will we have lost by the time the day is done? Thirteen years ago at Halidon Hill we lost an entire generation, annihilated in a single day. We waited for their sons to grow and replace them, and now their sons are dead or dying too. How many times will we repeat this folly, Sim? Until every family is wiped out, every future obliterated?'

'The same is true of England,' Merrivale said, thinking of de Lisle. 'It takes two to make a war, Archie. Come. Let us get you away so you can rejoin your own people.'

The Scots were fleeing down the slopes towards the Browney now, the English howling after them, and some of the men-at-arms were calling for their horses. Merrivale spotted Warin leading his own horse and called to him. 'Fetch another mount for Lyon Herald. Quickly now!'

The horses arrived. They mounted and rode down towards the river, seeing little parties of Scots fighting desperate actions here and there across the meadows near Beaurepaire. David Bruce's party had not managed to get him to safety; they passed the king being led back towards the English lines on foot, John Coupland gripping him possessively by the arm. He had not surrendered tamely; several of the Englishmen around him had fresh wounds and Coupland's face was covered in blood. The blackened stump of an arrow still protruded from the king's head.

On the far side of the river another company of Scots was making their last stand, English hobelars and archers howling around them. Beyond them Merrivale spotted two riders on the skyline.

With a cold shock he realised one of them was Tiphaine.

'I may need your help, Archie,' he said.

—

'I need to see,' Tiphaine said.

The three women sat on their horses by the pilgrim cross, the baggage train parked behind them. The cathedral bells were ringing again; it was vespers now. Lady Mary listened to the cries of the wounded men coming from the field ahead and shuddered. 'I don't. I'm not moving, and I don't advise you to either.'

'I have seen battlefields before,' Tiphaine said. 'Mora, will you come with me?'

They rode forward, skirting the edge of the field, Tiphaine scanning the bodies for Brus's saltire. She did not see it; she did not expect to. No matter how fierce the combat, Brus would find a way to survive. She turned the other way and looked down into the meadows along the Browney, and spotted his device at once. He had found his horse, and had collected a small band of mounted men around him; Guy of Béthune was one of them. As she watched they cantered away across the meadows towards Beaurepaire, easily outrunning the English who pursued them.

'God's death,' Tiphaine said sharply. 'He is getting away.'

She kicked her horse down the slope towards the river, Mora close behind. Scottish fugitives ran down the hill too, trying to escape; one made a lunge for Tiphaine's horse but Mora clubbed him down with the flat of her sword. English soldiers came plunging down with bloody knives and spears in hand, and men screamed as they fell; for a few moments death was all around her, but all she could think about was that red saltire banner. If Brus escaped, the plotting and killing would continue. She would be in danger, and so would Simon, so long as Brus lived. She had to find him, and somehow, she had to find a way of killing him.

They had left the stream of fugitives behind now. A quarter of a mile ahead, Brus and his companions rode on, every minute taking them further towards safety. Tiphaine and Mora followed them.

—

'What do you intend to do now?' asked Guy of Béthune.

'We carry on,' said Brus.

They rode past another string of coal pits, black holes like smallpox scars gouged out of the ground, piles of coal heaped up at their edge. 'Are you mad?' Béthune repeated. 'The army is destroyed. The king is probably either dead or a prisoner.'

'Hopefully the former,' Brus said. 'It doesn't matter either way, Guy. When we reach Edinburgh, I shall proclaim myself king and take the throne. The English will invade, of course, but they don't have enough men or money to do much damage, and in a few months King Edward will be dead as well and the whole country plunged into chaos. We'll have everything we planned, and more.'

Béthune nodded. 'Have you ever wondered why I came to Scotland?' he asked.

'To see what spoils you could gather for yourself, I imagine. Don't worry, you will have your heart's desire. I had intended to give Carrick an earldom. Now he is dead, I shall give it to you instead.'

'You honour me too greatly,' said Béthune. He raised his hand and hit Brus a powerful backhand blow that knocked him out of the saddle. Flailing, Brus fell onto a heap of coal beside one of the pits. The heap collapsed, pitching him ten feet down into the bottom of the pit. An avalanche of coal followed him, crashing down across his legs and burying him up to the waist. Pain lanced up his side as his broken ribs gave way once more. Stunned, he looked up to see Béthune standing on the edge of the pit looking down. The count's gauntlets were black; it was he who had pushed the coal down on top of Brus.

'You disobeyed orders,' Béthune said. 'Had you succeeded, you might have got away with it. But our friends don't tolerate failure, Brus. You killed the Traceys, who were useful to us. You failed to protect Blyth, who was essential to our plans. And now you have broken Scotland, and all for nothing.'

He paused. 'There is no profit in this, Brus, not for any of us save you. You thought only of yourself. That is not acceptable.'

'Get me out of here,' Brus gasped.

'No,' said Béthune. 'Your blind ambition led you to this hole, and you can remain here. What the English will do to you when they find you, I don't know and I don't care, but don't expect us to pay your ransom. You've flouted orders for the last time, Brus. Time to pay the price.'

Béthune turned away. The weight of coal pressing down on Brus was almost unbearable; already his legs had gone numb. He scrabbled at the coal with his hands, trying to pull the hard black lumps away, but more came cascading down on top of him. Even the slightest effort brought more blinding pain in his ribs. A shadow fell across the pit and he looked up, hoping beyond hope that Béthune had changed his mind and returned to rescue him.

His hope turned to ash. Tiphaine stood on the edge of the pit, looking down at him.

–

Tiphaine and Mora had seen Béthune mount and ride away with the other horsemen.

'They've abandoned him,' Mora said. 'Why?'

'Perhaps he is dead,' Tiphaine said. They rode past the pits to the one where Brus had fallen and dismounted. Brus lay on his back, half-buried in fallen coal, pinned and unable to move. For the first time in her life, he was helpless before her.

'Get me out of here,' Brus said.

'No,' said Tiphaine.

He scrabbled at the coal again, gasping in agony as he tried to pull himself free. 'For God's sake, Tiphaine. I'll give you anything you want. Money, houses, land, anything. It's all yours.'

'You don't have any money,' Tiphaine said. 'Not any more. The Traceys are dead and Blyth has fled away to Flanders. You're empty now, Rollond. You are a husk, nothing more.'

'We were lovers once,' Brus said, still trying to pull the coal away. 'Does that mean nothing to you?'

She heard hoofbeats on the ground. From the corner of her eye she saw the herald dismount and come forward, along with another man in a red lion tabard.

'About as much as it did to you, when you gave orders to burn me alive. Three times you tried, at La Roche Guyon, in Liddesdale and at Lanercost. There will not be a fourth.'

Brus looked up at her and he must have seen the expression in her face. Anger exploded in his voice. 'You filthy stupid little bitch. Burning is about all you are good for. Well? Are you expecting me to beg?'

'No, Rollond,' she said. 'I don't want you to beg. I want you to die.'

His anger faded quickly. He screamed in frustration, clawing at the ground. Tiphaine turned to the two heralds.

'Is there any reason why I should not kill this man?' she asked.

'Can you live with yourself afterwards?' asked Merrivale.

She thought for a moment, her face serious. 'Yes,' she said. 'I can.'

The wind whirled coal dust around them. 'His intrigues and ambition have destroyed a kingdom,' said Lyon Herald. 'Hundreds of good and noble men are dead. Hundreds of widows will grieve, hundreds of children will grow up as orphans. An entire nation will drown in its own grief, because of him. The Seigneur de Brus no longer deserves to walk upon this earth.'

Mora came up beside her, holding a stone jar and a torch. 'I found these in a mine just down the hill. The jar is full of oil. It is up to you what you do with it.'

Tiphaine took the stopper from the jar and poured it over the coal in the pit below her. Brus saw the oil falling and shouted at her, raging, cursing her for a witch and a whore; she barely heard him. 'I need to light the torch,' she said.

'Allow me,' said Lyon Herald. He took a tinderbox from a pocket of his cloak and lit the torch, handing it to her. Oily flames licked up, pale in the dying daylight. Tiphaine held the torch out over the pit, looking down into Brus's eyes. She held his gaze for a long moment, and then opened her fingers and let the torch fall.

The oil burned quickly, flames rushing up, and the onlookers on the edge of the pit felt the heat on their faces. Drops of burning oil fell on Brus's armour and surcoat, burning for a minute or so and then dying away. When the flames passed they saw the coal beginning to turn white in places. Brus tried again to pull himself free, but the coal was too hot to touch now and he could not shift it. Time passed, and as darkness fell the white heat turned to red. Very slowly, the furnace glow spread towards the man trapped in the pit below.

It took a long time for Rollond de Brus to die.

33

The Narrow Sea, 6ᵗʰ of November, 1346
Morning

The roundship *Grace-Dieu* had sailed from Greenwich the previous day, making its way downriver by daylight and anchoring off the Isle of Sheppey for the night so as not to risk the treacherous shoals of the Thames estuary in darkness. Dawn saw them underway again, the ship's single huge sail billowing in the uneven north-westerly wind. Whitecaps lifted on the seas around them.

The herald stood on deck between the two fighting castles, gazing out towards the coast hidden in mist and spray. Ahead was Calais where the English army lay camped, besieging the town; the *Grace-Dieu* was carrying supplies to help make their camp secure for the coming winter. It was nearly three weeks since the slaughter at Neville's Cross and its gruesome aftermath, but some of the memories of that day would remain forever; more memories, adding to the ones already crowding in on him.

After every battle came the administration. He had written his report the day after the fighting, laying out the losses the Scots had suffered; the earls of Strathearn and Moray, Bruce of Carrick, the Marischal and the constable dead along with thousands of others; David Bruce and most of the rest of the earls, including Menteith and Sutherland, prisoners in English hands. It was a victory even more complete in some ways than Halidon Hill. His report also commended the very important role played by the northern barons, Lord Percy and his son Sir Harry, Lord Neville,

Lord Wake and Sir Gilbert d'Umfraville, and expressed regret over the loss of the gallant Sir Robert de Lisle. No word, no hint of possible treason entered his report; it was as if those days of doubt and uncertainty had never existed. In his mind's eye he saw again *The Dream of Scipio* lying on the table, its cover boards gathering dust.

A second, private report for the king noted that Rollond de Brus and Thomas Clennell were dead along with Hugh and Gilbert de Tracey, but William Blyth and Guy of Béthune had escaped. Some of the tendrils had been cut down, but others were still flourishing. The conspiracy was still alive; the threat to King Edward was real and immediate.

–

He had come down to London by sea, travelling with Lady Mary and Tiphaine. In London there had been a long and wearying delay. The queen had crossed to France to join her husband at Calais, but there were still interviews with Stratford, the president of the council, and Ufford the lord chancellor, and various clerks and officials at the Treasury and Chancery who were slowly unravelling the financial affairs of the Traceys and William Blyth. Lady Mary had handed over Blyth's accounts and gone back to her family, after a gently emotional farewell with Tiphaine.

'What are you going to do?' Mary had asked her.

'Go with the herald, I suppose. There is nothing else for me to do.'

'You could come with me. We would welcome you at Hargate.'

'But what would I do there? I love you for the friendship you have shown me, Mary, but prison and war have changed me. I cannot live life as you do.'

She was beside the herald now, wrapped in a black cloak and staring at the dark waves sliding past the rail. Merrivale watched her, quietly. Over the course of the summer and early autumn they had grown closer together, a little, but now there were shadows between them. Seeing Yolande again had shaken him, badly; guilt and remorse had eaten into his old wounds and reopened them. For her part, she had said she could live with killing Rollond de Brus in such a manner. She had not said she could live comfortably.

He had not burned Yolande alive, but at times he thought he might as well have done; Brus's suffering had lasted for a few hours, but Yolande's had endured for years. But he still did not know whether he could trust Yolande. When she asked him to run with her, had that been a trap to deliver him into the hands of her husband and Brus? Perhaps.

'What will we find at Calais?' Tiphaine asked finally, breaking the silence.

'By all reports, not very much. The French are sitting inside the city, the English are camped outside, and it is hard to tell who is more uncomfortable. We have closed off the land approaches to the city, but the French are still able to run in supplies by sea. It's what Archie Graham would call a staring contest.'

'Archie. Are all you heralds so friendly?'

'We get along,' Merrivale said. 'We get to know each other well during our travels. There is a kind of fellowship that binds us, or most of us.'

'I wonder what that feels like? To find a place where you belong?'

He wanted to say to her, *perhaps you have already found it*, but he held back. Too much was uncertain in both their lives, too much darkness and pain. Perhaps the moment would come when they could talk openly of their past. Or perhaps it would never come.

She hesitated before speaking, as if she could sense his own dark mood. Probably she could; she could read him well by now, better perhaps than she realised. 'Will you find another apprentice?' she asked.

Another wound, another pain, though this one was something they could share. 'I don't think I could bear it,' he said finally.

'No. I understand that. It was like losing a member of one's family.'

He wondered briefly about Yolande's son — their son — and then slammed and locked that door in his mind.

'While you look for a new home,' he said, 'you are welcome to remain with me. I warn you this winter is likely to be a hard one.'

'Harder than last summer, or the past two months? You have always been kind to me. I cannot think what I have done to deserve it.'

'Nothing,' he said. He turned his head and smiled at her. 'Kindness isn't something that is deserved, Tiphaine. It is not bartered or exchanged. If it was, it wouldn't be kindness.'

'When you start to talk like a philosopher, I know you are trying to cheer me up. You don't have to, you know. I am not sad, my spirits are not depressed. But I am not the same person I was a month ago.'

The ship was rounding the North Foreland now, setting a course for Calais. They felt the change in the motion of the ship, pitching and rolling in the strong currents. 'Do you still think Bishop Hatfield is the man from the north?' she asked.

The change of subject came as a relief to him, and he suspected to her as well. 'It is possible. Of course, that might be too obvious. But I shall certainly begin with him.'

'Let me know how I can help.' She looked up at him, fore-stalling any possible objection. 'Don't hold me at arm's length, Simon, or tell me I need protection. I am already part of this story, and I will be there when it ends.'

'Whatever that end may be,' he said, and they stood in silence, watching as the dark shape of the coast of France began to slide out of the mist.

Acknowledgements

It is impossible to remember and thank everyone who has helped us with a series of books so long in the making. First and foremost we must thank our wonderful agents, Jon Wood at RCW and Heather Adams and Mike Bryan at HMA for all their support and thoughts going forward. The team at Canelo have been great as usual; thanks to Kit Nevile for editing, suggestions, advice, support and encouragement, and especially for making things easy for us during a time of chaos. Elodie Olson-Coons has done a brilliant job of copy-editing, and Nick Venables has done a superb cover illustration; as Kit says, he knocked it out of the park. Thanks to Gary Beaumont for his last-minute work on the map.

Thanks as always to Cogito Books in Hexham; sorry we had to burn your town down, but we hope you will think it was worth it! Thanks finally to Steve, Bat, Xav and Raf for a wonderful lunch just down the hill from the battlefield at Neville's Cross; one of the highlights of the year. And finally, thanks to the Scottish borders, Northumberland and Durham for providing such a spectacular backdrop to write about, and a wonderful place to visit.